LANCELOT

Her Story

Carol Anne Douglas

Hermione Books

Washington, D.C.

Book Layout © 2013 BookDesignTemplates.com

Lancelot: Her Story/ Carol Anne Douglas
ISBN 978-09967722-0-4

*This book is dedicated to Mandy Doolittle,
who brought joy to my life.*

ACKNOWLEDGMENTS

I express my gratitude to the writer whose story about Lancelot as a woman I read as a college freshman. I have searched for many years to find the story or the writer but have not been able to do so. That story inspired this book, and I have drawn on aspects of it, such as Lancelot's friendship with Gawaine.

I want to thank many people, especially Sherwood Smith, who gave me years of encouragement while I worked on this book, and Betty Jean Steinshouer, who lovingly prepared the manuscript for publication.

I thank the friends who read the manuscript, especially Tricia Lootens, who read several early drafts, and Ken Louden, who read a very early draft when he was dying. I thank Virginia Cerello, Russell Cox, Liz Quinn, Victoria Stanhope, and Stephanie Wynn for reading the manuscript. I thank Amy Hamilton for helping me find the wonderful listserv ARTHURNET and for her encouragement of my writing.

I thank Viable Paradise for providing a great environment for writers, and everyone at VP XV, especially those who provided comments, including Stephanie Charette and LaShawn Wanak. I am particularly grateful for comments from Debra Doyle and Jim MacDonald, to Debra for her editing, and to Jane Kinsman for last-minute advice on the cover design as well as interior details.

I want to thank the wonderful friends and family who have given me emotional support over the years: Lois and Nancy Brown, Ned Cabot Sr., Suzie Carrigan, Tacie Dejanikus, Beth Eldridge, Colleen Flannery, Daniele Flannery, John S. Flannery, Carolyn Gage, Barbara Gardien, Julie Gerard Harris, Alice Henry, Marlene Howell, Jackie Hutchinson, Edward P. Jones, Sue Lenaerts, Vickie Leonard, Elizabeth Lytle, Colise Medved,

Trudy Portewig, Luanne Schinzel, John Schmitz, Delores Smith, Liz Trapnell, and Judith Witherow. Above all, I am grateful to my wonderful mother, Joan Flannery Douglas, who always gave me love and encouraged me.

I am also grateful for the kindness of Mary Frances Moriarty, who has been like a second mother to me; Jim Bethea, who was my first unrelated male friend; Tom Field, a King Arthur who has reigned with genius and compassion; Dean Ahearn, who was a true knight, loyal and excellent in all he did; and Lissa Fried, the bravest knight of all.

Part I The Path to Camelot

1 THE CHANGELING

Anna lived in the forest, as much as she could. Animals spoke to her, telling secrets lost for a thousand years. Birds guided her home. This morning she was eager to be outside, walking with her mother.

She looked through the window at the endless waves of trees that grew beyond her father's holding. She longed to feel pine needles under her feet, to touch soft moss.

Magpies that lived at the wood edge screeched, beckoning her to join them. She imagined that she could smell the pines, but only the scent of baking wheaten bread strayed up from the kitchen. She wanted to see the early morning light, still slanting through the trees, not the ordinary light of midmorning.

A deer, or even a bear, might appear in a sunlit glade. In the villa, there was eternal sewing and spinning, and nothing magical ever happened. Twisting vines and bunches of grapes were painted on the walls of the room where she was supposed to be sewing. What would happen if they suddenly came to life, if vines took over the villa?

Seeing her mother make her way across the cobbled courtyard, Anna jumped up from her stool. The crimson gown she had been mending dropped to the floor. Anna picked it up and flung it onto the stool.

"I never knew a girl whose mother let her sew and spin so little," her plump nurse sniffed. Rathtyen had a small, upturned nose, and often sniffed as if discontented with the very air, though she never wanted to exchange the air indoors for the air outdoors. "What kind of wife will you be?"

"I'm going to walk in the forest with Mother now," Anna darted away from Rathtyen and her question. Life was a song, after all. She warbled one of the hymns she had heard her mother sing. She made it sound much more cheerful than her mother did.

In the courtyard, her father and his men mounted their horses to leave for a hunt. Her father's roan stallion tossed his head and pawed the ground while her mother glided across the cobbles to bid him farewell.

What splendid horses, Anna thought, leaning out of the window as far as she could. If only she could ride mounts with that much spirit, but girls never could. She wanted to tame wild horses and travel to faraway lands. She couldn't bear to stay indoors another moment.

"Mother! Father!" Anna called. She waved to get her parents' attention.

"Don't lean too far," Rathtyen warned.

Finally, Anna's mother signaled that Anna could join them in the cobbled courtyard. "If I find any mushrooms, I'll pick them for you," Anna said to mollify her nurse.

As she rushed out of the room, Anna began to sing another hymn. She would go among the trees. She would be free of sewing and other chores.

Anna hurried out of the old stone villa, through the atrium where men were repairing the floor tiles left from Roman times, and met her mother at the gate in the wall that surrounded the villa.

She felt a surge of pride at the sight of her beautiful mother, Lucia. It was good to have a mother who walked in the woods often and sang hymns while she sewed, Anna thought. And it was good to have a father who seldom raised his voice.

Lucia gazed at Anna's father as if he were going away for a month instead of a day.

Anna hoped he would look at her.

Three of his men-at-arms were with him, all of them clad in chain mail because the forest they must travel through might hold creatures more dangerous than deer. The men made little noise because her father scowled at them if they were rowdy. But he rarely frowned at Anna.

She wished that she could ride out with them into the forest's darkest recesses, rather than just visit the safest part near the villa. If she rode far enough, she might even be granted a vision of a holy saint. No, she was unworthy of such a blessing.

She wondered how sharp the swords hanging from the men's baldrics were, for she was not allowed to touch weapons.

"God grant you a safe hunt, Marcus," her mother said to her father. Lucia's voice made the words sound full of meaning, as if no one had ever said them before. Her black hair strayed from her headdress.

"Don't worry, we'll be safe, and we will bring back a fine deer."

Marcus clasped her hand. He smiled at Anna, then went on his way, leading his men.

Anna and her mother began their more modest journey on a well-marked path, though the trees and bracken on either side were almost impenetrable. Anna wanted so much to investigate the tangled way among the trees, but her mother would never let her do that.

Anna scampered through the woods ahead of her mother. The children of other noble families had sometimes asked her if she minded not having any brothers or sisters, but she thought the question foolish. Of course she did not. She had her mother to herself, while other children's mothers were always having more babies, sometimes leaving the older children entirely to their nurses. Besides, in her tenth year she was old enough to know that girls with brothers had to defer to them, and she did not want to defer to any boy.

Anna breathed in the welcome scent of the pines. Why didn't Mother walk faster? They might miss something. Ladies never ran, and that seemed foolish. A red squirrel chattered, and Anna chattered back at it. Her mother caught up with her.

"What if that wasn't really a squirrel? What if it was a little man with a squirrel's head? This squirrel seemed to be just a squirrel, but the next one might not be," Anna said, staring up the pine that the little animal had climbed. She touched the bark and rubbed her fingers in the sticky resin.

"Has Rathtyen been telling you impious tales?" Lucia chided. "I must tell her to stop. You must never confuse people, who have souls, with animals, who do not." The slightest of frowns appeared in her forehead. "And don't get the resin on your gown."

"Yes, mother," Anna agreed, rubbing her fingers on a stone to scrape off the resin.

A tremulous birdsong filled the air.

"Not many birds sing this late in the summer," Lucia mused.

"Can you tell me what song that is?"

"The wren's," Anna replied, proud that she remembered the many songs her mother had taught her.

"Good girl. Yes, it's the wren." Lucia's smile transformed her face until it glowed like the faces of the angels painted on the walls of their chapel. Her tender look made it seem that Anna had done something remarkable.

Anna felt as if she had sprouted wings. She wanted to be just like her mother when she grew up. When she walked in the forest with her own daughter, would her mother be there with them? She hoped her father would not marry her to a lord who lived far away.

"It is important to know all the different songs," her mother said.

"Can we go as far as the lake today?" Anna begged.

"Yes, to be sure we can." Lucia caught hold of her hand and squeezed it. "You always want to go to the lake. You're my little Lady of the Lake, aren't you?" She frowned and looked around as if someone could overhear them. "Don't tell your father I said that. That is the name of a pagan priestess across the sea in Britain, and he wouldn't like me to call you that, even in jest. But, my water-loving girl, you are my child of the lake." She clasped Anna to her, then let her go.

"I'll remember, and I won't tell, I promise."

Anna felt important because she was sharing a secret with her mother. She bounced along the path and wondered what water-fowl they would see at the lake. She let out a squawk. "Listen to me, I'm the heron of the lake."

"Don't go too far ahead of me. Stay within sight," her mother called out. Anna ran ahead as she usually did, reveling in the crisp air that foretold the coming of autumn. She ignored her mother's warning and sped on. Mother never punished her for running ahead, as long as she stayed on the path.

Anna flapped her arms. Perhaps feathers would sprout on them and she could become a heron in truth. Perhaps if she ran fast enough, she might begin to fly. She ran further and further into the woods.

Small white butterflies fluttered through the trees like spots of light in the dark forest. "I am flying, too," she told them.

Anna found some golden chanterelles, the most delicate of mushrooms, and began to pick them. They would taste so good at supper, and Rathtyen would be pleased.

In the forest behind Anna, crows cawed wildly, as if trying to drive off a hawk or an owl.

A terrible scream made her drop the chanterelles. Was it her mother? Anna ran back through the trees. When she came to a clearing where she found wildflowers in the spring, she saw a huge man writhing on top of her mother. Only shreds of clothing, sleeves and stockings, still clung to Lucia's body. Blood poured down her legs. Her screams had stopped. No sound came from her.

Anna flung herself on the man's back. He smelled rank, like carrion. She pounded on his shoulders and kicked his sides, but he only growled and tried to shake her off. She bit through his ear, and he reached up, grabbed her, and threw her to the ground. Only slightly bruised, she staggered up. He returned to grinding himself on her mother.

Looking around desperately, Anna found a long branch several inches thick. She rushed again at the man and thrust the pointed end as hard as she could into his eye.

Shrieking in pain, the man thrashed out at Anna, but she leapt away from him. His hands clutching his bleeding face, he jumped up from her mother and, still screaming, lumbered off among the trees.

Anna knelt beside her mother and touched her cheek. Lucia's neck was snapped; her head hung at an awkward angle. Her brown eyes stared unseeing at the sky. Anna collapsed beside her mother, clutched her, and sobbed.

"Mother! Mother! Mother!" She screamed, she moaned, but her mother made no reply. Anna knew that she would never hear that sweet voice again, but she begged anyway. She buried her face in her mother's dark hair as it spilled on the ground, along with the blood that pooled on the pine needles.

Mother was dead. Dead like her first horse, which had gone lame and had to be killed. No, Mother had a soul. Mother must be with the Christ and his Mother.

Come back, come back, Anna begged. I need you, I need you. I never should have left you.

Why did she have to run off alone? She reproached herself. Perhaps she could have saved her mother. Perhaps her mother's death was her fault. Tears covered her cheeks.

Why had God let the man kill her mother? Why didn't He freeze the man's hands before they could strangle her? If Anna had prayed more often and more fervently, if she had been a better girl, would He have saved Lucia?

Anna begged God to raise her mother from the dead as He had Lazarus. She would never ask for anything else in her life, just this one miracle, please.

No voices answered her. The clearing was silent, except for a squirrel's chatter. How could squirrels still chatter in this nightmare world? People said that weasels could bring the dead back to life. She looked around the clearing, as if a weasel might emerge from a hole, but none did.

Two carrion crows flew down to investigate her mother's body. Screaming at them, Anna waved her arms to keep them off.

Her thoughts became less and less clear. She felt nothing but pain, in her chest, in her head. Surely no one could feel this much pain and live. Perhaps she would die, too, and be with her mother in heaven, if only she were good enough.

Then Anna was empty. Perhaps she had died. No, she was not with her mother, not in heaven, but nowhere, just someplace black, the smell of blood mingling with the pine scent. Could there be pines in hell?

Voices cried out, "Lady Lucia! God's wounds! Is the child dead, too? Who did this?"

She did not speak, but struggled when arms lifted her away from her mother's body. A strong man was carrying her somewhere – it didn't matter where.

Later, voices prayed beside her, but there was only blackness.

"Anna, speak to me."

She heard her father's voice. She was lying in a bed, probably her own. She did not open her eyes.

"Be merciful, Lord," she heard Marcus pray. His voice was solemn but desperate, far different from his ordinary calm tone of authority.

"Let my child speak." He sobbed. "I vow that I'll never wed again. I'll spend all of my days praising You, Lord, only let my child live. Anna, Anna, listen to your father." He clasped her hands in his.

She knew she ought to open her eyes, and so she did. She saw her father, tears streaming over the stubble on his usually clean-shaven cheeks.

"My little girl. Are you well, Anna?"

She looked at him, but could not speak.

"Your mother is in heaven with the holy angels. All the priests from miles around came to her funeral. And the vile murderer was soon found. His head is on a pike on our wall. He'll never harm anyone again. No one will ever harm you again, little one." He chafed her hands as if they were cold, but she said nothing.

She noticed they were in a room she had never seen before, with an unfamiliar hanging on the wall.

"I have taken you to my brother's villa," he told her. "I shall explain later."

She remembered that her uncle had died fighting the Franks.

At last, her father left and she was alone again. It didn't matter whether she was in her own bed or another.

Her nurse brought her warm possets to drink and tried to tempt her to eat. Anna picked at the food, but still she did not speak.

"Don't you want to get up, Lamb?" Rathtyen said. "It's a bright day. You've always been so fond of walking about. I'll go out with you, if you'd like."

Anna shook her head. The world would never be as it had been. The rivers and lakes would be dry. The trees would lose all their leaves and never grow new ones. There would be no flowers in the world without her mother, no birds to sing her home.

Then her father was there again. "You must speak, Anna. I see that you don't want to live, but you must. God has given you life, and you must accept his gift.

"I have sworn to be pure for the rest of my life to thank God for saving you. No doubt you want to be pure, too, after this horror, my little one. I cannot bear to send you away to a convent but I can raise you as a boy, so you will be safe forever. And it will be easier for you to inherit my property, for I shall have no other child. Was it you who put out the murderer's eye?"

15

Anna nodded. She didn't want to go away to a convent. Pretending to be a boy sounded far better.

"Brave girl." He patted her hand. "I'll train you to fight to protect yourself. Do you want to learn?"

She nodded again. She never wanted anyone to do to her what the murderer had done to her mother.

Marcus sighed, apparently in relief. "You will be Antonius, as if reborn. I'll tell everyone that my Anna died, and that you are my brother's son come to live with me. Only Rathtyen and Father Matthew will know. Is that well, Antonius?"

There was so much anxiety in his voice that she had to speak. "Yes, Father. It is well."

He embraced her. "In front of others, you must call me Uncle Marcus now, but I shall always be your father."

It wouldn't be so bad being a boy, she thought. She wouldn't have a nurse following her around and she wouldn't have to sew. And when she was older, she could have a fast horse, like father's.

Not marrying didn't matter. She had never thought about what a husband would be like, except that he should live near her parents. Babies were strange, crying things, and she wouldn't mind not having any.

Rathtyen brought her a boy's breeches and tunic, and helped her dress. She cut Antonius's black hair off at the shoulders. Rathtyen sniffed while she cut the hair, but Antonius did not.

"Poor Lamb, won't you mind giving up your pretty gowns?"

"No, Rathtyen," she said honestly. She hadn't given the gowns a thought. "Anna must be reborn. I'm Antonius now."

"You're such a beautiful girl, too, even more so than your poor mother. I never said much because I didn't want to turn your head, but what a shame to try to make such a beauty into a boy."

"I don't care," Antonius said. She knew she had brown eyes like her mother and a long face and Roman nose like her father, but she didn't think she was beautiful.

Rathtyen shed a few tears. "This is the last time I can dress you, Lamb, but I'll be near whenever you need me. Poor thing, you've become so much thinner that people will believe you're a different child. You must eat now and be strong so you can learn to use weapons as your father wants."

"I shall." Instead of being like her mother, she would learn how to be like her father.

In a few days, Antonius's father brought her and Rathtyen back to his villa. Antonius rode in a cart with Rathtyen and took little interest in the hills and trees they passed. They arrived late at night. Antonius looked away from the gate because she knew the murderer's head would be there.

Rathtyen took Antonius to a room that had been arranged for her. It was much like her old room, with a warm brazier in the corner and fur coverings on the bed. The straw mattress was just as comfortable as the old one and the down-filled cushions were just as fine. But there was a wolfskin rug on the floor instead of the sheepskin rugs in her old room.

"I must leave you now, Lamb," Rathtyen told her. "I can't sleep in your room anymore. Pretending to be a boy means that you'll always have to sleep alone."

Anna said nothing, but she stayed awake for a long time. She felt as if she were in a cavern all by herself, for the rest of her life.

The next morning, Rathtyen knocked at the door. She escorted Antonius through the villa as if showing it to her for the first time. Antonius pretended not to know where anything was because she was supposed to be new to it all.

She must act like a boy, she thought. Would a boy be more excited than she was by the weapons and shields hanging on the walls? Would a boy notice the stitches in a wall hanging? She used to think she might make one someday, but now she knew she would not, and the thought relieved her. No need to spend years stitching. Would a boy speak in a louder voice to the serving people? Would he be less careful about not bringing mud inside? Could she ever be exactly like a boy? And did she want to be?

Rathtyen told her the servants' names, as if she had not known them all her life. She must act like a boy, she reminded herself again and again.

They passed through the kitchen, where a haunch of mutton was roasting on a spit. The smell nauseated Antonius, though it never had before, and the blood dripping from the meat made her turn away. She looked without recognition at Gwella, the old cook.

"Give young Antonius a bit of wheaten bread," Rathtyen ordered.

Staring at Antonius, Gwella cut a slice and handed it to her.

"Thanks," Antonius muttered, in a voice that she hoped sounded different than it had when she was Anna. She chewed the bread, but it had less flavor now that her mother was dead.

When Anna walked out of the villa, the first thing she saw was the head stuck on a pike near the gate. Though the head had shriveled and been picked at by birds, she recognized it all too well. Shuddering, she averted her eyes. A wave of nausea made her feel that perhaps the bread had been too much to eat. Her legs threatened to buckle under her, but she forced herself to keep standing because she must be Antonius, who had not witnessed the murder. Now that she knew where the head was, she could avoid looking in that direction, but she felt that the killer had invaded her life. The thought that the man was burning in hell gave her little comfort.

She would go to see her horse. That would soothe her.

Entering the stable, she enjoyed the mingled smells of horse sweat and hay. Even the smell of horseshit was not unpleasant after her long confinement in bed, too far away from horses.

"I am the Lord Marcus's nephew, Antonius," she announced to Duach, a stablehand who walked with a limp.

She tried to make her voice slightly haughty, so she would not be questioned. He nodded. "I heard you were coming."

"My uncle says I am to have a horse called Shadow," she said, naming her own horse. "Where is this horse?

"She's in that stall." Duach pointed to Shadow's stall.

"Where are the brushes for grooming?" Antonius asked, though she knew very well.

He pointed to the brushes hanging on the wall. She selected one and approached her mare, who was such a dark brown that she was nearly black.

Shadow whinnied in greeting. The mare was not fooled by seeing her with short hair and breeches. Looking about, Antonius hoped that Duach did not hear and did not guess that she had been Anna. She did not see him, so perhaps he was not near.

She patted Shadow's neck, and the mare nuzzled her shoulder.

While Antonius was grooming Shadow, she heard low voices.

"The boy's the lord's bastard, I'm sure of it, brought here now the lady's dead and can't object," said Macon, a serving man of middle age.

Antonius crouched down in the straw in her horse's stall and listened.

Duach pitched in. "He's a bastard, all right, but I'd say he's King Ban's son, and our lord has brought him here to curry favor with the king," he said. "A clever man, Lord Marcus."

"King Ban's son, my ass! He's Lord Marcus's own by-blow!" Macon insisted. Both he and Duach laughed.

Pressing her cheek against her horse's flank, Antonius was only a little dismayed. She did not want to be thought of as a bastard, but there was nothing to be done about that. She would not tell her father because he might have the men whipped.

When they had gone, Antonius led her horse out of the stable and mounted her. She could ride out alone! That was what it meant to be a boy. The villa no longer confined her.

She rode into the woods and found that the lake was still there. Traitorous waters! How dare they still ripple, though her mother was gone. She threw herself on the ground and wept, angry at the lake. But as she pressed herself against the cool and still earth, it seemed to welcome her. Perhaps her mother's spirit had passed with her blood into the land. This was the closest she could come to being at her mother's bosom again. The thought comforted her.

Father Matthew, the balding old priest of Marcus's chapel, sat with Antonius in the library, where Marcus kept his many books. One had a sewn leather cover and the rest were scrolls.

"Your father wants to raise you to be a nobleman, so you must learn more than a girl would have had to," the priest said, nodding as if teaching a girl to be a boy was something he did every day. "You must learn a little history and even some theology. You may go to a court someday and hear men discuss religion, so you must know enough to be safe from heresy."

"Yes, Father. Just tell me what to believe. I don't want to be a heretic," Antonius said. She vowed to be holy, as her mother had wanted her to be.

"Good child." The priest smiled paternally and picked up a scroll. "We shall read The Acts of St. Paul and Thecla, for the holy Thecla dressed as a man, the better to serve Almighty God as a virgin."

Anna squirmed as she tried to read the scroll, for she was not fond of book learning and wished that Latin words did not have so many different endings. The library's musty smell was not pleasing to her.

Later, Antonius knelt in the villa's chapel, repeating every prayer her mother had taught her, until the words seemed almost magical, a link that bound her to her mother, and a way that her mother's voice could speak through her lips. Could her mother hear her? If the saints could, why not her own mother?

Marcus brought Antonius to the practice room, which was empty of furniture but had weapons hanging on the walls. She wondered whether swords and spears, blades marked from use, might tell of her father's and grandfather's battles if she listened hard enough.

"Here is where I practiced when I was young, before I crossed the sea to Britain to help King Uther Pendragon fight the Saxons," her father said. "I was retracing the journey of my own father, who left Britain to come here to Lesser Britain."

Antonius remembered her father's tales of how her grandfather had married the daughter of their villa's owner and become the overlord.

The practice room was the one room in the villa that did not seemed filled with her mother's spirit, and that was a relief.

Her father showed her a wooden sword, a steel sword, some small throwing spears, and a long thrusting spear.

"This is the room where my father taught me to fight. You must become a fighting man in order to be safe," he told her. "You no longer look like a girl, so you will not incite any man's lust." His face was unsmiling, grimmer than it had been when her mother was alive. "Nevertheless, you must always be prepared for an attack. First, you will learn how to use this wooden sword, which is weighted with lead. Then we'll move on to the steel sword, and finally the spears. Try holding each of them."

The wooden sword felt good in her hand. The two-edged steel slashing sword felt even better, though it was heavy. She was proud to touch it, for she never had been allowed to when she was a girl. She ran her finger along the edge to learn how sharp it was. A small cut gave her the answer.

Then she took hold of the thrusting spear, which was wooden with a metal head. It was awkward to hold such a long weapon. She wondered whether she could ever fight with it.

"Any lad of ten summers would have such difficulties," Marcus assured her. "Just keep trying to lift the spear into a fighting position, while you learn agility with the wooden sword and good aim with the throwing spears."

She took up the wooden sword again, and he put his hands over hers to show her how to hold it properly.

"I've had some chain mail made for you, also," her father said, handing her a heavy coat of interlocking rings sewn on leather.

Antonius fingered it curiously, enjoying its roughness compared with the soft gowns she had worn. This would be her new skin, which would save her life someday, no doubt.

"It won't keep out the fiercest slash of a sword or throw of a spear, but it will be a good barrier," Marcus told her. "It's best if you can put on your own chain mail, so I had the armorer make the kind that ties on the side, rather than going over your head."

He showed her how to put it on and she almost fainted from the weight of it. She staggered and grabbed hold of a window ledge to steady herself.

"You'll learn to wear it in time," her father assured her. "Just have patience."

Each day they practiced fighting with the wooden sword and throwing the shorter spears at a straw-stuffed target, and each day she tried to hold the long spear in fighting position.

Her father was gentle with her, but he never smiled. Sometimes she heard him sigh.

The seasons came and went. Snow covered the ground where her mother's body had lain, and, though Christmas at her father's holding was subdued, they did roast some geese. Violets appeared in the spring. Antonius felt no desire to pick them. Birds returned and sang, but her mother was not there to hear them. Not even the summer sun could warm the chill in her heart.

She visited the forest at times, but she no longer saw it as a place where squirrels might speak and magic might happen. Beams of light among the trees still wove a spell around her, but the rotting leaves reminded her – the forest was a place of death.

Antonius woke at first light, stretched, and flexed her muscles. The spring breeze blew through the window. She was proud of how strong she had become. Her body pleased her, except for her chest, which wasn't flat anymore. She had hoped it would stay that way.

Rathtyen came to Antonius's room and closed the door. The nurse's brown hair, which was graying slightly, strayed out of her braid. Before Antonius's mother had died, Rathtyen had always taken greater care of her appearance.

"You've grown very tall for a woman, but you'll need this to bind your breasts, if you persist in pretending to be a boy," the nurse said, presenting Antonius with a long cloth of white linen.

Antonius looked at the wolfskin rug on the floor.

She was glad that she was slim and straight, with buds smaller than other girls', but still they were growing. At least they didn't interfere with her fighting practice, which now seemed to tire her father more than it did her.

"Of course I shall continue," Antonius replied. "Will you show me how to wrap the cloth?"

So she took off her woolen bedgown and Rathtyen, sighing, wrapped the cloth tightly around her.

"What if this prevents your milk from coming when you have a child?" Rathtyen asked, shaking her head and making a disapproving sound with her tongue.

"I never will have a child," Antonius assured her.

Rathtyen groaned. "I hope your father knows what he's doing."

"Don't worry yourself," Antonius insisted. The cloth pressing down her breasts was uncomfortable, but she would not say so.

"What would your mother say about this pretending to be a boy?" Rathtyen mumbled, tying the cloth.

Antonius bit her lip. "Surely she would understand, wouldn't she? I wouldn't want to displease her."

"Of course, of course." Rathtyen looked sorry she had spoken.

Antonius put on her tunic, which was crimson. Though she did not wear gowns any more, she still cared about colors, and preferred to wear any shade of red, which Rathtyen said best suited her. She prayed to be forgiven for that vanity.

Antonius went to the practice room, where she found a strange man standing beside her father. He was an aging man with powerful muscles and numerous scars that his sweeping moustaches could not hide. His hair was brown, with a trace of gray.

"Here is my nephew, Antonius." Marcus's voice was full of pride. "Antonius, this is Dinias, a warrior of great reputation. You have learned all of fighting that I can teach you, but you have the promise to be a better fighter than I, so I have engaged Dinias to train you."

"Many thanks, Uncle." Antonius apprehensively surveyed the stranger. Surely her father would not have engaged him if he were not a good man. The prospect of more lessons excited her, though being around a strange man sounded less pleasing.

Dinias eyed Antonius skeptically, as though teaching a boy was not what he most wanted to do.

"Let's see what you can do, boy," he said wearily, picking up a wooden sword and a shield. "Come at me and make me defend myself."

Antonius picked up her wooden sword and advanced on him. She struck his shield even before he had fully raised his sword.

"How did you do that?" Dinias exclaimed.

"Pardon me, did I move too fast?" Antonius feared that she had done something wrong.

Dinias chuckled. "No, I moved too slowly. Let's try it again."

Again Antonius struck his shield before he could parry the blow.

"Swift, isn't he?" Dinias said to her father. "I don't think I've ever seen anyone faster. And agile, too, aren't you, lad?"

"I'll wait and give you time to get into position," Antonius said, deferring to him.

"Hmpf." Dinias did not sound so pleased at her words, but he raised his sword and moved on Antonius.

She moved away before his blow could strike, then leapt into position and dealt a blow to his shield.

Dinias smiled. "What have we here? Your father was right. You could be a fine fighter. I shall teach you everything I know."

The weather grew hot, and she learned how to fight, sweating in her chain mail. As well as swordplay, she learned how to charge on horseback, thrusting the blunted long spear at her instructor's shield and avoiding his weapon.

25

After many a fall, she was able to sit well enough on her horse to keep from plunging off when her own shield was struck. She also learned the use of a bow and arrow.

"Some say that the bow and arrow are not weapons for noblemen, but only for robbers," Dinias told her. "That is foolish. If you are in a caer that is attacked, there is no better way to fend off the attackers than to shoot arrows from the stone walls. You should learn to use all weapons."

When Dinias advanced on her with a sword, the picture of the murderer's face flashed into her mind. She shuddered, but she fought fiercer than ever. She was not just fighting Dinias, she was fighting off a rapist. She could not lose.

When he bested her, she was so stunned that she could barely speak. If this were an attacker, he could be tearing off her chain mail.

"Don't be so downcast, boy. Everyone loses sometimes," Dinias said, clapping her on the back.

But she shook her head. Defeat was too terrible; she could not accept it. She would not be satisfied until she always won.

She would not settle for being fierce. No, every move must be perfect. Even when her lessons were over, she practiced each stroke again and again. She must wield her sword as carefully as a goldsmith used his fine tools. Only what she wrought would not be fine rings and cloak pins, but wounds.

One autumn afternoon, Dinias let her off early, and she went to visit the lake. She rode past her father's fields into the forest, though it still was haunted for her.

Her new black gelding, Arrow, was as swift as his name. She still liked to ride Shadow for old times' sake, but Arrow was the horse who was being trained to carry her into battle, if need be.

At the lake, Antonius threw herself on the ground and watched a gray heron stalk fish and a brilliant blue kingfisher hover above the water and dive down, returning with a fish in his beak.

She watched the kingfisher, then noticed that the heron had flown away without her seeing it leave. A dragonfly landed by her knee. She observed its delicate black wings.

Antonius saw that the pines surrounding the lake lived twice, on the land and reflected in the water, as she lived twice, once as a boy and, secretly, as a girl.

A fish splashed. The creatures that lived below, in the blue-green waters, seemed to call her to join them. It was warm for autumn, so she risked revealing herself by slipping out of her clothes and sliding into the waters. Diving so the water covered her whole body, she wished she were a fish or a frog instead of a girl. Once she had passed by a river and accidentally seen her father's men swimming. She now reached out her arms and kicked her legs, in imitation of what they had done.

The water soothed her as if it were magicked, as if she were a sojourner in an enchanted land. Perhaps the fishes swimming all around her were people long-entranced who waited for someone to end the spell. She had thought that after her mother died she would have no more such fancies, but they were part of her.

Emerging, she threw her clothes back on, swung herself onto Arrow, and rode further into the forest. The water had lessened her fears. She must be brave. How could a fighter be afraid of the forest? She dreamed of birdsong weaving a spell of protection, in a forest where no one could be killed as her mother had been.

Antonius came to a place where oak trees gleamed with yellow leaves. Cobwebs stretched between the trees and acorns covered the ground. She dismounted and sat on the moss under a large oak with pale green lichens growing on its bark. She was careful not to touch the oak because Rathtyen said that oak trees had great power.

Antonius could not forget the sight of her mother's body. The pine needles and oak leaves on the forest floor were not covered with blood, but she remembered that once they had been.

A large gray wolf appeared through the trees not far from her.

Antonius froze. The hairs on her arms prickled. Her throat tightened. Wolves were killers, as she had heard in many tales, and this one was large enough to kill her. Her hand clasped the hilt of her sword.

The wolf stood still and regarded Antonius with its cold yellow eyes. I could get a spear from my horse and throw it, she thought. Immediately, she was sick with fear not of the wolf but of herself. She knew that most boys her age would try to escape. But the bravest ones would try their skill. There would be much rejoicing if she brought home a fresh wolfskin.

Her stomach revolted at the idea of the wolf, now so alert, lying bloody on the pine needles. She knew she would fight the wolf if it attacked her, but not otherwise. The golden eyes looked so intelligent.

The wolf was a female, and might have young waiting for her. Even if they were weaned by this time of year, they might still need a mother's care.

The wolf walked away in another direction.

"Well done. You're a fine lad," said a voice behind Antonius.

Antonius nearly jumped. She turned and saw that an old crone had walked up behind her. She had concentrated so hard on the wolf that she hadn't heard the woman.

"Weren't you afraid?" she asked the thin, bright-eyed old woman.

"Of the wolf? No. Were you?"

"Not of that wolf."

"You were right there, lad. That wolf did not want you for a meal."

28

"I would have fought it if I had to."

The old woman, whose clothes looked as ancient as she did, sat down beside Antonius. "It is good to be able to fight. It is even better to know when not to fight," the crone said. "You don't have to be afraid in the woods. The wolves aren't the fiercest animals in the world."

"I know.'Lupus est homo hominis,'" she said, quoting Plautus as Father Matthew had taught her. "Man is the wolf of man." The old woman wouldn't know Latin, Antonius thought.

"That's the very truth," the crone said. "And men don't just strike in the woods. They can strike anywhere."

Antonius shivered.

The stoop-shouldered old woman patted her arm. "I know who you are, child. I saw you in the woods with your mother when you were a little one. I am Creiddyled, and I have seen many things, in these woods and elsewhere. Evil can happen anywhere. Let me teach you about the woods so you won't be afraid."

Antonius sneaked out of the villa before dawn because Creiddlyed had told her to come to her hut at that time. The air was chilly, so turning away from the warm brazier in her room was difficult. In the stable, Duach snored loudly, and did not wake when she saddled Arrow.

A sliver of moon provided little light. Trying to accustom her eyes to the dark, Antonius made her way through the trees to the crone's wattle-and-daub hut. A slight wind rustled in the leaves. An owl hooted not far away. The scent of damp earth and leaf mold filled the air. The old woman was waiting near the hut.

"Tie your horse here," she commanded.

"This morning we shall follow the deer. Take off your chain mail, because the rings would chime."

"But surely when I am in the forest I shall usually be wearing my mail," Antonius protested.

She believed her mail was like a turtle's shell. She longed for the day when she could put on a hard casing of mail even when she was not taking fighting lessons or riding in the forest. The mail restricted her movements and its weight tired her, but that did not matter.

The mail was familiar, comforting. It added to her weight as well as protecting her. She wished she could sleep in the chain mail. Without it, she felt like a peeled turtle. She kept it on until the last possible moment, even on hot summer days.

"You will learn to move quietly even in mail, but first you must learn how to move silently without it," Creiddlyed told her.

Antonius removed her mail shirt and left it in the crone's hut, which was permeated with the smells of the herbs hanging on the walls.

"We must always stay upwind of the deer, so be alert to the wind's course," Creiddlyed said. "Now, step softly, as I do. Feel the forest floor so carefully that even when it is dark you can anticipate roots before your feet touch them."

First they walked on a path, then they made their way through trees and bracken. Antonius felt ahead of her for branches, but when her arms moved them aside, they swished noisily.

"No, imagine you are a deer and wolves may be nearby. Or that you are a wolf trying to steal up on a deer or a wildcat on a hare," the crone said. "We are coming to a pond where deer usually drink at dawn, so we must stop talking. We will approach the pond from the east, since the wind is blowing from the west."

Antonius marveled at how silently Creiddyled slipped through the trees. Following the old woman through the first light, she spotted a pond with morning mist rising from its waters. A stag with many-pointed antlers stood by the pond. She held her breath. A night heron, still lingering by the pond after its night of fishing, squawked and flew off. The stag bent his head to drink, then raised it and walked away, leaving an empty clearing.

Antonius and Creiddyled continued silently, rounding the pond until they came to the stag's tracks, then following them. The ground was dry, so the tracks were hard to follow, but Creiddyled always found them, or broken twigs that told her the way stag had gone. Finally, the old woman clutched Antonius's arm and pointed. There, off through the trees, the stag was visible again, munching on grasses. They stood motionless, watching until he wandered off.

"As a man I must hunt and kill the deer." Antonius sighed, foreseeing the use for the skills she was learning.

"You must become both the deer and the wolf. You can never rest entirely, but must always be ready for danger," Creiddyled said.

"We also will spend days tracking foxes," she added. "You must learn how the fox changes its course, doubles back on its tracks, and crosses streams. Like a fox, you must have many strategies, for you never know which one will work. You are learning to fight, but it is also good to know how to evade attack."

"You must learn to kill." Creiddyled put her hand on Antonius's arm. "But you should pray to the spirit of the animal you are killing, thanking it for giving its flesh so you can live."

Antonius crossed herself. "That sounds pagan. I cannot pray to animals, but only to their Creator."

"Then pray to whatever spirit you believe in to show your humility at taking life," the crone told her.

"You must not be an unthinking killer."

Antonius nodded. The old woman's words made sense to her. Much as she thrived on her lessons in sword fighting, Antonius wished that they were less demanding, so she could spend more time learning from Creiddlyed. She was coming to feel at home in the woods, less afraid than she felt within walls. But even beautiful things made her think of death. She knew the leaves and flowers would die, but still she loved them. She watched the fish, though someone might catch them, and smiled at the deer, though someone might hunt them. She went hunting with her father, but took less pleasure in it than he did, for she kept thinking herself kin to the prey.

While she rode through the forest, she tried to calculate what her first move would be if someone attacked her.

Tired after a day of practice with Dinias, Antonius went to her room. Kaethi, a serving girl, was fussing with the brazier.

"The fire is lit," Kaethi said, turning to Antonius. There was a grin on the girl's red-cheeked face. Her auburn hair stretched down to her waist. "Can I light your fires, too, young master? You shouldn't have to live like your uncle, with no kisses."

Gasping, Antonius stepped backward. She had never thought that pretending to be a boy might mean that girls would want her.

"Don't be afraid. It's great fun." Kaethi approached her. "You're so handsome, and I know you'd be gentle. Would you like to touch my breast?" She started to pull one breast out of her gown.

"No! Please don't!" Antonius cried, averting her eyes. She fled from her room and returned to her father's hall, where she sat staring into the fire and pretending to listen to a long discussion about sin that her father was engaged in with Father Matthew.

She hardly dared to return to her room, but when she reentered it, Kaethi was gone. Fearing another invasion, Antonius barred the door.

She tried to console herself with the thought that at least the serving people did not guess that she was a girl. But she realized that this was not the last time that a girl or woman would approach her. She could not always run away, so she would have to be prepared with polite words of refusal. She tried not to think about pretty Kaethi.

Antonius rode with her father to a festival in a town that was not far away. Apple trees were blooming, scenting the air. White petals covered the ground in patches. Antonius thrilled to the sound of a lark's song.

A woman's scream pierced the air. Antonius's heart seemed to stop. Reminded of her mother's terrible screams on the day she died, Antonius rode away towards the sound. She heard her father calling after her. Turning her head, she saw his horse stumble and Marcus slip off. She hesitated, but she saw him scrambling to his knees. The screams compelled her to ride on. Another man might be holding down a woman as the murderer had held down her mother.

Antonius urged Arrow to gallop faster than ever before. She passed the apple trees and came to a newly planted field where a girl of fourteen or fifteen was struggling with a clean-shaven young man who was dressed like a noble and wore a sword. He flung her down and she kicked him. He struck her across the face and pulled up her skirt.

Antonius yelled "Stop!" and jumped off her horse. Nothing existed in the world but this rape that she must prevent. She could almost feel the man's hands grabbing her legs instead of the girl's and smell his stinking breath.

The man glared at her. "Get away, boy, she's mine. Find your own girl." She pulled her sword from its scabbard, and he turned from the girl and pulled his.

33

All at once her sword's metal was meeting flesh, different from the feel of a wooden blade touching her teacher. Heart thumping, Antonius did not hesitate. She cut the man's shoulder, but he moved away fast enough to prevent too great an injury. His sword flashed back at her, and metal clashed on metal. She fought as if she had been the one he had thrown on the ground, as if it had been her legs that he had pried open. One of his blows nearly struck her head, and she realized that he would kill her if he could, but she pressed on. He tried to push her back, and she, pretending that he was too strong for her, stepped backward. He raised his arm a little too high, and her sword went into his chest. Furious, she pressed against the resistant flesh and felt the life go out of him. Blood poured from his chest.

He fell to the ground. She pulled out her sword and stared at the blood covering it. She wiped the sword on the earth. Holy Virgin, this was what it was to kill. The stench of blood mingled with the scent of the newly planted earth. She almost retched.

The girl on the ground watched wide-eyed. She moaned. Tears streamed down her face. She struggled to pull down her torn gown.

Marcus rode up and leapt from his horse. He flung his arms around Antonius and kissed her on both cheeks. "My brave one! My Lancelot! I shall name you after a weapon. That's a name for a fighter." Letting her go, he frowned. "I am glad you didn't get yourself killed. You were right to protect the girl, but did you have to kill him? I shall have to find his family and pay a large sum to keep them from retaliating and to satisfy the magistrate."

"I did have to kill him," Antonius replied, not apologizing. She believed her father would be able to settle the matter.

No, she must not think of herself as Antonius any longer. Her father had given her a new name, and she would use it.

Lancelot turned to the girl and extended her hand, just as gently as she would have wanted if she had been the one thrown onto the furrows.

The girl allowed Lancelot to help her rise. "Thanks," she said faintly, barely able to speak.

Lancelot was no more able to speak than she was.

Marcus said, "Let's find your family. What is your name?"

"Braca, the silversmith's daughter, lord."

"We'll take you back to your father," Marcus told her.

Lancelot mounted her horse and Marcus helped Braca up behind her. With Braca's arms around her waist, Lancelot could feel that the girl still trembled.

Lancelot trembled too. She had killed. And someone had tried to kill her. She had almost died. She might not have been here, sitting on her horse, riding away. She might not be smelling the apple blossoms. She might have been gone forever. But she knew that, even if she had had time to think about challenging the man, she would have done the same.

Townspeople filled the street near the silversmith's shop. The wiry smith came out and Braca ran to him, crying, "Father, a man assaulted me and this lad saved me!"

"God be praised!" exclaimed the smith, pulling Braca into the shelter of his arm. He bowed to Lancelot's father, then to Lancelot. "I thank you, noble lords." He hurried the disheveled girl into his shop and closed the door.

A crowd began to gather, and many people clapped Lancelot on the back. Dogs began to bark and jump about in the excitement. "We must find the magistrate," Marcus said.

But Lancelot said, "Please, I want to be shriven first."

Her father took her to the lime-whitened church.

Lancelot genuflected at the altar. She saw a rosy-cheeked young priest and begged, "Please shrive me."

35

"Very well," he said, raising his eyebrows at her urgent request.

She could scarcely wait until they had gone into the vestry.

Among the priest's fine embroidered robes, which smelled of incense, she sobbed, "I've killed a man. He tried to rape a girl, and I stopped him."

"Why, that was no sin," the priest assured her. "You're a good lad."

She trembled, uncertain that she deserved the praise. "But I was so angry that I truly wanted to kill him, not just to prevent him from hurting her. Wasn't that wrong?"

"Your conscience is too tender." The priest's voice was soothing. "Not many men would have risked their lives to save her as you did."

Lancelot shook her head. "Oh no, I had to fight him. There was no other course that I could take."

The priest absolved her. But she still thought of the ugliness of the body lying raw on the field. She wondered if the man was in hell.

Her father took her to a magistrate, a man they had known for many years. Lancelot barely heard her father's words.

"Fortunately," the magistrate said, "the man you describe was a rogue from many miles away who has plagued us with attacks. I have heard that his father disinherited him. So you won't have to pay the father much, if anything."

That night Lancelot shared a straw bed in the town's inn with her father, who slept as far from her as possible. She stayed awake into the night, wondering whether Braca could sleep. How did she bear what had happened? Lancelot thought that she would rather die than be touched as the man had touched Braca.

Reaching up to her face, she found it still the same, though her name was new. It seemed right to have a name to denote her transformation to a killer. She had changed from Anna to Antonius, and now she was Lancelot. In her short life, she had been three people.

What would it be like to be Lancelot? If she wounded and killed, it must be only to help others, she vowed. She would have to risk her life many times, but if that was necessary for her to fulfill her role in life, she would accept the danger.

Mother, help me to save others, though I could not save you, she prayed. Let me never fail again. Tears dripped down her cheeks.

After this, Lancelot often was asked to help people when a sword might be of use.

Marcus shook his head and said privately, "What life have I prepared you for, my daughter?"

"A better one than any other father would have." She smiled and pressed his hand.

2   THE KING'S DAUGHTER

"One day I shall be Queen of Powys," Guinevere mused, sitting on her gray pony at the top of a hill where she overlooked the woods and farms of her land. All of this would be hers someday, when she was grown. The oaks and the beeches, the rowans and the alders and the elms, all were her trees. The glens were hers, and likewise the lakes and streams and the golden fields of wheat. The people in the mud-daub huts and the stone caers were to be her subjects, and she would care for them. Her chest swelled with pride.

Sion, the pockmarked stableboy who accompanied her on a slightly larger bay, nodded. "I don't doubt you'll be queen, Lady Guinevere."

"I shall be a kind queen, a just queen," she announced, letting her pony, Bramble, eat some of the summer's lush grasses. Her people would call her Guinevere the Generous.

If she had been a boy, she could have talked openly about her desire to rule, but because she was a girl and her father, King

Leodegran, still hoped for a son, she knew instinctively that she could talk about it only with the stableboy. "I shall put you in charge of all my father's horses."

Sion whistled. "They say your father has the greatest herd in Britain, so that's no mean gift, Lady Guinevere."

"You may also have someday a tunic embroidered with gold as thanks for teaching me to jump Bramble."

He gave her an impish grin. "I'd get that fine tunic terrible dirty looking after the horses."

She wrinkled her nose. "For feast day use, of course."

Rain started to drip on them and a cloud of mist began to rise over the countryside she surveyed.

"I suppose we had better go home now." She rolled her eyes to show that she would rather not. "My mother will be expecting me. I'll race you down the hill."

"It's too rocky for a race, Lady Guinevere," he reproached her.

"So it is. Very well. I'll race you when we get to the glen." She urged Bramble down the narrow path through the heather. A startled grouse flew up on whirring wings, but Guinevere was able to keep Bramble from rearing.

Guinevere loved the motion of the pony. Sometimes she wished she could be a centaur, and have hooves instead of feet with silly toes. Then she would never have to worry about tearing her clothes, because she wouldn't wear any. But if she were a centaur, she couldn't become a queen.

She slowed Bramble's pace as they approached the caer. Even with the drizzling rain, she had no great wish to go indoors.

Her father's huge timber hall with its high thatched roof loomed before them. They passed through a gate in the stone wall that surrounded the caer. Smiling, Guinevere answered the guard who greeted her. Surely her father's wall was tall enough to keep out any invaders, and all of the buildings were in fine shape, their thatch roofs as well repaired as the very roof of the hall. No one lived meanly at Leodegran's caer, she thought with pride. She had visited other caers where the servants were too thin.

"Guinevere! Your mother wants you!" called Gwynhwyfach, a serving girl of her own age, as soon as they reached the stable yard.

Guinevere reluctantly dismounted and handed Bramble's reins to Sion, who grinned with sympathy. She drank in the scent of the damp pony and patted her in parting. Her mother sometimes complained that Guinevere smelled too horsey.

"Very well, Gwynhwyfach," Guinevere replied in a voice that was sharper than she had meant it to sound.

Gywnhwyfach flinched, and Guinevere felt a trifle guilty. It was the need to go indoors that bothered her, not the serving girl. Gywnhwyfach's plain, undyed gown was so tight that she seemed to be bursting out of it. She was growing and should have a new one.

Aware that her own wet black hair must be tangled from her ride, Guinevere patted it down.

"Tomorrow we'll jump more ditches, Lady Guinevere," Sion promised.

Gwynhwyfach stared with evident longing at the stocky pony.

"You may pat my pony," Guinevere told her.

Gwynhwyfach gave the pony's side a quick, awkward pat. "It would be grand to ride." She sighed.

Guinevere frowned. Should she ask Sion to teach Gwyn-hwyfach how to ride, too? But why should she grant such a favor to a serving girl? Bramble was hers and she didn't want anyone else riding her. Why was it that however kind to Gwynhwyfach she was, it never seemed to be enough?

"Perhaps someday when all of your chores are done," she said, thinking that magnanimous. "On one of the old horses that have been put out to pasture," she added, so Gwynhwyfach would know that riding Bramble was Guinevere's prerogative alone.

"Thank you, Guinevere." Gwynhwyfach dared to pout and her voice held a hint of sarcasm. "But when are my chores ever done? There's always something else to do. Never mind, I don't care."

Annoyed at this ingratitude, Guinevere bit her lip to keep from making a retort.

How strange it was that Gwynhwyfach's face looked just like her own. She hadn't realized it until recently, when she started using her mother's copper mirror. The black hair was the same, and so were the nose and the mouth. The main difference was that Gwynhwyfach, like most of the serving people, had gray eyes, whereas her own were blue like her mother's. They were both short like the serving people, some of whom were descended from the Old Ones.

Guinevere wiped her face with a bit of linen, then dropped it in her hurry to leave the stableyard. With a resentful air, Gwynhwyfach picked it up, as usual. Why was Gwynhwyfach more sullen than the other servants? Guinevere wondered.

"I'll race you to the door," Guinevere said as she headed for the fine thatched-roofed building where her mother sewed.

Guinevere sprinted forward, running with all her might, but the serving girl outpaced her and reached the door first. The girl laughed triumphantly. How simple it was when they were younger and just played tag, before Gwynhwyfach had become her servant. Catching her breath, Guinevere patted her hair down again, and entered the room where her mother, Rhiannon, was generally to be found weaving or spinning with her women.

Rhiannon was sitting near her loom, tying a thread on a piece of blue wool in her lap. She raised her head and smiled, and Guinevere wished that she could be tall and fair-haired like her.

"Your new gown is finished. Let me see how you look in it." Holding the gown up to a window's light, Rhiannon's eagerness was much greater than Guinevere was able to feel. A gown was all very well, but dull stuff compared with her pony.

Nevertheless, the deep blue wool was very fine, she had to admit, and her mother had embroidered some pretty flowers on the sleeves. Guinevere thanked her and carried the gown off to her own room, down a passage from her mother's.

Macha, Guinevere's gap-toothed old serving woman who had been nurse to her mother before her, helped her out of her riding breeches and into the gown.

"About time you dressed like a daughter to the king of Powys, now that you're ten summers old," Macha scolded.

When Guinevere ran back to her mother's room, her father, Leodegran, was there with a hand on Rhiannon's shoulder. Rhiannon was now embroidering designs on a tunic intended for him.

"Isn't our Guinevere beautiful? She's the loveliest girl I've ever seen," her mother exclaimed.

Leodegran smiled and twisted his long black mustaches. "You're very pretty, Guinevere. No doubt every king's son in Britain will seek your hand some day."

"But I'm not any prettier than Gwynhwyfach. She looks just like me," Guinevere said.

She was glad that her parents liked how she looked, but she thought it only fair to point out that Gwynhwyfach looked the same.

Rhiannon dropped her needle. "No, she doesn't, child. Your eyes are much bluer. Hers are gray."

Guinevere shrugged. "My eyes may be bluer, but what of it? She looks just like me."

Rhiannon pulled away from her husband and retrieved her needle. "You see, Leodegran," she said, in a voice much bolder than usual, "it can't be hidden. It will shame Guinevere when she is older."

Leodegran grunted and frowned. "Of course you're much fairer than any serving girl, Guinevere. You mustn't say such things."

The next morning, Gwynhwyfach burst into Guinevere's room and dared to knock the gold-tasseled cushions off the bed.

"I hate you!" Gwynhwyfach cried, glaring at her.

Guinevere stared at her. "Why ever would you?" she gasped.

"We have to go because of you! My mother and I are being sent away to some old farm of your father's because you said I look like you."

"Why? I don't understand." Guinevere shivered at the idea that she was hated, but Gwynhwyfach just ran off and wouldn't say anything else. No one had ever said they hated her before. Guinevere had always believed that everyone liked her, and the thought that they might not made her blink away tears.

She hastened to her mother's room and asked, "Why are Gwynhwyfach and her mother Effrdyl being sent off?"

Her mother only said, "Never mind." She wouldn't look Guinevere in the eye. Guinevere ran outside and saw pretty, red-haired Effrdyl and Gwynhwyfach climb into a cart. Effrdyl's face showed no emotion, but Gwynhwyfach was pouting.

"You can have my old shawl," Guinevere said on impulse, taking it off her shoulders and handing it to Gwynhwyfach. Its red color was faded, but it was good, warm wool. Her new plaid one was enough for her.

"I don't want it."

Gwynhwyfach wouldn't reach out her hand, but Effrdyl tool the shawl and said, "Thank you, Lady Guinevere."

Then the cart rolled away, taking them out of sight. Guinevere shrugged. She would not miss them. No matter how generous she was, Gwynhwyfach dared to resent her kindness. She was sorry that she had given the girl her shawl. But who would she run races with now?

The great hall was warmed with cheerful flames in the fire pit. Leodegran's men jested and jostled each other at trestle tables, but they subdued their voices a trifle while Guinevere poured mead for them. The scent of mutton whetted her appetite.

She slipped back to her place beside her mother at the great oak high table and took her share of mutton stew, which she liked exceedingly.

Soon she saw that it was time to pour for the men again, and took up the jar to fill their drinking horns. She paused by Gwythr, her father's chief man at arms, a grizzled veteran who often told her stories about giants.

"I'll tell you another story tonight, princess, about a giant who made a coat of the beards of men he had killed," Gwythyr said softly while she poured his mead.

If only she were a giant, instead of being short, even for a girl.

A harper sang her father's praises. Leodegran had led his men to take many of the fat cattle of Gwynedd, the song proclaimed.

Why was taking your neighbors' cows so glorious? Guinevere wondered, but she enjoyed the spirited tune.

As she walked past the firepit, the hem of her gown caught fire. Guinevere screamed and dropped the jar, which broke on the floor. Gwythr grabbed her and beat out the fire with his leather cloak.

Guinevere exhaled. She must not cry. She was a future queen. She could see that only a bit of her skirt was ruined.

Her father and mother rushed to her.

Her father reached her first. He squeezed her hand. "Stay away from the fire, my usually clever girl," he said. "Gwythr, I'll give you a fine new horse for your quick action."

"Thank you, my lord." Gwythr bowed his head.

"Thank you for helping me," Guinevere said to the warrior.

Her mother hugged her. "Your skirt can be mended more easily than you can. Be careful around fire."

Leodegran resumed his seat at the head table. He signaled the harper, who had stopped playing, to begin again.

"Go and change your gown," Guinevere's mother told her.

Rhiannon then resumed her seat and smiled at the company as if to say that all was well. A serving woman began to clean up the mess from the broken jar. The door to the hall opened and a dirt-streaked warrior entered. He motioned for Leodegran to come aside, so the king went off with him.

Guinevere lingered because she sensed that something unusual had happened and she wanted to know what it was.

When Leodegran returned, his face was grim. His eyes were narrow and the veins bulged on his forehead.

"The Saxons have raided my old farm on the eastern part of our lands. They burned it to the ground and killed everyone there." He called out to the men eating at the trestle tables, "Come off with me, we must plan a raid to retaliate."

The men leapt up, waving their arms as if they held swords.

Guinevere froze. She imagined the fire that had just frightened her, magnified a thousand times.

She went up to Rhiannon, who sat frozen, holding her spoon in her stew. "Mother, does that mean Gwynhwyfach and her mother were killed, too?"

"Yes, child." Rhiannon's shoulders sagged; her eyes were dull.

"I hate fire!" Guinevere exclaimed.

Rhiannon rose from the table and wrung her hands. "Oh, Blessed Mother, it was the only time I ever stood up to my husband, and I was wrong! We should go and pray for them. It's all that we can do now." She grabbed Guinevere's hand and dragged her to the chapel.

Guinevere paid little heed to her mother's prayers. What good were prayers? They couldn't bring people back from the dead. Somehow she had caused Gwynhwyfach's death by saying the girl looked like her. Gwynhwyfach had burned to death. No one had saved her.

"Remember Gwynhwyfach in your prayers," Macha ordered Guinevere when she knelt by her bed that night.

"I didn't like her so very much," Guinevere admitted. "She was always sulking. But of course it's terrible that she's dead."

Macha frowned. "Do you think it was easy for her, looking like you and always being reminded that she couldn't have what you have? It's always hard for lords' bastards, but not all of them wear their breeding on their faces."

Guinevere felt dizzy. Her voice was shrill. "What do you mean?" Macha grumbled and fussed with the bed covers.

"Now, don't tell me you didn't guess. She was your father's daughter, of course. And don't say I told you, unless you want me to get in trouble."

Guinevere held onto the side of the bed to keep from falling. "She was my sister? A serving girl?"

"I just said she was, didn't I?" Macha snapped. "She was your father's daughter. Most men take their pleasure where they will. That's a serving woman's life."

"My father loved Effrdyl?" Didn't he love her mother, then?

"Love's rather a fancy word for it. Don't carry on so, child."

Macha squeezed her shoulder. "Mayhap I shouldn't have told."

"So I have a sister? I had one," she corrected herself, dazed at the unfamiliar thought. "Why didn't anyone tell me? I always wanted a sister to play with."

"You did play with her. Then she waited on you, as was only proper," Macha explained.

"But if I'd known she was my sister, I would have treated her differently," Guinevere protested. "I would have let her ride my pony." Oh, why hadn't she allowed Gwynhwyfach to ride Bramble? Was she mean and selfish?

"What's done is done." Macha's withered hand patted her small one.

"My father couldn't have loved Gwynhwyfach. He treated her just like the other servants, as far as I could see."

Guinevere tried to imagine what it would be like if Leodegran never smiled at her or told her how proud he was of her. "What if I had been born a servant? I could have been, couldn't I?"

"Nonsense, you mustn't have such thoughts. Your mother was daughter to the king of Dyfed." Macha's arms enfolded Guinevere.

Guinevere buried her face in Macha's shoulder. "I never even knew she was my sister. I just gave her orders. I don't blame her for saying she said she hated me."

"She said that? She'd have gotten a beating if you had told anyone. It was good of you not to tell. Now, be calm, my girl." Macha rocked Guinevere as if she were still little.

Guinevere clutched Macha – how she wished she had given Gwynhwyfach her new shawl instead of her old one, even though the Saxons would have gotten it. If only Gwynhwyfach had owned just one thing that was new and beautiful.

Gwynhwyfach's resentment at being a servant looked different to Guinevere now. It was just how she would have felt if she had been in Gwynhwyfach's place. Her half-sister had been bold and restless, as Guinevere was herself. She resolved that she would always be kind to serving women, in memory of her sister.

She looked at her father in a different way. He had always seemed so fond of her, but he must be cold to have ignored his other daughter. How could men love some children and not others? She wondered. Didn't they have the same feelings she did?

Guinevere still kissed her father dutifully, but she no longer ran up with excitement when he rode into the courtyard.

She wondered whether he had other mistresses, and whether her mother was angry and ashamed. How could her mother bear it? Rhiannon was so meek around Leodegran. Macha said many men did the same, but Guinevere vowed that when she married, she would never let her husband be unfaithful.

Rhiannon dragged herself painfully across her room and slumped in a chair as far from the brazier as possible, though it was late autumn and Guinevere almost shivered from the cold. Guinevere winced at seeing her mother's evident discomfort.

"Are you well, Mother?" Guinevere asked anxiously. Her mother never looked well when she was great with child, and now her face was pale. Guinevere scarcely thought about what it would be like to have a brother or a sister because her mother so often bore dead ones.

"Well enough." Rhiannon tried to smile.

The hanging on the wall showed the Virgin Mary holding a plump baby Jesus, no doubt inspiring her mother to go through another childbed. Guinevere frowned at it.

No one else was near, so Guinevere burst out with the question she had held back for so long. "Why must you have another baby? It makes you so weak." And they never live anyway, she thought but did not say.

"It is important for your father to have a son to rule Powys after him," Rhiannon said, as if that should be obvious. She did not hold back a sigh.

"Why can't I rule Powys?" Guinevere made bold to say, though she wouldn't have dared to ask her father.

"You might have to." Sighing again, her mother took off her shawl. No one else would leave off a shawl on such a day. "But I shouldn't say that. This time I may have a fine brother for you." She patted her stomach.

Guinevere did not think it so fine that a newborn child would be seen as more important than she was, but she did not bother her mother by saying so. She hoped for a sister.

The thought of a sister reminded her of Gwynhwyfach. Did her father have more children by other women? Did her mother love him?

"Are you happy, Mother?" she asked, because she could not ask about love.

Rhiannon started in her chair as if wakened from sleep. "What strange questions you ask. Happy, indeed! I'm married to a king and have all that I want, and I'm a Christian woman with a hope of salvation. That's more than enough for anyone."

She wasn't happy, then. Guinevere's heart constricted. She was embarrassed at knowing so much about her mother. She turned back to the cloak she was mending.

She wanted to be happy, not just a queen and a Christian.

Leodegran burst into the room. "When will my new tunic be ready? I need it for the ceremony next week."

Rhiannon's wan face looked up at him. She reached for the red tunic that she was trimming with embroidered gold wildcats, Leodegran's symbol.

"Yes, Leodegran. It will be ready." She picked up her embroidery hoop.

"Good."

He left the room as unceremoniously as he had entered.

Guinevere almost jumped off her stool. "Can't someone else finish it? You're so tired."

"No one else can do fine work as well as I can. You certainly can't." Rhiannon's brow creased. Guinevere's lack of skill at the womanly arts did not please her. "Leodegran likes me to make the finishing touches on all his better clothes, as you well know." She took her needle and began to make couching stitches, putting down the first thread over which others would be laid.

Guinevere stirred restlessly. Why must her mother always say "Yes, Leodegran," so meekly? Guinevere had no intention of learning fine work. She could not even do chain stitching well. She would never wait on a husband as her mother did — never.

Screams woke Guinevere in the middle of the night. At first she thought it was a nightmare, but she pinched herself and knew that she was awake. Those must be her mother's screams! Her mother must be giving birth. Guinevere jumped out of bed and, still wearing her woolen bedgown, ran to her mother's room. The room was full of women, Macha among them, crowded around the bed. At first Guinevere could barely see Rhiannon. Then she saw her mother, legs open, sweating and twisting.

Guinevere wanted to cry out and tell her mother not to have babies if it hurt her so.

Macha caught a glimpse of Guinevere and said, "Go back to your room. You're too young for this sight."

"No! I want to stay with my mother!" Guinevere hated the sight of her mother in pain, but leaving would be even worse than staying.

Rhiannon's agonized eyes focused on her. "Let my daughter stay," she gasped.

Guinevere prayed much more fervently than she ever had before. "Let my mother be well. Mother Mary, please let my mother be well."

The room smelled of blood, sweat, and excrement. The windows were open, but Guinevere felt as if she would never breathe clean air again.

"Push harder," one of the women told Rhiannon.

"I am pushing," Rhiannon moaned. "Oh, Blessed Mother!"

Rhiannon screamed, wept, and groaned, but the baby still would not come.

"Are there knots tied somewhere in the caer?" an old midwife asked in a stern voice, staring around the room.

"Of course not. Do you think we are fools, careless of our lady's life?" Macha demanded, glaring at her.

Guinevere bit her lip so hard that it bled. She wanted to clench her hands into fists, but that would bind her mother. Instead, she dug her nails into her own arms.

Finally, her mother gave a shriek, and the baby came, along with a great deal of blood. Guinevere saw a limp red bundle. One of the women cleaned it, slapped it, and tried to breathe into its mouth, but the baby was as limp as ever. The dead boy was the most wretched-looking thing Guinevere had ever seen.

"She's gone, too," the midwife said, and Guinevere quickly turned her gaze to her mother.

Rhiannon's eyes were staring, and Macha closed them.

"No!" Guinevere shrieked. She grabbed Rhiannon's hand, but no pressure answered her own.

Her mother was gone. One moment she was there, and the next moment she was not. Guinevere could not breathe. It was too terrible; it could not be true.

Guinevere fled to her room. She flung herself on her bed, put her head under a pillow, and sobbed.

Macha came after her. Guinevere saw tears flowing from the old woman's eyes.

"Poor girl," she said softly to Guinevere. She tried to put her arms around Guinevere, but Guinevere shook off the touch.

"Oh, my poor child," Macha moaned. "I pray that you won't die the same way as your mother. You are so much smaller and more delicately made that I fear you won't survive as many child-beds as my lady did."

Guinevere sucked in her breath. So this terrible death that had claimed her mother threatened her, too! She could not make any reply to her nurse.

Left alone, Guinevere vowed that she would never lie scream-ing like that. She would never bear a child. Why die to please a husband or bear him an heir? Tears streaming down her cheeks, Guinevere decided that she did not want a husband.

"Let me become queen of Powys, never marry, and never bear a child," she prayed. "I will be kind to everyone." But she doubted that Mother Mary heard her prayers, or cared, if she did hear. If prayers could not save her mother, what good were they to her?

"Father, won't you please teach me a little more Latin? I've learned some, but I don't know enough words to read well." She approached Leodegran in his office, where he was looking over his steward's accounts. The caer's few leather-bound books and scrolls were kept in this room. They had belonged to Guinevere's grandfather and had been neglected since his death.

Leodegran looked up from his wax tablet. "You know all the Latin you need to know, and more. Your mother couldn't read. You should go off and spin with your ladies."

"I have already been spinning for hours. It's always the same. You can't imagine how dull it is!" Guinevere dared to tell him. Her fingers were sore, but not as weary as her mind.

53

She tried to make up stories while she spun, but then she broke the thread.

"And is it dull to have clothes? You're a willful girl. I indulge you too much," he said, shaking his head.

"Could I help you with the accounts, then?" she ventured.

Leodegran chuckled. "Very well, but mind you don't make any mistakes." He handed her one of the tablets.

She sat down, moderately content, for she liked figures better than spinning.

Counting with the abacus, she pondered the numbers. "How much barley is enough to supply the caer for a year, Father? And how much wheat?"

There was no answer. She looked up to see that Leodegran had gone. She could find the steward and ask him.

Instead, her eyes strayed to the books, one in particular. She picked up the heavy volume and carried it to her table.

The story of Aeneas was the only book in the caer that was not religious. The leather cover smelled good to her.

Guinevere opened to the part to which she always felt drawn – about Dido, the African queen. "Perfide!" she whispered aloud, raging with Dido over her abandonment by Aeneas. It was magic that a story was on vellum. She wished for more of them, and she longed to know all the words.

But there were other reasons to want to learn.

She might be a queen someday, and surely a queen should know more than any of her subjects. She did not want to depend on priests, or any other men, to tell her what books said.

The sound of horses echoed on the cobbles, and Guinevere ran out of the hall to meet the warriors. Her father had been fighting for Arthur, the man who was trying to become High King of all

Britain, and against Ryons of Norgales, who had entered into the war of succession to try to seize part of Leodegran's lands.

Leodegran's horse was in the lead of the returning warband, and Guinevere sighed with relief. She had scarcely admitted to herself that she had feared he might never return. She ran to him, as she had not done in ages.

Many other girls and women, both noble and common, were hurrying to see whether their fathers, brothers, husbands, sons, and sweethearts had returned.

Leodegran looked weary and had a new scar on one hand, but he seemed handsomer than he ever had to Guinevere, though his black mustaches were turning gray. He smiled at the sight of her.

Leodegran dismounted in a dignified manner. She flung her arms around him, as she used to, when she was little. He reeked of unwashed clothes, horses, and other smells that were strange to Guinevere, but she did not mind. Though he laughed at her fussing over him, he allowed it.

Then she asked, "Where's Gwythr?"

Leodegran's smile faded. "Dead. He was the best warrior I had, and he died a hero's death."

Guinevere's stomach rebelled. A hero's death? What was that? Just a death. She would never again hear him tell tales, which he had done better than anyone else. She could not even attend his funeral, for he had been buried in some far-off battlefield.

She looked around the warband to see who else was there, or was missing. She saw that other men had but one arm or leg, and their faces were grimmer than they had been. One young warrior who had been handsome now had only one eye.

Guinevere bade the injured men come into the hall and be tended. It was only later that she realized that Sion the stableboy had not come back, either. So this was war. She shed tears for him and for Gwythr.

That night Guinevere wanted comfort, so she asked Valeria, a fosterling and highborn orphan, to sleep with her. Guinevere asked that often because she liked the girl.

Guinevere snuggled beside Valeria, not gossiping as they often did. She wept, and her friend held her. Valeria smelled sweet as a meadow. Guinevere fell asleep, her cheek resting on silken brown hair, her arm flung around Valeria.

Guinevere made her way across the courtyard to the stables. Spring was in the air and she had no mind to stay inside and spin. She wanted to see the first wildflowers in bloom.

Whecca, a plump, brown-haired girl who had been Guinevere's servant ever since Gywnhwyfach was sent away, trailed behind.

"I'd rather have a good horse than a good gown any day," Guinevere declared. "A gown can take me nowhere, but a horse can take me anywhere."

Whecca giggled. "But if a girl could have only one or the other, it's better to have a gown."

Guinevere tossed her head and refused to concede. "I'd still rather have the horse. I could ride naked, if I had to." And she would do so with dignity, despite her growing breasts.

Whecca choked with laughter. "You'd best not let your father hear you say that, my lady." They continued on to the stables.

Clusters of Leodegran's men were readying their horses for returning to the war. Shining Star, her mare, whinnied when Guinevere came up to her and presented her with an apple. She patted the white star on the brown horse's forehead.

Leodegran, wearing chain mail, strode up to his stable. He grumbled at the sight of Guinevere making ready to ride out.

"What do you mean, trying to go riding when there's a war on? I've told you that you have to stay home." Though his voice was gruff, it was not unkind.

"But Norgales' forces aren't still in our territory, are they? I thought King Arthur's warband had driven them out?" She tried to reason with him, though she knew that she could not convince him to let her leave the caer. The hepatica in the woods would bloom without her.

"I think Norgales' men are gone, but the High King's men will be through here today to gather supplies. It's true that his warband is helping us, but any warband has men who might bother a girl. It's better for you to stay at home." Leodegran smiled a little and twisted his mustache ends in his fingers. "However," he added, "there is no harm in your walking outside for a moment and greeting the High King when he comes to water his horses. I would invite him to dine with us, but he is in pursuit of Ryons's warband and cannot take the time. Perhaps after the war he will do us the honor.

And put on your best gown," he added, looking with disfavor at her riding breeches. "See to it that all of your ladies stay inside, and only you stand by the well."

Guinevere said, "Yes, Father," in a dutiful voice.

She saw no great need to hide away because of the warriors. She was used to her father's warband, and none of the men had ever bothered her.

Frowning at the cloudless sky because she could not ride under it, Guinevere made her way back to the women's quarters. Whecca, still trailing her, babbled with excitement,

"The High King will ride this way today, my lady! I can't believe we'll see the High King!"

"I suppose that's interesting," Guinevere acknowledged. She had never seen any king with a territory larger than her father's. "Help me dress in my green gown, and then go back to the courtyard and let me know when you hear that he's come. I suppose I have to see to the making of cloaks for the soldiers."

After Whecca had helped her dress and braided green ribbons in her hair, Guinevere went off to join her attendant ladies and serving women, who were weaving woolen cloaks for Leodegran's fighting men. Even now, Guinevere had little patience with the weaving. She knew it was necessary, but couldn't she leave the task to others? She kept breaking her woolen thread and having to tie it.

At midday, there was a great clamor in the courtyard, and Whecca ran up to her, calling, "He's coming!"

The ladies rushed to hang out of the windows. It was odd that her father had said they all should stay inside. Guinevere shook her head over her father's peculiarities.

She went to the well, where serving men were eagerly drawing water for the High King's party. A number of warriors rode up.

The High King was dressed not much differently from the others, in chain mail, but he wore a gold torque around his neck. His white stallion was the finest of the horses, and the other men held back deferentially as he rode up.

He was dusty, but had a handsome face, shaven in the Roman way, red-gold hair, and large shoulders. He rode well.

The king dismounted and a stable boy took his horse to water.

Arthur smiled at Guinevere as he accepted the dipper of water that she offered him. "You're Leodegran's daughter?"

"Yes, Lord Arthur." She was displeased he had not called her "my lady," for she thought she was old enough to be addressed that way. She was as calm and cool as she might have been with any other stranger who visited.

He drank deeply, then returned the dipper and declined her offer of another drink. His voice assumed a light tone.

"Well, my lady, you have leave to ask the High King three questions, as in a fairy tale. What would you like to know?"

This suggestion pleased Guinevere, for she wanted to learn what sort of High King he would be. She would have to decide whether to swear allegiance to him when she was queen of Powys, if he was indeed High King then.

"When will you win the war?"

He laughed. "I shall win it as soon as I can."

She continued, rather fiercely. "How many people will die?"

Arthur gave her an ironic look. "It will claim as many lives as it takes to win."

Guinevere demanded, "Is there any way that you can keep down the numbers of the dead?"

Running his fingers through his red-gold hair, the High King stared at her for a moment, then laughed again. "Such a clever young lady! The best way to keep down the numbers of the dead is with a show of might that will make my enemies give up."

"Are High Kings always so evasive?" Guinevere asked, for she had not liked his answers.

"That's a fourth question, and I must depart. But I trust that we shall meet again. I see that Leodegran did not exaggerate about his daughter's cleverness, or about her beauty." He inclined his head, smiled, then mounted his horse and rode off.

Guinevere fretted at his answers. She was not sure whether she should follow her father's example in pledging the loyalty of Powys to him. But perhaps he would wage war against Powys if she did not.

She scarcely noticed the other warriors riding by. Then her gaze was caught by a lady riding with the men. She did not ride up to the well.

The lady was as dusty as the other riders, but to Guinevere that mattered little.

The lady's roan horse matched the magnificent red of her hair.

Guinevere had never seen such cheekbones, such a noble fore-head, such a fine bearing, such long hands. The lady's eyes, green as the forest, regarded her, and the lady smiled a strange and wonderful smile.

Guinevere's whole being was concentrated on watching her. Silently, she willed the lady to ride over to her and speak.

Seemingly in response to Guinevere's longing, the lady veered and rode over to the well.

At a closer glance, her skin was flawless, which embarrassed Guinevere, who had a few flaws like many girls of fourteen years.

Was her hair well combed? Was her gown becoming? She had seldom worried about such things before. She felt awkward.

"Will you have some water, my lady?" she asked, for the king and his warriors had not drunk all of the water that the servants had drawn for him.

"Water is the most sacred of drinks," the lady replied, extend-ing her arm. "I give you thanks."

Guinevere reached up and gave her the dipper, but felt that she could never reach high enough for this lady.

The stranger drank Guinevere's water, and, without introduc-tion, asked, "What did you think of the High King?"

Her eyes fixed on the noble face, whose every line she was committing to memory, Guinevere asked without hesitation, "Does he truly want peace?"

The lady lowered the dipper. Drops of water still sparkled on her lips. Her eyes searched Guinevere's. "You answer my question with another one. Very good. Yes, Arthur is the only one who can bring us peace, though he must do it through war. He will lead just as well in peace as in war."

"I am not pleased to see our fighters dying in battles with other Britons," Guinevere said, surprised at her own boldness.

The lady smiled with approval, making Guinevere flush. "What a pity that your father is a Christian. You could have served the Goddess well." She reached down and handed back the tin dipper as if it were a sacred vessel. As Guinevere took it, the lady's fingers touched hers, and she trembled. The lady's hands felt warmer than anyone else's.

Nevertheless, Guinevere spoke her mind. "I am a Christian, but I wonder what good prayers do. They didn't save my mother's life, or the lives of some of my father's best men."

The lady's beautiful forehead wrinkled. "Indeed? But women at Avalon, where I was raised, truly spoke with the Goddess. War leaders used to seek the blessing of the Lady before they went out to fight, and even Arthur was pleased to have her support."

She sighed. "But the Lady is dead now, and all that is gone, but I hope not forever. I hope I can bring it back."

"May you do so if it would please you. But as for me, I do not want to spend my life praying. I want to be — I shall be — a queen." Guinevere wondered whether she had been too bold, but she wanted the lady to know what stuff she was made of.

"You will be a queen," the lady replied solemnly, as if she could foresee the future. "But do not despise women's prayers. I hope you will use your power to help other women. Did you know that in Ireland there is a council of women? Of course, they speak only of women's matters, but they say a great deal." The lady's voice was not soft, but it drew Guinevere to another world.

"Would that we were in Ireland," Guinevere answered. "Who are you, my lady?" she finally managed to ask.

"I am Lady Morgan of Cornwall, the king's sister. I have traveled across Britain with him. I must go now. Remember me always," the lady told her, and rode off through the caer's gate to follow the High King.

Guinevere wanted to run to the stables, leap on her horse, and follow, but she could not.

His sister, she thought. How wonderful to meet a woman who had seen much of Britain! For the first time Guinevere thought it might be very good to see places besides Powys. A woman could view the sea, see snow-capped Yr Wyddfa, and visit cities with markets crowded with far more stalls than a fair. When she became queen of Powys, she would travel like the High King's sister.

While Guinevere still was standing in the courtyard and looking in the direction that the lady had gone, Leodegran rode up.

"How did your meeting with the High King go?" her father asked, scrutinizing her face.

"Well enough, I suppose," she said, shrugging.

Her father sighed.

"I also met his sister," Guinevere ventured.

"She's only his half-sister," Leodegran said in a voice that showed little interest. "But I am surprised that he hasn't married her off by now."

Guinevere returned to the women. Her mind was full that day, but Valeria frowned and did not seem interested in talk.

"The High King let me ask him questions," Guinevere said.

Valeria did not look up from the green plaid wool she was weaving. "Don't you want to know what I asked him?" Valeria murmured slightly, not sounding as if she cared.

Chastened, Guinevere nevertheless continued. "The High King has a sister who's the most beautiful lady I ever saw."

"I have to concentrate on my weaving or I might make mistakes," Valeria insisted. Guinevere fell silent, but she resented Valeria's lack of interest.

When evening came, Valeria still failed to speak, so Guinevere came up behind her and tugged lightly at the long brown hair that flowed down her back. "I want to speak with you," Guinevere said. "Come to my room tonight."

Valeria came to Guinevere's bed, and Macha scolded them. "Go to sleep, girls. Don't talk all night. You'll lose your beauty if you don't get enough sleep, Lady Guinevere, and then where will you be?" Guinevere giggled.

"Ah, well, soon enough you'll be married, so you might as well spend the nights in girlish giggling while you can," the old woman shook her head. "Blow out the candle soon."

As soon as the door was shut, Guinevere said, "I'll not marry."

Valeria's pout had turned to a frown, and she snapped, "Of course you will. I'm the one who'll never marry. I'm going to be shut up in a convent with a lot of pious old women."

Guinevere couldn't help giggling again. "You won't enter a convent. You aren't pious enough."

"It's no jest." Valeria's face was unsmiling. "I have no father or mother to find me a husband. My uncle is a priest, and he says that's what I have to do. Whatever you do, you'll at least be in the world, but I'll be shut up like a prisoner." She buried her head in the pillow and wept.

Sobered, Guinevere put her arms around Valeria and held her tightly. "I won't let you be shut up," she said. "My father's a king. I'll ask him to persuade your uncle to let you stay here with me."

Valeria stopped weeping and rubbed her hand over her wet eyes. She pulled away from Guinevere. "No, Gwen, I don't want to spend my life in your shadow. You'll be married, and I'd have to go to your husband's caer and spin by the fire like one of your serving women. At least in a convent I'll have a life of my own, even if I don't want it."

Guinevere drank in those bitter words.

She felt no impulse to be falsely cheerful, or to imagine lives for Valeria that she could not provide her.

"When are you going away?" she asked.

Everyone always went away and left her.

"I'm going to the Convent of the Holy Mother this summer," Valeria said. "I asked my uncle whether it was one of those abbeys where they have both women and men, and he frowned and said it was not, and that my asking showed an impious attitude." She sighed, and then she let Guinevere snuggle up to her and sleep close, as usual.

In Guinevere's dreams, the king's sister came, with a caer that appeared and disappeared into the air, but it was no more magical than the Lady Morgan was.

Peopled with men and women with the faces of birds and other creatures, the caer was dazzling to Guinevere, and she longed to live there, but it vanished.

Guinevere turned away from the road where Valeria and her uncle had disappeared, once the dust from their horses settled. Her eyes teared, and she felt as if she were strangling. Nothing but the death of her mother had hurt this much. There was no one else she wanted to be with as she was with Valeria. She couldn't giggle with anyone else or confide in them. What good was it being a king's daughter if she must be alone?

Not wanting anyone else to see her weep, she walked in the garden. The lilies brought her no comfort. Their fragrance reminded her of the scent of Valeria's hair.

When Guinevere returned to the room that had once been her mother's domain, where the women still spun under the shadow of the Virgin and Child, Macha made clucking sounds.

"No mournful looks. You mustn't carry on. You're a king's daughter. Someday you'll have a husband who must go off and fight, and then you'll know what it truly is to miss someone."

Guinevere didn't look at her. She did know what it was to miss someone. Her heart ached, as she had not known hearts could really do. Missing a husband could not be any worse than what she now felt.

On a hot summer day, Guinevere was called to her father's office, where she found him speaking with a grim-looking priest with grizzled hair. The priest scrutinized her through narrow eyes.

"This is Father Jerome. He'll improve your Latin and teach you some Greek," her father said.

Guinevere stared at Leodegran with amazement.

Many times she had asked for such lessons, only to be told they were not fitting for a girl. Why had her father changed his mind? Had he returned from the war with a new respect for learning? Deciding not to question a blessing, she did not ask.

Father Jerome frowned at her.

As soon as Leodegran left them alone, the priest said, "You will be attempting to learn more than any woman should know. It will be like trying to teach a horse to play the harp, but you must behave yourself and do the best you can."

Guinevere liked him little, but the languages delighted her, even though the tracts he gave her were generally those that cautioned against the wiles and weaknesses of women. She was determined to make no mistakes, just to spite him.

3 THE WITCH'S SON

Gawaine leapt off his horse, tethered him, and scrambled through heather and broom to the rocks of the seabird colony. When he was younger, he had raced his horse through the colony, but he did that no longer. He ran, waving his arms to protect his head from the terns that dove at him to keep him from their nests. A tern struck his arm, and he laughed, though it hurt.

Puffins, their beaks full of fish for their young, flew into the crevices and burrows that held their nests. Their screams sounded like demented cows, far stranger than the cries of the gulls and kittiwakes. Bird droppings covered the rocks and made them slippery. The stench was overpowering, almost enough to cover the salt smell of the sea.

Gawaine glanced at a puffin standing on a rock and laughed at its comical face.

"I'm not hunting you. I leave such pursuits to the boys, and besides, we're roasting a sheep today," he told the bird.

Another tern struck his arm.

By the gods, these terns were fiercer than any opponents he had met in fighting practice. He could best any of his father's men, and defeating his younger brother Agravaine was almost too easy to be worth the trouble. When would he face a real challenge?

Here on Orkney's main island he could not even ride for any great distance. Islands were all very well for boys, but as he grew older it was better to be in a place where he could ride for many days without coming to the land's end. He was too old to live in a place where his mother expected him home for supper every night. Climbing on rocks was not bad exercise, but wasn't it a bit too boyish for one who was nearly sixteen years old?

He loved the islands of Orkney, but he wanted to visit his father's lands in Lothian. It would be good to see forests again, for there were few trees on the islands.

Staring out to sea, he tried to spy a dolphin or a whale, but there were none. A seal's head emerged from the waters, and Gawaine thought of the tales he had heard about selkies – people who could change into seals – or seals that could change into people. Most of the tales were about women, but some said that a man also could be taken off to live with the seals. Gawaine half wished the seals would come for him and teach him to live in the kelp beds. He wanted to taste all that life had to offer. He ate Orkney's oysters and mussels as eagerly as venison from the hunt.

No doubt in some life he had been a seal, darting through the waters. He had been a stallion galloping over the moors. He had been a wolf bringing down the deer. He had been a hawk soaring above the clouds. He thought with pride of his childhood name, Gwalchmai, Hawk of May.

Gawaine clambered over the rocks until late afternoon, when he reluctantly turned his horse towards home.

As he approached the caer, he saw that a ship had landed in the harbor and men were carrying boxes away from it. He hoped they might have exciting cargo, such as new swords.

The sandstone slab caer was small and damp compared with his father's caer in Lothian. Men milled around outside it and his tall mother, unmistakable even from a distance, was in the court-yard. She wore a rust-colored gown and her red-gold braid hung far down her back. The gold in the torque around her neck was not as glorious as the color of her hair.

He dismounted and hurried over to her. Hounds rushed up to him and begged for his attention. Laughing, he scratched the ears of one and patted another's head.

"Gawaine, where have you been? Everyone's been searching for you," his mother complained, but her voice was not harsh. It never was to him, though Queen Morgause was often sharp with others.

"He's been tumbling a girl as usual, no doubt," grumbled his brother Agravaine, who had just recently grown nearly as tall and muscular as Gawaine, and whose hair was just as red as Gawaine's own.

"No doubt." Gawaine laughed and tossed his head. His breeches were torn in several places, and why not pretend that a girl had done it because she was so eager to be with him? "I have to make them happy, don't I? Mother, can you make a charm for Agravaine so some of the girls will look at him? I do believe he's getting bitter."

Agravaine howled at this insult. "Just wait until we practice swordfighting and I have a chance to get even."

"How? I always win. Mother, can you give him a potion so he can beat me, just once, poor lad?"

Agravaine tried to cuff him, but he held the boy off.

69

"Boys, stop your horseplay at once, or I shall turn you into toads!" Their mother tousled both their hair. They ducked away, and she led them toward the caer. Guards saluted as they passed. "No wonder the world calls me a witch when my own sons jest about this calumny."

"No more than you do," Gawaine retorted. "But if any man dares to slander you in earnest, I'll have his hide."

"And that you won't." She sighed. "You must curb your anger. I can survive the Christians' vile lies. They say I am a witch because I am the only woman north of Hadrian's Wall who can read."

"Oh, I won't be angry." He put his hand on his knife because he wasn't wearing a sword. "I won't stab such a man any more than ten times."

"Gawaine!"

"If you like, Mother, I'll be gentle and make it only five times."

She looked into his eyes, which were blue as her own, and her gaze was the steadier. "You'll do no such thing. If you killed every man who called your mother a witch, you'd have to kill more of our people than the Saxons have. Why do you think I jest about it? To calm your nerves on the subject. You cannot spill blood over these old insults, Gawaine. Too many people have heard the tales."

"About sacrificing dogs and cats? They've never seen the way you cosset our hounds." Several of said hounds were leaping about them, trying to reach up to lick his face.

She shrugged. "If they knew that, they'd say I consort with them, no doubt."

Gawaine growled and drew his knife, cutting the air. "No man dare say anything so vile, or his life is forfeit."

But his mother did not sound overly dismayed.

"The name of Queen Morgause of Lothian and Orkney will always have rumors attached to it, and there's nothing you can do to stop that. You must learn to feign indifference, especially now that you will go south to fight for your father."

His heart raced. "My father has sent for me?" Perhaps he would finally have a chance for a real fight. He saw himself defeating a stream of warriors. Lot was a stern father and Gawaine had tried to stay out of his way, but he was proud that his father was a notable warrior.

"Didn't you see the ship come in the harbor? Are you blind?" complained Agravaine.

"I was off riding. There's a message from father?" He would make the name Gawaine resound with glory. Both his mother and father would be proud of him.

"Now that King Uther Pendragon is dead, some boy who claims to be his son is trying to gain the throne and become High King of all Britain. Of course your father will fight him," Morgause explained, glancing at the ship in the harbor, then turning back to Gawaine. "And it's time for you to join the fighting, too."

Gawaine let out a yell of excitement. "At last! I'll win victories for you, Mother, I swear it!"

"Indeed!" Agravaine glowered, shoving him. "Father has hundreds of men, but you'll be the one who wins the victories! Don't boast 'til you've won them."

"Well, you'll never win anything except perhaps tavern brawls," Gawaine countered, shoving back.

"Stop this childishness! Agravaine will go next year, if the fighting continues. Agravaine, be good enough to let me speak with your brother about his journey. Go find Gaheris so we can have supper sometime this evening," Morgause commanded.

"The child is off watching the men unload the ship."

Agravaine spoke as if he were overwhelmingly superior to twelve-year-old Gaheris.

"Well, find him then." She dismissed him with a smile and, grumbling, he went off towards the dock.

Morgause walked with Gawaine to her room, which had a faint scent of rose petals mingled with the ever-present smell of the sea. There were no very good hangings or furniture because the sea air spoiled them. The best were all at Din Eidyn, his father's fortress in Lothian. Even in summer, a peat fire was burning to keep off the chill. The Orkneys' weather was seldom very cold, but neither was it hot.

"Try not to tax Agravaine too much. You excel in ways that he never will, so you must be gracious."

He shrugged. "But it's only because I'm older."

"No, son, it's not." She looked into his eyes.

Gawaine was silenced. He had suspected that he would always be a better fighter than Agravaine, and now his mother confirmed it.

Her eyes were bluer than the skies on this fine summer day. When she looked at him with admiration, he could almost burst out singing.

Morgause put her hand on his shoulder. Her touch was gentle, though nothing about her was delicate. Her long, graceful fingers smelled like roses. "Would that I did have the power to predict the future. Yours, at any rate."

"So, do you think that father will become High King? Who is it who contests him?" He tried to sound like a grown man. Now that he was going to battle, his mother must not think of him as a boy any longer.

"A boy called Arthur, a bastard son of Uther's, and the son of my sister Igraine, or so Merlin claims. Yes, the sage Merlin is on his side, unfortunately, even though the boy has been raised Christian." She grimaced. "I do not see why Merlin should favor the bastard."

"But is he then my cousin?"

Her face relaxed slightly. "Yes, he's likely your cousin. Your father thinks this Arthur is no match for him, but Lot is not always the best judge of men."

"But my father is a king in his own right who has fought many battles. How could a boy be a better king?"

"I know one young man who might be. One who is a king's trueborn son." Morgause smiled and gazed at him as if he were the only person in the world. "Why do you think I want Lot to be High King? For his own sake? Or for yours?"

Gawaine's jaw dropped. "Could I be High King? You don't want my father to be High King?"

"Your father and I get along well, particularly when he is in Lothian and I am in Orkney, but I can see that you will be greater than he. That much I am safe in predicting." She gave him the smile that made people believe she was an enchantress.

Well, he hoped that he would at least yell less than Lot. His head spun with pride at hearing that his mother thought he would be greater than his father, even though he had always guessed she did. He could not imagine sitting on a throne and having to give orders. He could perhaps manage in Lothian and Orkney, which he had known all his life, but he had no idea how he could rule all of Britain. He did not tell his mother about his misgivings.

"Listen, son," she said, her hand on his arm, "I am not sure what will happen in these battles. If Lot wins, that is very well. And if he does not, I want you to go with the next High King. Whoever he is, he cannot fail to be impressed with you."

Gawaine gasped. "Go with someone who defeated father?"

"If he proves to be a greater war leader, why not? You can respect him. And if he is your cousin, well, he will understand that you fought for your father and should be glad if you make peace afterwards. But perhaps you will win this war for your father. We shall see. Would that I could have been at the conclave of kings when Uther died! Why did Gareth have to be born this spring?"

Morgause shook her head, but, apparently reminded of the baby, she stepped to the door and called out to her serving woman to bring him to her. "Bring Gareth!"

A red-faced girl soon hurried in with the baby, who let out a wail. Morgause sat in a chair, dropped her gown off her shoulder, and took him to her breast. The baby quickly grabbed hold and began to suck.

"Another fine son, aren't you?" she chortled. "I am much too fond of my boys to give them to wet nurses," she told Gawaine, as she had many times before. "I can raise them to be big and strong better than any peasant woman could."

Also seating himself in a chair, Gawaine was at a loss for conversation. How beautiful she still was, though she had turned thirty the year before. No other woman could compare with his mother.

"The girls, high-born and low-born alike, all smile at you, my son." Her gaze moving from the baby to Gawaine, she gave him a tender look. "You are gentle with them, then. Always remember that the woman should have some pleasure as well as the man." She sighed.

Gawaine felt himself flush with embarrassment as well as with anger, at the sigh that implied his father was not a tender lover.

He had taken it for granted that his mother and father were not overly fond of each other, but now he began to see that his mother might have deep grievances.

"Your father wants you to leave soon, so part with any girls in the next few days." Morgause shifted to a more serious tone. "Let me tell you more of the South, for as you well know I was born there."

Gareth choked, so she held him to her shoulder and patted him, then put him back at her breast.

"Uther was much like your father," Morgause said, "a fierce warrior and a strong king, but he was not as great a king as Ambrosius Aurelianus before him. With the Saxons on the eastern shore, who have lived there for generations and cannot easily be dislodged, and with other Saxon and Angle sea wolves continuing to come from the North, and Irish raiders pillaging from the West, Britain needs a strong leader. But the kings are not of one mind as to who that should be. The strongest kings are your father and Uriens of Rheged, but the kings of Gwynedd, Powys, Dyfed, Dumnonia, and all the smaller kingdoms also want a say. Many of them apparently may back the boy because they fear the strong kings of the North almost as much as they fear the barbarians. Some of these kings are Romanized, and some are Christian. But what matters most is to have a good, strong man as High King. And I hope that will someday be you."

He did not argue with her, but he thought it was enough for him to be a great warrior, whose deeds were sung by the bards.

Gawaine had battled his way into a town, ahead of his father's other warriors. He had dodged the archers' arrows, and he had fought he knew not how many men. The tide of men that had rushed at Lot's forces had ebbed. The streets were littered with the bodies of dead and wounded fighters. A few women, mostly old, crept out of hiding to look for their kin among the bodies.

Stunned to be alive and with no serious injuries, Gawaine found a well, hauled up some water, and drank. The warriors of Lothian and Orkney were passing around northern liquor, and he gratefully took a flask offered him by one of his father's men. His own had disappeared in the fighting. The man clapped him on the back and praised him, and the liquor warmed Gawaine as it poured down his throat. Pausing made him realize that every muscle ached. He was covered with blood, but it was not his own. He lived, he had won, and that was all that mattered. He wanted to collapse on the cobblestones, but pride kept him standing.

"This way, your father's this way," a warrior called, and Gawaine followed him into a thatch-roofed wooden building. He wondered if there was a treasure in it.

Lot was there, surrounded by his men. Though his beard was graying, he was nearly as large and strong as his son. His huge hand grasped the arm of a girl of about Gawaine's age who was dressed in undyed homespun. She screamed and flailed about. Several of the other men also held girls or women.

Gawaine saw his father tear the front of the girl's gown with one large rip. Gawaine pitied her, but he knew he could not stop Lot. Gawaine had always imagined that if he ever saw a man trying to rape a woman, he would prevent it, tell his mother what he had done, and win her praise. He had never guessed that he would confront a group of warriors all bent on rape, or that one of them might be a king, much less that it would be his own father.

"Get one for yourself, son." Lot laughed and grabbed the girl's breast. "This is the best part of the battle."

Gawaine reeled, not just from the liquor. He longed to free the girl, who had a round, young face that should feel only gentle kisses but was now contorted with terror. Her screams unnerved him. "Nah." He wanted to vomit.

His father glared at him. "What, is my son a woman? After that fighting, can you be so limp?"

That he was not, not at all, just sickened. How could he possibly want to force himself on one of these screaming women who were trying to get away? How could the other men bear it?

"The hair barely covers your chin, but I didn't know you pissed squatting! This is no way for my son to act," Lot yelled at him, then laughed. Some men laughed along with their king. Others stared as if they could hardly believe what Lot had said.

"I won the fucking battle for you!" Gawaine moved to strike him. He wanted to kill his father, then realized that he easily could, and held back at the last moment.

Some men looked to Gawaine as if they were waiting to see what he would do. He could challenge his father for kingship, but he really would have to kill Lot for that.

Lot's face reddened.

"Go fight with beardless Arthur, why don't you? They say he doesn't take the women when he's won a town."

Seeing Lot distracted, the girl broke away, but Lot grabbed her and struck her so hard that she fell. He jerked her back up.

Gawaine spat in his father's direction and staggered out of the building. He didn't want to be a kinslayer. He hurried down the town's one poor road, now crowded with warriors drinking and looting. Where was his brother Agravaine?

He saw the familiar face. Agravaine was hurrying towards the building that Gawaine had just left.

"Brother! Hero!" Agravaine cried out, saluting Gawaine.

The brothers clasped shoulders. It had been Agravaine's first battle, and his still fairly unstained garb suggested that he had fought only a little, but he beamed at his brother, basking in Gawaine's glory.

"Come away from here." Gawaine took his arm and tried to change his direction.

"Away from the celebration?"

"Away from Lot. They're raping all the women they can find. I'm off to fight for Arthur, if I can. You should come with me, too." He tried to hold onto Agravaine, but let him shake free.

Agravaine's blue eyes bulged.

"Desert father and go to the other side? You can't. You must be mad from all of your fighting. They nearly killed you so many times."

Gawaine could hardly keep the frenzy out of his voice. "This is an evil place. Come with me, or they'll make you part of all this horror."

They saw some warriors doing in the street what their father was doing behind the walls. The struggling women shrieked like the gulls of Orkney.

Agravaine laughed, his voice heavy with liquor. "We won, did we not? Come on, Gawaine, have you never hit a girl or shoved her down to make her open her legs?"

"No. I'm going. Come with me." Gawaine tried to make the words sound like an order.

"No." Agravaine darted to the door of the building where their father was.

Gawaine found his gray war stallion and rode away. A few of the men stared at him, but they no doubt assumed that he was on some mission for his father.

He was so tired that he could hardly stay in the saddle. His empty stomach protested that it wanted food. His horse, Storm, was no more pleased than he was at riding away, and Gawaine knew that he would have to rest the stallion soon. He had chosen a gray because Cuchulain's battle horse had been of that color.

Gawaine found a stream with blue gentians growing on its banks and let the horse drink a little.

Never had he thought of being anything other than the fighting son of King Lot of Lothian, and his heir. Not knowing what to think, he rode across bleak moors and on, over heather-covered hills. He paused only to avoid killing his fine horse. The pink of the heather, so fresh and harmless, reminded him of the cheeks of the girl his father had assaulted. Lot had no pity. What would it be like to have no pity in your heart?

He had not risked his life so some old men could rape girls. But what had he risked it for? So Lot could be High King? Or just to prove how brave he was?

Why, after all, had it been necessary to devastate a town just because its lord had supported Arthur? The fight seemed inglorious compared with attacking Arthur's warband.

Where could he go now? His mother would have welcomed him and understood, but he could not go back to her. He had to make a name for himself.

His mother was married to a rapist. The thought sickened Gawaine.

His father must not have imagined that Gawaine really would go to fight with Arthur, but there seemed to be no other choice.

What would he do if Arthur did not want him? All he had was a good horse, a good sword with his emblem, a hawk, carved on the hilt, and what he was wearing. The golden torque around his neck and his golden armrings had been gifts from Lot, and the large garnet ring on one hand and the amethyst ring on the other had been gifts from his mother. She had made the many-colored plaid cloak on his back and the embroidered scabbard that held his sword. He supposed he could sell or trade the jewels if need be.

If Arthur did not want him, perhaps he could serve Uriens of Rheged? But it would be humiliating to go to a king no greater than his father, and he wondered whether Uriens was any better than Lot. Gawaine touched his chin with regret. He would grow a thick beard as soon as he could and would never shave it, though many men in the South had picked up the habit of shaving from the Romans. He would woo so many women that no man would ever cast doubt on his virility again.

When Gawaine finally found the tents of the young man who called himself High King, Arthur's warriors eyed him suspiciously. Having fought against Gawaine, they glared while he waited to hear whether Arthur would see him. Gawaine was aware that his clothes and his mail were still covered with the blood of men who had fought on Arthur's side, and he was sure that he stank from the battle. Some of the soldiers were eating venison. The smell made him want to tear it from their hands.

A soldier escorted Gawaine into a tent with a red dragon pennant hanging in front of it. Inside, he saw a young man, tall, though not as tall as he, with a shaven chin, red-gold hair, and steady gray eyes. Arthur rose from a pile of rugs, and moving like a soldier — no, like a commander — he greeted Gawaine.

"My cousin, are you not? Does my Uncle Lot send a message?"

Of course, it was their mothers who had been sisters. Gawaine thought he saw a trace of Morgause's looks in Arthur's face, and a bit of his young brother, Gaheris, who was still at home. Gawaine bowed slightly. Arthur invited him to sit on the rugs beside him and offered him some wine.

Gawaine drank it, though it seemed too sweet.

While he told his story, Arthur regarded him thoughtfully. Then the High King shook his head.

"Surely you can see that Lot will never be High King. He could not act that way in Lothian, or his people never would accept him. The people will look to a ruler who protects them rather than pillaging them. You were wise to come here, Gawaine, and most welcome."

The gray eyes also bade him welcome, and Arthur clasped his shoulder. "I've heard that my father, King Uther, did such things as well. We'll be better than our fathers were, and our sons will be even better than we are."

Gawaine nodded. He had come to the right place, after all.

4 THE KING'S SISTER

Morgan walked past the half-finished caer, which resounded with noises of men carting stones and piling them. Arthur was reconstructing a hill fort, making it larger and stronger. The workers had repaired the outer wall first, as protection, and now they were working on the citadel's inner dwellings.

Swallows swooped by her as she looked out over the fields and forest at the foot of the hill. Her arms were full of violets she had gathered that afternoon. She drank in their scent. In the west, a red sun was fast disappearing. She missed the sight of the sun's red streaks fading into the sea at her own caer, Tintagel, on the Cornish coast. A sea of tents for Arthur's men surrounded the half-built fort. She went to the one beside a white banner with a red dragon.

Morgan opened the tent flap and found her brother, away from his builders for once. Arthur's red-gold hair fell over his face as he looked up from his building plans. She let the violets scatter over his vellum drawings.

With a cry, he shoved the flowers off.

"Put aside those plans. It is Beltane tonight." She smiled at him and extended her hand.

Arthur pulled her down on the rugs beside him. "It is always Beltane for you and me, sweeting," he said.

He tried to kiss her, but she pulled away. "Beltane is sacred. Our love then is different from other times."

"You can't expect me to go rutting on the ground among the common folks." He laughed, showing his strong white teeth, and reached for her again.

She jumped up, disgusted. "Don't speak of it so. It is a holy ceremony. We celebrated it together in Cornwall."

"But now we are in the place where I shall rule." He spoke as if explaining to a child. "I must be dignified. I am a Christian." He grimaced, as if he found there were drawbacks to dignity, and perhaps to piety.

Morgan felt as if he had struck her. "I have always celebrated Beltane, and I always will. Must I ask some other man to celebrate with me? I suppose I could ask our cousin Gawaine."

Gawaine she had met in Arthur's camp, and she liked him, though not in the way that many other women did.

Arthur's usually pleasant face reddened and distorted. He leapt up, glaring at her. "Don't you dare! I won't let another man touch you. I'd lock you up first."

He reached for her, but she evaded his grasp. She was now glaring as much as he was. "Lock me up in a tent? Or would you confine me in one of your mud-and-wattle churches? You'd never see me again afterwards. If you object so much to my lying with a man you know, I'll just go to the fires and lie with any man there, it doesn't matter whom."

He collapsed on the rugs and buried his head in his arms.

"Please don't, I can't bear it."

The sight of his misery filled her with tenderness, as his anger never could. How young he looked, though he was more than twenty, four years younger than she was, and so often foolish. She had known him for little more than two years, but she could imagine what he must have looked like as a child. Perhaps the Goddess would understand if she pampered him.

She slipped down to the pile of rugs and put her arms around him. "We can celebrate here, by ourselves, in your tent."

Arthur lifted his head and embraced her tightly.

"I never want to lie with any woman but you." He pressed her head to his shoulder.

Morgan wriggled out of his grip. "Don't talk nonsense. I know that you write to Leodegran of Powys more than to Maelgon of Gwynedd or even Uriens of Rheged, and I can guess why. That daughter of Leodegran's would make a good wife for you."

Arthur reached for her and groaned. "I don't want to marry, but I must. You know that you are my true love."

He attempted to kiss her, but she playfully resisted. "Do you understand why I would choose Guinevere?" he asked, seizing Morgan's hand. "She seems dignified, clever, even thoughtful, and has been raised to be a queen. And yes, I admit that she's pretty, too. Her father's a wily old cattle-thief, but he's a good ally."

"I am not quarreling with you. The girl would make a good choice." That was true enough, Morgan thought, kissing him. Guinevere had seemed much taken with her, and would be a good sister-in-law, who might listen more to her than to Arthur.

"You're so kind. You forgive me everything," he said, as if he had not just shown how lacking in forgiveness he would be if she displeased him. "I shall always be glad that you do not hate me because my father killed yours and took your mother for his own."

Strange that he seemed to feel more guilt over that than over anything he himself did. She settled into the curve of his arm.

"I was only a small child then. I never knew my father."

"I'm glad I came looking for my sister. You're the fairest woman in the world, and the best lover." She smiled because she remembered how disconcerted he had been that she had been with other men before him.

"Only at Beltane and Midsummer," she had told him, which was not quite the truth. But no doubt he often lied to her, also.

He unlaced the front of her gown and fondled her breasts. Morgan sighed with pleasure.

Arthur suddenly pulled back. "Lace up your gown. We can't act this way in a tent. Someone might discover us."

Morgan glared at him. "Are you a coward? You're a king! You can do as you please."

"Do not dare to call me a coward. Do you know how many kings I have vanquished?" Arthur's eyes narrowed. "Lace up your gown," he repeated. "I won't be caught up in scandal."

"If you want it laced up, lace it up yourself!"

"Arthur, may I enter?" The voice belonged to Bedwyr, one of Arthur's warriors.

"In a moment." Arthur's voice was full of displeasure.

Morgan laced up her gown. After a pause, Bedwyr entered. He was an unattractive man, older than Arthur, an ordinary warrior with little to recommend him except his loyalty to Arthur.

"Pardon me, Arthur, but your voices could be heard outside the tent. I had to let you know." Bedwyr looked only at the king. "There is already too much gossip."

"Is there indeed?" Arthur's voice was steady, but he twisted the amethyst ring that was his seal of office. "And what is the nature of this gossip?"

"That you and your sister are lovers." Bedwyr's voice was unflinching. "I wouldn't bet on keeping it secret much longer."

Since Bedwyr bet on anything and everything, that was a damning phrase, Morgan knew.

"Petty people will always gossip about the great," Morgan said, her voice dripping with disdain.

Arthur ignored her. "And what more are they saying?" he asked Bedwyr.

"That she is a witch who has bewitched you. I've heard that these rumors have reached the ears of the priests. This could be dangerous, Arthur."

"Indeed." Arthur poured himself a cup of mead and drained it.

"Nonsense." Morgan felt her pulse quicken. She pulled herself up to her full height. "How dare you bother the king with such trivia? No one has the right to question him or spread rumors about him. Whoever does should be punished."

"I need to know everything that is said about me." Arthur spoke in his state voice. "Thank you, Bedwyr. You may go now."

"Yes, Lord Arthur." Bedwyr bowed to him. He left, still having said or done nothing to acknowledge Morgan.

"How insolent!" she said.

Arthur looked at the mead jar and poured another cup. "This is serious."

"No one can challenge you!"

He put his hand to his forehead. "Can they not? Haven't I had to fight years of battles for the throne? I can't throw all that away now."

"You are the greatest fighter in the world. Nothing can change that." She could scarcely believe that he needed her to remind him of his power.

"Perhaps I am tired of fighting."

He seemed to be looking through the tent cloth, far beyond her. "Perhaps there are battles that I cannot win. We still face the Saxons, who will attack us again someday. I must think of the future."

"Of course a king must think of the future." Morgan touched his hand. "We have often spoken of the future."

Arthur slowly moved his hand away from hers. "We have no future together. I regret that deeply. I have tried to hide our love, but it is impossible. You must go back to Tintagel and never come to Camelot again."

Her heart seemed to stop beating. "You cannot mean that."

His voice was dead serious. His face lacked any trace of warmth. "I do. Believe me, I do."

"Traitor!" She slapped him.

"Never do that again." He was colder than winter.

Morgan trembled, too angry to shout. She looked at Arthur as if he were a creature to be trod under her foot. "You have betrayed love. My curse is upon you. May you never again know happiness in love" She swept out of the tent.

She was determined not to weep. All of her sorrow would be anger.

Morgan could not keep herself from screaming. Her screams blended with the shrieks of the gulls outside her caer by the sea. Pain, more pain than she had imagined possible, wracked her body. Finally, she took one great shove and the child came out. She sank back onto the pillows. "Bring me the child!" she demanded. At last she had a son who would avenge the wrongs done to her.

One of her woman carried the red, squirming thing to her. It was a girl, a frail girl. Morgan groaned and closed her eyes. Her child would never grow up to overthrow Arthur. Never would she have her revenge. This girl was only a daughter of incest, the daughter of a witch, a girl the Christians would despise.

"Give her to me." She took the poor thing to her breast. She must find a better life for the child. Her daughter must not grow up to be hated, to be scorned and discarded as she had been.

She felt the small lips fumble at her nipple, then pull, although she had no milk yet. The pulling pained her, but she ached so much already that a little more did not matter. She knew that her breasts would ache far more when the child was gone. Her cousin Elaine, niece to her father Gorlois and therefore no kin of Arthur's, wanted a daughter and did not have one. She lived with her husband, Bagdemagus, only one day's journey from Tintagel. This girl she would name Elaine, like her cousin, and give to her. "If I love you, I must give you up," she whispered to her child.

Gawaine bounded surefooted from rock to slippery rock. "Your Tintagel reminds me of Orkney," he called out to Morgan. "I'm glad to smell the sea again."

She laughed and followed him, scrambling easily on the rocks she had known since childhood. Sea spray splashed in their faces.

"You know the sea well, don't you, seal girl," he teased her. Gulls screeched over their heads and sandpipers flew up when they approached too close.

"Of course. This is my home." She smiled at him. Fool that he was, he thought that she had sent for him out of great desire, when it was because he might give her a son she could claim was Arthur's. As Gawaine was a close relation to both of them, it would not seem strange if the child resembled him. And when the child was grown, no one could tell that the age was short by a year.

"You are clever, like my mother," he said. "You resemble her a little, too."

Laughing, he touched her red-gold braid. "She would be fond of you, no doubt."

Morgan did not echo his laughter. She had no wish to meet her aunt. Morgause might be shrewd enough to guess her plan. "It's not likely that we shall meet."

"We have much in common, cousin." He gave her a foolishly fond look.

"Much," she said sharply. "I have lost Arthur, and you lost your young wife. Did you love her?" Morgan had heard that in the year she had been gone from Camelot, he had married a girl in Lothian, who nine months later had died in childbed. How much could he have cared about a girl he had barely known?

Gawaine winced. His smile faded, and he sat down on a rock. "Yes, I loved her." His voice cracked. "She laughed more than anyone else I have ever met."

A little fool then, Morgan thought with disdain. Despite his thick, red beard, Gawaine looked young to her, which he was, being not yet twenty summers old. "You were fortunate. Your love did not betray you, as mine did me. Many women die in childbed. You'll find another wife soon enough." She had no great belief in the love of men.

"No doubt." He rose again, turned from her, and, heedless of the waves crashing around the rocks, jumped further out, away from her.

It was just as well for him not to become too fond of her, because his stay with her would be brief, and she did not want him to return and learn that she was bearing his child.

Her blood had not come, so it was time for him to go. He was pleasant and attentive, especially in bed, and some might have thought him handsome, but he was not like Arthur, whose face had been shaped by a god. More important, she could not love a man who would gladly let another man rule over him. She longed for Arthur, who ate and drank power.

It had occurred to her that Arthur might not be able to keep her in exile if she were Gawaine's wife. He had no wish to lose Gawaine's loyalty. It would drive Arthur mad to see her belong to another man, and she would enjoy that. But though it might be possible to cajole Gawaine into marrying her, his mother was reputed to be fierce. No doubt Queen Morgause would see that she did not love Gawaine. Morgan might sit down to supper one night and never rise from the table.

No, raising a child to claim Arthur's throne was the best plan.

Exhausted, Morgan leaned back on her cushions. She let the new baby suckle, but she frowned at the child. Why did she have to be another girl? At least this one looked sturdier than the last one, and drank from her more greedily. This one she would send to a convent, but not to be raised by an ordinary nun. Ninian, who had been one of her teachers at Avalon, had gone to a convent, and she would raise this girl to be whatever it was she might become.

Surrendering to the little blue-eyed creature, Morgan sang her a song of the sea and called her seal girl.

5 THE FUTURE QUEEN

"It's a boy!" Macha cried out.

The circle of women surrounding Sarran, Leodegran's new wife who was only two years older than Guinevere, exclaimed with pleasure.

Guinevere did not press to be closer. The crowded room with its smells of blood and sweat almost took her breath away. The birth reminded her too much of her mother's death. She caught a glimpse of her new half-brother, red-faced and crying lustily. She felt no surge of sisterly affection.

Macha cleaned him off and handed him to Sarran, who looked weak but smiled.

"Leodegran wanted a son to be called Cadwallon," Sarran said in a voice full of pride.

Knowing she must congratulate Sarran, Guinevere came closer up to her. "He looks healthy. Father will be so pleased," she said, hoping her voice did not sound as insincere as she felt, now that she could never be queen of Powys. She was sure that she could be a fine ruler, just and compassionate. She choked back tears. Even though she could not be a queen, she must always have dignity, and never weep.

Guinevere rushed about the caer, for Leodegran was holding a feast to which all of his lords and their wives were invited. It was early winter, but there was no snow and the guests were able to travel.

She helped Sarran make arrangements for the feast. Little as she liked attending to the details, Guinevere made sure that all her father's favorites were served. Beef, pork, and mutton made the table a farmyard, while venison provided a touch of the forest. There were also many varieties of honeycakes, which Guinevere much enjoyed, and she sampled them in the kitchen.

Of course the guests also had to be housed. Everything that could be made into a bed was used, and every covering was needed for bedding for the women. The men would just sleep in the great hall.

The household had not been so lively since Leodegran and Sarran's marriage the year before. Guinevere wore her finest gown, which was made of green wool, and her best jewels, which were garnets. She must look like a king's daughter, even if not his heir. She wanted to the guests to admire her, not pity her.

"You look beautiful, tonight, my daughter," Leodegran said, smiling at her. "Everyone will admire you, as well they should."

Had her father already drunk too much? He seldom praised her looks, and his smile was wider than usual.

The great hall was ablaze with many rushlights and a roaring fire in the firepit. Gliding among the trestle tables, Guinevere poured Leodegran's best wine, saw that all the guests were fed, and listened to reports of the latest marriages and childbirths.

She savored the smell of venison and longed to sit down and enjoy the feast. Leodegran then called her over to the highest table. He put an arm around her shoulders.

"Great honor has come to Powys," his voice boomed. "I am proud to announce the betrothal of my daughter, Guinevere, to the High King of all Britain, Arthur Pendragon." He beamed at her.

Guinevere's head spun as if she would faint. She could hardly believe his words. Why had he not told her sooner? Her father kissed her cheek. "You will be a great queen, my girl," he proclaimed.

Guinevere felt as if someone had died, and as if that someone was herself. Numb, she managed to be gracious through the long evening of toasts and congratulations. People smiled at her with more admiration than usual, but she did not feel complimented. Ladies oohed and aahed, girls giggled, and men asked her to recommend them to King Arthur.

Guinevere's appetite was quite gone. She had difficulty forcing herself to eat a few bites. Her head ached from the wine, and from her father's news as well. A harper played a cheerful song often heard at weddings and she knew she would never like that tune again. She thought Sarran smirked at her and would not be sorry to see her go. Perhaps Sarran even envied her for marrying a man who was young and handsome, and a greater king than Leodegran.

The guests consumed many jars of mead and reduced the meats to bones. The ladies finally went off to bed and the men began to lie down by the still-glowing firepits. At last Guinevere was able to go off to her room, which would be shared with other highborn ladies. Her father followed to speak with her privately outside her door.

"You must put aside your girlish ways now, Gwen," he said, placing his hand on her shoulder. "The High King was much impressed when he met you, but he has been occupied with securing his kingdom and building his new caer. Now he has time to wed. I'm so proud of you, chosen over every other girl in Britain. That is why I had you learn Latin and a little Greek, to please him because he liked your cleverness. I thought he would want his wife to be the most learned girl in Britain, and I was right. Remember your duty and be a proper consort to him. But I know you will." He squeezed her shoulder.

She longed to tell him how little she wanted this marriage, but she looked at the rushes on the floor and controlled herself. "You didn't even ask me whether I wanted to marry him." There was no expression in her voice.

"How could you not? Of course you're overwhelmed, my girl. You might thank me a little more for getting you the finest husband in Britain."

"Of course I thank you, Father," she said, because she must.

He kissed her cheek and left her. His mustaches tickled and she thought that at least Arthur didn't have mustaches, or hadn't had them when she had seen him nearly three years before.

No longer having the strength to stand, Guinevere slumped on her bed. Two ladies sharing it were already snoring. She could hardly believe what was happening to her. She knew such things happened to other highborn girls, but somehow she had imagined that she was exempt. She had meant to tell her father that she did not want to marry, but when he had never mentioned the subject she had guessed that he somehow understood or wanted to keep her at home. She had longed to become a queen, but in her own right, not through marriage. She had never thought of the High King as a possible husband, nor did she want him now, no matter how handsome and powerful he was. She was not entirely sure why she didn't. She should be grateful that he wanted an educated wife. If the High King had wanted a wife with no learning, her father never would have hired a teacher for her, but instead would have told Arthur that she was the most ignorant girl in Britain.

It was useless to protest. After such an announcement, her father would never change his mind. She had heard about Julius Caesar crossing the Rubicon, and it seemed that she had been carried across in a litter while she slept.

If she had been the daughter of a farmer or a blacksmith, she would have been a free woman at fourteen, and never would have had to wed. There were disadvantages to being a king's daughter, she realized for the first time.

But even if she did not much want to be Arthur's wife, she would be able to be near his wonderful sister at the court. The thought made her shiver with pleasure. Guinevere recalled that Morgan had told her she would be a queen. Had Morgan foreseen how that would come to be?

Truth to tell, Guinevere thought she would not have minded seeing the High King's court and learning more about the world than she could at Powys, but she did not want to have to marry to do so, nor did she want to leave Powys forever. She buried her face in her pillow and tried not to sob at the thought of marrying Arthur and, still worse, the thought of bearing a child. Perhaps she had only another year to live. She was smaller than her mother, so she might not live through as many childbeds as Rhiannon had. Macha's warning about pregnancy still rang in her ears.

Pain stabbed Guinevere below her stomach, pain worse than any cramps she had ever felt. The room was close, smelling of blood and sweat – her blood and sweat. Women she had never seen before surrounded her. Her legs were open. It was birth! She was giving birth! She thrashed. She screamed. She would die like her mother. She was passing out. She would never see the world again.

Guinevere woke. Tears streamed down her cheeks. Now she was sure that this marriage would kill her. She would have to bear a child and die. There was no escape. Perhaps if she had wanted to marry Arthur the pain would not seem so needless.

Oh, let him find some other woman he longed to marry, let him end the betrothal, even if everyone would think Guinevere disgraced forever.

Spring came to everyone but Guinevere. The sight of the first violets and primroses angered her, for they seemed to promise a happier world than the one she knew.

The months had not calmed her ire over her impending marriage. She could barely refrain from snapping when her ladies cooed over the new garments they made for her.

New leaves were greening the trees, but the spring was winter to her on the journey to Camelot, the High King's caer. If the journey had a different purpose, she would have enjoyed crossing the hills of Powys and heading south, but Guinevere held back tears at the thought that she might be seeing her home country for the last time. She insisted on riding her horse – no litters for her. Even when rain drizzled on her party, she did not complain. There was nothing worth complaining about but the dreaded marriage, and she could say nothing about that.

Her guard included many of Leodegran's men-at-arms who were being sent to Arthur as part of her dower, and some of the High King's men he had sent to escort her. They were led by a gentle-faced warrior named Bors.

When she said that she wanted to stop and spend the night at a convent where a friend of hers was a nun, Bors looked at her reverently and nodded.

"How good it is that such a holy maiden will become queen, Lady Guinevere."

Guinevere had little mind to ask the solemn man much about the court, but she decided that the question she most wanted to ask would sound only courteous.

"Is the king's sister well?"

Inexplicably, Bors turned pale. "What, have you heard of her? Don't be troubled, my lady." Shuddering, he made the sign of the cross. "She is long since gone from Camelot, thanks be to God."

"Gone? What do you mean?" Guinevere felt as if someone had struck a blow to her stomach. Could the beautiful lady be dead?

"The king sent her away. She's a witch. She's no fit subject for decent conversation, my lady," Bors replied, crossing himself again. "Keep your heart serene and do not think on so terrible a subject."

Guinevere found these words exceedingly troubling, but she saw that she could not ask any further questions of him. More wretched than ever, she rode through the forest without taking in its beauty. Though she noticed the many patches of bluebells, she did not enjoy them.

Guinevere was in no cheerful mood when her party approached the gray stone Convent of the Holy Mother.

She bade good-night to the men who had accompanied her. They would camp outside while she rested in the convent.

Seeing Valeria might be pleasant, she thought, but perhaps her friend had changed and they wouldn't like each other any more. Besides, nothing could cheer her as she went off to this marriage.

But a plump sister opened the great oak door and exclaimed, "God grant you good evening, Lady Guinevere!" so pleasantly that Guinevere could hardly refrain from smiling.

The convent was like others she had seen, except for the statue in the passageway, which was of the Virgin holding a book in her hands instead of an infant. Guinevere noticed it with amazement.

A tall and dignified nun swept in, and said, "Welcome, Lady Guinevere, I am the Abbess Perpetua." Thick eyebrows and an aquiline nose made her look a little fierce, but she smiled. "We shall do our best to make you welcome. Our Sister Valeria will be so glad to see you."

Guinevere was shown to a small and plain room where she washed, and then a sister led her down to the refectory, where, after only a few prayers – to her relief – supper was served. Good fish had been prepared, as well as wheaten bread and honey, and Guinevere wondered whether they always ate like that, or the food was in her honor.

The sisters dressed in black and white, which suited Guinevere's mood. Although Guinevere had no great desire to retreat from the world, she wondered whether it might be better to live in a convent than to be touched by a husband she did not want and risk her life to bring him children.

A hanging on the wall depicted the miracle of the loaves and fishes. She wished a miracle would make another bride appear and take her place.

To Guinevere's great relief, no one talked about her marriage. She had not been free of such talk since she had been betrothed. The abbess discussed Ireland, which had been her place of birth, then gradually shifted the conversation to books. She asked what Guinevere had read and nodded with pleasure at her answers.

Valeria — now Sister Valeria — was permitted to sit next to Guinevere at the long oak table. It was strange to see Valeria in that setting. She said little, but smiled and squeezed Guinevere's hand. Guinevere had expected her friend to be thin from fasting and have a downcast look, but instead Valeria was plumper than she had been and her eyes sparkled. Could nuns be happy? She wondered whether she would be able to talk with her friend alone.

Toward the end of the meal, the abbess looked Guinevere in the eye. "You will be living in a large court. You must not let yourself be swayed by gossip, flattery, gowns, and jewels." Her voice was stern but not unfriendly.

Guinevere nodded in agreement. Surely such things were far from her mind.

"You will be a queen," the abbess said, "and being a good one will involve much work. You must always think of the poor as well as the nobles."

"I shall," Guinevere promised in a steady voice. "I know that is the true work of rulers."

"The true work of each person, whether ruler or peasant, is to keep her own soul whole. Remember that always." The abbess looked as if she could see into Guinevere's heart.

"I shall." Guinevere clasped her hands together under the table. She did not know how she could keep her soul whole while she belonged to a man she did not want, but she vowed to try.

The abbess nodded. "And we shall pray for you, to help you do that."

She rose from the table. "Now we must do our evening prayers. You may go to you room to rest."

Guinevere bowed her head in response and wished that she had many more days to listen to the abbess. She was relieved to have a room to herself, and bade her serving women go off to their own room and leave her alone. Whecca had not come with her because she loved a young man who worked in the stable, so Guinevere had said she could stay in Powys, and Macha was too sickly to accompany her. Saying farewell to the old woman had tested Guinevere's determination not to weep.

Guinevere sat on the hard little bed, and thought she would prefer it to a fine bed shared with the High King.

There was a knock at the door and a plump old nun entered. She was wrinkled, but the lines on her face seemed like works of beauty. Guinevere had hoped her visitor would be Valeria, but tried to keep her disappointment out of her face.

"I am Mother Ninian," the nun told Guinevere. "I can see that you are one who will find no temptation in gowns and jewels."

"That is true." Guinevere nodded, relieved to be understood.

"Mother Perpetua could see that about you too, of course." Mother Ninian smiled. "She has already told the nuns to copy books for you, so your mind will not grow dull."

"How kind!" Guinevere's heart pounded with gratitude. But then she recollected that the books would probably all be religious tomes that told how women were lesser than men, like the books Father Jerome had given her.

"The books will not just be religious works." The old nun seemed to read Guinevere's thoughts. She touched Guinevere's hand. "For you know some Greek and can therefore read plays and philosophy that most never see."

"Thank you a thousand times." Guinevere held the wrinkled hand, which was even stronger than her own.

"The true temptation is bitterness. You must never succumb to that," Mother Ninian warned her. Guinevere was too astonished to speak. How did the old nun guess that she might be bitter about her lot, which most women envied?

"Learn all you can. Blessed are those who ask questions—and who can bear the answers," the old nun said. Then she quietly departed from the room.

What questions must she ask?

What answers should she seek? How fearsome were they? Guinevere wondered.

At the moment, the question most on her mind was whether she would see her dear Valeria.

There was another knock on her door. This time, Sister Valeria walked into the tiny room.

Guinevere leapt up. "I didn't know whether I'd have a chance to see you alone. You look so content." She was unable to keep the surprise out of her voice. Her friend had been so sad at the thought of entering a convent.

"I am." Sister Valeria smiled more brightly than Guinevere had ever seen her smile, even when they were young at Leodegran's caer.

"So you have become pious after all. Perhaps I should, too."

"You don't seem so happy." Her old friend gave her a tender look.

Guinevere laughed sharply. "I'm not. I would give anything to escape this marriage, but I cannot. Perhaps I'd have been better off in the convent like you, never thinking about love."

"Oh, Gwen, I do have a love." Valeria blushed.

"It's Sister Fidelia, did you see her? The tall one with the gray eyes and the beautiful voice who said the blessing."

Guinevere stared at her. Her head spun, and she sat on the bed to keep from falling. Could women love other women? If they could, then she was one such woman. That was why she found the Lady Morgan's beauty so much more compelling than King Arthur's handsome face. "Of course I noticed her. You love a woman? I thought I was the only girl who thought much about women." Her voice was full of longing. Now she could see why she had grieved so much when Valeria had left.

Valeria smiled the more, and said, "So you feel these things, too? And we never knew it." Sitting on the bed, she put her arms around Guinevere, and Guinevere sank into them, and wept on Valeria's shoulder.

Guinevere thought of all the years they had slept in the same bed, snuggled up together, and wished that they had known then what they knew now. She longed to kiss Valeria's lips.

"Do all the nuns have such loves?" Guinevere asked.

"Only a few of us, and we love privately. I think the abbess might guess, but I would never speak of it."

"She bade me keep my soul whole, but how can I do that if my duty is to go to a man I don't love and risk my life bearing his children?" Guinevere swallowed her tears.

Valeria hugged her. "You are not a tree whose only purpose is to bear fruit, or a creature whose purpose is to bring forth its young. I am sure you have other work. You have always tried to learn as much as you can, and I am sure there is other work you can do. I am not as clever as you, but I take joy in copying books."

"But you live in a community with other women who do the same." Guinevere complained as she would be ashamed to do with anyone else. "You have a dear friend. I am so alone."

Valeria stroked Guinevere's hair. "I believe that my friend would understand, Gwen, if just this night. . . "

Guinevere clasped her. It wasn't too late, then. She still could kiss Valeria.

Guinevere turned away to undress. She did not put on her woolen bedgown, but left herself unclothed. Embarrassed, she got into bed and pulled the rough wool covers over her.

Valeria climbed in beside her and kissed her mouth. Guinevere thrilled at the soft touch of her lips. Valeria's tongue entered her mouth, filling it with sweetness. Valeria's hands covered her, and then her tongue touched her in ways that Guinevere had never imagined. Tears of joy moistened Guinevere's cheeks.

When she loved Valeria in return, she was the more amazed that the power had passed into her, and that Valeria moaned in joy as she had.

Why, touching and being touched could be grand! It was like the ecstasy spoken of in the psalms, only more real. At last she knew it was possible to know joy in this world. But her time with Valeria was so short.

After Valeria had fallen asleep, Guinevere listened to the sound of her friend's sleeping for the last time, and wondered whether she would ever have a love of her own. She wasn't sure whether it was a blessing or a curse to learn what she really wanted.

6   LANCELOT ALONE

One morning Lancelot woke to see that snow had fallen during the night. She roused herself from bed and pulled on her boots and her cloak so she could be the first to ride through the snow.

But when she was leaving the villa, her father followed her.

"I'd like to go riding with you," Marcus said, yawning. "I want to try out my new horse."

Lancelot was pleased because her father so seldom enjoyed anything. His face had long since wrinkled into a frown.

When they went to the barn to get their horses, Duach the stablehand was sleeping. Marcus shook him. "Who is to keep watch over the horses if you sleep?"

"I'm sorry, my lord." Duach jumped up and rubbed his eyes.

Lancelot gave the man a smile. Surely no horse thieves would dare to come to her father's stable. She had routed the brigands for miles around.

She and her father rode out across the snow. Marcus's new horse, a fine bay gelding, pulled ahead of Lancelot's Arrow.

The horse stumbled on the slippery ground, and Marcus flew off, landing in the snow. Lancelot dismounted to help her father, but she saw that he had fallen at a strange angle. His neck was twisted. He had fallen so many times before. How could it be fatal now? She could scarcely believe that she had lost another parent. This time she did not sob or scream, but stood frozen like the world around her. Then she knelt in the snow beside her father and prayed.

Lancelot walked listlessly to her daily session with Dinias. Every room reminded her too much of her parents. Her mother's chair. Her father's sword. Why did she have to outlive both of them? At times it seemed there was little to do but follow them to the grave.

She sighed as she passed the window where Rathtyen used to sit, until she died of the ague. Now no one Lancelot loved was still alive, except for Creiddyled. She respected Dinias and Father Matthew but she did not love them.

Everything she saw, her parents had also seen, except for a few animals that were born after they had died. Every spoon she touched had been used by her mother. Every book had been read by her father. She sighed again.

Every view in the woods they had also seen. She thought it might be pleasant to ride in a forest other than the one where her mother had been killed.

She remembered resenting her father's gloominess. She told herself not to follow his example.

She greeted Dinias and picked up her sword. At least she had that routine. After they had practiced for some time, the fighting master said, "Enough sparring for today."

He put down his sword and wiped his face.

"I'm getting too old to spend all day fighting with you."

"Nonsense. You're far more skilled than any of the young men I've fought," Lancelot protested. "You don't look any older."

She believed that lie was innocent. The fighting master's hair was much grayer than it had been.

"So you always thought I looked ancient." Dinias chuckled. "None of the younger men will enter contests with you.They're tired of losing."

He poured some water from a jar in the practice room and drank deeply. "Why don't we go riding?"

"A grand idea." The thought made Lancelot feel as if the wind already blew through her hair. She could never turn down a chance to go into the forest, which of course was where they would ride.

The leaves were drying on the trees because the summer had been hotter than usual. But even the wilted grass was finer than the stone floors of the villa, or so she thought.

They rode for some distance. A hawk called out, and Lancelot wished she could soar far away. Then she saw smoke, off in the distance — far more smoke than could come from a hearthfire.

"Perhaps some brigands have set fire to a peasant's hut," Lancelot cried, making her horse gallop as fast as it could along the forest path towards the smoke, which she could smell even when she could not see it. Dinias followed.

But when they reached the source of the smoke, they found a group of men slumped on the ground, resting by a hut with one blackened wall.

"Have you put out the fire?" Lancelot asked.

A stoop-shouldered man she recognized looked up at her.

"Yes, my lord. My son dropped coals on the straw bed, but by good chance my neighbors came running and put out the fire before it destroyed the whole house."

"I had feared that brigands had set the fire," Lancelot said.

"No brigands will come this near your lands, Lord Lancelot," the man told her.

"Yes, you've driven them all away," said Dinias, whose horse had just pulled up in the clearing.

That was good, of course. Lancelot thought she must be wicked to wish that she had some other challenge to face.

7   THE QUEEN COURTED

Camelot's gray walls jutted against the sky. It was much larger than Leodegran's caer. This caer stood on a high hill, with a commanding view – at least when there was no fog.

Guinevere drew near late in the day, as an evening haze was settling in. Several dozen warriors rode out to greet her party and escort her inside the town walls. Perhaps she would never again go anywhere without men in mail escorting her. She nodded to the warriors.

The huge gates in the outer walls stood open. In the caer's cobbled streets, farmers and tradespeople cheered her. Ladies and children, along with a still greater number of warriors, also crowded the streets. When Bors helped her dismount, the people cheered still louder. "Huzza! Guinevere!" they cried. "Our new queen!"

At last she was saluted as a queen. Guinevere's heart throbbed over that as it did not thrill at the thought of Arthur. She smiled with dignity, as was appropriate for a queen.

She saw the dragon pennant, Arthur Pendragon's symbol, flying from the tower, and thought she would be guarded as if by one that breathed fire. Clever of Arthur and his father before him to use the dragon symbol, which had been Julius Caesar's and, more recently, the Emperor Constantine's. If she must marry a man, at least he seemed to be one who knew how to be a ruler.

She saw the king, wearing a golden circlet on his head as well as the gold torque around his neck, walk up to greet her to the roar of loud cheers. Feeling that many eyes were appraising her looks, Guinevere wished that she could be queen back in Powys, where everyone already knew her.

Arthur's voice was deep, but she could scarcely hear it over the uproar. "You are well come, Lady Guinevere. I am glad to see you here at last."

"Thank you. Greetings, my Lord Arthur." However much he believed that he was her lord, he would never have claim to her soul. She smiled at him calmly, without flirtation, as if he were still a visitor at her father's well. He was as handsome as he had been, and she was just as unmoved by his looks. She was pleased that he had not grown a mustache or a beard.

He took her arm. "You're even more beautiful than you were three years ago."

"You are much the same," she replied, scrutinizing him and thinking that soon he would touch her everywhere. Supposedly, he would know her, but she vowed he never really would. There on a snowy mountaintop, she wrapped every part of herself in coldness. Her fine green gown and her elegant embroidered green cloak were layers of ice. She told herself that she must make her skin also a layer of ice, to keep herself from feeling.

People seemed to like to stare at the two of them together. There were endless smiles, bows, and cheers. The crowd, smelling of sweat, pressed at them, and many hands reached out to touch them as if they had the power to cure infirmities. Guinevere was afraid to think about what ailments the people who touched her cloak and even her hand might have.

Then Guinevere saw the joy on so many faces and marveled that she was the cause of their rejoicing. She wished that the people knew her and cheered for that reason, not just because she was Arthur's bride. And because they believed she would bear him children. Smiling and waving, she silently vowed to do anything she could for these people, so they would love her as they loved Arthur.

That evening they had supper in the largest hall Guinevere had ever seen. The trestle tables were set up in a circle, with spokes like a wheel, rather than laid out in parallel lines like those at any other caer.

"This is what I call my round table, where all can be seated equally," Arthur told her.

Guinevere smiled at the impossible idea of seating all of the caer's many nobles at one round table. No great hall could ever be large enough for such a table. The diners would scarcely be able to see each other, much less talk to one another. And, if there was one giant table, how could the serving people clear it away so the king could use his great hall for matters other than dining? But she appreciated his wisdom in trying to make his men feel that they were equal to each other.

Myriad torches set the huge room ablaze with light, although smoke from the great firepits permeated the air before finding its way out through the hole in the ceiling. She stayed at a distance from the firepits. Fire was all very well, but she did not like to get too close to it. Shields hung on the walls, and the clatter of the place made the gathering seem loud as a battle. Her father's men had not been quiet when they dined and drank their ale, but they had never made such a clamor.

There were not nearly as many ladies as warriors in the hall.

With Arthur, she met the lesser kings, like large Uriens of Rheged. Some of them she had seen at her father's hall. Greeting them was second nature to her.

There were a great number of dogs, of which the king seemed inordinately fond, prancing about in the rushes on the floor. She imagined how much trouble it must be for the serving people to clean up after the dogs. The grayish dogs with a dignified air were the tallest she had ever seen, and their heads were huge.

"What are these dogs?" she asked.

"Irish wolfhounds. Aren't they splendid?" Arthur beamed at them as if they were his children.

She muttered some acknowledgment.

A whole roasted boar sat on the table, alongside many lesser meats. At least the dogs did not leap up to grab at the meat, though they eyed the table.

Arthur introduced her to a great number of warriors. She was polite, but aloof, as befitted a queen. She had heard of the most famous warriors, of course, but were they so different from her father's own warband?

Bedwyr, whom Arthur said was his first follower, had a harsh-looking mouth. Peredur, who looked to be some years older than Arthur, was thin and plain. Arthur's tall cousin, red-bearded Gawaine, son to Queen Morgause of Lothian and Orkney and the late King Lot, wore a golden torque that was almost as fine as the king's.

They all seemed to have an air of self-satisfaction, a sense of themselves as great men that her father's men-at-arms had not had. She found it unattractive.

"And here is my good foster brother Caius, my seneschal, who manages the treasury and the running of the caer as well," said

Arthur, indicating a slim, well-groomed, handsome man who smiled slightly.

"Welcome, Lady Guinevere," he said, inclining his head more than necessary, showing the fine waves in his chestnut hair. "I am Arthur's Martha, who takes care of the details so the Marys can attend to his words and think on higher things, such as the killing of enemies." His lips twitched as if he suppressed laughter. "I suspect that you are a lady who will be glad to have me as your Martha also."

She returned his smile. She had heard many women compare themselves to Saint Martha, but never had she heard a man do so. "True, I am little fond of the details of administering a household, although this seems more like a barracks, about which I know still less."

"Pardon our barracks. No doubt its martial roughness will seem strange to you," he said smoothly. He slurred the word "martial" so that it almost might have been "marital."

For an instant, she wondered whether he might guess things about her that no one else knew, but she dismissed the thought.

Arthur turned to a gray-bearded man. "Ah, here's my adviser Merlin, who guided me when I was a boy and more than anyone else helped me gain the throne."

The aging man, shorter than most other men at court, eyed her coldly, nodding his head almost imperceptibly. "Greetings, Lady Guinevere. I opposed this marriage. I hope it will go better than I have foreseen," he said, and walked away.

Used to hostile remarks from Father Jerome, Guinevere was able to remain as calm as she had been meeting anyone else.

Laughing, Arthur squeezed her arm.

"Unperturbable, aren't you? Don't let Merlin's words bother you. I'm sure he'll never be unkind to you. He's unhappy when I don't take his advice. He didn't want me to marry you, but he had no other ideas, so in the end, he simply sighed and said, 'I know what you'll do, Arthur.' Merlin never married himself, so he doesn't understand these matters as he does battles and king-craft."

Guinevere rather wished that Arthur had paid more attention to Lord Merlin's advice.

Then Arthur led her to a wooden chair with dragons carved on the arms and legs, and she seated herself in it. Next to it stood the large wooden chair where he sat. It was covered with dragons, and a large dragon wearing a crown seemed to grow out of the back.

After the king seated himself, everyone else sat. All of them, even the lesser kings, sat on benches. She was pleased that she had a chair.

Later, Guinevere surveyed the room that had been prepared for her. A large bed was draped in more fine coverlets than anyone would ever need, with wool covers and furs for warmth and embroidered stuff for elegance. There were two chairs with cushions. A huge tapestry of girls picking apples hung on the wall. She was pleasantly surprised by that, for she had never seen tapestries depicting anything but biblical scenes, battles, or hunts. The room was something she could change a little and make her own. She would banish the oil lamp because she disliked the smell and would use only beeswax candles for light and rushlights if she wanted to read in the evening. A brazier drove off the worst of the night chill.

There were iron bars in the window, and, though Guinevere knew they were there to protect her, they intensified her feeling that she was a prisoner.

She was determined not to give in to weeping, although she wanted to. She must not be weak, not even for a moment.

116

There was a knock on her door. Arthur.

He sauntered in as if he belonged there. The light from the lamp made his flame-colored hair shine. "I'll stay just a short time, of course. It wouldn't be seemly otherwise until after the wedding." Arthur gave her a smile that said that she was his, and he was just waiting out of courtesy.

"I'm afraid that I look worn from my travels," Guinevere stood in a very straight posture, as if she were troops being reviewed.

"Nonsense, you look beautiful. Do you like it here?" Of course, there was only one answer she could give.

"It is grand." She knew that it was probably nothing like as grand as the Emperor's palace in Constantinopolis, or the one in Rome, if that had not been destroyed entirely by barbarians, but never mind. "It is impressive that you built this."

"You will grace it nobly." Arthur took her hand. "Such poise and calm. Your father told me that you can read and write, and you surely speak good Latin."

"Many thanks. I can read and write, it is true." Guinevere did not like the pressure of Arthur's hand on hers, but she steeled herself against showing any reaction other than a polite smile. She would have to learn to endure much more intimate touches.

He nodded. "I remembered the clever questions you asked me. Other kings' daughters flirted with me or used charms and spells to try to win me. That is not the sort of woman to be queen. I need a wife who can think and help me in my work."

Guinevere inclined her head to him. She was pleased that he wanted an intelligent woman, but surely she would have used spells to fend him off, if she had thought such things had any power. "I shall try to help. I have heard of your great deeds in war and am much impressed, and even more impressed that I hear you want to keep peace."

That much was true.

He smiled broadly. "Only a fool wastes lives when he can have peace. It's far wiser to rule with as little bloodshed as possible. I'll keep peace as long as the Saxons let us, although I think they won't for long. And I'll discourage the lesser kings from warring and stealing each others' cattle. But surely war and ruling are not the subjects that are most on your mind, Lady Guinevere." He squeezed her captive hand.

She remained outwardly tranquil. "They are important to you, my lord, and therefore they must be to me," she said, as if that were the only reason. Her eyes looked straight into his, but she did not flirt. Of course he knew well what was on her mind, but she was determined to show that she was not nervous about it. She ignored the implied criticism of her father's cattle stealing.

Arthur planted a kiss on her cheek. She politely kissed his cheek in response.

"A modest maiden, aren't you? I daresay you have never been kissed before." He seemed to take her coolness as a sign of purity, and that relieved her.

"No man but my father has ever kissed me," she replied, telling the truth if not all of it.

He squeezed her hand. "I'll not disturb your modesty, then. Good-night, my dear." He left, and she cherished the thought that she could spend the night alone.

He was handsome, and seemed to be a good man, she kept telling herself, so why did she mind his kisses? She must learn to accept them and to pretend that she liked them. She tried to banish the thought of Valeria's soft lips.

Guinevere woke, her body covered with sweat. She had had the dream again, the birthing dream.

One day it would not be a dream. She would give birth and she would die. Probably the baby would be born dead, too, like

118

so many of her mother's, and all her suffering would have gained nothing.

When Guinevere retired to her room on the night before the wedding, Fencha, a gray-haired serving woman who had been among those who dressed her, entered the room.

"I served the Lady Morgan of Cornwall, and now I'll serve you, Lady Guinevere," said the woman in a soothing voice. She dared to look the queen straight in the eye.

Guinevere stared back at the woman, whose eyes were as gray as her hair. The old woman put her hand over her mouth, as if she were holding something back. Guinevere shivered, and not just from the night air blowing in through the window.

"What happened to her? Why is she gone?" Finally there was someone Guinevere could ask.

"The king sent her away." The old woman frowned, making deeper creases in her forehead. "You must never tell him I told you."

"Of course not," Guinevere reassured her. "I met her once and liked her well. How could the king bear to send her away? Why does that Bors call her a witch? I must know."

"Yes, you must know." The old woman took the liberty of patting her hand. "Did you never hear that she was more than a sister to the king? He loved her well, for a time."

Guinevere gasped. Feeling as if she had been struck, she sank down in a chair and put her hand over her face.

"I have never heard of such a thing," she said when she could speak. She pictured Arthur and Morgan embracing — no, she must not think of that.

What kind of man was she about to marry? One whose desires knew no boundaries? And did he still desire or love his sister? Would he compare Guinevere with her?

119

Guinevere had no brother, but she could not imagine any of the brothers and sisters she had known doing such a thing.

She was flooded with envy. He had touched Morgan as she could not. Guinevere no longer thought it was strange to desire such a beautiful, clever woman. It seemed more natural for her to want Morgan than for Arthur to be with his own sister.

So this was why the Lady Morgan was still unmarried though she was well past twenty summers? What a fool Guinevere had been to dream of her, when the lady loved her own brother.

If Morgan's old serving woman wanted to make certain that Arthur's bride did not love him, she was succeeding admirably, Guinevere thought.

"They did not meet until they were both grown," Fencha continued, telling her secrets in a low voice. "She was the older. He came to her caer, Tintagel — it's a grand place by the sea — and he was smitten, as so many other men had been. He wasn't the first, and he won't be the last. I'm sure that galls him." She smiled, but it was a smile to make one shudder. "He was so jealous of her that he glared at every other man who looked at her."

"But why then send her away? How could he?" How could he bear to lose her? Guinevere wondered. If she had the love of such a woman, she would never let her go.

The old woman's mouth was drawn and bitter. "There were too many rumors about their love. Many people were scandalized. The king was not man enough to defy them. And my lady had too many thoughts of her own. When people labeled her a witch, he did not discourage them, but finally said he agreed.

"When Arthur sent her away, my Lady Morgan cursed him, swearing that he would never find love again."

"It may be that she was right," Guinevere replied, her fingernails digging into her hands.

The old woman searched her face far more than was proper.

"She sent you a letter, Lady Guinevere. Do you want to see it?"

"Oh, yes." Guinevere extended her hand, and the serving woman drew a letter from her bosom and handed it over.

Guinevere wondered whether Morgan had already cursed her for marrying Arthur. She was half afraid to read it.

Trembling, Guinevere opened the missive. The writing was large and elegant, and of course, in Latin.

My dear sister,
Do not be afraid. Would that I could be there with you. No doubt he will be kinder to you than he was to me. I am your friend, though there is little that I can do for you from remote Tintagel in Cornwall. Now that I am called a witch, there is no place else that I can go. Remember me always. I shall write you at times, in secret, and I beg you to write me also.
Your poor sister,
Morgan

Guinevere shook with anger. Her stomach tightened. If she hadn't wanted Arthur before, she wanted him less than ever now. If he could treat a woman he supposedly loved that way, he must have no heart. "So I must go to the brute who sent his own sister away? I must bear his children?"

She looked at the old woman, who had just revealed how little she liked the king. "Must I? I saw my mother die in childbed, and I have no wish to follow her. My nurse said she believed I was likely to die if I bore a child, and I have often dreamed it."

Fencha shook her head. "What nurse would tell a girl such a thing unless it were true? What a terrible fear for you to have."

Guinevere dared to speak further. "They say that old women sometimes have ways . . ."

Fencha's face was unreadable.

She passed her hand over her mouth again, then said, "Of course, my lady. There are brews, if you want one."

"I shall drink it." Guinevere rose, pulling herself to a height that felt taller than she had ever stood before.

"Shall I bring it to you every morning after the king is with you, Lady Guinevere?"

Guinevere nodded.

"It would hurt nothing to drink some beforehand as well. I can fix you some now, if you like, my lady." Fencha did not smile, yet she did not seem hostile to Guinevere.

"Please do so."

While the old woman was away bringing the brew, Guinevere pondered what its contents would be. She wondered whether the old woman could truly like the new queen, or whether she might hate her for replacing Morgan. Was it possible that Morgan hated her for marrying Arthur, and Fencha would give her poison?

Fencha returned, bearing an ordinary stone jar. She poured the contents into a silver cup on Guinevere's table.

Despite her doubts, Guinevere reached for the cup and drank from it. The brew was not tasty, but not noisome either. No burning pain or nausea followed. Guinevere felt that the potion would give her life, not death.

The next morning was truly her wedding day, and there was nothing Guinevere could do but acquiesce. She had never seen as many candles in a church as those burning in Camelot's lime-whitened chapel, and there was enough incense for the investiture of a bishop. She held her breath to keep from choking. A choir of priests sang, but the saints painted on the walls seemed to frown at the couple, or perhaps just at her. The wedding was a pageant of bright robes and jewels. Guinevere's white gown sewn with pearls gave her little satisfaction, and neither did her gold-embroidered mantle. The incense made her dizzy. She trembled as she said her vows, and Arthur, dressed in a white tunic and cloak embroidered with gold dragons, said his.

As they departed and walked into sunlight that was even more dazzling than the chapel, Guinevere heard a robin sing for an instant before cheers drowned out the sound. The song seemed to mock her.

Even birds might choose their own mates, but she could not.

After the wedding and more feasting came the bedding. A number of the higher-ranking ladies escorted Guinevere to her room, undressed her, and helped her put on her new white linen bedgown. They were strangers, so she held off from them.

Claudia, wife to Arthur's man Peredur, teased her. "Now you'll learn what all women know, that men are just boys who want one thing only, and are pleased once they have it."

Claudia's hair was gray – she must know all about marriage.

"Don't worry," said smiling, brown-haired Lionors, who was married to Bors. "It doesn't hurt much. And it's a hurt you'll be glad to have. After the first time, it hurts not at all."

Guinevere felt only rising nausea as the ladies tucked her into the bed. She thought it might be easier to be like these women, calmly accepting men, but she was certain that she never could. Even when she was broken for riding, she would never be truly tame, she was sure.

Arthur was escorted into the room by some of his warriors and a few lesser kings, who did not refrain from jests.

"Well, Arthur, are you strong enough to please this pretty lady?" one man said.

"Don't stay in bed so long that you leave the land without a king," another jested.

Guinevere tried not to hear them, or even see the men's faces.

She must bear the humiliation of having them see her in the bed, waiting. Thus it seemed as if they, too, were having their way with her.

Arthur was wearing a kind of long tunic, and sat on the curtained bed beside her. Then he waved everyone off, and the men and ladies drifted out of the door. Someone shut it behind them.

"Now you are married to Britain," Arthur said, putting his arm around her.

Those words stunned Guinevere. She felt that he did not mean simply that she was queen and would rule beside him, but that he embodied Britain and she must see his body as the nation.

He stroked Guinevere, and she gritted her teeth. He had bathed, of course, but his breath smelled too strongly of wine. His touches were not ungentle, but she did not want them. He seemed practiced at these matters. Trying not to think of Morgan or Valeria, Guinevere opened her legs when he reached between them.

This was Britain lying on her, and the weight was heavy, but she must think of the good of the nation and bear it.

Guinevere pretended that nothing hurt, although her blood on the sheets said that it had. It didn't hurt terribly much. She only wanted it all to end.

Arthur smiled at the stain and said, "You were a good maiden and you'll be a good wife. It will be much better after the first time, I promise you."

She was sure that it would not. The minor physical pain mattered much less than the fact that she did not want him at all.

She became convinced that the delicately twisted Irish band on her finger was a living creature, a golden leech, eating into her flesh and leaving nothing but bone.

Arthur left the queen's bedchamber and retired to his own room to dress for the new day. She was beautiful, but cold, even for a maiden. He had little faith that he could warm her. No other virgin he had been with had showed so little enthusiasm. Purity was all very well, but there should be limits to it.

He was pledged to her, and would make the best of it. She was as intelligent as he had hoped, and would do him credit.

If only Morgan could be beside him. He let a groan escape his lips, then stifled it with the morning ale his body servant brought him. Even if Morgan truly had cursed him not to know love, he must continue in his course. He did not have her, but he had Britain. That was what mattered most – to bring peace to his land. And to be the one whose name might live forever.

How could he let that name be tarnished by rumors about his sister? Besides, it was likely that she loved power as much as he did, and therefore could be dangerous. No, it was best for power to reside in one man. Guinevere would complement him, he was sure, not challenge him.

But the memory of Morgan's embraces made his ale bitter. Perhaps he could have kept her near him if she had married one of his men, but he could not bear the thought of that, and she had probably been too angry at him to have done it even if he had asked.

8   GUINEVERE THE WIFE

Guinevere longed to speak with other women. She thought she might befriend some of the ladies. Perhaps there were none like her friend Valeria, but surely one or two would be congenial.

Dark-haired Cornelia's bright eyes had some spirit. Guinevere tried to catch her glance at one of the endless suppers. Cornelia gave her a brief nod, but Guinevere noticed that the lady was looking past her, at Arthur. She was actually trying to attract Arthur's attention, right in front of his wife, and Guinevere saw that she gained it. He smiled briefly at Cornelia, but his glance lingered.

When Arthur did not come to her room that night, Guinevere guessed that he was with Cornelia, and hoped that he would visit the lady often. She slept better than she had since her marriage.

He returned the next night, and Guinevere resigned herself. She was a new bride, and he would not leave her alone for long. A few nights later, Guinevere was alone again, and she slept well.

Arthur returned to her bed, sporadically, and of course she had to greet him as if she wanted him. Her life was, of necessity, a series of lies. She grimaced when she remembered that as a girl she had thought she couldn't tolerate a husband's infidelity. Now she wondered how many women were pleased that their husbands had mistresses.

Sometimes when Arthur began to caress Guinevere, she let her mind travel back to her father's caer. She imagined that she was walking from room to room, revisiting everything, not where she was, in Arthur's arms. She did not dare to think of what it might be like to be in the arms of someone she wanted.

But all of life was not to be lived in bed – she was glad of that. Guinevere found pleasures where she could. Food pleased her. Cai saw to it that the finest of fish, meat, fruits, and sweet things were on the table, and she thanked him for his efforts. She particularly liked breads and cakes, but she had to be careful because Arthur might not mind a rather plump queen but would not be pleased with a fat one. So she ate of the honey cakes enthusiastically but sparingly.

The food and the music were even finer than at her father's caer. The greater use of herbs was no doubt due to Cai's influence.

When the harpers played and sang of love, Guinevere at times was able to shut out the sound of the warriors' voices and imagine that she was free to love a woman. The songs resounded with the cries of women dying for love or suffering a lover's death, but they filled Guinevere with a wild longing. She feared that she would never know what it was to love and be loved. Oh, let love come, no matter how it wounded her. She felt sure it never would.

She had thought that love was foolish, far inferior to kingcraft, but now she yearned, like the giggling girls she had disdained, for passion. The thought that no lips but Arthur's ever would touch hers made her want to beat her fists against the walls, but she kept her face serene and gave the harpers furs and arm rings.

In the hall one rainy evening when Guinevere was wishing for someone to talk to, Gawaine asked her whether she would like to play gwyddbwyll.

She nodded and smiled at him, for she liked exercising her wits. She was good at board games.

As they set up the board, Gawaine picked up one of the pieces. "This side is fighting because it believes that only bread made with wheat can be sanctified," he said, "and the other side fights because they believe the heresy that oat cakes also can."

Guinevere laughed, surprised that she still could. Good, here was someone else who was not overly pious. "They are both wrong. Only barley bread can be holy," she said.

"This side believes that one god is three," Gawaine went on, rubbing his red beard, "while the heretics believe that three gods are one."

"Let me take the heretical side. You clearly should take the orthodox," Guinevere said, relaxing as she seldom did now.

"I was baptized not two years ago, because Arthur wanted all his men to be, so pardon me if I make mistakes about Christianity," he told her. He rolled his merry blue eyes as if to say that he had not been converted at all.

So men, too, had to obey Arthur's wishes, she thought with sympathy. She found that she enjoyed the game, and defeated him handily, for he seemed to care more about his jests than about the moves in the game.

He shook his head and gave her an exaggerated frown that clearly was not serious. "The heretics have won, so their doctrines now become the one truth. You play very well, Lady Guinevere, as well as the king does. I should warn you that he hates to lose, especially to a woman. His sister often defeated him, and it made him angry. Arthur is genial, but it is best to avoid angering him."

Arthur walked up to them. "Did you do well, my dear? Shall we play a little?"

"Oh, no, Lord Arthur, I have heard that you are much too good for me," Guinevere replied. She determined that she would never play with him, rather than lose deliberately. But perhaps it was better not to let the king know that she could play at least as well as he could.

She decided that she liked Gawaine the best of Arthur's men, even better than Bors, who always spoke to her reverently, as if she were an abbess.

But it was Bors she chose to accompany her on her rides. Her fear that Arthur wanted her to ride only with an armed escort proved correct. She longed to explore the new countryside, though the forests seemed less beautiful to her than those in Powys because they had fewer hills. A day when she could ride her mare was a fine day, but she found that a queen was expected to abide mostly at the caer, with a thousand matters needing her attention.

At least Arthur had concern about his people — for that was how he saw them, as his — and had a brain in his head. She could have been married to a man who was far worse. He wasn't bad-looking, or bad-tempered, but was always pleasant as long as people did things as he wished, which they cheerfully did.

All in all, her life was commonplace, much like other wives', with a bit more luxury and plotting. And Arthur, too, though a man among men, was commonplace, with breath that sometimes was better, sometimes worse, like her own.

Perhaps she could have some influence over him.

One night he came to her room complaining that the Bishop Dubricious, who ruled the Church from Londinium, had sent a petition demanding a harsher stand on pagans. Arthur groaned as he sank down on her best chair. His brow was furrowed, showing that he would not always look young.

Guinevere immediately exclaimed with sympathy, "How dare that bishop make demands of you? Does he want to make the Christian Church more powerful than the king himself?"

Arthur smiled at her, and said, "Thank you, Guinevere. I like that you are always thinking of me."

"I want to be of service to you," she said, refraining from saying that she would prefer that service to be out of bed rather than in it. "I worked on my father's accounts. Perhaps I could do the same here?"

He leaned back in his chair, touched his chin where a hint of stubble had grown since morning, and looked at her thoughtfully. "Cai is nearly buried in a mound of vellum, and I have far too much to read myself. The Romans had an army of administrators, but I do not. Would you like to help Cai in reading the reports from our magistrates and tax collectors? He has several assistants, but it would be good to have someone else who can read as carefully as he for hints that men are not entirely loyal to me, or that tax collectors might be keeping too much for themselves or helping the wealthy to pay much less than they should. Most of the men I have around me have come to fight, and I can't burden them with such tasks. A man like Gawaine won't willingly read anything but reports on troop movements. But you could help Cai. Are you as good with figures as you are at Latin?"

"Surely, my lord," she said. She preferred numbers to spinning. As queen, she could bid any priest to read aloud while she spun, but she would prefer to read for herself, alone, not in the company of bored ladies who would rather talk about men than listen to books.

"I am grateful that you are willing to undertake such tasks, my dear." Arthur inclined his head to her.

Guinevere was somewhat less glad when she discovered the sea of vellum and wax tablets that awaited her, and had to plot her course through it. There were endless pleas from the outposts for more aid, and endless reasons why they could not send more taxes to the king. She tried to guess which of the writers were merely selfish, and who was so self-seeking that he might cheat or even betray. She watched for boastful phrases amidst the pleas of poverty and asked Cai to describe the lords he knew among them.

"People's best natures seldom are revealed when they are paying their taxes," Cai observed with a grin as she worked at a table near his in his office. Though the room was small, it was well lit and had good chairs as well as a rug on the floor. "Are you sure you want to wage this battle with me, Lady Guinevere?"

"Onward," she said, flourishing her stylus as if it were a sword and returning his smile. His perfume smelled better than the warriors' sweat. "Though we wound only their purses, let us make them feel besieged and fear to cheat."

Arthur sometimes asked the opinions of his warriors, some of whom were quite dense, about matters such as how to treat the lesser kings or the Saxons, while Guinevere sat silent. He seldom heeded what the men said, but they were overwhelmed with the honor of being asked.

"Should we sweep the Saxons from our shores, or wait until they next attack us?" Arthur asked each one in turn. The fighting had abated, but everyone knew it was not over.

"We should sweep them from our shores," exclaimed Sangremore, a warrior with a scar snaking down his cheek.

"Do we have enough men to do that?" asked Gawaine. "The Sea Wolves have been established here for several generations now, curse them. Driving them away wouldn't be so easy."

"Perhaps if we keep building our army we can," Bedwyr suggested.

"My Lord Arthur, I have no idea of the answer. I must leave such strategy to you," Bors said, so humbly that Guinevere wanted to groan.

Unasked, Guinevere spoke later in her room, "I am sure that you are so clever that you won't fight your major battles against the Saxons until you know that you can win decisively."

Arthur chuckled. "You're getting to know me well," he said, embracing her. "I am glad I married you."

At least he valued her opinion, she thought. That was something. Actually, it was a great deal.

Arthur's men talked endlessly about battles, past and future. Guinevere soon learned all about Hannibal and Caesar's wars, and the fighting methods of the Saxons and the Picts. She had to watch the warriors' seemingly endless tests of strength.

She sat in the royal stand, with Arthur's red dragon pennant flying, as men fought each other in pretended deadly combat. They rushed at each other with spears outthrust, trying to knock each other from their horses. Then they stood on the ground and fought with swords.

The fighting contests continued from dawn to dusk, and she must sit there, applaud, and give prizes to the victors, though she cared little which man fought better than the other.

They never seemed to tire of fighting.

They fought for war, and they also fought for sport.

She wondered that more of them did not want to learn to read.

While they risked their lives or at least their limbs for glory on the contest field, she wondered how it would be to be able to hold a sword and fight. She saw herself riding against some proud warrior and unhorsing him, then getting down and battering at his shield, and, when he yielded, taking off her helmet to reveal — Guinevere!

It was a foolish game, this fighting without war, but it was the thing that won the greatest honors, so she half wanted to take part and win. She wished that she could defeat every one of those proud warriors.

Perhaps it was going a little far to imagine that she could defeat someone as tall as Gawaine. If only there could be women warriors, to keep the men from swaggering so much and feeling so infallible in their powers! The futility of her wishes made her head ache.

Often, Arthur held court, and his people came to him with petitions. Guinevere watched how he sat tirelessly in his huge carved chair, listening even to petty disputes as if they interested him. Sometimes he twisted the great amethyst ring with a dragon embossed on it that he wore on his right hand.

She could do this work herself, she thought. It was hard for her to keep still and not offer her opinions about the petitioners. She noticed that all those who came before him were men of property. After one such session, she pulled Cai aside.

"Why do the common people not come to ask the king's aid? And why do I never see women bring petitions?"

She could hardly keep the annoyance out of her voice.

"Cai raised his eyebrows. "No doubt they are intimidated."

They should not be." Guinevere shook her head, as if to say the court was not so grand after all. "See that your serving people go into the town, and into the highways and byways, and tell the people that anyone can bring a petition to the High King."

A faint smile appeared on Cai's lips. "Very good. Arthur will like that. He thinks much about the common people."

"He will think more if they can speak to him," Guinevere said, eyeing the shields and weapons on the walls of the great hall that emphasized the king's might, rather than his benevolence.

And so the common people began to bring their petitions to the king, and Arthur was pleased.

After he had decided the case of a man whose land had been stolen from him by a neighbor, Arthur turned to Guinevere.

"How many troubles people have," he said. "I wish that I could hear all such cases, though I cannot. What good is a kingdom without justice?"

She smiled at him. "That is true," she said, letting him hear the pride in her voice.

It was good to be part of a reign that was more than an excuse to accumulate wealth and hold fine feasts.

A lady struck a serving woman's cheek so resoundingly that Guinevere could hear it down the passageway. The serving woman fled from her mistress.

Guinevere hurried up to the pretty, fair-haired lady. "How could you do such a thing, Calpurnia?" she demanded.

In her father's dun, servants had been beaten rarely, only for stealing excessively or injuring one another. Guinevere had never struck a serving woman, nor had her mother.

"She deserved it," Calpurnia snapped, eyes glaring. "But if I offended you, I beg your pardon, Lady Guinevere," she added, in a tone that pretended contrition.

That evening, Guinevere spoke to Fencha, as the serving woman combed her hair before supper. "I saw Calpurnia strike her serving woman today. Do many of the ladies do such things?"

Fencha sighed. "The Lady Calpurnia is not kind, my lady, but she was in pain herself. She was married young to her feeble, old husband, and she seeks from other men what he cannot give her. She is fond of Gawaine, and was sorely vexed to discover that her serving woman had been with him also. Gawaine is the cause of many of the quarrels among the ladies, and the serving women, too. He charms many of them, but each likes to think she is his favorite."

"Indeed. What a lecher." Guinevere set her lips.

"Don't be too hard on him," Fencha said, smiling as if she, like everyone else, was fond of Gawaine. "The poor young man has been married twice, and both wives died all too soon, in child-bed."

"That excuses nothing," Guinevere said, shuddering at the thought of such a death. She felt sorry for the women, not Gawaine. He might have spent a little time mourning them before bedding other women. Nearly all the noblemen she knew, her own father included, had mistresses, but Gawaine's venery seemed excessive. She had thought him kind when he played gwyddbwyll with her, yet now she thought his kindness was nothing but the charm of a practiced seducer. Of course he would not dare to try seducing the queen, but perhaps he thought she would be another of his many admirers.

She determined that she would be cool to Gawaine. Let him learn that some women saw through him.

"I wonder how the serving women bear it here," Guinevere asked as Fencha plaited her hair. "The men are always after them."

"It's much like anywhere else, my lady," Fencha muttered, appraising the state of the braid and then redoing it. "At least here they are not supposed to force or beat the women. Lord Arthur does not like that."

"But there are so many more men here," Guinevere observed.

The old woman worked carefully, not pulling the hair. "Not many ladies think of it as you do, Lady Guinevere. Most of them think that pleasing the men is just part of a serving woman's work, or something that doesn't concern them. As for me, by the time I came here I was too old to interest any of the men."

Guinevere winced. Being at the beck and call of many men seemed unimaginably awful. It had been only a generation or so at best since most of the serving people had been called slaves, and many still were. As for the others, there hadn't been much change in condition. The word "slave" had gone out of fashion, that was all, Guinevere thought. Many of them were small and dark-haired, like the Old Ones. Or like herself.

That night, Gawaine asked Guinevere if she wanted to play gwyddbwyll.

Guinevere frowned. She did not want to play games with a man who saw women as toys. She said "No" in a tone of such disdain that he pulled back in surprise and stared at her.

A few nights later after supper, a pretty young serving woman passed Gawaine's chair and he pulled her onto his lap. The girl laughed, kissed his cheek, and went back to work. Serving women often threw their arms around Gawaine, kissed him, or flung themselves in his lap for a moment.

Guinevere looked at him with contempt.

He saw her look and turned away from her.

Guinevere decided that she would always give him looks that showed her disapproval of lechery.

One morning when Fencha came to help Guinevere dress and fix her hair, she noticed that the serving woman's eyes were red.

"What is the matter?" Guinevere asked in her gentlest voice, which she seldom used.

"Has someone dared to speak harshly to you?"

"No, Lady Guinevere. My only daughter died ten years ago this day." A few tears dripped down her cheek and caught in the furrows of her wrinkles. Her hand covered her mouth as if to suppress a sob.

In an instant, Guinevere's arms were around her. Imagine going through the pain of bearing a child and then seeing it die. So many women lost child after child. She had no idea how they endured the loss. "That must be a grievous hurt," she said.

"It is that. Why couldn't the Goddess have taken me instead of her? Why, I keep asking myself?" Fencha said, in a voice as heartbroken as if her daughter had died only a month earlier.

"How did it happen?" Guinevere asked, sitting down on the bed, gesturing that the woman should sit beside her and holding the wrinkled, spotted hand.

"It was a fever took her," Fencha recounted, rubbing her eyes. "It happened so quick. She was still a girl, and so bright. You never saw such a bright girl."

"That's very hard," Guinevere said, listening. Here was someone who felt real things, and said them, unlike so many at Camelot, who said only what they thought would please the king or the queen. "Tell me more."

"My sons are dear to me," Fencha said, "but sons soon go off to fight with the other men. Two of them died fighting the Saxons. The other two still live, but they don't know what to say when they see me. My daughter I could talk to. We could chat all day and not know the time was passing. She had such a cheerful laugh, she did." The old woman smiled through her tears.

Sitting there holding Fencha's hand, Guinevere could almost picture laughing with a daughter. She carried the image with her.

In the courtyard, she watched Lionors, wife to Bors, run after her young son and daughter, both of whom had darted off to follow a disreputable-looking mongrel. Lionors caught them in her arms, laughed, and tousled their hair.

"Your children seem to be a handful," Guinevere remarked.

"They're such a joy," Lionors said. "They grow too fast."

The boy tugged away from her and ran after the dog, which took him through a mud puddle and a pile left by a horse.

"You wicked child!" Lionors cried, but her voice still was warm.

There was something after all to children, besides bearing them in pain, Guinevere reminded herself as she walked slowly back to her room. Was she missing something grand? Would she love them although she did not love her husband? Perhaps many women preferred their children to their husbands.

Lionors did look sweet holding her little ones. Could Guinevere enjoy such moments? Had she been born with no tenderness? Was she made all of bones with no marrow?

Then she imagined handing a girl of about sixteen over to some ally of Arthur's to bind the alliance, and she dismissed the daughter's picture. Why bear a daughter to be as unhappy as she was? And she pictured a little boy, cheerfully running about the caer, then spending his days with savage men, learning how to be like them. If she died giving birth, she could not influence such a son. Even a nun like Valeria had told Guinevere that she did not need to be simply a tree bearing fruit. Was that not a kind of permission not to give birth to an heir for Arthur? What child could rule better than Guinevere herself? She continued to drink Fencha's potion. But she had doubts.

Guinevere woke to the sound of Arthur tossing and turning in his sleep. He woke and wiped sweat from his brow.

"Are you well?" she asked him.

"What a dream." He trembled.

"I keep having the same dream. It is so terrible that it shakes me more than a battle."

"Would you like a warm posset to drink?" Guinevere asked.

"Do not summon a servant. I hate for anyone to see me like this. Could you get me some of the wine on the table?"

"Yes, of course." She slipped out of the bed, poured wine into a goblet, and brought it to him. She sat on the bed beside him. It shook her to see the High King of Britain so unnerved by a dream.

Arthur sat up and drank the wine. He moved his legs so that he was sitting beside her.

"Pray light candles."

Nodding, she went back to the table and lit some of her beeswax candles.

"I must tell you of my dream," he said.

Guinevere wished that he wouldn't, but it was a wife's duty to listen. She worried that his fears might spread to her and she might have similar dreams about whatever monsters disturbed him.

But she sat on the bed and said, "Of course, Arthur. What is it?" He stared beyond her at the candlelit shadows.

"I dream of an infant," he whispered hoarsely. "An infant son."

Her heart sank.

"The child glares at me with unnatural ferocity," Arthur said, shuddering. "Then he leaps at my throat and tears at it with his teeth."

Guinevere gasped. She dug her nails into her arms.

"I push him away, but he comes back again and again, attacking first my throat, and then my heart. My blood pours out." Arthur's voice quavered. "I grab up my sword, strike at him and kill him. He vanishes, but he is not gone. He attacks me when I least expect it.

"Finally, in desperation, I order that all baby boys in the land be killed."

"That is King Herod's command!" Guinevere cried. "You are not King Herod. You must not listen to this evil dream." It took all of her strength not to leap up from the bed and dash across the room to get away from him.

"But it keeps recurring. What if it is a prophecy?" He shook his head. "What if my son will kill me?"

"Infants do not murder their parents. Try to be calm." Guinevere attempted to keep the terror out of her voice. "You should talk to a priest about this."

"No, no. I cannot tell a priest." He waved his hand in dismissal. "I have asked Merlin." Arthur paused. "And he says it is possible that I might have a son who would kill me."

Guinevere felt as if a blast of cold blew through her. "Anything is possible." Her speech faltered. "But he should not have told you that and fed this terrible imagination."

Arthur stood and paced about the room. "No, if anything, he was sparing me, Gwen. I believe that he sees it happening."

She wished that Merlin were at the bottom of the sea. "My lord, have you been reading the Greeks? This sounds like the story of Oedipus. The difficulty was not that he was born, but that he was sent away."

"I see the resemblance to Oedipus and to Herod," he said. "As always, I am glad that you are so well read. We must discuss this intelligently, my dear." He tried to smile at her, but there was no happiness in the smile. He took her hands.

Reluctantly, she allowed him to hold them.

"I fear this evil dream," Arthur said. "I think it may be best if we do not have a child. I fear that a son might murder me, and I do not know how I would treat him. Of course I would not deny you the conjugal acts, my dear, but I think that at least for a time I should try not to get you with child. I hope that no one will blame you for that, but they may. I am sorry to disappoint your natural hopes with this burden."

Guinevere's head reeled. "It shall be as you say, my lord," she managed to tell him.

He put his arms around her, but she was relieved that he did not want anything more intimate at the moment.

She redoubled her vows never to bear this man a child. What man could think of murdering his own son?

She could not tell this secret to anyone, not even Fencha. Guinevere thanked God and Mary that she had the potion.

But Guinevere did ask her old serving woman, "Are you sure the potion will continue working?"

Fencha took the liberty of patting Guinevere's hand. "My lady, there is more than a little magic in the potion. It cannot fail." Guinevere did not believe in magic, but the old woman's strong certainty reassured her.

One morning, when Fencha came to her room, Guinevere continued to sit on her bed instead of rising to be dressed. She looked in the old woman's face, which held such maternal warmth that it gave Guinevere the courage to speak.

"I have learned to be guarded with everyone here, but I am becoming fond of you. Foolishly, I wish that there was one at least with whom I could be honest. If you served Morgan and loved her, can you truly be fond of me?"

"Do you doubt it?" Fencha's voice sounded offended, but she sat on the bed beside Guinevere and took her hand. "You are not the one who hurt her. Have you never had more than one friend, Lady Guinevere?"

"Do queens have any? I'm glad if I have you." Guinevere leaned to embrace her.

"I am your friend, my lady, and I want to let you know a secret." Grinning, the old woman went to the huge hanging on the wall and pulled it back, revealing a hidden door. "This room has a secret passage because it was intended for Lady Morgan. That way, the king planned to visit his sister at night without anyone knowing. Perhaps someday you might need the passage."

Guinevere laughed and shook her head. "I might not mind escaping, but I have nowhere to escape to. Many thanks, though."

The thought that she had a secret way to leave did comfort her. She smiled to herself, imagining darting out in the middle of the night, getting on her horse, and riding away. In truth, she was a little afraid of the dark, but she still could enjoy her dream. She also pictured having a visitor – Morgan herself – pass through the secret door. Fencha sometimes brought Guinevere messages from Morgan.

Guinevere devoured the Latin words on the vellum, as if they were food that might sustain her, although they were cryptic and generally brief. Morgan addressed her as "sister," but thinking of how it was that they were related, Guinevere flinched at that.

She spent days pondering her responses. She tried to turn the lines into poetry, but failed.

Could she write of the redness of the lady's hair, or the greenness of her eyes? No, not when Morgan did not write her in that manner.

Could she tell of the emptiness of the court, and the shell of her marriage? But Morgan apparently had found joy where she found none, and perhaps envied her what she most disliked. She decided that she must be brief.

Dear Friend,
I am doing all I can, which includes working on the accounts with
Cai to be sure that no lord is cheating on his taxes. I ride as

much as I can, though I am always supposed to have an escort. Truly, a woman's lot is hard. I watch the women at court bear children year after year and wonder how they can keep on.

I think often of the women's councils in Ireland you told me about. It would be a good thing if we could have such gatherings here.

Would women squander their sons' lives in warfare as recklessly as men do? I doubt it. We would fight the Saxons, of course, but not other Britons.

The men here speak of little but warfare, the women of little but their children. But surely they could learn greater wisdom.

If only I could speak with you, I know that we would find much to discuss.

I hope for that day.

Your friend

So she wrote of women's troubles, but tried to make it seem as if they were not her own. Some weeks later, an answer came.

Dear Sister,

As well as meeting in women's councils, Irish women join in their own clan councils to discuss important matters – taxes, for one, and so you would know well what to say. And you could teach many others your wisdom.

But who knows what may happen? Perhaps one day you will be even closer to the throne than you are now. Couldn't you decide matters as well as he can? You were raised to be a queen. Do not let anyone persuade you that you need to produce an heir. Who could succeed him better than you could? Such an outcome would not be unprecedented. After all, my Aunt Morgause rules Lothian, and all the world acknowledges that she is a better ruler than Lot.

I rule my little Tintagel with a firm but gentle hand, and the people of Cornwall love me.
Of course I do not believe that a woman's hands were made only for holding infants.
Your sister

Guinevere smiled to herself at the compliments. She was pleased at the thought that perhaps she could rule after Arthur's death, although that day was no doubt many years distant. How good it was that another woman understood that a queen was capable of ruling. And the thought of Queen Morgause was reassuring, though Guinevere had heard that fear of witchcraft might be the reason no one challenged Morgause.

Much as Guinevere liked the letter, she wondered whether Morgan hoped to be the one to rule. Burning Morgan's letters hurt, though Guinevere quickly learned the words by heart, for they were all that was hers. But clearly Morgan would never love Guinevere as she longed to be loved.

Guinevere liked some of the women at Camelot, and others less, but she saw none who stirred her heart. She stopped thinking about what it might be like to love. It was foolish to pine for what you could never have.

9   QUEEN OF LIGHT AND DARKNESS

Pelting rain did not diminish Gawaine's happiness in the least. He was back in Lothian, on his way to visit his mother, who had ruled Lothian and Orkney for the past several years, since his unlamented father had died. He was determined to enjoy seeing his mother and being in his own country.

Gawaine chose to travel with Lamorak, a young warrior who was pleasant to a fault. Arthur had suggested that Gawaine might want a companion, no doubt because Arthur wanted a report about Lothian from someone other than the queen's son.

But Lamorak, who was from the South, proved not to be overly fond of Lothian. Gawaine thrilled at the sight of the heather, but Lamorak complained about the frequent rains, and found the air chilly. The cool air felt good to Gawaine, and he had no objection to water streaming down his face and shoulders. His horse might not have been equally pleased.

The day was fine when they came to his mother's caer, Din Eidyn. Looking up at the tall stone battlements, Lamorak said, "It looks forbidding."

Gawaine laughed. "Not if you come as a friend."

When they rode into the courtyard, the warriors of Lothian, men Gawaine had known all his life, cheered at the sight of him.

"Here's the hero himself!" they called. "Our own Gawaine, greatest warrior in the world!" "Tell us who you've fought lately!" "And tell us about the women, too. Are they really hotter in the South?"

He anticipated sharing many a good jest with the men. Leaping down from his horse, Gawaine showed that he remembered them by speaking of this one's old wounds, that one's habit of fighting with his left hand, and yet another's liking for buxom women.

Many of the men had told him on previous visits that, rather than resenting him for leaving Lot to fight with Arthur, they were proud of his fame as a warrior.

And he was proud of them for changing their ways. He recalled that on his first visit home after his father died, he had gathered the leaders of Lot's warband and told them that he and Queen Morgause would not punish them for anything they had done under Lot, but they would have to act from that day forward as if they were Arthur's own warriors, abiding by similar rules. As far as he knew, they had done so.

Some of the men called out the words "King Gawaine." But Gawaine shook his head at them. "You have a fine queen. You do not need me here. It is better that I am at Camelot with the High King to keep up the prestige of the North." He could scarcely say that he liked Arthur's court better than Lothian and Orkney.

And though he little liked the thought of ruling, he knew that Morgause enjoyed it more than food, wine, or any other thing.

Queen Morgause herself came to the courtyard to greet him. Gawaine threw his arms around her.

Her embrace was lingering, and she asked him how he was – many times.

"I am well," Gawaine assured her, "and so are Agravaine and Gaheris." His brothers, too, had joined Arthur's warband after their father had died. "They send their regrets that they could not accompany me."

"I'm glad to hear that they're well," Morgause said without undue concern. The truth was that Gawaine had not brought them along because he knew she would rather visit just with him.

"Where's Gareth?" Gawaine asked, looking about for his youngest brother.

"Off in the hills somewhere. He'll be upset that he missed the first moments of your homecoming," his mother said, still clinging to him.

"And here is a fine warrior of Arthur's, Lamorak," Gawaine told her.

Drawing herself to her full height, Morgause smiled at Lamorak, who bowed more deeply even than he had to the High King at Camelot.

Gawaine gazed at his mother. She was beautiful as ever. The sunlight sparkled on her red hair, which had not yet started turning gray. She was buxom and tall for a woman, although not as tall as her sons.

They were interrupted by loud shouts, as if from an enemy attack, and a boy hurled himself at Gawaine.

"Gareth!"

"Gawaine!" The boy, redheaded like the rest of his family, was tall for his years. What was he now? Seven, perhaps?

"Take me hunting, will you? I've caught some hares lately, but nothing worthwhile. Let's go after a bear."

Laughing, Gawaine caught him in a wrestling hold. "To be sure, I'll take you hunting. I don't know about the bear. Are there any around here? Let's go off and wrestle. Show me how strong you are."

Gawaine spent the afternoon with Gareth, but Morgause decreed that the boy could not linger after supper. Gawaine made a promise to take him hunting soon, to make up for it.

Supper in the great hall was a far more magnificent feast than could have been expected with just a day's preparation. Lords and ladies sat at the lower tables, and only Lamorak had the honor of being seated at the high table with Morgause and Gawaine. After the meal, while the harpers still were playing, Morgause indicated that the three of them should go to a smaller room where talk was easier. Servants brought wine for Morgause and northern liquor for Gawaine, as well as sweets and fruit. Lamorak hesitated over what he wanted to drink, and chose wine.

Morgause spoke almost entirely with Gawaine, but Gawaine noticed that Lamorak never took his eyes off her.

Finally, she turned her attention to him. "Do you like Lothian, Lord Lamorak?"

"It's the most beautiful place I have ever seen, Lady Morgause," he said in fervent tones. "I wish I could stay here forever."

Gawaine stared at him. Why this change in attitude? Lamorak was handsome, with long, flowing brown hair — and perhaps not distasteful to his mother.

Morgause smiled, and her smile was like no one else's, Gawaine thought. It appeared that Lamorak thought so, too.

"I was born in Cornwall," she said.

"True, Cornwall is even more beautiful than Lothian," Lamorak added hastily.

"You should visit Cornwall sometime, Mother," Gawaine said. "You would like your niece Morgan. She's clever, like you." He smiled to himself. What pleasant memories he had of Morgan. Surely it wasn't wrong to lie with a woman Arthur had discarded, even though it would anger Arthur if he knew. But by sending Morgan into exile, Arthur had given up his right to her.

Morgause turned pale. "I never want to meet a woman of my family. Don't ask me why." She sipped her wine, but the hand holding the winecup trembled.

Gawaine almost fell out of his chair. He had heard that women of his mother's age sometimes had strange humors, but he had never seen her so disconcerted. "Are you well, Mother?" he asked anxiously.

"Well enough." She drank more wine.

"Perhaps I should retire. Your hospitality is splendid, noble lady, as suits this majestic caer," Lamorak said, bowing, but with a very different look on his face than he had when he bowed before Arthur.

"Such a gracious guest is always welcome, for as long as he wants to stay." Morgause spoke in a throaty voice, and Lamorak left the room slowly, as if he found it unbearable to depart.

"An admirer." Gawaine grinned at his mother.

He had chosen well — much better than he could have foreseen — in bringing Lamorak. Morgause rapped Gawaine on the knuckles.

"What about you? When will you marry again?"

Gawaine's stomach muscles tightened. He thought of the two wives he had married, and their deaths in childbed, especially his first wife. "Keri," he mumbled.

"Keri was a sweet girl, but she died years ago."

"Not yet three years." He sighed.

"That's a long time for a young man."

His mother's voice was not ungentle. "You can't mourn her forever. You don't grieve so much for your second wife."

151

"I thought of her as a little mouse because she scurried about and said so little. Before we were married, I thought her silence was just maidenly shyness, but it was not. I tried to encourage her to talk, but to no avail. And she never laughed. I didn't want a little mouse." He shook his head. "Perhaps I wasn't patient enough. Poor Little Mouse. I think she liked me. I asked her whether she wanted to marry me before I discussed it with her father, and she said yes readily. And she looked at me fondly sometimes."

"Of course she was fond of you. Do you think any girl you asked to marry you would be foolish enough to refuse?" Morgause chided him.

"Probably not, because I am a king's eldest son." Gawaine snorted.

"Not only that, but for many other reasons as well." His mother smiled at him. "You should have good memories of your little mouse. There are worse things than quietness in a wife, I assure you."

"I know that. But believe me, I have no intention of trying marriage again for a good long while. I can't replace Keri, and it's madness to try." He took a long drink. "And I don't want any more women to die bearing my children."

"Not all women die in childbed," Morgause said in a deep voice, as if showing how strong she herself was. She patted his arm. "You need sons. You needn't look to a wife for pleasure," she scolded. "You can find that elsewhere, as you already do, of course."

"Of course." Gawaine felt his face redden. "No doubt I'll find another wife someday." He took a long swallow of northern liquor, better than any he could get in the south. "I'm certain Arthur would let Lamorak stay here to help you in case there are any incursions from the Picts."

"Nonsense, I'll never look at a man again. I had quite enough with Lot." Morgause's smile belied her words. She passed him an apple.

Gawaine took a bite of the apple. Of course, it was tasty. His mother knew how much he liked the fruit and always saved the finest for his visits. "I believe Arthur will want Lamorak to send reports," he said.

Morgause shrugged. "I doubt that he'll say anything bad."

"I'm sure he won't," Gawaine agreed. "Not that there's anything bad to say. You aren't plotting against Arthur, are you?" he teased.

"Not as long as he's a friend to you." Morgause handed Gawaine his horn of liquor as if he were still a child she was feeding. Not minding his mother's coddling, he drank from it.

Arthur entered Guinevere's room for his night's leisure. He kissed her cheek and sat down in a chair by hers.

Guinevere poured wine into a silver goblet for him.

"I miss Gawaine," he said with a sigh. "It's good having the support of kin. When I was a boy and didn't know that I was King Uther's son, I thought I had none." He sounded rather sad, which was unusual for him.

Guinevere pressed his hand and saw her chance. There would never be a better opportunity to ask him to allow Morgan to return to Camelot.

"It is sad indeed for kin to be parted. Perhaps someday your sister might return here? I would make her welcome." She spoke sweetly, as if she were concerned only for his sake, not her own. Arthur jerked his hand away. "Never!" He knocked over a candle.

Guinevere jumped backed from the table. She could not forget that her sister had been burned. "Fire!" she gasped.

"Never fear, it's nothing."

Arthur put the candle, which had singed the table, back in the candlestick. He softened his voice. "I am not angry at you. You don't understand what she is like. But do not speak of her again. I have promised Bishop Dubricius of Londinium that she would never return."

So Guinevere gave up that hope. She guessed that his own mixed feelings about Morgan mattered more to him than the bishop's. He could not bring himself to face his sister again, and no wonder, after the way he had treated her. Seeing how he could hate frightened Guinevere. What would it be like if he ever came to hate her?

He was gentle only as the leather scabbard that covers the sword is soft, she figured, but unbending as the metal within.

Although Gawaine left Morgause a little time with Lamorak, she made it clear that she wanted to spend most of her hours with Gawaine while she could. He often went out riding with her.

On one such ride, a cold rain began to pour down, so they rested under a rock ledge.

The rain did not bother Gawaine. He was glad to be back in Lothian, glad to see the flowers that did not grow near Camelot. The people's voices, with their familiar accents, sounded good to him. He was surprised that his mother seemed to mind the rain. She seldom had in previous years.

Queen Morgause looked bleaker than the day. Her shoulders drooped, and a few wrinkles showed on her face. She really is getting older, Gawaine thought, and barely stifled a sigh.

"Can I tell you the most terrible thing that I have done? Would you still love me?" she asked him.

"Of course." He fidgeted, not wanting to hear about whatever it was, but he thought he had to. No doubt it was some small matter, such as lying with a man other than his father.

"You shouldn't feel so bad if it was some man. You know how many women my father had."

She dismissed that with a bitter laugh.

"Nothing like that. The men around Lot were just like him."

Thunder sounded in the distance, and lightning appeared far away. Gawaine wondered what she had done.

It had seemed passing strange that Lot had died at home so soon after Gawaine had told his mother that Lot was a rapist.

He would not blame Morgause if poison had been involved. How could she bear to be married to such a man?

She shook, although the cold usually did not make her do so. "I had always thought I would like a daughter for company. Then, a few years after Gaheris was born," she said in a hollow tone that was strange to him, "I gave birth to a girl."

He nodded. "The baby who died. I remember."

"The midwife handed her to me. A madness came over me, and I feared what her life might be like, with Lot as her father, and three older brothers, and a husband like Lot in her future. I turned her face to the pillow and pressed it in. That is why you have no sister."

Feeling as if he had been thrown from a horse, Gawaine reeled. He gasped, "Gods, mother, I wouldn't have touched her."

"I know, but I could not be sure about the others," she said, shuddering.

"I did not trust Lot, though perhaps he would not have stooped that low. Agravaine and Gaheris have always been too much like him. They listened to their father, not to me. I can scarcely believe that they came from my body. I have never been able to bear being around another woman since then. I especially never wanted to meet your cousin Morgan, because I was afraid she would look like my daughter."

He tried to mutter consoling sounds, but what could he say?

"Do you hate me?" she asked anxiously, more subdued than he had ever seen her.

"No, no, of course not." Gawaine patted her cold hand and wondered whether his father really would have mistreated a daughter. He couldn't bear to be angry at his mother. Instead, here was another reason to hate his father.

"The worst part is that I was wrong," Morgause whispered. "I realized later that I was powerful enough to protect her, to make my husband and my sons fear to harm her, but it was too late." Exhausted, she sank back on the stones, her head in her hands.

Gawaine also staggered back and sat on a rock. His mother had always seemed to be the tenderest woman in the world – the arms where he had sought refuge as a child – as well as a fierce queen.

He could easily imagine her knifing a man if any attacked her, but he could not picture her killing a baby. Causing the death of an innocent child seemed worse to him than killing Lot would have been. He knew his thoughts about that subject were different from other men's.

If I had been a girl, I would have died, he thought, but the very idea was foolish because he never could have been a girl.

Gawaine wanted to put his wineskin to his lips and drink, but somehow the moment seemed too solemn. He thought of his own little girl, his second wife's baby, who had lived only a day. How much he had longed for the midwife to save his daughter. He had begged, promised anything in the world, if only she could save his little girl's life. Had the little sister his mother killed looked like her? Best not to think of that.

Keri's child had been a boy born dead. In a way, Gawaine had been relieved not to have to love a child who had cost Keri her life. But no, her death was his fault, not the child's.

Now he often tried not to get women with child. But he was not always that careful, he admitted to himself.

After a little while, Morgause lifted her head. "I did teach Lot to fear me. Do you know how I came to be called a witch? I started the rumors myself."

Staring at her, Gawaine took a deep breath. He groaned inwardly at the thought of hearing more revelations. Now the rain made him feel like a wildcat with soaked fur. It was all he could do to keep from saying, "No more, Mother, please."

"It was the first time Lot tried to beat me," Morgause went on, leaning towards her eldest son.

"Surely he never dared to beat you!" Gawaine could not fathom anyone striking his majestic mother. Why, she used to silence even Lot with a glance.

"A girl of fourteen summers, completely under his power? Of course he did." Her laugh was hollow.

"But I could think quicker than he could. I cursed him and told him that I had great powers. I would make his cock wither and his heart stop beating. I showed him a little simple magic I had learned from a jester in my father's caer, making things disappear. Lot believed me, or decided that he had better not risk learning whether I was telling the truth. He soon told his men to beware of his wife because she was a witch." She reached out to Gawaine, but did not touch him. "That was how I protected myself, and you. That was why he never beat you as hard as he might have."

"Mother!" Gawaine leapt up and threw his arms around her. Her skin felt so cold from the rain. He could remember being a shivering little boy, with Lot looming over him, and Morgause demanding, "Don't dare to injure my son." Lot had listened to her. Now Gawaine knew why.

His mother had had to take on the name of witch to protect herself and him.

She had always seemed so proud and powerful. Now she felt fragile, and he wanted to protect her. He held her close.

"You are the only one I did not want to fear me. You are the only one who never has," Morgause said, putting her head on his shoulder in a gesture that was far softer than was her custom.

"Of course I haven't."

"Now I hope that Lamorak will not fear me. Do you think he'll stay long in Lothian?" she asked, an unaccustomed anxiety in her voice.

"Of course he will. How could he not?" He patted her rain-drenched shoulder. "Never fear, I'll tell him how you came to be called a witch."

He had been right to see his mother as a protector, Gawaine thought. She had been even more of one than he had reckoned. He wished, now that Lot was dead, that the rumor that she was a witch could be dispelled.

"Lot was so angry that you went over to Arthur," Morgause said, raising her head and looking her son in the eye.

Gawaine tensed. That had been years ago. Why did she want to mention it now?

"I told him that he should not curse his first-born son, but he did." Morgause touched Gawaine's cloak, as if he were still a child and she wanted to wrap it tighter around him. "He demanded that I never speak with you again. I said, 'You should not seek to separate a mother and son, but you are my lord. I must obey your orders. I will never speak to Gawaine again during your lifetime.' Then I ordered a fine dinner for him. He ate and drank heavily, as he so often did. The next morning he did not awaken. He didn't have time to call his men together and disinherit you."

158

"Gods, Mother, I should have killed him so you wouldn't have felt you had to!" Gawaine gasped.

"No. People should know you as Gawaine the Good, not as a kinslayer. It's far better for any blame to fall on Morgause the Witch." She pressed his hand.

Gawaine returned the pressure. "Poor brave Mother," he said, his voice trembling as hers no longer did.

Of course, Lamorak would never hear about what she had just told him.

10   The Barren Queen

Guinevere could scarcely hide her delight whenever she received packages of books from the convent. She already had read every book that was to be had at Camelot, almost all of which were about war. Caesar she knew too well, and Thucydides, Tacitus, and Plutarch's lives of the Roman emperors and the noble Greeks. The Roman writers insulted the Celts in ways that angered everyone who took the trouble to read them, but Arthur said it was important to learn about their tactics nonetheless.

The Greek plays were more to Guinevere's liking. When she spoke with Arthur about Homer, he beamed at her.

"How clever you are, my dear," he said, kissing her cheek as they talked alone in his room. "I'll never leave you alone as much as Odysseus, but I have no doubt that you'd be as faithful as Penelope."

Seeing that she was in his favor, she made bold to say something that she had pondered for a long time.

"Women need rules to live by, my Lord Arthur, so that the Penelopes can counsel their sisters. I have heard that in Ireland there is a council of women, who decide women's matters only, of course." She thought it better not to mention that Irish women also joined their clans in councils at which matters such as taxes were discussed.

The king frowned. "What foolishness. They just gather to gossip, no doubt."

"Oh, do you think so?" Guinevere asked, struggling to keep the disappointment out of her voice. "But aren't there some subjects that are too trivial for men to ponder, that women could discuss with profit?"

"And what would they talk about but men and children, and they could not make any decisions concerning those." Arthur's voice was disdainful. "You are so intelligent, my dear, but few women are." His arm pressed against her. "I count on you to see who will always serve me and who might not, and to help me bear the burdens of the throne."

"I am glad to help you, my lord," Guinevere replied. She was pleased to help him, for he was a good ruler. But it was difficult to be resigned only to be a helpmeet, not the ruler herself. She must not imagine what was unlikely, she told herself. She had far more power than any other woman, except Queen Morgause and some abbesses. She had to become inured to the aspects of the marriage that she disliked.

Guinevere did not want to hoard the pleasures of reading, like a miser's gold. She asked Lionors, the lady she liked best, whether she wanted to learn to read, but Lionors only laughed and said a mother had no time for such distractions.

Guinevere watched the unmarried girls to see who among them was clever. She called Ailsa, a girl who made no mistakes in her few Latin phrases, away from her spinning and asked whether she would like to learn to read.

Ailsa shook her head. "Lady Guinevere, many of the warriors cannot read. I am afraid that I would not find a husband then. I had rather listen to the tales the bards tell in our own language."

So Guinevere left her alone. Someday she would find women who wanted to read Latin books with her, she vowed.

What she liked least about being queen was that her body was the subject of discussions, increasingly frequent as the years passed and there was no sign of a child. Every man and woman in the kingdom felt the right to stare at her stomach and silently sigh. Only the women commented to her, of course, expressing their sympathy or proposing charms or remedies, but she knew that the men talked about it too.

Lionors was one of the most insistent. "Don't go to pagan women with their terrible charms, Lady Guinevere," she ventured to say when she saw the queen alone in the room where the ladies did their sewing. "But you might eat plenty of eggs. I am sure the Blessed Mother will hear your prayers someday."

"No doubt," Guinevere said, smiling the required smile.

Guinevere still shuddered at Arthur's grisly reason for not wanting a son, and she still took the potion in addition to the means he used to prevent conception.

Guinevere wondered whether someday Arthur might present a child that some mistress had produced for him, or whom he claimed the mistress had. Guinevere hoped that he would just adopt the child and proclaim it legitimate, not put her aside and marry the mother. She vowed she would be a kind stepmother, and perhaps she could be regent if Arthur died.

11 BEFORE THE JOURNEY

One winter's night after a long and quiet dinner, Father Matthew cleared his throat and looked sternly at Lancelot. "Perhaps you should give your lands to the Church, and turn this villa into a convent, where you could live a suitable life."

Lancelot spilled her wine on her tunic. "I have no thought of doing such a thing." Never would she let herself be confined behind four walls. She was so irked that she soon went off to bed.

Though the land was now hers, Lancelot had little interest in the fields. But she did make certain that in good years her farmers stocked up what they could for years when harvests were poor. She knew the farmers' labor fed her, so she let it be known that they could snare whatever game they wanted. On feast days, she ordered that pigs or oxen should be roasted to feed all of the people on her lands.

On a spring day Faustinus, a friend of her father's whose lands were near, came to visit, and Lancelot of course asked him to stay and rest. Faustinus had long, graying moustaches and a nose that ran like a stream — it always had, Lancelot recalled — and a mouth that ran just as readily. They dined on quail, and she gave him the best wine from her father's stock.

"Good old Marcus. I'm sorry he's gone. I never saw a more pious man in my life," Faustinus mused, wiping his nose with his hand. "There's too little good in this world, young man. You seem to take after him, and that's a good thing."

"Many thanks. There is nothing I would rather hear." Lancelot threw some bones to the hounds that waited around her chair. She told herself it was unkind to be disgusted by the old man's perpetually running nose, but her appetite was not as keen as usual.

"They say Arthur of Britain is a good king," Faustinus told her. "He's called Arthur the Just because he cares about his people, not only his own power. He's gathered together a warband of the finest men, like the famed Gawaine of the Matchless Strength. They're more than a match for the Saxon Sea Wolves. A good Christian army is just what this world needs. The so-called Roman Empire has too many men from savage tribes to suit me."

"So King Arthur is looking for good men to serve him?" Lancelot asked, wondering whether there was a place where she could do something other than gather dust at her own villa.

Faustinus looked into Lancelot's eyes. "Are you thinking of venturing out from these shores? Consider it carefully. Your uncle left you all that you need, all that any man could want." He gestured around the room, which indeed was a good one, with a fine tapestry of the Marriage Feast at Cana from her parents' wedding still on the wall and clean rushes, somewhat disarranged by the dogs, on the floor. Some of the plates were red Samian ware, a good stock. "But I know young men often want to see new lands, and your uncle, God save his soul, served in Britain under Uther, who wasn't such a bad king either. They say that

166

Arthur's the son of King Uther, although there's been some question about that."

Lancelot sipped her wine. "I am of course grateful for the bounty of being my uncle's heir. This land is dear to me, but I think I might be of more service elsewhere, if it is God's will. If I go, would you see that this land and the people on it are protected?"

Faustinus laughed, coughing and choking a little as he did. "I was a friend to Marcus, and I know he would have wanted me to. It's natural for a young man to be restless." He leaned closer to Lancelot. "But perhaps a wife would keep you at home."

Lancelot gasped.

"Now, don't tell me you're going to be monkish like your uncle. Remember, he was married before you knew him, and was mad about his wife."

Lancelot sucked in her breath at the mention of her mother.

"I wanted you to marry my daughter, but Marcus wouldn't hear of it," Faustinus continued, sighing. "Our lands are so close together. She was married long ago, as you know, but I have a niece . . ."

Lancelot turned to throw scraps to the dogs. "Please, say no more about that subject. I am monkish like my uncle, as you said. Pray tell me more about King Arthur."

Shaking his head at Lancelot's folly in refusing his niece, Faustinus nevertheless obliged by telling tales of daring.

After he had left, Lancelot thought much about Arthur the Just. Perhaps her skill at fighting could be more useful in Britain than at home. Besides, she thought it might be pleasant to be in another country. She liked the idea of being in a place where no one had ever heard of her. And perhaps if no one knew how much land she had inherited, men would be less eager to marry their daughters to her. She hated to admit it, but she even liked the thought of being in a place where her parents had never been, where she could escape her memories at times. Perhaps she could gain fame like that of Gawaine, so someone would remember her when she was dead.

To make her disguise more complete, she began rubbing her cheeks with pumice every morning so they would look raw, as if she had shaved. When she was preparing to leave, Lancelot spoke one last time with her old confessor.

Father Matthew made the sign of the cross over her. "May the Holy Virgin keep you. You must stay pure, living around warriors. If you ever find that you are tempted to lose your innocence, you must enter a convent."

Lancelot had no intention of ever being so confined. "Oh Father," she said in a scandalized voice, "of course I shall be pure. I've never even been tempted not to be. None of the men I have seen has seemed the least bit tempting, and I cannot imagine that the others I meet will be any different. I am not made for such earthly things."

The priest cleared his throat. "It is rare for anyone to live a whole lifetime without temptation. Don't become arrogant about your purity. It is only through resisting sins that attract one that one becomes virtuous. There's no virtue in not doing what you don't want to do anyway."

She smiled, which she rarely did with her stern confessor. "It's true, there's no virtue in being pure, because I want to be. Don't worry about me."

He handed her a small scrap of bone encased in wood. "Here is a relic of St. Agnes. She died to preserve her virginity, and you should do the same, if you must."

Lancelot took the relic reverently and nodded her assent. She felt like a bird about to fly off for the first time, with only instinct to guide her on a path she did not know. She trembled when she parted from Creiddyled at her hut. The old woman moved so much slower now. Perhaps she would never see Creiddyled again.

"Do not try to come back," Creiddyled told Lancelot while pressing her hand. "Your future is not here. Your mother's soul and mine can fly anywhere to watch over you." She scarcely paused to allow Lancelot's kiss to brush her cheek.

"Won't men soon discover that I am a woman?" Lancelot asked anxiously, before she mounted her horse.

The old woman shook her head. "To them, man is strength, so as long you are strong, you will seem to be a man. Most people see things only as they seem to be. As you seem, so you shall be, in their eyes." Creiddyled held out a black feather. "Keep this raven's feather in memory of me."

"I shall." Lancelot took the feather as if it were a jewel and put it in a small bag hanging from a chain around her neck, where she carried a ring that had been her mother's and the relic Father Matthew had given her. As she set off, Lancelot tried to keep her mind on prayer, but she feared she just imitated her mother's prayers without any piety of her own. Life was no doubt a vale of tears and human beings were poor, weak creatures who had to try for unachievable perfection. She tried to feel the unimaginable essence of God, but, as was usual when she prayed, she thought of her mother. She would begin by picturing the Christ on his cross, as she had been taught to do, but as soon as she thought of the wounds she saw her mother lying on the pine needles. Lancelot feared she was less than truly religious because even when she thought of Mother Mary, the Blessed Mother had her own mother's face.

12　The Reluctant Warrior

Gawaine stared through the window at the rain-drenched court-yard. He played at dice with Bedwyr, but the game was not on his mind.

"The fighting contest shouldn't have been postponed because of rain," Gawaine grumbled. "Have Arthur's men become weak-lings, that we can no longer fight in the rain? We did so often enough in the war of succession."

Bedwyr took a swig of ale and stretched. "As for me, I'm glad to be indoors. We can fight tomorrow."

Of course Bedwyr would rather gamble than fight. Indeed, there were jests that he even preferred gambling to bedding women. Bedwyr was not the most interesting of companions, but he was devoted to Arthur, Gawaine thought. All of them were, of course, but Bedwyr had never fought in any other warband and never would, even if, the gods forbid it, Arthur died. Gawaine made a sign to ward off that evil.

Merlin appeared, noiselessly as always.

Are you willing to cease dicing, Gawaine? Arthur would like to speak with us." Gawaine jumped up.

"My luck was just going to turn," Bedwyr complained.

A private interview with Arthur at midday, much less in Merlin's company, was no common occurrence. As they crossed the damp courtyard to Arthur's quarters, Gawaine's heart raced. What troubled the king?

The door to the king's chamber opened. Arthur sat at his small carved table and bade them to join him. He smiled cordially, and Gawaine relaxed. At least no attack was imminent. The wall hanging depicting warriors fighting was the only hint of the king's martial strength.

Arthur's body servant, Tewdar, poured them ale. Tewdar, who limped, then cleaned up a puppy's mess and carried the puppy outside.

"I suppose you wonder why I wanted to talk with you." Arthur spoke in a matter-of-fact manner, as if the subject did not concern him too closely. "I have wondered whether I should put Guinevere aside and marry another woman, who might not be barren."

"Poor Guinevere," Gawaine said without pause, although he little liked her. She clearly enjoyed being queen and discharged her duties with great dignity.

Arthur shook his head. "But no other woman has had a child that is believably mine. So perhaps the fault is not Guinevere's. What do you think?"

Gawaine looked away. He had, of course, sometimes thought of that, but he never would have mentioned the subject to his cousin. "True, that is very strange. If you put away Guinevere, and married some other woman, and that one also failed to bear a child, she would go to some other man so she would not be put aside also. It might be better to leave things as they are."

"Guinevere certainly won't go to another man," Merlin said.

"No man would be fool enough to try to seduce her, and if he did, he'd be rebuffed sharply." Gawaine added, downing his ale. He hoped the discussion was ended.

Arthur smiled. "Yes, Guinevere is the woman least likely to commit adultery, and of course I'm glad of that. But I need an heir." He looked into Gawaine's eyes. "The only solution is to ask some man, one related to me . . ."

Gawaine spluttered, nearly falling out of his chair. "The idea's mad. Put it out of your mind. Guinevere would never agree."

Arthur remained calm. "But perhaps she might be persuaded."

Gawaine thought of trying to bed Guinevere while she looked at him with contempt. The picture was far from pleasant. And why must he be the one? His two wives had died in childbed, and they had both been larger than little Guinevere. Was he supposed to kill her, too?

He was still pained by thoughts of the son who had been born dead when his first wife had died and the daughter who had lived only a day after his second wife's death. Having a child he could not acknowledge, who looked to Arthur as a father, would tear the heart out of him, and having his son become High King was no compensation. Nor did he wish to have a daughter raised by haughty Guinevere to be just like her. But he did not want to tell Arthur those reasons. Arthur had never been a father and would not understand.

But it was only too plain that Guinevere would refuse, Gawaine thought, so he should stop this plan before she heard of it. He shook his head. "What do you think you're talking about? Horses? Guinevere's not a mare." Nor was he a stallion, much as he liked to present himself as one, to breed at another man's whim. "She doesn't even like me."

"Of course she doesn't like you, that's all to the good." Patting him on the shoulder, Arthur spoke as if to a child. "If I thought my wife was mad for you, do you think I'd encourage it? Do you think I like the idea? But I'm talking about kingdoms, which are more important than likes and dislikes. Guinevere thinks about kingdoms, too, as much as a woman can, so she might agree. She's a sensible woman, not the kind who falls in love."

"Guinevere cares about likes and dislikes, and perhaps I do, too," Gawaine said, pulling away from him. "It would be dishonorable to lie with a woman who detests me."

Arthur frowned. "Why must you balk? Perhaps you don't care whether I have a son because you know my secret will names you as my heir if I die childless."

Gawaine jumped up from his chair and yelled, "How dare you accuse me of disloyalty! I've saved your life many times, and this suspicion is the thanks I get! I don't lust after your throne, or after your wife, either!" He shook with anger.

"Be calm, Gawaine. Sit down," his cousin said, maintaining his royal composure.

Gawaine remained standing. He wished Merlin would speak up, but Merlin said nothing.

"Poor Guinevere must be longing for a child," Arthur said in a coaxing tone. "Would you deny a child to a woman who is desperate to have one?"

Gawaine groaned. "If she's truly so desperate that she wants to lie with me so she might have a child, I suppose I'd agree, but I doubt that she is. Please don't mention it to her. She'd think I schemed to seduce her, playing on your weakness."

"What weakness?" Arthur demanded. "I don't have any."

"Your weakness is that you care about nothing but ruling. Don't bother to deny it. You have just shown that it's true." Gawaine had thought that Arthur cared about Guinevere, but now he doubted it.

174

"Of course I think of my people. Would you want a king who didn't?" Arthur twisted his ring.

"Let's just leave the question of an heir to history," Merlin suggested, speaking up none too soon.

Gawaine left and went out in rain. He thought of his first wife, Keri. He would have died rather than ask another man to lie with her so he could have an heir to the throne of Lothian. Perhaps he was not ruthless enough to be a king. The rain splashing on him soothed him.

Guinevere heard her door open. Arthur was the only person who ever failed to knock. The time was earlier than usual; he must not have spent much time after supper drinking with his men.

A small gray kitten sat in Guinevere's lap. She put the kitten on the floor.

"My dear, I need to speak with you," her husband said, his voice more formal than usual for his evening visit.

Guinevere rose. "Yes, my lord?" She brushed cat hair off her skirt as if that were the only thing on her mind.

"I regret that we have no child . . ." He hesitated.

Steeling herself to hear that he wanted her to try again, which she had no intention of doing, Guinevere merely said, "Indeed?"

Arthur gave her a benign smile. "It does worry me that there is no heir. But we could fool people into believing that a child was mine. Gawaine is my closest male kin . . ."

Guinevere shrieked and backed away. "No!" she shouted. She stared at Arthur as if he had just turned into the dragon for which his family was named. She had never imagined that her failing to bear a child would lead to his asking her to lie with another man. One man was bad enough, but two seemed beyond

175

endurance. The thought of lying with Gawaine made her stomach heave. She shuddered.

"My dear, I understand that you are a good and loyal wife." Arthur's voice was soothing. "Of course I don't like the thought of that bedding either. But think of Britain. An orderly succession is the greatest gift I can leave my people. And I believe that your bearing a child by another man would avoid the possibility that my own son would kill me. I have no bastards, so far as I know."

"My lord, I cannot." Her voice shook as she tried to keep rage out of it.

"It's no sin, my dear. St. Paul said a wife has no authority over her body but her husband."

"Surely St. Paul did not mean that adultery was permissible." She knew that St. Paul had also said that a husband had no authority over his body but his wife, but she did not say so because she did not dare anger Arthur.

"Just a few times, my dear. That would probably be sufficient." Giving her the smile that he believed no one could resist, he spoke in a paternal tone. "Many women like Gawaine very well, I believe."

Guinevere crossed her arms over her chest. "My Lord Arthur, if you insist that I lie with any man but you, I shall have to kill myself, or enter a convent if you permit it."

Arthur stared at her, then swept her into his arms. "I had no idea you loved me so much. Never mind, you don't have to lie with any other man. Gawaine told me you wouldn't agree, but I understand that only now."

She had to let Arthur believe she was motivated by great love. Her reward was that he spent the night with her as usual. She felt greater repugnance than ever because he had made such a disgusting suggestion. She was cold to his touch, but he didn't seem to notice.

The next morning she saw Gawaine in the courtyard and gave him such a look of hatred that he turned red, perhaps from embarrassment, and walked away.

She knew from Arthur's words that the idea had been his, not Gawaine's, but she could not show her anger to her husband. Gawaine might well be king one day, if Arthur died childless and she was not allowed to succeed him. But she trusted that despite her obvious dislike, Gawaine would do no worse than send her to a convent, and she knew which convent she would choose.

13 A Strangely-made Warrior

Sea birds shrieked like devils, while waves far greater than any Lancelot had ever seen lapped at the ship that carried her to Britain. She did not want to get out of sight of land. The ship was old and she had no way to know whether it was seaworthy. At least the leather sails looked to be in good shape.

Was it worth this terror to go to Britain? This water was called the Narrow Sea, so surely the journey could not be too long. She stayed with her horse in the hold, patting Arrow down, trying to be calm so he would be reassured. Lancelot's stomach lurched with every motion of the waves. She tried to eat a bit of wheaten bread, but that proved to be a mistake. The salt breath of the sea permeated it and everything else. Salt she smelled, salt she tasted. The sea was no doubt a place like the forest, like the lakes, that existed in a world beyond time. She felt that she should appreciate it, but it was too vast for her.

She wished she could escape from the sounds and smells of the crew and the other passengers, who yelled and cursed when the ship pitched. Better get used to curses now that she was going to live among warriors. Yet surely good King Arthur's warriors would be different, rather like fighting monks?

But warriors are not monks. Was she doing the right thing by dedicating her life to fighting, to killing? She had the gift for fighting. It seemed that she had no others. She intended to kill only in just causes, but would she always know what cause was just? She prayed for guidance, but no revelations came to her.

"Land ho!" the men shouted, but she could not see any land. All she could see was a fog so thick that she could almost believe that she had left the world and was journeying to heaven or hell, not Britain. The pelting rain was real enough, though.

The ship pulled in to a fog-bound shore, and it was all she could do to keep from jumping off before it had landed properly.

After landing at Llongborth in the south, to the west of the Saxon-held territories, she decided to ride north on Arrow, though the ship's captain assured her that the sea came close to her destination on the west, if she would only stay on board for the rest of the journey around the island. But she had had enough of the sea. Her feet embraced the land, and she bade the captain unload her horse, who whinnied when he touched earth. Stopping only to visit a mud-daub church and eat a meat pastry at a tavern, Lancelot set forth for the king's caer, Camelot.

Would Camelot be a place different from any other? She wondered. Would the warriors' voices, full of devotion, be softer than other men's? Would the very birds sing sweeter at King Arthur's command?

Britain seemed to be full of morning fog and later drizzle. Lancelot rode through marshes, where harriers looking for prey sailed low over the reeds. In the evening, they were replaced by short-eared owls on similar missions. She came to forests of oak and beech, which also were damp. It rained every day, although not for long, and it was always moist. She worried that her chain mail would soon rust. Warriors in Britain must continually need new mail.

She rode past fields yellow with buttercups, then through the woods of Britain, trying to learn their ways. New leaves covered the trees in a yellow-green haze. "Look at the leaves, child. You can tell a tree by its leaves," she could remember her mother saying. "Look up to the sky and down at the moss. Don't miss anything. The works of the Lord are meant to be enjoyed." Her mother would have wanted her to feel happy at memories of her, but Lancelot could not feel entirely tranquil. She still saw the poor broken neck and the blood on the pine needles.

She tried singing hymns to keep her mind clear. She believed that her mother's soul had entered the forest when it left her body and stayed there instead of moving to the special crypt her father had built. Of course her mother must be in heaven, but part of her was in the forest, too. Not just in that forest in Lesser Britain, but here in Britain, too, as Creiddlyed had said.

Lancelot passed shrines, stones where people had left cloths tied to nearby bushes to worship some local god. But surely in whatever form, their prayers also went to heaven, she hoped.

Each new sight pleased her — patches of primrose and bluebells, a woodcock flying up suddenly, a darting stoat, or a red fox crossing the path. Thrushes sang from the trees, cheering her. Then the notes of a wren's song filled the forest, and she decided she liked that song even better than the thrush's because it was the last song she had heard with her mother.

The damp earth smelled of new life. She filled her lungs with spring air. On the first morning with only a little drizzle, she saw a doe nursing its fawn and was flooded with tenderness. Did the fawn feel the same sense of safety that she had in her mother's arms? If so, it was no doubt as much an illusion.

She heard whistling, a haunting tune she had not heard before. As she followed a bend in the path, she came upon a red-bearded warrior who was as tall as any man she had ever seen and broad-shouldered as well. He rode a massive gray horse with bronze harness trappings. His shield was enameled, with a hawk depicted on it. The many colors in the man's plaid cloak and the gold torque around his neck showed that he was high-born. It was he who whistled, but he stopped when he saw her.

"God grant you good morning," she said.

"God grant you the same," he replied in a friendly voice. His merry blue eyes showed no hostility. "Want to fight?" He put his hand on the hilt of his sword.

"Whatever for?" Lancelot asked, startled by the incongruity between his tone and his words. "Are you a brigand who accosts all travelers?"

"Of course not," he replied, seeming to scold her. He rubbed his beard. "It's just the thing to do when men meet, to keep us in shape for real dangers. I'm Gawaine ap Lot, a warrior pledged to King Arthur."

Must she test her skill so soon against the most famous warrior in Britain? "I also want to serve King Arthur," Lancelot told him.

"Very good," Gawaine said. "We can drink afterwards. You need not be afraid. I'll hold back my strength so you won't get hurt."

She bristled and reached for her spear. "I am not afraid. Let's joust, then, as friends. No wounds."

"Never fear, no wounds," he replied, grinning and moving his horse into position.

They rode at each other, spears raised. Knowing that she would meet a forceful blow, Lancelot tried to calculate how to strike so as to use his weight against him.

They struck each other's shields with a great impact and both were knocked off their horses.

Shaking herself from the blow, Lancelot jumped up and pulled her sword from its scabbard.

The red-bearded warrior leapt up and drew his sword also, attacking sooner than seemed possible for one who had just fallen. She had never before encountered a man who could rise from a fall as quickly as she could.

She parried the blow, though it was powerful. The passion she generally felt in fighting came back to her. The man who had raped and killed her mother had been large, too. She must win; there was no other choice.

They fought for a long time, neither gaining much advantage over the other. She moved faster, but Gawaine had great strength behind his blows.

"Your sword dances like lightning," he said with apparent admiration.

The earth was wet from the rain, so they sometimes slid in the mud. Though her opponent was large, he moved well and did not trip. No doubt he was used to fighting in mud.

Finally, she saw an opening, and moved her sword past his shield to show that she could have slashed into him, but did not, for she remembered that he was not a murderer after all.

"Good move!" Gawaine cried out with enthusiasm. "You're a fine fighter. I never saw anyone so fast."

"Can we end this foolishness, then?" she asked, with considerably less warmth. The fighting passion ebbed out of her.

"Surely. I'm glad to meet you." He sheathed his sword. "I seldom meet a man who can stand against me. What is your name?"

Also sheathing her sword, she inclined her head. Gawaine of the Matchless Strength was strong indeed, but she had done well against him. She was a fine fighter after all. Her heart beat faster with pride.

But what name should she give for herself? In Lesser Britain, she had called herself ap Gaius, son of her father's brother who had died fighting the Franks for King Ban when she was a child. Should she give the name Lancelot ap Marcus? But even in Britain, someone might know of her family and remember that her father had no son. Her mother had told her to remember that she was "of the Lake," so perhaps she should use a name that honored her mother. "I am Lancelot of the Lake," she said, listening to herself to see how it sounded.

"Glad to know you, Lancelot." He clasped her hand. "And I'm grateful that you didn't wound me. Many men would have, so they could boast that they had wounded Gawaine ap Lot."

"Why are you are you so eager to give them the chance, then?" Lancelot asked, puzzled.

"Why, indeed? Not very worldly, are you?" Gawaine grinned and took a wineskin from his saddlebags. "Let's rest a while and have a drink, Lancelot."

"It is not yet midday," she objected. "Am I close to Camelot? I am eager to go there."

"It's not many miles from here. Have a drink, and we can ride together."

"I have no wish to linger," Lancelot said, wanting to approach the sacred Camelot alone. She mounted her horse. "Godspeed."

Gawaine laughed and replied, "Godspeed. I'll see you this evening, then." He sat on a log and began to drink.

Lancelot rode on, shaking her head at how readily this warrior wasted his time in unnecessary fighting. No doubt she would have to fight many others to prove herself.

She soon went into the bushes to change her tunic and breeches, for the clothes she wore were much splattered with mud from her fight. She did not want to arrive at Camelot in such disarray. She thought the earth did not smell as fine on her clothes as it did in the forest.

Guinevere had had a thousand tasks that morning, a thousand ceremonies to attend to, a thousand sick ladies begging her leave to let them rest, a thousand servants asking questions, a thousand matters from Cai needing her approval. All she wanted was to escape somewhere, scream and sob out the bitterness that was inside her after Arthur's words the night before, suggesting that she lie with Gawaine.

She would not weep in the caer lest someone hear her. Finally, in the afternoon, she was able to put on her riding breeches and slip away to the stables. She took her favorite horse and, despite the surprised look on Cuall the stablemaster's sun-browned face, rode off alone.

"I shall ride alone for a while," she said in a haughty voice, as if it were quite usual for the queen to do so, and of course there was nothing that he could say.

She was married to a man who cared so little about her that he wanted her to lie with another man. She was married to a man who imagined killing his own child.

When she thought she was deep enough in the forest to be away from any passers-by from Camelot, she flung herself on a rock and began to sob noisily.

After some time, she heard a voice saying, "My lady, why are you distressed? May I help you?" Guinevere looked up, annoyed at being interrupted, and grew even more irritated when she saw a warrior in chain mail. Was there nowhere she could go to escape men for a short time?

Then she saw the concern in the long, angular face. And what a face it was, handsome beyond anything in a bard's tale.

185

Those soft brown eyes – could it be that this was no man, but a woman? The warrior was taller than any woman she knew, and looked far stronger. Guinevere stared, taking in the glossy black hair, the slender but muscular build, the face that showed no beard or even stubble. The skin was a trifle weather-worn, but smoother than any man's, and this warrior was not young enough to be a boy.

Guinevere rose and took a few steps closer, moving so close that she could smell the warrior. Her heart leapt. Despite a kind of horsey odor, this warrior smelled like a woman – in fact, like a woman having her monthly flow.

There actually was a woman who had learned to fight! She marveled at the muscular arms that contrasted with the woman's large, gentle brown eyes, with lashes longer than most men's. There was a hint of sorrow in those beautiful eyes.

How had this woman ever managed to live concealed as a man? She must be daring beyond all measure. Could Guinevere ask the woman why she pretended to be a man, and tell her how she admired her bravery? No, the woman would not be pleased that someone had seen through her disguise. She would be alarmed, and might go away.

Guinevere wished she could confide in this woman, tell why she was weeping, about the conversation with her husband.

Guinevere had thought she could never tell anything so terrible to anyone, not even Fencha. But there was so much sympathy in the woman warrior's eyes.

Then it occurred to Guinevere that she must look red-eyed and haggard. "Oh dear, I've never looked so ugly," she exclaimed.

Lancelot reached out a hand to wipe away the lady's tears. She was moved by the warmest expression she had seen on any face since her mother had died.

"You are beautiful beyond belief," she told the lady. She touched the damp cheek and found it the softest she had ever felt. "Why are you so sad?"

Lancelot withdrew her hand, and the lady's right hand enfolded it.

"I'm not sad anymore."

The dark-haired lady looked at her in a way that encompassed her whole being. Her hand made Lancelot's feel warm — and the rest of her felt warm also. Her heart raced. Somehow this lady was different from any other.

For a while, they simply looked at each other.

"Who are you?" the lady asked.

"I am Lancelot of the Lake, from Lesser Britain. I have come to fight for King Arthur because I have heard that he is the best and most just king there is. And what is your name, my lady?"

The lady dropped Lancelot's hand. "You will see me every day at Camelot. I am sure the High King will accept you into his service."

Lancelot's heart raced even faster at the thought that the lady lived at Camelot. "Let me ride there with you, my lady. It's not safe for you to ride alone."

The lady raised her eyebrows and pursed her lips.

"I know you did not mean to be discourteous, but that is not a pleasant thing to say to a lady. Please never say that to me again."

Lancelot nearly stumbled over a log. "Pardon me, my lady. I am rough and ill-mannered. I meant no discourtesy. I shall never say such a thing again." The lady smiled the most wonderful smile that Lancelot had ever beheld.

Neither of them spoke. Finally, Lancelot shook herself like one awakening from a dream and pulled back. The lady would think she was rude for standing so close.

"I suppose we must go to Camelot." The lady sighed.

Lancelot helped the lady onto her horse. The touch of her hand was enough to make Lancelot's face hot. She realized that she must be blushing. As they started off, Lancelot said, "Pardon me, my lady, but I still do not know your name."

"I like to hear you call me your lady. That suits me very well." The lady smiled again. "I am the lady from Powys."

Lancelot was full of joy at the marvel that she would see this lady every day, and perhaps talk with her. She might even touch her hand again.

"It seems that you are fond of the forest. Tell me what you like about it," the lady requested. She looked much in command of her horse, more so than any woman Lancelot had seen except herself. Perhaps the riding breeches the lady wore made that easier than a skirt would.

Lancelot was glad she had changed out of her mud-splattered clothes and wore her best breeches and a crimson tunic under her chain mail.

"The forest is the grandest place in the world, my lady," Lancelot began. "Moss is finer than marble, and flowers are far lovelier than jewels. At every turn, there is something unexpected. When you wake in the morning, you never know what you will see, whether it might be a red deer, or, if you are lucky, a fox or a badger."

She went on in this way, and forgot her shyness. Too soon they came out of the forest and approached the caer on a hill, but the lady asked her to tell about other hills that she had seen, and so she did. They rode to the outer wall of the town and the guards let them enter without asking who they were. To Lancelot's surprise, the guards saluted and many townspeople bowed. The town smelled rank from the ditches that ran through it, and Lancelot shuddered at the thought of living with that smell. Then they went through the second wall, to what must be the king's own dwelling place. A great number of warriors and serving men crowded up to them in the courtyard, and the men jostled each other to get to the lady's horse and help her.

The crowd drew back as a tall man with red-gold hair, one of the handsomest men Lancelot had ever seen, approached the lady's horse. He was perhaps not as tall as Gawaine, but he walked as if he were the only person in the courtyard. Around his neck was a golden torque that was finer than Gawaine's, and his tunic was embroidered with designs in gold. The nobly dressed man offered his hand to the lady, and she took it.

"Here is a new warrior who wants to serve you. He kindly escorted me through the forest. Thank you, Lancelot," the lady said, turning her head briefly towards Lancelot.

"Did you ride off alone, my dear? You know you shouldn't. It isn't safe for a queen to ride alone."

King Arthur pressed the lady close and kissed her cheek.

The king and queen were a very attractive couple.

Lancelot felt her stomach muscles clenching. Her heart was a lump of clay. She felt unable to speak. She almost wanted to turn away and leave Camelot forever.

The king looked up at her. "That was a good start, protecting the queen." Then Gawaine strode up beside the king and bowed his head briefly to the queen.

"You'd better accept Lancelot before one of the lesser kings does, Arthur," he said in a loud voice. "He's a formidable fighter. He bested me in a match earlier today."

"Did he indeed?" The king smiled at Lancelot. "I hope you will join us at the fighting contest tomorrow, and we'll see how you do then. But of course you must dine with us tonight first, and my seneschal, Cai, will find you a place to stay."

Queen Guinevere touched her husband's arm.

"What about the house that Casnar left when he went back to Dyfed to take over his father's property? No one lives there now, and surely a fine warrior like this Lancelot should have a place of his own."

"A good idea." Arthur nodded. "We have a few small houses. Not all the men have them. But if you do well enough at the contest, perhaps the others won't object to your getting a house."

"Thank you, my lord," Lancelot managed to say. She remembered she should bow deeply, and inclined her head as far as she could. But Lancelot was reeling as if a great spear had hit her shield. She got down from her horse and surrendered Arrow to a stablehand because there was nothing else that she could do. She now noticed that Queen Guinevere wore a ring of twisted strands of gold. She looked away from the queen, but felt vaguely betrayed, or at least much aggrieved, though she was not sure why. She resolved never to look into the queen's beautiful blue eyes again, and certainly not to touch her.

Guinevere saw the misery in Lancelot's eyes and tried to give her a reassuring smile. But it was too late. The woman warrior averted her gaze, and Guinevere regretted withholding the truth about her identity. She went off to change her clothes.

14   A WARRIOR AMONG WARRIORS

"Come to my great hall," the king said, gesturing towards the largest building, a round stone structure. Overwhelmed at being invited by a king, Lancelot followed Arthur and Gawaine.

When she entered the stone building, she saw that warriors were standing about, chatting or lounging against the walls. Gawaine went to speak with another red-headed man.

There were hundreds of men, and the hall was far larger than Lancelot had imagined a room could be. Perhaps as many as fifty torches blazed from the walls. She felt like a wild animal that had wandered into the hall by mistake and did not know how to find its way out.

"So many warriors!" she exclaimed.

"Most are mine, but some of the lesser kings have brought their men to show their skill in tomorrow's fighting contest," Arthur said.

A gray-bearded man wearing white robes that showed the marks of time approached them.

"Here is Lord Merlin, the sage, who has advised me all my life," Arthur said, touching the old man's arm. "This is Lancelot, who wants to become one of our warriors. Gawaine says he is a fine fighter."

Merlin peered at Lancelot and nodded. "You will do great things. But still, I wish you had never come." He looked at Lancelot sorrowfully, as if he could see into her soul and discover sins that were unknown even to her. She shivered.

Arthur spoke in a mock scolding tone. "Well, Merlin. That is a poor welcome."

"Lancelot is to be pitied. And so are you, Arthur," Merlin said, with tears forming in his eyes. He then hurried off, not waiting for the meal.

Lancelot was so unnerved that she had to restrain herself from shaking. Her jaws were clenched tight and her hand gripped the hilt of her sword, but she relaxed it. How much did this Lord Merlin see?

Arthur frowned. "Let us hope that Merlin does not see that you will be wounded in battle. I can't believe that even Merlin can see the whole future. Don't let him disturb you."

The king bade her admire his great table, which had spokes like a wheel. "I have a round table to lessen the jostling for position," Arthur said proudly. "At a round table, all are equal."

Lancelot had heard of the table and was a bit disappointed to see that it was a series of trestles placed like spokes, rather than the single huge table she had imagined.

Lancelot stood quietly by a wall and watched the gathering. She noticed that many of the other warriors wore jeweled rings and gold, silver, or bronze armrings. She had never wanted jewels, but now she wondered whether she looked odd, being so plain at court. Her crimson tunic, at least, was a good quality and color.

Warriors and ladies began to seat themselves at the table, and Lancelot could see that the ladies, who were far fewer in number than the men, sat at the spokes more remote from the king, except the queen, who entered the hall and sat in a dragon-carved chair beside his.

Though the table was round, Lancelot saw that everyone watched who was close to the king. They must believe the seats near to him the best.

"Guinevere at times sits next to me rather than with the ladies. That way, I can hear everything she says," Arthur jested. "Sometimes I call the warriors here, and speak to them as if they were a council, and then of course no women are present."

After Guinevere had entered, it was difficult for Lancelot to notice anyone else. But turning her gaze from the queen, Lancelot wondered where she should sit. Of course everyone besides the king and queen sat on benches, as in any other caer.

"Come sit by me, Lancelot," said Gawaine.

Surprised, she moved to sit beside the tall warrior, who sat close to the king. Only the visiting lesser kings sat closer.

"I should warn you that some of the men play foolish pranks on those who are new to our company," Gawaine said in a low tone.

Lancelot's body went rigid. Some of those pranks might be ones that would reveal her sex. "Tell them that anyone who tries to play tricks on me will greatly regret it," she said in her harshest voice.

Gawaine nodded. "I thought as much. I'll tell them."

How fierce would she have to be — or seem to be? Lancelot wondered.

She felt that someone was observing her, and looked up to discover that it was the queen. Guinevere was wearing a blue gown that matched the blue of her eyes. Ropes of pearls were threaded through her shining black braids, and a magnificent golden torque around her neck proclaimed her high station.

. Guinevere's glance met hers, but Lancelot turned away.

Lancelot felt great embarrassment at having been so moved by a woman who had seemed to have a particular interest in her, but who was married – and married to such a great king.

The crowd at the contest field was greater than any Lancelot had ever seen. Never had she been near so many men in chain mail. Nor had she seen a contest with so many onlookers eating, drinking, cheering, and staring at the fighters. She had never had to fight in front of so many people. Nor had she seen so many horses in one place. How many of them were as fast as Arrow, or faster? She wished she had time to watch each of the horses, instead of the men who were riding them.

But her gaze was drawn to the royal stand, where the dragon banner, larger than all the other colorful pennants with various lords' insignias, floated in the air — and where the queen sat.

As Lancelot walked out on the field, the king called her over.

"Do well and I will swear you in as one of my warriors," Arthur told her. He wore a fine white tunic embroidered with golden dragons and a cloak of badger pelts, but his eyes were bright as a boy's, apparently with anticipation of the contests.

Then the king turned to speak with Merlin.

Guinevere looked at Lancelot as if she were the only warrior in the field, but Lancelot could barely meet her glance.

"All of my strength, such as it is, shall go with you, now and whenever you fight, Lancelot." Guinevere's voice was solemn. "Let me be like a rock to hold your feet, let me be a wind to speed your arm, let me be lightning to strengthen your blows to your opponents."

Lancelot was overwhelmed at these noble words, but perhaps ladies often said such things at fighting contests. The only response Lancelot could think of was "Thank you, Lady Guinevere." She vowed that even if she never again spoke alone with the queen, she would gain her admiration by fighting well.

It seemed that none of the men saw that Lancelot was a woman. True, no man in Lesser Britain had known, but she had wondered whether the great men at Camelot would be sharper-eyed. It was fortunate that she had defeated Gawaine the first time they met — everyone who met her spoke of it. But she had better keep on winning, so the men wouldn't look at her too closely.

Her muscles tensed at the sight of all those loud, sweating warriors, many of whom, unlike herself, had fought in wars. But she drew into herself and made herself calm. She had trained all her life to face such men, and much worse.

Several warriors — men named Bedwyr, Gryffyd, and Sangremore — challenged Lancelot. They all proved to be good at fighting, but she was swifter than any of them. Her spear met their shields before theirs could touch hers. Her sword cut the air before they had drawn theirs. She fought courteously, not battering them or causing any unnecessary injuries, but she defeated each in turn.

When Lancelot came up to the royal stand after her victory in the jousts, Guinevere smiled and said, "You have done well."

Lancelot replied only, "Thank you, Lady Guinevere."

"I shall be proud if you take the oath to be one of my warriors," the king said, beaming at Lancelot.

Lancelot bowed to him. "Thank you, Lord Arthur. I appreciate the honor, and I will serve you all of my life."

That evening when the warriors and the guests gathered for supper, Lancelot longed to speak with the queen, but avoided her. When Lancelot was leaving the hall, Guinevere walked over to join her. "Did you enjoy the contest, Lord Lancelot?"

Lancelot shook her head. "Not very much, Lady Guinevere. It was strange fighting with men I must live among."

"I hope you will like it here and not miss Lesser Britain." The queen's voice was friendly, but Lancelot warned herself not to make too much of that. Of course, Guinevere was gracious to everyone at court.

"I am grateful that the king will allow me to stay at Camelot, Lady Guinevere. I have pledged him my service until the skies fall and water swallows up the earth." Lancelot looked down at her boots like a shy child, and the queen nodded, giving her leave to move away.

Guinevere watched Lancelot's departing back until the warrior was gone. Lancelot's walk was just slightly different from a man's, not enough so that anyone who believed she was a man would notice.

Lancelot's cheeks did not really look like a man's cheeks, but fortunately no one else appeared to see that. No doubt it was unthinkable that a woman could defeat three of Arthur's warriors, one after another — much less that she had defeated Gawaine.

The men literally would not be able to think it, and Guinevere prayed that they never would.

That night the duty of lying with her husband seemed much more hateful to her. She could not keep herself from imagining what it might be like with Lancelot.

Guinevere was certain now, beyond any doubts that she might have entertained before, that she would never bear Arthur's child, even if Arthur decided he wanted one. She could not endure the thought of Lancelot seeing her with child and knowing that it was Arthur's. Guinevere longed for the woman warrior to love her. That must be her destiny. She could have only one love, and she knew whom she would choose. A child would drive her even farther from Lancelot than she already was.

If Lancelot never came to love Guinevere, then at least she would have someone to cherish in her heart, someone for whom she would do what little she could do to help.

Sleep eluded Lancelot as she tossed and turned on the straw-filled mattress on the bed in her new stone house, which had just one room. She was shaken at having had to fight so many men — and when there was no cause for it, too! Her muscles ached from the contests, but she was used to that.

Try as she might, she could not keep Guinevere's face out of her mind. Every word that Guinevere said, no matter how inconsequential, ran through her head again and again. She remembered the thrill of touching Guinevere's hand, and longed to touch it again. She wondered what it would be like to kiss her soft cheeks. The queen had been close enough so Lancelot could catch her scent, which was like an orchard. Not like perfume, but like fresh apples.

Lancelot tried praying to banish these thoughts, but the prayers had little effect. How could it be that she felt this way about a woman? Did pretending to be a man give her the feelings of one? Should she go off to a convent? She shuddered at the thought of being shut within walls. No, surely her skill at fighting was God-given – being a warrior was her mission.

She had never wanted to have a man's body, just to be slim enough to pass for one. Now she thought it might be a good thing indeed to be a man, for it meant that one could kiss women, and not just in a sisterly way. As a pretended man, she could not even kiss women in that manner. But even if she were a man, she could not kiss a married woman, much less one wedded to her king.

She remembered Guinevere's sobs in the forest. What might a queen have to weep about? Perhaps she had lost a family member not long ago?

Lancelot knew of course that coveting a man's wife was a sin, but was it a sin that she could confess? She had already decided that she would not tell any new priests who shrove her that she was a woman.

She went to the leading priest at Camelot, Father Donatus, who was plump and balding but looked to be no more than thirty. His voice was gentle, but Lancelot put a sort of chain mail on her soul. She confessed only to having impure thoughts, vague enough words to cover a great many sins.

At Mass, Lancelot often saw Bors, who was one of the younger sons of King Ban of Lesser Britain. Fortunately Lancelot had never met him before. She soon decided that it was not much of a risk to trust him, at least a little bit. When they were leaving the chapel after an early Mass that no one else had attended, she dared to ask him a question.

"Does the queen have some private sorrow?"

Lancelot nearly shook at asking anything about Guinevere, even of this man who looked too mild to frighten a nervous cat.

Bors's eyes widened.

"The queen is very guarded. Why do you ask?"

Lancelot thought she had to tell a little of the truth. "I saw her weeping once."

Bors shook his head. "I'm astonished by that. She never shows her feelings. The poor lady. She must have wept because she is not able to bear a child for her great husband. May the Virgin Mother have mercy on her and help her bear a child, if it be God's will."

Lancelot nodded. Of course that must be the reason for the queen's tears. And, if Guinevere flirted, perhaps it was because she sought someone to bring her a child. Well, Lancelot could not do that. The queen would have no interest in her if she knew that Lancelot was a woman.

So when the queen's gaze sought out hers, Lancelot felt herself blush and was unable to speak.

But she could not refrain from listening when Guinevere spoke at supper on some learned subject.

One evening, a short, dark-haired warrior named Lucius who often spoke in Latin said effusively, "Lord Arthur, you are another Caesar."

Arthur gave a shake of his head, but he smiled nevertheless.

Guinevere raised her eyebrows and put down her spoon. "That is a poor compliment, for the Caesars were mostly tyrants. Which Caesar did you have in mind? I hope not Tiberius or Nero?"

"Certainly not. I meant Julius Caesar or Augustus, of course," sputtered Lucius.

"What do you know of such as Tiberius? I hope you have not read my copy of Suetonius, my dear," Arthur said, but he grinned. "He details the Caesars' vices most explicitly."

"I have read all of your books, of course," Guinevere answered.

Bors wrinkled his forehead. "You, my queen, are noble enough to read such books, but it is better for most to avoid pagan books altogether, I am sure."

"But why?" Guinevere asked in the mildest of tones. "For the pagan authors condemn sinners, whereas the Christian ones often forgive them. Is it not more corrupting to learn that one can do whatever one pleases and still be forgiven?"

"In Christ, all things are possible," said Bors, bowing his head.

Lancelot had been watching the queen, but when Guinevere's gaze met hers she turned away. Guinevere was more learned than anyone but a priest. How good it would be to listen to her always, Lancelot thought, pretending to have an interest in the salmon on her plate. She dared not speak with the queen lest her voice show how she felt.

One morning as Lancelot walked to the practice field, the king approached her. Although Arthur was not going to participate in the fighting practice, he dressed simply when he watched the men in their exercises. "I've heard that you can jump from your horse to another man's, grab hold of him, and fight."

Lancelot nodded. "I can."

"Very good. You must show the others how to do that."

"Of course, my Lord Arthur, if you wish it."

They had arrived at the practice field and Lancelot swung up on her horse. Eager to work with her as always, Arrow whinnied and pawed the ground.

Peredur, a man of formal manners, was the one chosen for her to jump behind and attack, and he looked not overly pleased at playing this part. Arthur yelled with enthusiasm when Lancelot leapt from one horse to the other, then did the same again, more slowly, showing the men how she did it.

The warriors tried out this new feat, some of them falling, but many landing on the horses, albeit a little awkwardly. After all, they were well-trained in fighting on horseback. Lancelot said that many of them would soon learn well the new skill.

After the practice, Arthur talked to Lancelot about horses, telling how he had only recently been able to breed enough tall ones descended from Spanish stock so that all of his warriors had swift, excellent mounts. They walked off discussing the best way to train a horse, and how much easier it was to guide a horse since the recent arrival of Scythian stirrups.

"Let us ride together tomorrow morning," Arthur said. "There's a horse I would like you to try."

Overwhelmed with the honor, Lancelot said, "Thank you, Lord Arthur." Her heart beat fast with pride.

"You'll need more than one horse, for many horses are killed in battle," the king told her.

Lancelot's heart sank. She would buy more horses if she needed them, yet she prayed that Arrow would be safe.

The next morning, the sun shone brightly, and they went for a ride. Arthur talked about many things, but Lancelot mostly spoke of horses and other creatures.

After a time, she needed to relieve herself. She begged pardon and went off into the woods. When she returned, Arthur chuckled. "Modest, aren't you? Were you taught in a monastery?"

"No, but my teacher was a priest," Lancelot was embarrassed.

That was the best explanation she could think of for her modesty. She knew that not all men went off so far.

They arrived at a lake. The waters rippled, and a fish jumped.

"This might be the lake where I was given my sword. The waters parted just like that," the king said, putting his hand on the pommel of his sword, which was covered by a great amethyst.

"Might be the lake? Surely you would remember which one," Lancelot asked, made bold by the king's graciousness and wondering about the strange story, which was told by every bard at court. "Did an arm really appear?"

Arthur's mouth twitched.

"Perhaps the lake was enchanted for one day only. Or perhaps I was under a spell and can no longer remember exactly which lake it was. Kings must put on a show for the people, Lance."

Lancelot looked away, appearing to watch an osprey soar overhead. There undoubtedly were different rules of honesty for kings.

She ought to appreciate him. He was a great ruler. She was annoyed at herself for feeling jealous whenever she saw him touch the queen.

Gawaine was drinking with Arthur and Cai late at night in the king's chamber. One of Arthur's dogs begged to be let outside – an exceptionally well-trained dog, Gawaine thought. Arthur sent his servant to take the hound to the courtyard. Yawning, Gawaine thought that if he were married to Guinevere, he too would prefer to drink far into the night with his friends.

"That Lancelot is strangely modest," Arthur said, pouring himself more wine. "He always goes off alone to relieve himself."

Gawaine nodded. "I've noticed that, too."

"He must be a Jew," Cai said, rearranging his embroidered sleeves. Gawaine stared at him. "A Jew? Why? I've never met one, so far as I know."

"None of us have," Cai replied. "I don't believe there are any in Britain. But I think they look somewhat Roman, as Lancelot does."

Arthur shook his head. "Lancelot is a pious Christian."

"Oh, Lancelot's a convert to Christianity, of course," Cai put in, pouring wine into Gawaine's goblet and then his own.

"Converts may be more pious."

"Sometimes," Gawaine said dubiously. "But why do you think Lancelot's a Jew?"

"Jews cut off baby boys' foreskins. That's why Lancelot doesn't want to be seen." Cai smirked at his own cleverness.

Gawaine winced, and he could see that Arthur winced, too.

"That would explain the modesty."

The king spoke slowly, as if pondering the matter. "But are Jews warriors?"

"What about King David? And many other warriors of ancient days. And of course, Lancelot's just part Jewish, and part Roman and Briton." Cai admired his own fine rings, and perhaps his hands as well. "I have also heard that Jews have difficulty growing beards, and that explains why Lancelot does not grow much stubble before his next shave."

"We shouldn't press him about it," Gawaine agreed, thinking it would be strange to look different from other men.

"Perhaps I should invite some Jews to come here," Arthur mused. "I'm curious to hear about their religion. I know little about it. But no, the bishops are so irritated about pagans that I suppose they'd quibble about Jews, too."

"Christians think they are the only people who can be good," Gawaine complained. "We shouldn't tell anyone else about Lancelot."

Cai sat back smirking more than seemed appropriate for the subject, Gawaine thought. If Lancelot didn't want anyone to know he was a converted Jew, it was best never to mention it.

Despite the songs of harpers, Camelot was not a place of enchantment or of shining holiness, Lancelot discovered. The world of Camelot was the same as anywhere else.

Lancelot felt almost as uncomfortable at Camelot as she had when she had met warriors in Lesser Britain. Her nerves were tensed every moment. She could never relax. At any time, a movement of her body or a note in her voice might betray her. Even when she slept, she was on edge, easily awakened by the slightest sound. Nevertheless, she wanted to stay at Camelot, for if she were ever to do great deeds, it must be there.

Every conversation at the king's table turned to the subject of fighting. Boasts were many. If all of the warriors' stories were true, Lancelot was amazed that there were any men left to fight them in the whole of Britain.

Harpers sang of willing women, reluctant ladies, and alluring mermaids, but their most popular songs told of the clash of swords. Hunts and jousts they also praised, but the fight to the death brought the greatest acclaim. Grand it was to spear enemies, and the best death was on the battlefield.

Harpers had a good deal to answer for, Lancelot thought.

Sitting at the round table, she looked at the other warriors and wondered what they would do to her if they learned the truth. She feared that many of them – but which ones? – would be enraged that a woman had defeated them in jousts. Bors seemed unlikely to attempt to rape or kill her, but which of the others might try? They spoke of swords and horses, battles and missions for the king, sometimes jesting and sometimes disputing heatedly. Lancelot sat quietly, for she was taking in every word, and, even more, the tones and gestures, trying to determine which of the warriors might assault her and which would not.

Would a man who drank more be more dangerous? Even if he laughed when he drank? Would a man who shouted much be more dangerous than one who habitually sneered? Did pounding the table indicate a tendency to battery? Would those who were the most boastful be the angriest at being defeated by a woman? Would the better fighters or the lesser ones be most enraged? These were the questions on which she meditated.

"Cheer up, Lancelot, you look too solemn," Gawaine said, downing mead from his gold-embossed horn and putting it back on its stand.

"Listen to Gawaine. He's a famed warrior," Peredur told Lancelot.

"I know," she replied. "Even in Lesser Britain, I had heard of him."

"But do you know what he's most famous for?" Bedwyr chuckled. "Not fighting."

Lancelot looked at Gawaine inquiringly.

"The most important conquests are those of women," Gawaine said, laughing.

What did women conquer? Lancelot wondered. Then she realized he meant that he conquered them. She frowned.

"What has this Lancelot done to deserve a house of his own?" said scar-cheeked Sangremore, loudly enough for Lancelot to hear.

"I fought for the king in his war of succession, and I don't have one. I don't mind Gawaine having a house – he practically won the war for us and he's the son of King Lot of Lothian and Orkney – but who is this Lancelot to be so honored?"

"He's one of the finest fighters I've ever met, and that's enough," Gawaine replied. "I don't begrudge him anything, except the women I'm interested in, and he's made no move towards them."

Lancelot stared at her venison. She was no more at ease with the ladies than with the warriors, although her fears of them were rather different. Many ladies cast admiring glances at her, but she worried that those eyes might see through her disguise more clearly than the men's did. She was courteous but brief when she had to speak with them.

The king invited Lancelot to drink wine in his room with a few favored warriors after they had left the round table for the evening. She felt honored to be asked, but she worried about drinking too much, and took less at the great table so she would be able to sip a little afterwards without ill effects.

The king's chamber was the finest room she had ever entered. Wall hangings depicted hunts and men at battle. Arthur's bronze lamp, formed in the shape of a dragon, amazed her. His brazier made the room warmer than the rest of the caer, and the wine his body servant poured was even finer than that served at the round table. She was so awed by the setting that at first she scarcely heard what the men were saying.

Camelot was much busier than Lancelot's villa had been in Lesser Britain. She walked from room to room and building to building, looking for a quiet place, but everywhere there were loud warriors, talking, laughing, arguing, and clapping each other on the back. Servants laughed and cursed while they took the old straw off the floor, spread the new, and scrubbed the corners where warriors too drunk to get to the privy had pissed. Harpers practiced their songs for the evening meal.

The courtyards were full of wagons coming and going with ducks and geese, stones and rushes, wheat and hay. In the practice yards, warriors' swords clattered. Boys who were training to become warriors shouted as they fought with their wooden practice swords. Ironsmiths worked loudly, repairing shields and swords and making new ones. A thousand smells, from the urine in the ditches to the turnips cooking in the kitchens and the wastes from hundreds of horses, pressed in on her.

Lancelot carried the forest in her head and tried to keep out the noise and smells. Having to greet so many different people was a strain. Any one of them might discover her secret and endanger her. But she wanted to be a hero, to hear bards sing her name in praise. That would not happen if she lived her life in some remote retreat.

And if she left, she would never see that lovely face again – Guinevere's face.

Lancelot tried to find the forest at Camelot. The robin redbreast in the garden cheered her. Swallows and swifts swooped around the caer, and doves pecked at grain spilled on the cobbles.

As she passed the kitchen building, which smelled of baking bread, Cai walked out and greeted her. His smile was not unfriendly, but his mouth twisted as if he might be laughing at her. "Good day, Lancelot. You really should have a serving man as every other warrior does. It seems odd not to."

"I need no one to serve me. I can dress myself," she protested, putting out her arm as if protecting herself from a blow. She had no desire to have another pair of eyes observe her.

Undaunted, Cai continued, his voice as smooth as his handsome face, "There is a very good serving man who was blinded helping a cook when a pot of boiling water overturned. No one else wants him, but you are so kind that you might. He knows the caer well and could be a fine body servant. I am sorry to keep him in the kitchens."

Lancelot hesitated. A blind man might not be so bad. "I suppose he might look after my clothes and my chain mail. Yet I would prefer to have no servant at all."

"You can say what his duties would be," Cai assured her, patting her shoulder. "I know that you are pious and would want no lewd man around you. Catwal is good-hearted, and I assure you that even before he lost his sight, he never looked at women."

"Very well, send him to me and I shall think about it." Lancelot agreed because she could think of no good reason to refuse.

Catwal came to her small house, in which she wanted no decoration. There was only her chest of clothes, a small bed, a small table, and a stool. The serving man was not especially young, but his features were handsome.

His light brown hair was plentiful and his face was clean-shaven. "The Lord Cai said that I might work in your service, Lord Lancelot," he said in a pleasing voice.

"I want no one to dress me or wash me, but you might look after my clothes and my mail and weapons if you will," she said.

207

"Of course, and I can have the water brought for your bath and have it taken away. I can keep the fire going and keep the thatch in the roof in good repair."

She showed him her tunics, so that he might learn from the feel which was which. "Here is my best, the crimson, and this one is the green. This wine-colored one is somewhat older. And here are the ones that I use only for riding or sword practice."

Catwal learned them immediately, and seemed swift at other matters as well. He went through the things in her chest.

"It's wise of you to use extra cloths as padding in case you might be wounded," he said. He was holding the cloths that she used to flatten her breasts, and she sighed with relief.

To her surprise, she found that her supply of clean rags was soon much increased.

Catwal said, "I thought you might need small cloths to polish your chain mail and your sword when you go off from Camelot and I am not there to polish them."

She of course disposed of her own rags as usual. She usually buried them in the forest, for fear that they would be discovered if she washed them and set them out in her room to dry.

Catwal never commented on Lancelot's returning to her house during the day to use her chamber pot instead of going to the privy where the other warriors went. But she still feared that even a blind servant might observe too much about her. Could he perhaps detect her sex by her smell? Weren't blind men's other senses more acute? Even if so, there seemed to be no malice in Catwal, so she decided to trust him.

At twilight, Lancelot walked through the courtyard and passed a lady she knew was married. Before Lancelot could even incline her head, the lady smiled at her and touched her hand.

Lancelot raised her hand and made a gesture in the direction of the chapel, so it would seem that she moved only for that reason and not just to take her hand from the lady's.

"God grant you good evening, Lady Calpurnia," Lancelot said in a voice that was polite but held no warmth. "I am on my way to the chapel to pray." She had not been, but she had no objections to doing so.

"Would you like company there, Lord Lancelot?" the lady persisted, smirking.

"I want no company when I pray, my lady." Lancelot's tone was cooler. "I am sure your husband would be glad to pray with you." She bowed her head and walked off. The lady's boldness irked her. How many wives at Camelot were unchaste?

She wondered. Such incidents happened with various ladies until Lancelot made it clear that she would always be politely disinterested.

"Arthur is a great king, is he not?" Lancelot said to Bors one misty morning when they were leaving the chapel.

"Of course," Bors said in a voice only slightly less reverent than the one he used to refer to the saints. "There was a time when his wicked sister had him bewitched, but other than that he has been a good Christian ruler." He crossed himself. "He redeemed himself by renouncing her and letting the bishop proclaim that she was a witch."

"What did she do that was evil?" Lancelot asked, not eager to believe that a woman could be.

"She bewitched him, as I told you," Bors said a little irritably, as they walked on cobblestones into the mist.

Lancelot simply stared at him. She was stunned at the thought that the king would let his own sister be denounced as a witch.

Reluctance evident in his voice, Bors added, "She seduced him, you know. Only a witch would seduce her own brother."

Lancelot gasped with amazement that the king would lie with his own sister. Was her own high regard for him misplaced?

Lancelot had heard that the rule of the Irish Church drawn up by the holy Bishop Patricius said that there were no witches and excommunicated anyone who brought such a charge until he withdrew it. However, she saw that it was not a prudent subject to mention at Camelot, so she simply walked off to the stables in the swirling fog. Perhaps the fogs at Camelot were enough to make anyone believe in witches. But she was left with the feeling that king was perhaps not as noble as she had believed after all. She wondered what his sister was truly like.

15   THE COURTLY LIFE

The rushlights in the great hall blazed bright as the company dined on trout and roasted fowl. Queen Guinevere was seated next to Arthur, all too close to Lancelot. Lancelot had difficulty concentrating on her food, and almost choked on a fishbone. Embarrassed, she took the bone from her mouth.

Guinevere smiled at her. "Would you accompany me on my ride tomorrow morning, Lancelot?" she asked.

Lancelot managed to refrain from gasping. "My lady, I fear that I have so many duties . . ." she began.

"But you will be courteous and attend to me despite them," Guinevere said, before Lancelot could finish her sentence. "Thank you for being so kind."

Lancelot choked more on this unwelcome duty than she had on the fishbone. Why must the queen require her company? She could hardly ignore Guinevere if they had to ride together. Did the queen see how affected Lancelot was by her presence and mock her because of it? She was not a jewel to be hung around a lady's neck or pinned to her cloak – yet what good was a jewel, if such she might be, lying in the dust in solitary splendor?

The next morning, Lancelot walked to the stables much more reluctantly than was usual for her. The day was fair, with only a few clouds in the sky, but Lancelot did not rejoice in it.

The queen was prepared to ride. She wore the same riding breeches and simple brown overskirt that she had worn on the unlucky day when Lancelot had first seen her. Even in her plainest clothes, the queen dazzled Lancelot.

"God grant you good morning, Lady Guinevere," she said, as graciously as she could manage.

"God grant you good morning, Lancelot." The queen's voice was far merrier, and she seemed to smirk with pleasure at forcing Lancelot to ride with her.

Instead of helping Guinevere to mount her horse, Lancelot hung back. Cuall the stablemaster hurried to assist the queen.

They rode past golden fields of grain, but the queen wanted to ride in the forest. Unsmiling, Lancelot entered the great woods with her. Her heart beat fast at returning to the place where they had met. She tried to stay as far from the queen as it was possible for a guard to ride.

Her hands ached to touch Guinevere, but she must banish such thoughts. A thrush poured forth its song, but it did not distract Lancelot from the queen's overwhelming presence.

"What ails you, Lancelot? Why must you look so solemn? What heavy thoughts burden your mind?" the queen asked, holding back her horse so that she would be closer to Lancelot.

"A Christian must always worry about salvation," Lancelot said, frowning at having to speak.

The queen laughed and shook her head. "Have I asked a priest to ride with me? Come, let us give our horses a chance to gallop. That may chase such gloomy thoughts from your head."

She made her mare go faster, with a pace that soon built to a gallop, bursting ahead of Lancelot and Arrow.

"My lady, this speed is not safe in the forest!" Lancelot cried, pursuing her. How willful the queen was – and how splendid, what a fine horsewoman. But what if Guinevere's horse stumbled on the roots, and the queen fell?

Arrow sped close to the queen's horse, but Guinevere would not slow her mare's pace. Ducking branches, they flew along, and covered a considerable distance. When Guinevere finally paused to rest her horse, she was still laughing.

"You could have fallen!" Lancelot exclaimed, pulling her horse up beside the queen's.

"Nonsense. I never fall." The look in Guinevere's blue eyes seemed far merrier than it did at court.

"Anyone can die in a fall from a horse," Lancelot protested. "My father did."

The queen stopped laughing. "I am sorry, Lancelot." Her voice was softer. Lancelot looked away from Guinevere's sympathetic expression.

"I did not intend to say that, my lady."

"The words we do not mean to say may be the truest," Guinevere said, reaching out her hand. But Lancelot did not move any closer.

Drops of water began to fall on them. Lancelot looked up. She had thought only of the queen, and had not noticed that the sky had darkened. The rain poured down at an ever faster pace.

"My lady, you will get wet! We must find shelter," Lancelot said, far more distressed by rain than she ever had been before.

"I shall not rust," Guinevere observed. "Your chain mail is in greater danger than I am." She drew her cloak over her head.

"If we leave the forest by this path, we shall come to a tavern," Lancelot told her, turning her horse.

The morning had been warm, so Lancelot had not worn her cloak. The rain soaked her, and nearly blinded her as well.

The ride to the tavern seemed long, but not as lengthy as the ride back to Camelot would have been.

The thatched-roofed tavern was in good repair, but Lancelot flushed with embarrassment at taking the queen to such a place.

"I fear this is no fit place for you, my lady," she said as she helped Guinevere from her horse. "There may be drunken men."

"I see drunken men often enough at the round table," the queen said, pressing Lancelot's shoulder more closely than seemed necessary. "Are commoners so different at their drink?"

Trembling from Guinevere's touch, Lancelot opened the tavern's door. A good fire greeted them, and no drunken men were to be seen at the trestle tables.

Indeed, there appeared to be no other customers, only the bald tavern keeper and a couple of serving girls. The place smelled of mead and grilling meats, and fortunately not of anything worse.

"The queen seeks shelter from the rain," Lancelot said, in the unlikely event that the tavern keeper had not yet recognized Guinevere.

Although he was neither slim nor young, the man bowed so deeply that his head nearly touched his knees.

"It is a great honor, your highness," he said. "I fear that our food is very humble, but we have good hot mead."

"Hot mead will do very well, thank you." Guinevere glided to a bench and seated herself.

She beckoned for Lancelot to sit next to her, and of course Lancelot had to do so.

Water dripped from the queen's dark braids. Even when drenched, she was beautiful.

Men had carved their names on the old wooden table. Some of the warriors from Camelot, who would not dare to anger the king by marring his table, had put their names on this one. Some ruder words had also been carved, and Lancelot rested her arm over one so the queen would not see it.

One of the serving girls quickly brought the mead. Lancelot was so agitated that she almost spilled hers. Guinevere sipped daintily.

Another serving girl moved nervously by the fire and muttered to herself. "What ails you, my girl?" Guinevere asked her in a gentle voice. "You seem troubled."

The girl turned to them. Her long, brown hair was fine, but her face was haggard enough for a woman of fifty though she seemed to be about thirteen. There was an air of hopelessness about her.

"Now I'll have to wait longer to get hot mead for my master, and he'll be angry," she said, cringing.

"Are we drinking the mead that was heated for your master? Is he cruel?" Guinevere scrutinized her face.

The girl threw herself on her knees before the queen. "He uses me cruelly. I fear he will get me with child, and then what will become of me? Please let me work for you, highness. Please take me away from him." Guinevere put her hand on the girl's head.

"What is your name?"

"Luned, highness."

"I shall do my best for you, Luned," the queen promised.

So the queen cared about serving people. She was good as well as beautiful and learned, Lancelot thought.

A large man with a brown beard burst into the room. He was dressed in fine clothes and wore a sword at his side. "Where's my mead?" he demanded, his slurred voice showing that he had already had his share of drink. Then, seeing the girl on her knees, he cried, "Luned, what foolishness is this? Come here and serve me."

His tone was the sort used to admonish a straying dog.

The girl jumped up to get him mead.

"You had better speak more respectfully. This is the High Queen, sheltering from the rain," Lancelot warned him.

The man nearly jumped. "Pardon, highness." He bowed his head. "I am Melwas, a lord who fought for the High King in his war of succession."

Guinevere gave him the barest nod of acknowledgment. "Melwas, I like your serving girl. I want her to come to work for me, by your leave."

The anger returned to Melwas's eyes. "What have you been saying, girl? You should not dare to speak to the queen at all." He shook his finger at Luned, drunkenly. "She is my daughter, highness, a mere bastard by a serving woman, but I shall keep her in my household."

Lancelot gasped. Could it be true that the man abused his own daughter? But how could she doubt the words of a girl with such misery in her face? Lancelot felt rising nausea at the thought of such a horrible crime.

The queen's eyes narrowed. "Your daughter, indeed? Where is your mother, child?"

Melwas answered her. "She's dead, but I am willing to care for the girl."

"Now that you no longer have the woman to use, you use the daughter." Guinevere shook with rage.

"Did she tell you that? The lying little wench! What have you been saying, girl?" Glaring at the girl, he raised his hand as if to strike her.

Luned shrank into a corner.

Her fear only increased his anger. "Come with me, now!" Melwas commanded the girl.

"You're not taking her anywhere!" Lancelot leapt up from the table. She grabbed the hilt of her sword. "We're taking her to Camelot."

"Are you mad? She's my daughter, I tell you." Melwas stared at Lancelot.

"We are taking her, nevertheless, so you cannot injure her any further." Lancelot's voice shook. She wanted an excuse to strike at him.

"So the little whore can be used by all the men at Camelot?" Like many people who have had too much to drink, Melwas leaned forward as if his listeners could not hear him otherwise. "Of course she opened her legs for me. She'd open them for any-one, if I'd let her. You won't take her." Drawing his sword, Melwas lunged at Lancelot.

She pulled her sword, and returned his blow. Their swords clashed. Lancelot moved to strike at him again, but he aimed a kick at her groin. She dodged it. She could not afford to take a blow that would show that she was not a man. She kicked his sword from his hand, and Melwas fell back against a table. His head struck the bench, and he appeared dazed. Hot with fury, Lancelot menaced him with her sword.

"Stop!" Guinevere commanded. Lancelot froze.

Guinevere leapt up from the bench. "Would you slaughter him in front of his daughter? Even if he is an unnatural father, such a sight would haunt her for the rest of her days. We shall leave him and take her with us."

"Yes, Lady Guinevere." Reluctantly, Lancelot sheathed her sword.

"I'll petition the High King to give her back to me," Melwas said, clutching the table and pulling himself up.

"He'll listen to me."

"Yes, the king will decide this question," Guinevere said in a voice that was like ice. "Come, Luned."

The girl ran to her.

Her arm around the girl, Guinevere swept out of the door. Luned did not look back at Melwas.

"Do not dare to threaten us on the road," Lancelot warned him, and followed the queen. Melwas glared at her.

The rain had ceased.

"You shall ride behind Lancelot, Luned. Don't worry, you'll be safe," Guinevere told her. "Lancelot is as concerned about girls as I am."

As they rode back through the forest and the fields, Lancelot heard the girl sobbing behind her.

Melwas arrived at Camelot soon after they did.

It was not long before they all were in Arthur's private chamber, for the queen had said that was where this matter should be decided. Guinevere had changed from her damp clothes, but Lancelot had not. Luned hovered behind the queen.

Arthur looked his most magisterial. He sat in a chair that was not much less grand than the one he used in the great hall, and it had more cushions.

"What is the question here, Lady Guinevere?" he asked in a formal tone.

Before Guinevere could speak, Melwas broke in. His voice no longer showed the effects of heavy drink. "Majesty, I bring a complaint. My foolish little daughter has persuaded the queen to take her away from me. She's only a bastard by a serving woman, but I have raised her and I am willing to feed and clothe her for the rest of her life."

"My Lord Arthur, he uses her as a father should not, and he admitted as much to us, probably because he was too drunk to be careful with his words," Guinevere said in her most regal voice.

Holding herself erect, she seemed much taller than she had before. "The girl is terrified of him. She asked to serve me, and I have brought her here to do so. Melwas attacked Lancelot to prevent her from going with us."

Melwas's face reddened. "It was Lancelot who attacked me. The Lady Guinevere misunderstood me. I was angry that they tried to take my daughter away. Of course I have not lain with her. The girl tells lies about me, but I won't punish her too severely. I pity her."

Arthur frowned and twisted his ring. "Lancelot, did you hear him say that he had used his daughter?"

"I did!" Lancelot cried. "Incest is the vilest of all sins!"

Arthur flinched.

Realizing what she had said, Lancelot sucked in her breath.

Guinevere cleared her throat. "Nothing is worse than a father who misuses his daughter," she said, as if to clarify that Lancelot was not casting the king's sins up to him.

"I did not!" Melwas bellowed. Arthur turned to the girl, who seemed to be trying to hide behind the queen.

"What have you to say, Luned?" the king asked. "Is this accusation true?"

Luned nodded and covered her face with her hands.

"Ungrateful slut!" Melwas yelled at her.

"Silence!" Wrinkles stood out on Arthur's face, making him look older. His posture was much more rigid than usual. "You are guilty, Melwas. The girl will stay here. My only question is how I should punish you."

"He should be executed!" Lancelot shouted.

Melwas paled. "My Lord Arthur! I have fought for you!"

Arthur did not hesitate.

"You have fought for me, and therefore you will only have to forfeit one-third of your lands to the crown."

Melwas gasped. "My Lord Arthur! You would beggar me on the word of a serving girl, a bastard?"

"I punish you because of your own words, which the queen and Lancelot witnessed. Go, now." The king gestured for him to leave.

Guinevere put an arm around Luned.

Melwas tensed for a moment, as if for a fight, then stalked off. He did not look at his daughter. At the doorway, he growled, "One day, someone will pay for what has been done to me."

Lancelot could almost feel his sword cut into her flesh.

She stared after Melwas with disgust. She thought the punishment too light, but she knew it was more severe than many another king would have given.

Lancelot went off thinking that she served a king with a better sense of justice than most. And a queen with a kind heart.

Lancelot did not want to admire Guinevere too much, but she did. It was easier to think of Guinevere's noble heart than to ponder how terrible Lancelot's own life could have been if her father had been a different sort of man. The thought came unbidden, and she dismissed it with a shudder.

When she was going to supper in the great hall, Lancelot saw Guinevere in the courtyard and bowed to her. "God grant you good evening, Lady Guinevere," she said more heartily than usual. "I am proud to serve you, and King Arthur, of course. What other king would care so much about a poor serving girl?"

Guinevere had smiled when she saw Lancelot, but the smile disappeared. "That is true," she said. "How nice that you like us both so well." The queen's voice was less warm than it had been earlier in the day.

Lancelot bowed and commended herself for refraining from saying that the queen was the most wonderful woman in the world. Lancelot almost envied Luned because the girl would now be able to spend a good part of every day in the queen's presence, and perhaps even help dress her. Lancelot must not think of that, she chided herself. She should do penance for even having such a thought. She must learn to rein in her heart.

Arthur entered Guinevere's room and smiled at her. Shafts of moonlight streamed through the bars on her window.

"I have not had the evil dream for months, my dear," he said. "Perhaps we should try again to have a child. It is important for me to have an heir, and I am sure you would delight in having a child of your own."

Guinevere managed a smile. "Whatever you wish," she said, bowing her head. Never, never would she stop taking the potion.

Lying under her husband, Guinevere tried to think about her childhood, racing with Gwynhwyfach, learning to ride a horse, learning to read. She should be grateful to Arthur because her father had hired the tutor for his sake. She tried to imagine that she was a tree. Although she believed Arthur was trying to be gentle, she felt as if someone was hammering nails into her. She tried to think of anything but Lancelot.

Lancelot dragged her feet on the way to the practice field, for there was to be a public execution of thieves and murderers. She had never attended an execution in Lesser Britain, and she did not want to see one now. But how could she avoid it? She feared acting in any way that would make her look different from the other warriors. She might as well attend this execution, because there would be many others she could not avoid.

The sun was hot and flies buzzed around her head. She thought of what the flies might visit later, and her stomach heaved.

Lancelot did not even notice that the queen had approached her until Guinevere was close.

But Lancelot was too distracted to feel her usual distress at seeing the queen.

Guinevere was more plainly dressed than on most days and wore no jewels. "I have little liking for executions," she said.

"Nor have I, Lady Guinevere." Lancelot sighed. "I know it is just to execute murderers, but I do not see why everyone must watch. Why must the poor wretches pass their last moments on earth before a jeering mob?"

A scaffold with a noose hanging from it stood on the playing field. Surrounding the instrument of death was a crowd, eating meat pies and drinking from flasks.

Lancelot winced. "It is true that I have killed several men, but only because they were attacking the helpless. I have no taste for butchery."

The queen nodded. "I appear only for a moment before the hanging. I bow my head to the public, then leave," Guinevere said. "I have told Arthur that it would not be fitting for the people to see the queen get sick. Will you escort me back to my rooms?"

"Willingly, my lady!" Lancelot sighed, this time with relief. She now felt no reluctance to be in the queen's company.

"You may escort me away in like manner whenever there is an execution. No one will think anything of it," Guinevere told her. There was no flirtation in the queen's voice or her face.

"Many thanks, my lady!" Lancelot smiled at her more gladly than she had in many a day. How good it was to be able to admit that she disliked executions and to have an excuse to avoid them.

But she was pleased that the queen said little when Lancelot led her back to her rooms. "You have my leave to speak or not to speak," Guinevere said. Lancelot chose the latter.

The king began sending Lancelot, like other warriors who were particularly good fighters, on missions to examine the defenses of the subject kings, try to estimate their loyalty to him, and, if they seemed loyal, to assist in training their men for war in case of a Saxon attack.

Arthur told Lancelot, "It is important to make the king's presence felt throughout the land. That is why my warriors cannot just stay and train at Camelot. You must travel, enforce my peace, and show what great fighters my men are. That is how I show how much I care about my people, and remind the subject kings that they have no chance of overthrowing me."

Guinevere, who was standing beside her husband, said, "And you can learn whether the people are hungry or treated badly by their lords, and report it to the king."

"Of course, my dear," Arthur said, smiling at Guinevere. "The queen always tells my emissaries that. Very thoughtful."

How much in accord the king and queen were, Lancelot thought with a pang.

They must be happy together, even if the queen was a little overly friendly to Lancelot.

Lancelot was glad when the king sent her to distant places or let her ride in the forest if she had no other duties. Truth to tell, she liked the journeys to and fro better than the destinations. In the forest, she was just another creature, being itself, like a badger or a marten. Having no desire to return to Lesser Britain, Lancelot felt that she had no home, other than Camelot or the wilds. She was learning many new kinds of terrain.

In some places, each tree was a forest, its every branch covered with mosses, like the beards of a thousand fairies. Here green ruled, allowing few other colors to share its realm.

She was learning to appreciate the frequent rain because it had wrought this lush world. She found bogs where she had to guide her horse carefully to prevent sinking, although startling orchids drew her to take her chances on foot. At times she was covered with peat when she sank while seeking out a tempting flower. If anyone had seen her then, wearing the bog, they might have thought her some weird creature haunting it. And during the season that the bog was most appealing, with many small flowers blooming, it appealed to many insects as well.

Just as alluring were sharp-cragged hills further north, with eagles flying near their summits, and snow on the higher reaches. Mountains with snow were far more magical than mountains that were bare. She felt they lured the traveler to climb, then struck with sudden storms those who dared. Encountering such a storm could be more difficult than fighting the fiercest warrior, she discovered. When Lancelot had the time, she climbed mountains, longing for the summit as if it were a lover, trying to know each stone of the mountain, each cliff, for she believed that there would be no other love for her. But no matter how far she climbed, she still thought of Guinevere.

Not seldom she came across old stones in strange formations. Were standing stones giants who had frozen, and had flat stones once been altars for terrible sacrifices? She wondered. Had the divine hand shaped them thus to indicate a proper place for worship? Was any church truly as sacred? She mused and questioned, though she knew she was flirting with heresy.

She felt ill at ease when she rode past farmland, because the fields provided no cover, unless you were a hedgehog who could dive into bushes or a fox who could disappear in a hole. She liked better the wildness of the moors, but feared their openness as well, if there were no trees to hide her.

Lancelot was not so fond of traveling to cities. She found the Roman ruins of Londinium dreary, but liked its bustling markets a little better. She managed to avoid being sent to Aquae Sulis, because it would seem too strange to avoid the old public baths there. The hypocausts that heated them now often broke down, but the other warriors praised the pleasures of bathing.

Arthur came to Guinevere's chamber. She cast down her eyes. "My lord, it is my time of the month," she told him.

He sighed. "Perhaps next month. Or perhaps it is not meant to be." He departed, and she resumed reading about Antigone.

Lancelot struck at Gawaine, but his sword blocked hers as usual. "Must you wear that grim look, Lancelot?" he teased, pulling back and attacking with his wooden practice sword. "Is my face so ugly that you can't bear to see it?"

She spun away from him and attacked his left. It was impossible to get into a fighting trance when she fought with Gawaine because he always jested while he practiced. Her sword grazed his arm, but she had meant to get in a better hit than that.

"Ah, if I were a real opponent that would only anger me," Gawaine chided. "Come on, I long for you to defeat me." He moved forward.

Lancelot stepped backward, then lunged at his left again, which he wouldn't expect because she had just done it.

Laughing, he strove for balance.

At the end of the warriors' practice session, Lancelot gladly put down her wooden sword. She mopped the sweat from her brow.

She was not the only warrior who was sweating. Despite an open window, the room was pungent from the men's exertions.

"You weren't quite up to form today, Gryffyd," Gawaine said, turning it into a jest by poking that comely warrior in the ribs.

"If you keep eating so much, you won't be in form either," Gryffyd replied with a responding poke.

"Gawaine is light on his feet for such a big man," Peredur said. "Not to mention the force in his blows. If he was as swift as Lancelot, he'd always best every one of us."

"But he isn't," Bors observed, flourishing his wooden practice sword. "No one moves a sword as fast as Lancelot. He'll win all the prizes again next Pentecost."

"Not so! Gawaine will win, I'm sure of it," Bedwyr countered, wiping his face with a towel. "All he has to do is weaken Lancelot in the jousting. Then Lance won't be as swift in his swordplay."

"No doubt that would be the way to defeat me," Lancelot agreed, for she was becoming used to the endless discussions about who was better than whom and who would win at the next fighting contest.

"Lance's moves are so unexpected," Gawaine said, either in complaint or praise. "I never know what he's going to do next. That's even more important than his speed."

He reached for an earthenware jar of water and poured some into a cup.

"You're better at unhorsing other men with the spear, though, even if you aren't quite as good at footwork," Bedwyr said. "I'm betting on you, Gawaine."

"You should not place wagers on us," Lancelot chided. "Gawaine's moves are sometimes surprising, too," she added.

"Indeed," Gawaine said, splashing some water from the jar on Lancelot, and everyone laughed, Lancelot loudest.

"Would you show me how you knocked my sword out of my hand today, Lance?" Gryffyd asked.

"Of course," she replied, toweling her face.

226

"For after all, we'll all be on the same side when we fight against the Saxons. That is more important than contests among ourselves."

She had shown them feints that were new to them, and they had shown her some that were new to her.

Bedwyr, who had also been splashed by the water that had showered Lancelot, grabbed one of Gawaine's arms and began to wrestle. Lancelot stood apart. One of her many eccentricities was that she refused to wrestle and said that it was undignified, Saxonish, and unworthy of the High King's warriors. The others laughed at that. Lancelot knew they believed that she was too accustomed to winning and didn't want to play at wrestling because a slim build made winning unlikely.

Gawaine's brother Agravaine, who was about the same size and looked rather like him but with a less pleasant expression, grumbled, "What's the matter, Lancelot, are you too good to wrestle? Or not good enough? You've bested me with your fancy footwork too often. You can't always avoid wrestling." He lunged at Lancelot and grabbed her.

Lancelot kicked him as hard as she could in the groin and broke away from him when he doubled over.

"You filthy cur!" Agravaine moaned.

Some other warriors laughed, but most retreated into silence.

Gawaine put an arm around his brother. "You're the most courteous warrior in the world with weapons, Lance, but you fight like a tavern brawler without them. What a temper you have! It would be wise to avoid angering you."

Lancelot just stalked away without saying anything. She had been coolly deliberate, not angry. She knew it was necessary to keep any others from trying to force her to wrestle.

Not for the first time, she wondered why men must live by fighting and whether it was worth it to keep proving herself again and again. What did these men have in life but their swords, their spears, and their horses? Though most of them had caers or villas at home, they stayed with Arthur because they feared the country would be weaker if they did not. And they clearly enjoyed each other's company. Or did they just love to fight, more than she did?

After that day, none of the other warriors tried to force her to wrestle. Although Lancelot thought the men discussed fighting too much, she preferred such talk to some of their other conversations, which touched on women.

"So how many women have you had, Gawaine?" a new warrior asked one day as they drank barley beer after sword practice.

"How many trees are there in the forest?" Gawaine replied, shaking his head and rolling his eyes. "How can I possibly know?"

"Hundreds, no doubt," Bedwyr said, in a voice that indicated that there might indeed be room for doubt.

"You insult me," Gawaine reproached him and pretended to reach for his sword to fight over the supposed insult. "Thousands, of course."

"As for me, I like women with large breasts," Bedwyr said, leering.

"Women with big tits are the best lays," Lucius said, downing some beer.

"I have bedded some fine women with small tits," Gawaine objected, pouring himself more beer.

Lancelot wandered off. It was times like these that she felt least like a man and that she least wanted to be seen as one. And she was grateful beyond words that she had not been married to a man. Surely women would not love them if men spoke this way in front of them. She thought her father had been different, and Bors was much like her father.

How men could bear to talk about women in that manner, she wondered. She was sure that she could never discuss Guinevere so. True, they did not speak of their wives' bodies, but if they saw other women that way, they must see their wives through similar eyes. She felt relieved that her breasts were bound and hidden, though the passing years did not make the binding any more comfortable. The men's talk made her want to curl up like a hedgehog, sheltering her tender parts.

She walked to the walled garden near the chapel for a moment. Although its few trees were denuded of leaves until spring and its rosebushes were bare, the garden was the closest she could come to the forest without riding off.

But solitude was not so easy to find. A pretty young lady followed Lancelot into the garden and gazed at her wistfully.

Lancelot bowed to her and hurried off to the stables. It was too often that the unmarried girls pursued her, and the married ones, not seldom, did as well. She wished she could feel as little passion for the queen as she did for the other ladies.

Lancelot also wished that she could speak with them without giving them the idea that she was courting them. It might be good to learn what girls thought when they spoke with other girls, or women when they spoke with other women. Was all of their talk about men? But she could never learn what they were like. That saddened her. She could not know women without living lives like theirs, and that she refused to do.

The rain drizzled on Camelot, bringing with it the scent of early spring. Guinevere peered out of her window and drew a deep breath. She spied Lancelot heading to the stables. Pausing only to grab a shawl, Guinevere walked through her door and descended the staircase. She moved quickly, but still had to preserve her dignity. She nodded to the guards and covered her hair with a shawl. Once in the courtyard, she accelerated her pace, but could not run. A few of Arthur's dogs bounded past her and she did not stop to pat them.

Guinevere avoided the puddles between the cobblestones. She headed to the stables, only to see Lancelot leading her warhorse out, already saddled.

Guinevere looked at Lancelot but did not hail her.

Lancelot did not acknowledge seeing her, but Guinevere was sure that the warrior was aware of her presence. Lancelot was far enough away to escape outright rudeness. She swung onto her horse and urged it out of the stable yard.

Guinevere raised her hand in greeting. Lancelot nodded to her, but rode away.

Guinevere sucked in her breath. She watched Lancelot's horse race down the hill, towards the forest.

Guinevere bit her lip. She had endured such slights many times. Why must she torture herself? Lancelot would never reciprocate her love.

Guinevere proceeded to the stable, where she told the stablehands that she just wanted to visit her horse. She agreed with their assessment that it was too rainy for the queen to ride.

She pressed her cheek to her mare's face and drank in the horsey smell.

Silently, she composed verses about longing, odes that no one would ever sing. She spun words describing Lancelot's hair, her eyes, her stance, her powerful grace. And her matchless courage.

Guinevere was wakeful in the night. She wished she could rise and read, but she could not while Arthur slept beside her.

He began to moan in his sleep.

After a time, she touched his arm to wake him.

He woke groaning.

"The dream again. The cursed dream again. The bloody boy. It is as well that you have not conceived. I am cursed with this dream."

"I am so sorry." Guinevere put her hand on his arm. Perhaps he was cursed, she thought, but whether he was or not, she was resolved not to bear him a child.

"We must stop trying to have a child," he said, taking her hand in his. "I regret denying you one."

"I am reconciled to that," she told him.

Lancelot rode through the woods not many miles from Camelot. It was midday, so there was but little birdsong. The day was so warm that she had not worn her chain mail. She thought it was foolish to wear armor when she rarely encountered danger.

But she heard a woman's voice. "No! Let me go!"

Lancelot turned a bend in the road and saw a man of some thirty years holding the reins of a horse carrying a girl of about fourteen or fifteen, who was thin as a beggar but dressed like a lady. "Let go my reins! Father, make him stop." The girl's voice was not strong, but her meaning was unmistakable. Her eyes were fixed on an older man who was turning his horse away from them.

"What's happening here?" Lancelot exclaimed.

"No business of yours." The man holding the reins, who wore a gold chain around his neck, moved away from Lancelot, thus forcing the girl's horse to move also.

"I am Lancelot of the Lake, a warrior of King Arthur's, so any acts against his law are my business. What are you doing with this young lady?"

"Help me, Lord Lancelot!" the girl cried.

The girl's father inclined his head to Lancelot. "There is nothing amiss, my lord. I am Cornelius, and I own this land. Myfanwy, my daughter, is foolish and willful. This is our neighbor, the noble

Flavius. Her mother and I have arranged for her to marry him. He is most prosperous, the finest husband possible. But Myfanwy has been stubborn. We locked her up in her room and allowed her no food, but still she refused to give her consent. We feared that she would starve from stubbornness, which would profit no one, so I told her I would take her out riding. I arranged for Flavius to meet us and take her away. Once she has gone off with him, no one else will wed her, and she will have to marry him. It's all for her own good."

"You mean you would let him rape her." Lancelot was enraged.

"If that is necessary. But he will marry her, as I said. All will be well. Please let us be." Cornelius nodded to Lancelot, as if in dismissal. Disgusted with him, Lancelot turned to Flavius.

"The lady does not want to go with you. Let her go!" Her voice and her face showed that her command was also a threat.

"Her family has consented. This matter has nothing to do with you." Flavius started to ride away, forcing Myfanwy's horse to go along.

The girl moaned, as if she had lost hope.

"Halt!" Drawing her sword, Lancelot rode after him. "Stop in the name of the king."

"Why, the king has no laws saying parents cannot arrange good marriages for their daughters," Cornelius argued. "She'll consent soon enough now." He put his hand on his purse, as if suggesting that he would bribe Lancelot to leave.

"I won't marry Flavius! Everyone knows that his first wife died from his beatings!" Myfanwy cried.

"Silence!" Flavius yelled at her. He reached for his sword.

"Let her be, or you must fight me." Lancelot's voice was like the steel of her sword.

"Come at me, then." Flavius drew his weapon.

Lancelot attacked.

As she rode at him, she remembered she was not wearing chain mail, and swerved so his sword cut only the cloth at her shoulder.

Before Flavius had again raised his sword arm, Lancelot had cut through it, not severing it but wounding him sorely. His sword clattered to the ground and he dropped the reins of Myfanwy's horse. Flavius stared unbelieving at his bleeding arm. "You're a madman," he cried to Lancelot.

"Come with me," Lancelot told Myfanwy. "I'll take you to Camelot, where you'll be safe."

"Don't listen to him!" Flavius clutched his arm. "He just wants you for himself, to abuse and abandon. I'll marry you."

Myfanwy rode to Lancelot's side. "I'll go with you," the girl said, her eyes wide with fright as if she were unsure it was wise to follow Lancelot.

Apparently not daring to get too close to Lancelot, Cornelius chided his daughter. "Foolish girl, this will profit you nothing. Going with this man will destroy your reputation just as surely as going off with Flavius, and you'll have to marry Flavius anyway, because he's the only one who will have you after that. But your marriage will be far less pleasant than it would have been."

Myfanwy shuddered.

"Don't listen to your father," Lancelot exclaimed. "I won't hurt you, and you won't be forced to marry anyone."

"Go with him then, you little fool," her father said, starting to help Flavius bind his wound. "But you can't take the horse. The horse is mine and isn't disobedient like you."

"You can ride with me," Lancelot told Myfanwy, dismounting to help her get down from her horse and ride behind on Arrow.

"The king won't let you stop a man from marrying off his daughter," Cornelius called after them.

"But the queen will," Lancelot murmured to the girl.

"Thank you." Myfanwy's voice trembled, and her body shook for the entire ride back to Camelot.

When they rode through the gates, they encountered Bedwyr, who called out, "Lancelot, I see you've finally gotten a girl for yourself."

Ignoring him, Lancelot took Myfanwy as quickly as possible to Cai's office, where Guinevere was likely to be working on tax records.

Both were poring over piles of vellum.

Cai raised his eyebrows. The queen hastened to the side of the girl, who looked as if she had been brought back from the dead.

Myfanwy tried to curtsy, but she shook so that she almost fell. Guinevere put an arm around her.

Lancelot told how Myfanwy came to be there.

"Her own father would have let that man rape her, then would have forced her to marry him." Lancelot spat out the words.

"Monstrous." Guinevere held Myfanwy. "You were very brave to go off with Lancelot. I promise you, you won't have to go back. You might lose your inheritance . . ."

"I don't care," Myfanwy gasped.

"I shall provide for you, never fear." Guinevere's voice was kind but resolute, and Lancelot had never admired her more. Her heart filled with pride that she served such a good queen.

"It seems that you need provisions as soon as possible," Cai said to Myfanwy. "I'll have some food sent to you. Not too much at first, though, or it could sicken you." He hurried off on that errand.

"Are you strong enough to go to the king now?" Guinevere asked. "It is better that we make your case before your father makes his." Myfanwy nodded.

"And you must come with us, Lancelot."

"Of course."

When they came before the king, Guinevere stood majestic and let Lancelot tell the tale, and Myfanwy confirmed it.

Then Guinevere spoke. "I ask an unusual boon, my lord, perhaps the most important I have ever asked you. I ask you not to send this girl back to her family. I know it is legal for them to try to starve her to press her to marry. But my heart goes out to her. Have mercy on her, and let her stay as one of my ladies. I shall provide a dowry and find a better husband for her in time, after she has recovered her strength. It will grieve me greatly if you do not grant this." She looked him in the eye.

Arthur frowned. "The last time you asked such a boon, the girl was a servant. But taking a lord's legitimate daughter – an heiress – away from his control is a different matter. The king cannot be involved in deciding every marriage."

"But, Lord Arthur, Flavius killed his first wife!" Lancelot exclaimed.

Arthur twisted his ring. "That would make this a question of the girl's safety, not merely her wishes. But we have only her word that Flavius injured his wife."

"Great king!" Myfanwy begged. "Please inquire in our village. The people will tell you the same."

Arthur addressed Myfanwy. "I shall make inquiries. You realize that if you continue to defy your family's will, you will lose your inheritance thereby, and the man you may marry may be much less prosperous than Flavius."

"Yes, your majesty. I understand fully." Myfanwy's voice was firm, but she went down on her knees before him.

"Very well. At the queen's request, I grant this boon. We will find you a suitable husband."

"A husband she wants," the queen said.

"A marriage you will consent to," the king said.

"Her father will claim that she was dishonored by riding off with Lancelot," Guinevere reminded him.

"Nonsense. That charge will bear no weight with me. Lancelot wouldn't take advantage of a whore, much less an innocent girl." Arthur smiled at Lancelot. "Her father won't change my mind. It is decided."

"Thank you, my lord." Guinevere inclined her head to him, Lancelot bowed deeply, and Myfanwy almost prostrated herself on the floor.

Lancelot's heart nearly burst with love for the queen. Nevertheless, Lancelot strove to keep from showing her feelings. She merely bowed and said, "Thank you, my Lord Arthur. Thank you, Lady Guinevere."

"I am glad you have so much concern for women, Lancelot," the queen said, smiling at her. "We share that concern. Myfanwy deserves to make her own choices. I do so admire brave women."

Lancelot bowed again. "I must go and tell the men not to be overly friendly to Cornelius." She turned and departed.

She wondered whether an open love could possibly hurt as much a covert one. Every moment that she was near Guinevere, Lancelot feared that the queen would catch her off guard and she would reveal the love that must be hidden.

Later that day, Guinevere stopped her walk across the courtyard to speak with Lionors, who had a child in tow as usual.

Lancelot passed them, and Guinevere smiled warmly.

"Good afternoon, Lady Guinevere, Lady Lionors." Lancelot bowed her head.

"Lancelot rescued a girl just this morning," Guinevere said, trying to keep her voice as warm as the occasion required but no warmer. She wanted to kiss Lancelot's cheek.

How splendid!" Lionors exclaimed.

"It was merely what needed to be done, my ladies. I must go to fighting practice now." Lancelot bowed her head once more.

Guinevere watched her walk away.

"Don't put that in your mouth, dear," Lionors said, taking a fruit that someone must have dropped on the cobbles from the small girl whose hand she held. "How handsome Lancelot is." She inclined her head in the direction the warrior had just gone. "And such a good man. Which of the girls do you think would make a good wife for him?"

Guinevere sucked in her breath. "I cannot think of any. I'm sure he can find a wife for himself, if he wants one."

"Not inclined to be a matchmaker, are you?" Lionors wiped her daughter's face, which needed it. "I've almost given up trying to find a wife who would suit Gawaine, but I thought Lancelot might be easier to please."

"I doubt it." Guinevere shook her head. "How are you, little one?" she asked Lionors's child. It was certain that Lionors would gladly turn the conversation to children.

The child pulled a fistful of crushed flowers from her apron and handed them to Guinevere. Guinevere smiled at her and banished the thought of Lancelot loving anyone other than herself.

As he crossed the courtyard, Gawaine laughed at the sight of a couple of serving boys fighting each other with broomsticks.

"Reminds you of your childhood, doesn't it?" he said to Lancelot, who walked beside him. Lancelot walked a bit stiffly, as usual.

There was no glimmer in Lancelot's eyes. "I never played with boys."

Gawaine felt a surge of pity and averted his face so his feelings wouldn't show. He remembered many games with his brothers on the shores of Orkney and in the hills of Lothian. No wonder Lancelot was so solemn.

A good man, but not very lively, almost more like an old man than a young one.

He grabbed Lancelot by the shoulder. "Let's challenge each other, always at unexpected moments. It will be good practice for hidden dangers."

Lancelot nodded, though his face still showed little expression. "Very well, if it's good practice."

The boys saw Cai approaching them, dropped the broomsticks so he wouldn't scold them for denuding the brooms, and scampered off around a corner.

"Just don't interrupt me when I'm with a woman," Gawaine added, though he was sure Lancelot would never do such a thing.

"But Gawaine, that's nearly all the time," Lancelot said, with a faint trace of a smile.

"How true." Gawaine fingered his beard and sighed as if being with women was a great burden that he shouldered reluctantly.

"You should spend a little more time with them yourself. Many of them steal glances at you."

Paling, Lancelot shook his head.

Poor Lancelot probably was shy with women because he feared to show he was circumcised, Gawaine thought. True, not every woman would be understanding.

That night when Lancelot was descending the stairs from the king's room, Gawaine stepped out of the shadows to issue a challenge. Lancelot leapt into a fighting stance, and they fought up and down the stairs. Other warriors wanting to use the stairs stood grumbling at the top and the bottom, but Gawaine laughed at them.

The next night, Gawaine had drunk enough mead to make his step a little less steady than usual – which was a great deal of mead. Lancelot challenged him as he left the great hall.

"So you would be proud to defeat a drunken sot," Gawaine jested, drawing his sword. The game had necessitated wearing a sword at times when he normally would not.

Lancelot smiled and appeared to be on the brink of laughter.

Gawaine staggered, pretending to be more affected by the mead than he actually was, and fought in that manner.

The serving people carrying trenchers out of the great hall ducked around them, but some stopped and cheered.

His brother Agravaine complained to him that such play-fighting was undignified for one of the king's warriors, but Gawaine merely laughed. He knew he had proved himself too often to have to worry about dignity, which was a concern only for mediocre warriors like Agravaine.

On another day, Gawaine had gone to get a little pie before supper, only to find that Lancelot had followed him. As they leapt around the kitchen, the serving people stopped their work and called out, "Get him, Lancelot!" "Pummel him, Gawaine!" Even the young man turning a haunch of mutton on a spit stopped turning, letting it burn on one side. A burned smell mingled with the scents of baking honey cake, roasts, and stews. Lancelot backed Gawaine into an open sack of flour, and a white cloud of the stuff flew up, covering him.

Cai burst in and shouted, "Are you warriors or fools? Take your games out of the kitchen!"

They stopped their fight, but Lancelot was laughing so hard that tears dripped down his face.

Gawaine was pleased that he had achieved his purpose. He wiped flour off his sleeves.

Finishing her mutton flavored with mint, Lancelot listened to the conversation at the table. The night was bitter, so she was glad to be indoors near the great fire in the hall. Mulled wine warmed her. She had to take care not to imbibe too much of the hot, spiced drink.

"Let's play gwyddbwyll," Gawaine said, turning to Lancelot.

"Very well," she agreed. Her plate was now as empty as his, though his had been piled much higher.

Everyone had plenty of food at Camelot, Lancelot thought with satisfaction. Even many of the serving people were plumper than those she had seen elsewhere.

In the evenings and on the worst days of winter, the warriors sometimes played at board games. Lancelot was not good at them, because she tended to see each piece taken as a man who was killed or wounded in battle, and she became too upset.

Gawaine saw the pieces in a different way. As he played, he devised ribald jests to go with each move. His tales started by saying, "This warrior had a beautiful daughter. . ." or wife, or mistress. He made the stories a little tamer when he played with Lancelot or Bors.

"Don't be disturbed when you see the warriors taken," Gawaine told Lancelot while he made his first move. "They aren't real men."

"Of course not, but I think of how many die in battle," Lancelot sighed." Though if we keep the commandments, we may hope for a better world to come."

To her surprise, Gawaine laughed at that. "I doubt that your Christian heaven would want me, so I must hope that I shall be reborn. I got baptized for Arthur, because the bishops pressed him to have all of his men become Christian, but I care nothing about it. My brothers did the same. Not everyone who converts wants to do so." He looked at Lancelot as if he were asking a question.

Lancelot gasped at the thought that anyone could treat baptism so casually.

"Surely religion should not be a mere matter of pleasing the king, or any man."

Gawaine shrugged. "I know you care about it. If I cared about any, it would be the one my mother taught me. I go to the Masses at times, but I would never tell my so-called sins to a priest. And I have never taken the bread because I would not profane what is holy to others. But I suspect that the gods just laugh at the forms we use to address them. Let us hope they see us as more than these game pieces."

A harper began to sing, and the warriors paused to listen. The songs now told of Lancelot the Swift or Lancelot of the Lightning Arm, as well as Gawaine the Strong. She felt the blood rush to her cheeks when the harpers praised her, but the words filled her with pride.

A bard told the tale of a king who had fooled a giant and stolen the giant's treasure. The men at the table roared their approval. "Some of us can tell tales as well as a bard, or better," Bedwyr cried in a drunken boast. "Gawaine can. Show him, Gawaine."

Flushed with pleasure as well as mead, Gawaine put down his drinking horn. "But I cannot sing; I can only speak."

"Go on, cousin," Arthur said, settling back in his chair. "Show what you can do. Tell that new tale about Lancelot."

Lancelot stiffened. What sort of tale could Gawaine have devised about her? Too many of his stories ended with the man – frequently Gawaine himself – bedding a woman.

Gawaine touched his beard, which was shining red in the glow from the many rushlights. "I shall do the best I can with my poor tale. Lancelot is such a handsome man that no one will be surprised to hear that he was a handsome infant – so handsome, indeed, that all the women wished that he was their son.

"One day his family was traveling near a lake – a large lake, shimmering in the sun. Lancelot's nurse put him down for just a moment because she had to go behind some bushes.

"Then out of the lake came an enchantress, beautiful but ageless. She appeared to be young, but in fact she was several hundred years old.

"She saw the handsome baby and knew that she must have him to raise as her own. She snatched him and carried him down beneath the lake's waters, to a magical land that she ruled. Of course she put a spell on him so that he could live beneath the lake. There he grew, far from the world, in an enchanted realm. But when he was a man, he learned that there was another, larger world, above the surface of the lake, so he left the grieving enchantress and came to live in the world of men. And that is why Lancelot is a little different from the rest of us."

"A fine tale, better than the bard's!" Arthur exclaimed, thumping Gawaine on the back. The warriors cheered.

Lancelot's face was so hot that she thought it would scorch any who came near her.

She longed to challenge Gawaine to a fight, but knew that she could not. When they left the table, she accosted him in the courtyard. The moon was bright enough to illuminate his face.

She grabbed his arm. "How dare you make up such a tale about me!"

Gawaine stared at her. "What ails you? It's a good tale. It flatters you, and there's nothing coarse about it."

"It makes me seem not human!" Lancelot's voice was low, but it showed her displeasure.

"Not human?" Gawaine shook his head. "Don't be foolish. No one could ever think such a thing. Why, I've told tales saying that I have been a selkie, changing to a seal and living in the sea off Orkney."

"Tell such tales about yourself, if you like, but not about me," Lancelot demanded, not calmed.

He shrugged. "If it matters so much to you, I'll cease telling the story about you."

"Pray do so," she said, and stalked away, furious that he had suggested she was different from the others, though he little knew how dangerous that could be for her.

Merlin paid little attention to Lancelot, or to anyone. He seemed to be communing with himself and whatever spirits spoke to him. He never looked at her when she sat at the table. Indeed, when he sat there, he generally stared into space. He ate little.

Was he just a seer of visions, who existed in some nether world, with no fleshy substance to him? Lancelot wondered.

Once Merlin encountered her walking about alone on the ramparts. Staring at her, he muttered, "Truly, no man is as brave as you are."

He shook his head as if he were in the presence of a mystery that was beyond his power of understanding.

She shuddered.

But to her relief, he did nothing worse. It might be that he saw that she was a woman, but if so, he apparently did not tell anyone.

Even though Lancelot did not speak much with her, Guinevere still rejoiced at the sight of the long, handsome face framed with black hair and the deep brown eyes that refused to meet her gaze. The sound of Lancelot's voice was much sweeter than anyone else's, even when the warrior said only "God grant you good day, Lady Guinevere."

When she said "good day" in return, Lancelot often blushed. And often at the round table – and even at Mass – Guinevere would look up and see that Lancelot was gazing at her. Whether Guinevere pored over the tax records or did a little sewing with the ladies, she thought about how she could woo Lancelot. She would have tried charms or spells if she thought they could win Lancelot's love, but she doubted that they were any more effective than prayers. And surely she could not pray for success in adultery.

How could anyone possibly be as good as Lancelot? Guinevere wondered. So kind, so handsome. Many of the women and girls stared at Lancelot, but only Guinevere knew something of who Lancelot truly was. Therefore, Guinevere was not jealous of the others. Lancelot blushed only when Guinevere spoke, not when other women did. And when Guinevere tried to touch her, Lancelot almost jumped. The years did not change that reaction.

Sometimes Guinevere wished that Lancelot wore the clothes of a woman, for it would be easier to ask a lady of the court to share her room and then embrace her. But how could a lady refuse marriage? Guinevere could not imagine Lancelot married to a man, and certainly did not want to picture that.

16 A Most Courteous Warrior

Guinevere visited the stable ten times a day because her mare, Shining Star, was about to foal. The mare moved about restlessly, getting up and lying down, rolling, and then getting up and lying down again. On the night when the birth was expected, Guinevere left the great hall as soon as possible after supper and hurried to the stable.

Births frightened her. She always said extra prayers when one of her ladies or serving women was lying in. Now she feared for Shining Star because it was the mare's first birth.

Guinevere twisted her hands. Why did she allow her mare to be bred? She should never have let Arthur persuade her. Shining Star was old for a first birth.

Guinevere entered the dark stable, lit only with a few lanterns.

"How is Shining Star?" she asked Cuall, the grizzled stablemaster.

"Have no fear, Lady Guinevere. She is doing well."

Guinevere went to Shining Star's stall. The mare was sweating, so Guinevere rubbed her down and spoke to her.

There was a clamor in another part of the stable. The stablemaster appeared at the stall. In a breathless voice, he said, "One of our finest war stallions has had a fit of madness and injured two of my men. The stallion also hurt himself thrashing around. I have subdued him, but I must see to my men and the horse."

"Who will help Shining Star?" Guinevere's voice was frantic. Her heart pounded.

"Do not worry, my lady," said a familiar voice. "I have watched many mares give birth. I can do anything that is needed."

Lancelot stepped into the stall, approaching the mare slowly.

"Can you truly?" Guinevere had never been happier to see Lancelot, but had never felt so uncertain about Lancelot's skill.

"The Lord Lancelot has spent much time with the horses, your highness, and he has often visited your mare to see how she is faring. He will be equal to anything that needs doing," Cuall said. "By your leave, I must go." He turned away.

"Of course you worry about your mare, but I believe that all will be well." Lancelot actually touched Guinevere's arm, which gave her a warm feeling. She wished Lancelot had touched her at other times and offered more than reassurance.

The mare was down, and moving with difficulty.

After a time, Guinevere said, "Her labor seems long."

"It is. A mare's labor is normally short."

Lancelot's voice was calm but serious. "The foal's position may be the problem."

Though Guinevere's every nerve tensed, she murmured soothing words and hoped that Shining Star noticed them.

Lancelot shoved up her sleeves, moved closer to the mare, and was midwife to her, thrusting her hands in to help.

Guinevere feared for her mare, but she also worried that one of the hooves might strike Lancelot.

The foal began to emerge, hind legs first. Guinevere worried that it might die, but even more that her mare would.

The labor was long and long.

Finally, the entire foal emerged. It was a colt. Guinevere prayed that it would stand. She was so pleased that the birth was over that she scarcely noticed the blood smell.

Shining Star licked the colt, and after what seemed a long time, he stood. The mare rose also, and the cord broke naturally. She continued licking the colt and nuzzling him.

Lancelot looked at Guinevere and smiled. Guinevere, feeling weak, smiled with all her heart.

Lancelot washed her hands and arms in water from a bucket. "It will be some time before the afterbirth comes. I shall wait if you need to go and rest."

"I couldn't bear to leave her now. I shall stay until everything is completed."

"Very good, my lady." Lancelot smiled at her again and wiped sweat from her own brow. "Giving birth is worse than a battle," she said. "I am glad that I shall never have to do it."

"So am I," Guinevere said. "I had rather see this foal than an infant."

Lancelot's eyes widened. She stared at Guinevere, then looked back at the mare. "I am glad to be of service, my lady."

"I shall never forget your kindness," Guinevere told her.

The old stablemaster approached the stall. "Did all go well?" he asked in a weary voice. "How is the foal?"

"All is well," Lancelot said. "It was a difficult birth, but all is now done except the afterbirth."

"Ah, a fine colt." Cuall nodded. "Good work, Lord Lancelot."

"How are your men and the stallion?" Guinevere asked.

"Young Pwyll died." He paused.

Lancelot made the sign of the cross.

Guinevere exclaimed, "Dreadful!"

Cuall shook his head. "It is that. He was a good man. Gwynlliw suffered only a broken arm. And I had to put down the stallion."

"I'm so sorry," Guinevere said, thinking of the times the young stablehands had saddled her horse. "We must see that Pwyll's family has compensation."

"It is terrible. Such a fine young man." Lancelot lowered her voice. "I shall see Gwynlliw tomorrow. You should go and rest. We will wait for the mare to pass the afterbirth."

"Yes, you should rest," Guinevere said to the old man.

"I'll look in on Gwynlliw again. Then I will." Cuall went off.

Lancelot and Guinevere waited in silence.

After a time, Shining Star passed the afterbirth.

"It is done," Lancelot said. "Shining Star will be fine."

Guinevere sighed with relief. "My good mare. I shall never have her bred again. May she enjoy this foal, for it will be her last."

Lancelot nodded. "May I escort you back to your rooms, Lady Guinevere?" Her voice held less of the special warmth it had had that night.

"You may." Guinevere felt tears coming, but managed to hold them back. She could see Lancelot retreating, and she wanted to retreat to sleep herself.

The next day, Guinevere went to the stable at a time when Lancelot was likely to be there. Lingering by Shining Star's stall was no difficulty. Guinevere looked at her with more love than ever.

Lancelot came to the stall as expected.

She bowed and said, "God grant you a good day, my lady. Your mare is looking well, and so is the foal."

Guinevere smiled as warmly as she could. "Thank you for your kind help with the foaling. I want to give you a token of my gratitude." She handed Lancelot a pearl. "This pearl came from an ornament my father gave me." Guinevere wanted to convey that it had not been a present from Arthur.

Lancelot's face flushed. She accepted the pearl, but her hand did not clasp Guinevere's. "Many thanks, Lady Guinevere. I shall place it in the bag I wear around my neck that holds my mother's ring, a relic of St. Agnes, and a token given me by an old woman who was kind to me." She bowed and turned away.

Guinevere longed to bid her not to go, but that seemed futile.

A few days later Lancelot went away on a mission for the king.

Lancelot left the king's rooms and walked to her house. The hour was late, and she had drunk more than she wanted. Gawaine's stories about the ghosts of Lothian, though entertaining, had gone on far too long. She was eager to visit her chamber pot.

Soon after Lancelot relieved herself, there was a knock at her door. She groaned. Who would want to visit her at this hour? She had never encouraged visitors to come.

She opened the door to find Cai, wearing a cloak with a hood that covered him except for his handsome face.

"Pray come in," she said, trying to keep the astonishment out of her voice.

"Thank you." He entered, cast his cloak on her bed, and sat in one of her two chairs. "Your modest dwelling reflects your taste, no doubt, but are you sure you wouldn't like a wall hanging?"

He glanced at her plain wood table and chairs, bed, and chest.

Her sword and shield hung on the wall. There was a fur rug on the floor and a similar coverlet on her bed. Candles, a pitcher, and a bowl stood on her table. Her slops jar was in a corner. That was all.

"Thank you, no."

The seneschal shook his head. "Catwal could do more to make this pleasant."

"He does all that I need." Surely Cai hadn't come this late to discuss her furnishings.

"As you wish." He ran his fingers through his well-cut hair. His smile faded. "I have come to ask you a favor."

"Yes?" She couldn't imagine what he might want.

"Would you please give me some lessons in fighting? I want to enter the next fighting contest."

Lancelot stared at him. She could not have been more astonished if he had told her that he planned to serve only bread for dinner at the round table the next day. "But why?" she asked. "You have so many other skills." Everyone knew that Cai lacked prowess at fighting.

"Some of the warriors mock me, and I've had enough. I just came back from Londinium, where I made sure the merchants who sell us imported goods are reserving the best for Arthur. Earlier today I was waylaid twice."

"Did robbers dare to attack you so near to Camelot?" Lancelot jumped up from her chair. "I'll take a party of men out to find and punish them."

Cai laughed bitterly. "Hah! If only it had been brigands. It was Arthur's own men, our dear companions."

Lancelot gasped. "How could they not have recognized you?"

Cai raised his eyebrows. "Don't you ever serve wine? Give me a cup, though I'm sure it's as poor as your furnishings. I'm sore from trying to fight those curs. And of course they knew me!"

250

"How dare they attack you? This is shameful."

Lancelot's pulse raced, but she poured the requested wine, which indeed was unlikely to be to the seneschal's taste.

Cai drank deeply. "It's worse than I thought." He grimaced. "Monks who have taken a vow of poverty drink better. I'm sending you something halfway decent tomorrow." He nevertheless drank more. "But I'm aching so much that I'll accept even this. Don't you know that the warriors belittle me?"

"I have heard slighting remarks, it is true." Lancelot tried to make her voice calm. "They value only fighting and fail to appreciate how much skill it must take to manage the caer as you do to make their lives comfortable. But I had no idea they would try to injure you. Why would they possibly do such a thing?"

Cai sighed. "I have always believed that you were woefully ignorant, but you are even dimmer than I thought. Some of them despise me because I like men."

"Oh." Lancelot stared at him. She realized that she had somehow known that Cai was different, but she had never understood the reason.

"Oh, indeed." Cai shook his head. "Oh, and again oh. Arthur finds it puzzling, but he cares about me as his foster brother. The men who hate me don't dare show it much at Camelot because that would anger him, but when I leave, they come after me and challenge me to fight. They know well that they will hurt me. At the moment, I am sore and sorely tired. I must prepare myself to challenge them and fight. It is the only thing they understand."

Lancelot trembled with anger. "How dare they attack the seneschal, who runs all things well! How dare they attack Arthur's foster brother! How dare they attack for no good reason a man they know they can easily defeat!"

"They do dare. I should see that they are served wine that all the servants have spit in, or worse. But that I cannot do. I must fight, and you must teach me to do better."

Lancelot paused.

"Do you think that is a hopeless task?" Cai asked, pouring himself more wine while making a face to say it was exceedingly poor.

"I have a better plan, if you will accept it," Lancelot said. "We are nearly the same size. Let me dress as you do, wear your armor, carry your shield, and ride your horse. Then if anyone challenges me, I shall fight in your place."

Cai raised his eyebrows. "And will they believe that I could fight like Lancelot?"

"I shall fight as much in your style as possible," Lancelot explained. "Indeed we shall have lessons, but I shall watch how you move and try to imitate you."

Cai laughed much more than seemed appropriate. "You are astonishing, Lancelot. Yes, I am sure you are capable of watching to see how another moves and imitating him. I am sure you are better at that than anyone else would be. Are you certain that you have no problem with pretending to be me? What if someone discovered it was you?"

"Why should I mind?" Lancelot found his excessive amusement puzzling. "I don't like men as you do."

At this, Cai choked. "I know that." He contained himself and shook his head. "You may pretend to be me and fight anyone who seeks to fight me."

Lancelot wondered whether he might perceive that she was a woman, but she said nothing about that.

They practiced in secret a few times, and she learned to move her arms as he did.

Then Cai announced that he was going on a journey to inspect cattle for purchase. Lancelot set out, wearing Cai's heavily braided cloak over his chain mail and doused with perfume like his, though it made her sneeze. Fortunately his helmet fit her. She carried Cai's shield with a key as its symbol, and rode his horse, which he had dubbed Taxes. She disapproved of giving horses foolish names, but Taxes was a fine gelding.

She left Camelot a little after dawn, and by midday a horse and rider blocked her path. The rider was Sangremore, one of the members of the round table whom she liked little.

"Cai, I'm giving you another chance to prove you're a man," the warrior called. He sneered.

Lancelot said nothing, but let him attack and dodged his blow.

"Good at avoiding blows now, are you? You won't avoid this one, Cocksucker."

Lancelot's blood surged with anger, but she let Sangremore come close to hitting her a few times, then struck him with a blow that looked as if it might have been struck by chance, but unhorsed him.

Sangremore raised himself from the ground, but Lancelot rode away. She proceeded for about a mile, and Agravaine ap Lot rode up to her. He called her what Sangremore had, and many other names as well. He charged her, and she turned Cai's horse away.

"Coward!" he yelled, pursuing her. She stopped Taxes suddenly, so that Agravaine's horse almost ran into the gelding. While he was reining in his horse, she attacked him and cut his right arm more than a little.

"You cut my fighting arm!" Agravaine shrieked, following that with a flow of curses.

Lancelot doubled back to Camelot. She hoped that she might have prevented more attacks on the seneschal.

The ugly words used against Cai hurt her. She sympathized with his love for men. She had heard of such things, but no one ever said that a woman might love other women. She thought herself lonelier than Cai.

Lancelot sat on a bench in the great hall, close to the fire.

It was winter, so everyone crowded there to find warmth. She was enjoying mulled wine that smelled as good as it tasted.

A harper sang of Orpheus, who tried to rescue his wife from hell. When he had finished, Lancelot decided to go off to bed.

As she was leaving the great hall, Guinevere approached her.

They stood in the doorway, alone for a moment. "Some wives may live in hell, Lancelot," the queen said in a low voice. "Would you rescue such a one?"

Lancelot took a step backward. "Surely she would prefer that her husband rescue her, Lady Guinevere," she said. "I would never do anything that would put a woman at risk of going there."

She bowed her head to Guinevere and moved to leave.

"How thoughtful you are," the queen said, with an edge to her voice. "Would you kindly take me riding tomorrow? Bors has caught the ague from one of his children, and there's no one else I can abide."

"Of course, your highness. It will be very cold."

She wanted to tell the queen that being alone with her was like a visit to hell, a place of longing and no hope.

"I have no fear of possible snow," Guinevere said. "Other coldness disturbs me more."

Lancelot wondered whether her own love sickness was so strong that Guinevere had caught it. Lancelot prayed that she could resist the folly of believing that the queen could love her as she was.

They rode through the forest. Lancelot was silent, and Guinevere talked almost as little. Wind cut Lancelot's cheeks like a blade. The sight of bare trees did little to cheer her.

When they came to a dell that was sheltered from the wind, Guinevere stopped her mare, so Lancelot halted also.

"Must you shy away from me?" Guinevere said. She brought her mare close to Lancelot's and touched Lancelot's hand. "You must know that there are rumors that the Sea Wolves will sail again to attack us next spring. Life is short. I am longing for you, and I believe you feel the same about me."

Lancelot pulled away her hand. She held back tears.

"My lady, how could I touch a woman who is wedded to my sworn lord? Please be kind and cease to tempt me."

"Do you see me only as a temptation? I thought you of all people could understand a woman's heart. Is the king so much more important to you than I am?" Guinevere's stance was dignified, but there was pleading in her tone.

"Vows are more important than wishes." Lancelot shook her head.

"I do not just wish for you. I vow that I love you." The queen spoke formally, as if she were standing in front of the court.

Lancelot almost reeled, but she forced her voice to be unyielding. "My lady, you are already vowed to another."

"I leave myself open to you, but you keep up your shield. Perhaps your heart is as cold as this wind." Guinevere turned her mare back in the direction of Camelot.

"Do not follow me unless you wish to comfort me."

Lancelot covered her face with her hands. She was alone. She would always be alone. Now the woman she loved despised her.

How much more would Guinevere despise her if she knew that Lancelot was a woman? She clutched the bag around her neck that held Guinevere's pearl.

Lancelot remembered the words that her nurse had said many years ago. Rathtyen had spoken truly when she told young Antonius that if she pretended to be male, she would always have to sleep alone.

Now Lancelot understood how terrible that knowledge was.

Guinevere came down with the ague, but she did not care. She was relieved that she could retreat into a daze and sleep alone.

Part II   War with the Saxons

17   A New Kind of Fighting

Guinevere's ague had lasted longer than she expected. She slept
through more than a week. One morning, she woke to hear many
warriors in the courtyard. Horses neighed, men shouted. Arthur
stood beside her bed. He wore chain mail, which was most unusual.

"A great force of Saxons and Jutes has landed and combined
with the West Saxons and the South Saxons. We're leaving to
fight them, my dear. I hope that you will be well soon." His eyes
had a distant look, as if he were half on his way already.

"This early in the year?" Guinevere felt a cold wind blow through her. Although she had known that a fight with the Saxons was imminent, she had not realized how soon it would be. The season for battles generally started in late spring, but spring had not yet begun. Ships usually did not cross the seas so early.

"They think they're putting us at a disadvantage by fighting before there's enough grass for our horses, but I have been storing up oats and hay for just such a chance," Arthur said. "We'll travel with wagonloads, and we have more grain and hay stored at places along several routes. Cai will take care of things here while we're gone, and of course I depend on you to help him."

"When are you going?" Shaking, she rose from the bed. She could hardly keep the distress out of her voice. Arthur and all of the men she knew would risk their lives, and so would Lancelot.

"Immediately." Arthur pressed her hand. "Don't worry, we are better armed and better fighters than the Saxons, and we will be joined by forces from Dumnonia, Rheged, Dyfed, Gwynedd, and Powys."

Guinevere realized she would have no chance for a private farewell from Lancelot. She might never be able to speak with Lancelot again. "Oh, Arthur." Her hand clutched his. "There is so little time for parting."

"Perhaps that's just as well," he said, putting his arm around her.

"I want to wish Godspeed to all of our brave warriors."

"They know you wish them well, my dear. But if you feel strong enough, you can come outside and wave."

"I must ask a favor of you." She tried to make her voice sound less desperate than she felt. "The day I came down with the ague, I spoke to Lancelot harshly. Would you tell him that I regret it, and that he should please disregard what I said?" She hated using a messenger who could so little convey what she wanted, but she felt there was no choice. She could not risk a written message, or send Fencha to Lancelot, who was doubtless milling around with other warriors. She could hear their sounds in the courtyard.

"You shouldn't worry." He smiled indulgently, as if her request were foolish. "Lancelot is fond of you and has been concerned about your illness. He has asked me about you every day. He surely won't hold whatever you said against you, but of course I'll tell him."

"Thank you." She reached up to kiss him. She appreciated his lack of suspicion.

Arthur kissed her, and tears came to her eyes. She wondered when she would see him again. He was often her friend as well as her husband, and she wished that he could be a friend all the time. The thought of his risking his life was terrible. What would Britain do without him? Had she been mad not to bear him an heir, despite his fears and her own?

When Guinevere was dressed and her hair was braided, she went down to the courtyard, where warriors shouted for men to bring their horses, and ladies clutched their husbands in hasty farewells. Stablehands scurried about and horses whinnied. The serving men carried bundles of food and casks of ale to supply wagons.

Guinevere saw Lancelot briefly in front of a hundred people and was able to smile only a regal smile. Lancelot bowed to her, but after the bow, the warrior looked up, and her eyes were so filled with longing that Guinevere felt a stabbing pain in her gut. She pressed her lips together in a gesture so small and brief that she thought no one but Lancelot could see it as a kiss.

Lancelot made a similar gesture. Guinevere's eyes filled, but she refrained from weeping.

She wished she could follow and protect Lancelot. But the queen knew she had not the skill to fight.

Arthur mounted his white stallion and yelled to the assembled warriors to be quiet and listen to him. The crowd hushed.

Standing by her horse, Lancelot watched him as if he were a priest speaking from the pulpit. Never had she so longed to hear his words. She hoped for reassurance, for words that would help her to have courage.

"You are all that stands between your people and death and slavery. You must no longer be a warband, but an army, the greatest army in our land since the Romans left," the king cried out. "Do not think of yourselves merely as warriors, but as soldiers, the soldiers not just of the High King, but of all Britain! Together, we will save this land!"

The men roared their approval.

Lancelot choked on tears. Here was a leader who had the strength and the heart to lead his people to safety. She would follow him until the end of her days, whether that came soon or late.

The troops mounted their horses and rode out of the gates. Men blew the horns that would sound the call to battle. Lancelot wondered when – indeed, whether – she would return. She could not look back at the caer that had become her home. She had been accepted as one of the king's companions. Men, and women, praised her deeds. And Guinevere was there, even if untouchable.

Lancelot rode her black horse near the king's white one, at the head of the troops. Never having ridden with such a great number of men before, she felt like one drop in a great river.

They had gone only a short distance when Arthur turned to her and said, "By the way, Lance, Guinevere told me that she was testy when she was coming down with the ague, and she wanted you to know that she regrets it."

Lancelot had to hold back to keep from weeping.

She felt an unbearable mixture of relief that Guinevere was no longer angry at her and shame at receiving the message from Arthur. She thought that she had committed adultery in her heart, if not in the flesh.

She made her voice as formal as possible. "The queen should not feel that she must apologize to me. She was feeling ill. Thank you, my Lord Arthur."

"I knew you wouldn't mind, Lance, so that's what I told her." He smiled.

As they rode through forests and across fields to meet the Saxons, Lancelot's mind was full of Guinevere. Perhaps it was no great sin to dream of Guinevere if Lancelot might never see her again. She thought of Guinevere's shining black braids, her smooth hands, the way those blue eyes flashed just before the queen said something particularly clever. She wished she had kissed Guinevere, just once. She might have missed her last chance. It would be sad to die without ever having kissed the one she loved.

Pulling her crimson cloak around her, Lancelot rode through the cold rain. Looking to make sure that none of the army's carts were stuck in the mud, she saw that some carried fairly poor-looking young women. She rode up to speak with Gawaine.

"Why are women in carts following us? Are their husbands foot soldiers? Isn't it dangerous for them to follow an army? Shouldn't Arthur send them home?"

Rain dripped from Gawaine's red beard. He stared at her. "Great Dagdha's cauldron, don't you know? They're camp followers, what else? A few may be attached to particular men, but most aren't. Even you must have heard of them. They'll cook, and nurse the wounded, and minister to the men in other ways."

Lancelot felt the blood drain out of her face.

"I had heard the term, of course, but I hadn't realized . . . They really do follow the troops? Even a good king like Arthur lets such things go on?"

"Of course." Gawaine rolled his eyes.

"The men are risking their lives, so why not? They'd bother the local women more if the camp followers didn't come."

Lancelot did not brush the rain out of her face. Her voice was not so pleasant, but neither was the subject.

"If they don't have some women to use, they'll use others? What a way to live!"

"Can't you be human for a change?" Gawaine's voice showed more irritation. "Maybe you should visit them yourself. You've been looking a little pale. You need a woman."

"Do you think women exist only for men to use?" Lancelot retorted, clenching her fists. "How can men need the body of someone they don't even know? Why can't they wait until they are with a woman they are fond of, and who is fond of them?"

Gawaine gave Lancelot a disgusted look. "No doubt that's pleasanter, but why must a man wait for that, especially if he might die fighting?"

"He will die more at peace with himself if he has just used someone?"

"No one forces the whores to follow us!" Gawaine shouted.

"Then why do they?" She realized that she had no idea of the answer.

"Because they'll have no way to support themselves, now that the men have left their towns." His tone showed that he thought Lancelot a complete simpleton.

"Is that what you'd do, if you needed money?" She glared at him.

"No doubt, if I were a poor woman," he said, shrugging.

"As you still believe in the old gods, and in many lives, I hope you'll be born so in your next life," Lancelot snapped.

"May all of the men who so console themselves at their deaths be so reborn."

"May you long for a woman and find not one who will satisfy you," Gawaine pulled his plaid cloak tighter around him.

She turned her horse away, for this curse seemed too close to the truth. What woman would ever want her? None, if they knew she was a woman, and certainly not the one she wanted. She rode on cheerlessly through the mud.

The next morning, when they were camped in a field, Lancelot forced herself to walk over to the camp followers' wagons. She did so early in the day, when not many men were likely to be about their tents. Her boots sloshed through the mud and were covered with it.

"It's Lancelot! At last!" a pretty redhead in a mud-splattered dress called out. "Come to me, handsome one." She held out her arms in invitation.

"No, to me! I'm much nicer," cried a dark-haired girl, wiggling her hips.

"Ladies, I have not come for that," Lancelot said quickly, feeling herself blushing. "I only wondered how you were faring, and whether any of you wanted to leave this place."

"With you, anywhere!" jested the redhead, jumping up as if to leave.

"No, I mean do any of you want to be rescued?" Lancelot asked.

An older-looking woman – perhaps about thirty – with greasy brown hair looked wearily at Lancelot. "Rescued to where? Where do you think we can go and find a living? If there were anyplace else, we wouldn't be here."

"Speak for yourself," said the redhead. "I did the same work at Camelot, so why not do it here? It's where the men are."

"Who are you to try to make us feel ashamed?" asked the dark-haired girl, her glance no longer inviting but hostile.

"I beg your pardon, I didn't mean to do that," Lancelot replied in a humble voice.

"Go off, then, if you're too good for us," the girl told Lancelot.

Lancelot bowed and went off, nearly slipping in the mud. It was only after she had left that she realized she hadn't asked them their names.

That evening, as she passed the king's tent, she heard Arthur jesting with Peredur, as he didn't with Lancelot, "Why not visit the camp followers? Your wife will never know. Wives are sensible about such things. Guinevere never even mentions them."

"She might not, but my wife does," Peredur said. "Claudia found out that I strayed during your war of succession, and I had to face a cold shoulder for nearly a year. I'm not chancing that again for some camp follower."

Arthur chuckled. "True, the camp followers aren't all beauties, but what does it matter? Women are pretty much the same in the dark."

Lancelot gasped. Of course, Arthur couldn't mean to include Guinevere in that remark.

Peredur left the tent, and Lancelot pulled back, not wanting anyone to see that she had overheard.

Gawaine's loud voice was impossible to miss. "Now you've scandalized Peredur. So, do you mean that Morgan was just like the others?"

Arthur groaned. "Of course not. There's no one else like her. Don't remind me."

"You were a fool to send away the only woman you ever loved," Gawaine chided him.

"Silence! Even you can't talk to me that way!" Arthur yelled.

Lancelot staggered away. The only woman he ever loved? Did Arthur care more about his sister than about Guinevere? No, that couldn't be true.

One day soon after, when Lancelot rode next to Dinadan, a handsome dark-haired warrior whose eyes and wit both were known to sparkle, he said, "We're approaching the main Saxon forces. The poor camp followers will have more work than they can handle tonight. The men keep them busy when a battle is nigh."

"Don't you go to them?" Lancelot asked. "I didn't know that you were so chaste. I thought that Bors, Peredur, and Peredur's brother Aglovale were the only others who didn't go."

Dinadan laughed and folded his hands as if in prayer. "I am offended that you didn't see my shining virtue. I am deeply devoted to St. Caius and spend many long hours in such devotions."

Lancelot started to say that she had not heard much about that saint, then realized what he meant and smiled. "I never guessed. You are a much better fighter than Cai."

Dinadan frowned at that comment about Cai's fighting skills. "It's well that one of us is. Although Arthur is good to us, many are not."

"I know. That is very wrong," said Lancelot, patting his arm in sympathy.

Strangely, Dinadan looked as if he were making an effort not to laugh. Rooks in the trees were calling, and Lancelot wondered whether they were doing his laughing for him.

Such men were often very pleasant, Lancelot thought. She found that she missed Catwal, whom she hadn't brought to war for fear that he might not see a Saxon stealing up on him.

She rode off to find a chance to relieve herself, safe from any eye. Constipation did not improve her humor. Finding a private place had been a problem before, but now that she was traveling with the army it was greatly magnified.

When they saw the Saxons from a distance, Lancelot winced at attacking men who were on foot, while she was on horseback.

Then the Saxons ran at them, shrieking battle cries, sticking close together, shield to shield. It was impossible not to feel fear, though she was on a horse and they were not, and only a few of the Saxon chiefs had chain mail, while most of their fighting men wore only leather and their helmets.

With the other warriors, she charged them. The horses' ears flattened against their heads, their nostrils flared, their tails streamed behind them. She slashed all around her with spear and sword, as if these Saxons were not men but a host of stinging insects with small throwing axes buzzing past her head.

There was no moment to pause after a death – the killing was endless. The stink of death was everywhere. The clatter of battle deafened her.

Lancelot could see the men nearest her, but otherwise she had no idea how the battle was progressing. If hell was a confused mass of men trying to slaughter each other, this was hell. She had no idea who was winning.

A Saxon slashed at her leg with his axe, and she killed him. As he fell, she saw that he was only a boy of, who knows, twelve or thirteen. She gagged, but charged on to attack the others.

Toward evening, she saw that the Saxons were retreating, with the British in pursuit. Arthur's warriors must have won.

The field was littered with the bodies of the Saxon dead and the British dead, most of whom were foot soldiers. There were many fighters who could not afford to buy horses, and they bore the brunt of the battle.

She had never seen so many corpses and men near death.

Her head reeled; her stomach churned.

Lancelot guided Arrow over the bodies. He balked. It was natural for a horse to shy away from corpses, but he had to learn to ride over them in battle. He had been trained as a warhorse, but like Lancelot, he was dazed by an actual battle. He whinnied at the sight of dead and dying horses. She jumped down and cut the throat of one poor stallion whose entrails spilled through his sides. Then she wiped her hand on her chain mail and patted Arrow to soothe him. He accepted her touch.

Men began carrying – or dragging – wounded British soldiers, some of them screaming in agony, off the field.

They did not move the wounded Saxons.

Lancelot rode up to Arthur, who stood at the edge of the field watching. "It is a great victory," he said.

Triumph was in his voice, though his face was covered with sweat and his sword and tunic were caked with blood.

"What about the Saxons? Shall we start carrying the wounded prisoners?" she asked. The king shook his head. "We aren't taking prisoners. Our men will dispatch the Saxon wounded." His face and voice were as calm as ever.

Lancelot stared open-mouthed at him.

"We're going to kill their wounded?"

Arthur nodded solemnly. "How can we take them with us? We have barely enough food for our own men, and we can't spare all the soldiers it would take to guard them."

"Oh." Lancelot closed her eyes for a moment.

"You'll soon get used to the brutality of war, as we all have." The king touched her shoulder. Lancelot rode off so she wouldn't have to watch this final slaughter.

After they had carried away the wounded, the British warriors began to bury their dead companions. Lancelot joined in. The lack of coffins broke her heart.

She buried one young man whose head she couldn't find. Some Saxon must have it for a trophy.

They did not bury the dead Saxons.

The night after that first battle, Lancelot went to her tent and sobbed. I am a killer, she thought. A butcher, rather.

Slumping down on the wolfskin she had brought to sleep on, she buried her head in her hands. Her body felt riddled with aches and pains, but they were nothing compared with the emptiness she felt in her heart. She believed that she would never be able to feel the least happiness again. She had stepped into hell and could never leave.

Lancelot told herself that she had been a fool. Why had she ever wanted to pretend to be a man? True, she did not want to wear skirts or spin, but was wearing breeches worth going through this horrible slaughter? Fighting a brigand here and there to save some victim was nothing like war.

For the first time, she felt ashamed of shedding blood. So much of it, so much. Surely when her father taught her how to defend herself he had never dreamed she would have to fight in such a war. But she could leave, and return to her lands in Lesser Britain. The thought tempted her.

No, her fame as Lancelot of the Lightning Arm was not worth all the killing, but how could she betray all the men she knew? She couldn't leave them when their lives were imperiled. How could she desert Bors, who had half a dozen children at home? Or Gawaine, who, whatever his faults, had entertained her with so many play-fights? She could still picture him covered with flour in the kitchen. Or Arthur, the king who let her call him by his first name?

And what would Guinevere think if she heard that Lancelot had abandoned her king? Leaving was impossible. She pulled the wolfskin around her and tried to sleep.

When Lancelot woke and pulled back the flap of her tent, the pink clouds of sunrise brought tears to her eyes. She took a deep breath of the damp and chilly air. She was relieved to still see the sun, though perhaps she should feel guilty when so many would never see it again.

Battles were like nothing else on earth. Crowds of men, rivers of blood. Everywhere she turned, there was another man trying to kill her, or kill Arthur, or kill one of the other British fighters. Lancelot kept wielding her sword again and again, amazed that it struck its targets so effectively.

She became used to the feel of Saxons under the hooves of her horse, and only feared their naked berserkers who dove under horses' bellies to stab them might slash into her horse's chest. The sight of hoof-crushed men became as familiar as the sight of turf. She learned the smell of guts spilling out of bodies.

She managed for a time the great trick of seeing the bodies of the enemy as empty shells and the bodies of her companions as tragic. But after a battle was done, when the British soldiers buried their own dead while finishing off those of the enemy who were not quite dead, leaving them to rot in the sun, she prayed. "Holy Mother, these are all your children. Forgive me for killing them." She avoided being one of those who sent the Saxon wounded to Woden. Bors also declined that task.

She saw her fellow soldiers strip Saxon bodies of their jewelry and weapons, and divide the plunder. Arthur's rule was that plunder be divided fairly. But if any man knew that he had killed a particular Saxon, that man could have the plunder from his body. The soldiers also took the jewelry, weapons, mail, and cloaks from their fallen comrades and buried the Britons in their tunics, unless the mail was so stuck to their bodies that taking it off would tear them to bits. Quartermasters took the armrings and cloak pins to be sent back to the men's families, but Lancelot thought she sometimes saw a warrior wearing a jewel that resembled one that had belonged to a fellow soldier who was now dead.

After the battle, she saw the carrion crows, red kites, and ravens come down looking for food. Heartless birds, she thought, trying to drive them away. A crow perched on a tree near her and cawed loudly. Lancelot looked it in the eye. How foolish I am to be angry at the crows when I am the killer, not they, she thought. They have to eat. If I die in one of these battles, I'd just as soon feed you, she told the crow.

The bloodshed she had joined in colored her every thought. She smiled bitterly at her red cloak and tunics. Yes, the bloody color was fit for her. Dawns and sunsets she saw as bloody skies. The spring flowers this year seemed to mock the many deaths. She took no pleasure in the bluebells and violets.

Guinevere longed for Lancelot more than she had ever longed for anyone. She felt like a bard deprived of his harp. Even though they seldom spoke with each other at Camelot, she had had some idea where Lancelot was – with the horses, with the warriors, in the chapel, alone in bed. And even when Lancelot had been off on a mission or a quest, Guinevere knew that her warrior had been much of the time enjoying herself in the forest or on the moors. It was terrible to realize that now Lancelot might be under attack by enemy soldiers.

Guinevere feared for Arthur, too. As she sat alone in her room, preparing for the day of attending to Camelot's needs, the thought that he might die made her stomach ache. He had tried to be good to her. He had been far better than most husbands. It was not his fault that she longed for a woman.

And what if the king died? God help them all if the Saxons won. She could not let herself imagine what it would be like to have to flee Camelot, or worse, to be there if the Saxons sacked it. Even convents were not safe from Saxon ravages. She had heard too many tales of Saxons raping nuns. She prayed that the Convent of the Holy Mother would be safe.

Even if Arthur died but the Britons won the war, the loss of such a strong, decent leader would be great. She knew her chances of succeeding him in wartime were even less than in peacetime. Gawaine would likely rule. God preserve the nation from losing him at the same time as Arthur, for there was no other man who could gain the throne without much bloodshed. She believed that Gawaine was more intelligent than he sometimes seemed, and that he played the jester, in part, to reassure the king, so that Arthur would not see him as a threat.

And, after all, Gawaine let his mother rule in Lothian. It might be that he had no taste for ruling and it was even possible that he would let Guinevere rule, with him as her war leader. That was, indeed, the only way she could rule. She would have to endure his lewd speech, but ruling would be worth the price.

Guinevere gasped. What was she doing, imagining Arthur's death? Not when he was in mortal combat. She didn't want him to die. Please God, let him not die. She threw herself on her knees and prayed, begging God to forgive her for imagining that she might benefit from her husband's death.

God protect him, she prayed. And Lancelot. And all the Britons, all the men of Camelot. Especially dear Lancelot. Lancelot is so good, too good.

Guinevere promised God to do anything if only Lancelot survived. But she could not promise to stop loving Lancelot. She would sacrifice anything else, but not the possibility of holding Lancelot in her arms.

There was a knock on her door. Guinevere rose and bade whomever it was to enter. Fencha came in bearing a message.

271

"It's from the king, my lady," she said.

Guinevere snatched the packet from her and tore it open. He was safe. She sighed with relief. He said the Britons were winning. He made no mention of particular dead, which he surely would have if any of the men close to him had died. Lancelot, then, was still alive, at least at the time Arthur sent the letter.

"Another British victory," Guinevere said."Thanks be to God."

How long would she have to worry night and day? She prayed that Arthur would drive the Saxons back across the seas.

Together with Cai, Guinevere tried to make the caer's routine seem ordinary, although there was much less ceremony and much simpler food, and all the ladies endlessly made cloaks and blankets for the soldiers. She had words of sympathy for those who loved warriors off in the battle, because she did as well.

On the night before a battle, Lancelot stood in a line of men waiting by the priests' tent to be shriven. She still hoped for heaven, but wondered how long her soul could stay clean after so much slaughter.

Bors also was waiting, so she asked him, "Even if fighting the Saxons is necessary, how can we be blessed when we are just about to kill?" Bors sighed and leaned against an alder. "At least we are not killing Christians."

Lancelot also needed to lean against the neighboring tree.

"It is not so bad to kill the Saxons because they are pagans? But some of our own men really are pagan, too. Like Gawaine."

Bors frowned deeply, as if the moonlight that streamed around them offended him. "Gawaine never should have been baptised. He damned his soul rather than saving it." Lancelot gasped.

"He isn't too bad for a pagan," Bors continued, "but he's pledged to be a Christian, and he breaks that pledge every day."

Lancelot made the sign of the cross. "May you be mistaken about his being damned."

Bors made the same gesture. "I hope I am. I like him."

After Lancelot had been shriven, she went off to her own tent and met Gawaine on the way. The red-bearded warrior grinned.

"Someone overheard you and Bors worrying about my soul. Have no fear. Haven't you heard that I was a fosterling to the pope himself, and that he instilled me with enough piety to save the souls of my whole clan?"

Lancelot couldn't help laughing, even on the eve of battle. The idea of Lot and Morgause of Lothian and Orkney sending their eldest son to be fostered by the pope was just as incredible as the picture of Gawaine learning scripture and praying.

"You should not laugh at my history, Lance." Gawaine wagged his finger at her. "I was so renowned for piety that the cardinals were jealous. That was why I had to come home to Orkney."

"More likely you caused the greatest scandal Rome has ever known," Lancelot said.

"I did not, because I left before I was of an age to bed girls."

"That explains your story." She continued smiling for a moment before she remembered that they would be killing and perhaps being killed in the morning. She hoped that God enjoyed jests and would pardon Gawaine therefore.

Lancelot saw Merlin walk painfully to his horse. Each morning the old man looked as if he had aged another year during the night. Arthur put a hand on his adviser's shoulder.

"You are too ill to see battle. You should rest in your tent, or perhaps return to Camelot for a time." Merlin shook his head. Even that gesture appeared to give him pain. "No, I must stay with you. The men believe I have magical powers, and it reassures them to see me riding with you. The Saxons believe it, too; they fear me."

"All the more reason that I cannot risk your life in battle," Arthur said, giving him a fond look. "You are the only true father I ever had. Show yourself to our men and the enemy, and then, I beg you, go to the back of the ranks where you will be safer from the onslaught."

The old man nodded. "Never fear, I know I cannot fight. I'll go where not too many men have to risk their lives protecting me." The king helped him onto his horse.

Lancelot felt more kindly toward Merlin than she had before. What did it matter whether he guessed she was a woman? If he did, he never told anyone.

Arthur called Lancelot to his tent one night. She entered the tent, heaped with fine rugs for the king to sit on, and he bade her be seated. A brazier kept out the night's chill.

"You are proving to be just as swift and skillful in battle as you are on the contest field," Arthur said, giving her a look of approval. "Therefore, though you are new to warfare, you should command a cavalry regiment, as Gawaine and Peredur do. Of course Bedwyr will continue to lead the foot soldiers, and some of the lesser kings will continue to lead their own men."

"Command a regiment?" Her stomach tightened. She wished that he had not said those words and that she did not have to respond to them. Of course this was an order, not a request. "But what do I know of commanding men, or of tactics?"

"You will learn, as we all have. I was only seventeen when I led my first troops. And I gave Gawaine command of many men when he was that age."

Arthur was encouraging, but implacable.

Lancelot stared at him. She knew that she had no alternative. She might be a disaster as a commander, but no, that was impossible, she could not fail him – or Britain. "I shall do my best."

"Of course. Your best is very good indeed." The king poured himself some ale, and gestured for Lancelot to take some also. "The first thing you need to do is appoint a second in command. Who will you have?"

She had never thought of such a thing, but an answer came quickly to her. "Peredur's brother, Aglovale, unless he would prefer to serve with Peredur."

Aglovale she had met only since the war began, but he was a gentle-mannered man who lived with his family, not at Camelot. She would not be embarrassed to give him orders, as she might be with an older or more seasoned warrior, and he seemed unlikely to resent her or be envious.

Dazed, she left the king's tent. The other commanders were veterans of Arthur's war of succession and numerous campaigns against the Saxons. Would she measure up? She determined to ask Gawaine and Peredur about what would be expected of her.

Lancelot wandered to the campfire where Aglovale and Peredur were eating their share of a deer one of the soldiers had killed that afternoon. Aglovale was a medium-sized, brown-bearded man, a decade younger than Peredur. She called him aside.

"I'm to command a cavalry regiment," she said, unable to mask the uncertainty in her voice. "Would you be my second in command?"

"Of course, if you want me." He smiled as if pleased to be asked.

"I'm a little surprised you would not prefer to be your brother's aide." He laughed.

"Even the friendliest of brothers have their rivalries. I'm just as glad to serve with you instead. Otherwise, Peredur might think he had to appoint me out of duty, as Gawaine had to choose Agravaine," he said with a grin.

She returned the grin, pitying Gawaine as everyone did, for no one wanted to deal every day with Agravaine's temper.

Aglovale proved to be a good choice. Lancelot had to worry about her regiment, be sure that the physicians saw to the wounded, that the fighters who lost their swords or spears had new ones from the armorers who traveled with the troops, and that new horses were procured through purchase or coercion for men who lost theirs and lived to tell of it. Aglovale helped her with this work.

After her first battle as a commander, she realized that she had to go among the men and talk with them.

One young man, Sawyl, sat staring at the fire at a distance from the others. Unlike them, he was holding his stew bowl without eating, though the food didn't smell too bad.

"Sawyl? Are you well?" she asked.

He stared at her vacantly. "Yes, commander."

"Indeed?" She paused, not leaving him.

"My friend Rhun died today." His voice was flat. "I couldn't reach him before a Saxon axed him."

"I'm sorry. Do you want to talk about him?"

"He . . . he was so foolish, always jesting. Never again." Sawyl's voice cracked. He bit his lips.

How strange not to weep, Lancelot thought, but she listened to him. "Rhun was a hero," she said, though she had not seen how he died.

"He didn't want to be one." Sawyl sighed.

What more could she say? Were all the men who died in the war heroes, or just dead?

She looked at the faces around the camp and wondered which ones would be gone by the next night.

Soon the men were dropping by her tent late at night to talk a little sheepishly about their fears of death, their grief over friends killed in the previous day's battle, or the wives or loves that they left behind. She was drained, afraid that the heart for battle would go out of her, but Aglovale listened as well as she did, or better, nodding with sympathy and saying little, so she left a good share of this work to him.

"Poor Gawaine," she said. "He has twice the listening, because no one would take his troubles to Agravaine."

"You could help him," Aglovale noted, but she shook her head.

"Could but won't. He makes a good mother." And they laughed.

Lancelot learned that being a leader of soldiers was indeed like being a mother – a mother who led her young to death and saw them wrenched, limb from limb, every day.

She could not save many. Even if she saved one young soldier's life, she turned to find another butchered not far from her.

As for herself, she woke every day wondering if it would be her last. She had aches and pains, callouses and blisters, it seemed by the hundreds, and her body felt sometimes like one giant bruise, but she had no wounds. Although she risked her life as much as anyone, and more, she had a terror of wounds that might require a physician to see her body. She fought the harder therefore. She must strike at the Saxons before they could strike her. It might be better to die than to be wounded and have her sex discovered. And it would be far better to die than be captured by the Saxons.

In the evening after a battle, when they had looked after all the men in their regiment, Aglovale sank down by the fire that an orderly had made in front of Lancelot's tent.

"I hope my sons never fight in such battles. My oldest, Percy, already has his head full of stories about warriors. He believes that fighting is glorious. May he never learn the truth." He groaned and splashed water on his face from a tin basin that the orderly had placed there. The water streaked through the dirt on his cheeks.

Lancelot splashed some on her face also, no doubt producing similar streaks, then rubbed a towel over them.

"Perhaps he'll never have to see it for himself, if you tell him."

Aglovale shook his head. "He doesn't listen to me, just to his own strange fancies. When Peredur and some other warriors came riding up to tell me that we must go to fight the Saxons, Percy insisted they were angels. He pretended not to recognize his own uncle, whom he's named after. His name, Percival, is a combination of my brother's and mine.

"My other son, Illtud, is clever, but he is of this world, not odd like Percy."

"Why shouldn't Percy dream?" Lancelot smiled. "Don't worry about it."

Aglovale poured himself some ale, and offered some to Lancelot, who accepted it. "But he's always getting into trouble, going off further than he should on his horse, and pretending that the horse sprouted wings and he couldn't stop it.

"When the war's over, why don't you come and visit us? My sons would be wild with excitement and my wife, Olwen, is always glad for company."

"Thank you, perhaps I shall."

Children she had thought of not at all, but perhaps it might be interesting to visit Aglovale's family. Putting more sticks on the fire, she felt as if she were hearing tales of some strange land.

What must it be like to have someone at home who thought of you and longed for you to return?

Lancelot wondered. Did Guinevere think of her?

But even if Guinevere did, and even if Lancelot returned, Guinevere was someone else's.

Still, it would be wonderful, even though painful, to see Guinevere's face again and hear her voice.

As Guinevere walked across the courtyard one morning, she heard a commotion at the gates. Cai, who had been talking with some guards, saw her and beckoned her. She hurried to him, and he to her.

"People who fear the Saxons are seeking shelter here," Cai told her. "A few are nobles and merchants, but many are farmers."

"We must give them shelter," Guinevere said, imagining what it would be like to flee.

Cai sighed. "To some, but we cannot take in the whole kingdom. Those nobles who can must protect their own homes and their own people. And Britain cannot hold out if all the merchants, smiths, and farmers cease their work. We must talk with these people to learn whether they have been driven from their homes, and whether they can stay near Camelot rather than within our walls."

Guinevere also sighed. "That is true, but we must err on the side of generosity. How can farmers tend their fields or shepherds herd their flocks if they live in terror? How can merchants go from town to town if the Saxons might attack them?"

She went with him to speak with the people, and ordered that the great hall be opened to those who needed to stay there.

The fear on their faces unnerved her more than had the sight of the soldiers riding out. Women in finely tinted wool and those in undyed homespun clutched their children. Though the wind chilled Camelot, merchants' faces dripped sweat as if they had labored in the sun.

"Your highness, pray shelter my family!" cried more than one man who wore a well-made robe and rode a good horse.

"And my children, too! We can't go home," exclaimed a woman whose face and hands were wrinkled from labor.

Guinevere smiled at frightened children and promised them sweets. She assured merchants who needed to travel that their wives could remain at Camelot. Together with Cai, she also decided that some of those who could not return home could stay for a time in the houses of men who did not have wives, such as Lancelot and Gawaine.

"Why don't you speak with Lancelot's serving man while I arrange matters with Gawaine's?" Cai said.

Guinevere marveled at his cleverness in guessing that she would want to see Lancelot's house, and his discreet manner of giving her the opportunity.

She went to the house and spoke with Catwal, who assured her that he would have no difficulty in learning to assist people who needed shelter. The plainness of Lancelot's furnishings touched Guinevere's heart.

When Lancelot woke bleeding, she cursed her lot. How could she find ways to hide her rags when camping with an army? She decided to bury them in the ground under her tent.

That evening, Lancelot joined the warriors gathered by the king's tent, where harpers played. She hoped to be carried away by the music to some different land. Though the songs often told of war, they clothed it in beauty, hiding the stench of death that enveloped the warriors. Would the harpers soon be singing of her death in battle?

Some of the warriors played the harp themselves, and those from the North played pipes. Faces glowed in the campfire as

Dinadan took up a harp and sang about the warriors of their own company.

There was a familiar tune telling of Lancelot's noble deeds, of fair ladies without number saved, then turning their beseeching eyes on the handsome warrior, who smiled at them but rode away. The song hinted that someday there would be a lady from whom Lancelot would not turn away.

She held back a sigh. If only that were true.

Then Dinadan sang of the ancient Irish hero Cuchulain, but he changed some words to say that Cuchulain had been reborn among them, as Gawaine, for who else fought so many battles and embraced so many women? Arthur and the other men, not least Gawaine, laughed at this comparison.

"Not so," Gawaine said, drinking his barley beer. "For if I had been Cuchulain, I'd not have fought Queen Maeve but would have found a better way to win her over."

Bedwyr wrinkled his face and spat. "Even you might not want some sword-wielding bitch. Besides, she was bleeding at the time of the great battle. All men know that's why she was defeated."

Gawaine chuckled. "What's the matter with bleeding women? We're all covered with gore in battle anyway. Almost any man here would be glad to have a woman, bleeding or not. Sometimes they're hotter then."

Bors gasped. "You wouldn't really lie with a bleeding woman, would you, Gawaine? Who knows what terrible things could happen? Some say that if a bleeding woman conceives, the baby will have leprosy."

"Or that it will have red hair," Gawaine retorted, touching his red-bearded chin.

"What a terrible thing to say about your mother!" Bors exclaimed.

"That she lay with my father? I always thought she had." Gawaine swilled more beer.

"Even the great Pliny said that women's blood is like a poison, and wine will turn sour if a bleeding woman pours it," said Lucius, showing off his knowledge as usual.

"That's a good excuse for having bad wine." Gawaine chortled. "According to the legends, all of those old Irish heroes were taught to fight by the woman warrior Scathach. I wouldn't mind having one of those women warriors around right now. The tales say that they have voracious appetites for men."

"You shouldn't believe everything you hear," Lancelot observed, trying to keep her irritation out of her voice. None of her companions looked even faintly appealing.

"I have a treat for all of you – good wine," Arthur said. Though he sat on the ground with only a rug to rest on, he bore himself as if he were on a throne. "Who will pour it?"

"I shall," Lancelot said graciously. She poured the wine and asked how everyone liked it. They all said it was very good.

The troops were camped by a river, and the commanders had allowed the men to bathe. Lancelot volunteered for guard duty, but she could hear the shouts and splashes in the background. How she wished she could swim! Her body felt so grime-covered that it seemed like someone else's.

Living in an army camp, she was now as used to seeing naked men as naked dogs or horses, and it mattered just as little to her. That is, seeing men she scarcely knew mattered little. Seeing her friends' bodies still embarrassed her, but it would look too odd if she obviously averted her gaze.

Why must it make so much difference who was male and who was female? She didn't understand why people had to be obsessed with thoughts about mating. Why couldn't they all just swim together?

The men sounded innocent as they splashed and dunked each other. It was strange that these were the same men who went to camp followers, much less the same who slew many in battle. Why must people lose their innocence? Lancelot wondered.

Guinevere comforted the young girls because there would be no gathering of hawthorne blossoms this spring. "You can make flowers out of scraps of cloth too small to use for the soldiers," she told the few who sniffled.

No one could leave Camelot for playful reasons. Guinevere longed to ride in the forest, but it was not safe, not even with a guard, and she could not take men away from guarding Camelot. She was confined to riding Shining Star around the pasture, and letting one of the men ride the mare further for exercise.

The great hall looked so strange, filled with people who had fled to Camelot. As she walked among them, she wondered whether it would ever be full of Arthur's men again. The sight of the unoccupied throne unnerved her. She could picture Lancelot walking across the courtyard, riding off from the stable, sitting at the table. Whenever someone mentioned Lancelot, the name sounded like music to Guinevere.

One evening when they were sitting by Lancelot's campfire, Gawaine pointed out fires on nearby hills. "See those?"

Lancelot jumped up and peered out anxiously. "Are we so close to the enemy's camp? I had not thought so. Does Arthur know?"

Gawaine hooted. "That's no enemy. Those are Beltane fires in the nearby villages."

Lancelot relaxed and sank back to the ground, but she wrinkled her nose with disdain. "I suppose it's that time of year. I hadn't thought of it. No doubt people still will keep their pagan customs for some years."

"Why don't you go?" Gawaine suggested, gesturing to the nearest hill where a fire burned.

"I certainly will not!" She spat out the words. Surely even if she were a man, she would never go where pagans threw themselves on each other on the ground.

"Why not? I mean it, Lance. A fine night like this in the midst of the war is a gift from the gods. If you're shy of women, what could be better? It's pleasanter than going to camp followers. All of the women will be there because they want some fun." He warmed his hands at the fire.

"Will they?" she asked suspiciously. What Gawaine thought was fun the women might not.

"Of course, it's a great time for women. Such celebrations are the only time that a woman can lie with a man other than her husband, and he has no right to protest." He shook with laughter.

"How could there be days when a sin is no sin? Adultery is always wrong," Lancelot insisted. Even if she were a man, she would never do anything so wicked with Guinevere and imperil the lovely queen's soul.

Gawaine poured himself some barley beer, and offered some to Lancelot, who turned it down. "Then find a maiden at the Beltane ceremony if you object so much to adultery. It's nothing to be afraid of. It's just a lot of people lying together in the dark."

"With no walls between them! How disgusting. No wonder the Church condemns it," Lancelot exclaimed, making a face.

This time Gawaine's laugh was a guffaw. He slapped his knee. "It's no Roman orgy. Our ancestors weren't decadents."

"Some of my ancestors were Roman, but they weren't decadents," Lancelot protested.

"Oh, of course, your ancestors weren't," Gawaine said in a teasing voice. "At a Beltane celebration you might hear sounds

284

from someone else, but no one pays attention to what anyone else is doing. It's no less private than peasants' huts, or many a noble's holding. Only the richest can afford to care so much about walls." He poked at the fire with a stick. The sparks shot up, shining in the dark like red reflections of the stars.

"I suppose you'll go," she said with some disgust.

He shook his head and groaned. "If only I could! Not this year. Arthur doesn't want the soldiers to go. There are too many of us. We would take all of the local women, and anger the local men, and that wouldn't help us win the war. Of course some soldiers will slip off to the fires anyway, but the officers should set an example. Everyone would understand if they found out that you went, though. You have to lose your virginity sometime."

"No, in fact I don't," Lancelot replied with some sarcasm.

"You're not dry and monkish, nor are you like Cai and Dinadan. You seem like a man who's longing for a woman."

Lancelot turned away from him and stared into the fire.

"True, I am longing for a woman, one I can never have, and I want no other. Don't mock me."

"I'm not mocking you. Are you sure she's so unreachable? Can I advise you on how to woo her?" Gawaine was unusually quiet.

She shook her head. "I want no advice. I know she can never be mine."

"Then I hope you find another woman you could love. Most would be glad to love you, you're so handsome and kind. Life is short, and it feels shorter than usual at the moment." Gawaine sighed.

Lancelot did not take her eyes from the fire. She was sure that her life was doomed to be nothing but ashes, with no flames. Even Gawaine would not sympathize about her love if he knew she was a woman.

Gawaine took up his northern pipes and began to play. The sad sounds soothed Lancelot, for they echoed how she felt.

Dawn streaked into the British soldiers' camp and cast its rosy light on tents. Stretching, Lancelot greeted the day. Aglovale asked if she wanted barley beer. There was a smell of porridge in the air, and that appealed to her more than the drink. But was there enough porridge for all the men? Unlikely. She should wait until the soldiers who served under her had eaten and then, if the porridge lasted, take her share.

"Perhaps beer," she said, extending her hand for the jar Aglovale held.

Throwing axes whirled into the camp, and one struck Aglovale in the shoulder. He dropped the jar and fell to the ground.

"Saxon attack!" Lancelot shouted. Many others yelled with her. Aglovale was conscious. He held his bleeding shoulder.

Lancelot pulled him into her tent for shelter.

"I'll be all right," he choked. "Go after the Wolves."

She rushed off to lead the men to fight. The camp was a flurry of running men and rearing horses.

They soon discovered that it was only a handful of Saxons. It did not take long to kill them all, but with the element of surprise, the Saxon band had killed a dozen Britons.

Arthur summoned his officers to join him outside his tent. He still held his sword, bloody from battle.

"Our scouts say that there is a settlement a few miles away. The men must have come from it. We'll burn it to the ground," the king said grimly.

"Burn it!" Lancelot gasped. "What about their women and children?"

"We'll let them flee, of course," Arthur told her. "Lancelot, Gawaine, take thirty men each. To your horses!"

Lancelot quickly ordered thirty of her men to join her, and they rode off. But she was reeling inside. She did not want to burn a village. Where would its people go?

They came to the settlement, some twenty huts. The soldiers rode into it, and women and children ran screaming from them.

A British scout who spoke the Saxon language yelled out commands, and the people fled to the forest. Wailing women grabbed up babies and small children. Old women and one ancient man hobbled off. There were no young men.

A soldier began to pursue one of the younger women.

"If any of you touch the women, I'll see that your worthless hands are cut off!" Gawaine shouted. The man returned to his fellows. Lancelot longed to help the women and children, but she could not. Some British soldiers grabbed up sticks and ran to a cook fire to light them. Lancelot's heart pounded.

"Don't burn the huts yet!" she yelled. "There might still be someone in them. I'm going to check." She jumped off her horse and ran to the nearest dwelling. Burning people alive was an unimaginable horror.

"Careful, Lance!" Gawaine called out. "There might be someone in there who'll try to kill you!"

"I'll be careful. Hold back the men!" Lancelot darted into the hut. She rushed through its two tiny rooms, separated only by a blanket strung from the roof, then out again and over to the next house.

"There's no one there. Let's burn the damn village now!" one of the soldiers yelled.

"No man light a fire until Lancelot is done!" Gawaine ordered. Lancelot ran into one hut after another. In one room, she heard muffled sobs. She opened a large chest and found a boy of about three years hidden there. He screamed at the sight of her.

"I won't hurt you," she said, reassuring him as much as possible, though of course he wouldn't know her language. She picked him up. He kicked and struggled, but she carried him out, set him on the ground, and pointed to the forest. "Go!" she cried.

The child stared at her, then at the mob of British soldiers, and ran off as fast as his little legs could carry him.

When she had searched the last hut, she knew she could not postpone the burning any longer.

"Done, Lance?" Gawaine asked. She nodded.

"Go ahead," he ordered the soldiers, and, like fire-bearing demons, they set upon the empty village.

Men shouted with terrible elation when the huts went up in flames, but Lancelot did not share their glee. When the soldiers herded the Saxons' pigs and sheep to feed the British camp, Lancelot thought of Saxon children going hungry. She felt like a brigand.

As they rode off, Gawaine brought his horse near hers and clapped her on the back. "You're a good man, Lance."

She had never felt so far from goodness. The image of the women and children running from her had burned into her brain.

"If it had been your decision, would you have ordered the village to be burned, Gawaine?" she asked.

He paused. "No."

"But you did it because Arthur ordered us." Her voice sounded dead to her.

"Yes, as you did." Gawaine's voice also was flat. "We must trust someone, and he's the best leader we can find."

Lancelot sighed. Gawaine's face sagged as if he had just heard of the death of kin. "Do you understand why we were the ones he asked to do it? Because we'd be less brutal than others would. And that's why we'll have to be the ones to burn other settlements, too, before this war is over."

Lancelot let out a strangled cry. She could barely keep from falling from her horse. "No! God have mercy on us!"

"I'm sorry, Lance." Gawaine reached out, but she rode away.

The only bearable part of the day was returning to camp and seeing that Aglovale's shoulder was bandaged and he was pale but able to walk.

"I heard you were going to burn a village to avenge the attack on us," he said.

"We did." Lancelot could hardly speak the words.

Aglovale sighed and shook his head.

As the war continued, they burned more villages, and Lancelot continued to search every house. Gawaine insisted that she take another warrior with her in case the hut held a Saxon fighter who might attack her. Sometimes she found an old woman or a child. They cringed when she discovered them, shook while she dragged them out of the house, and were wide-eyed with astonishment when she let them go.

Once a hut held a Saxon warrior who lunged at her with his axe. She fought and killed him but was not sorry that another British soldier had come in with her and could have helped her if need be. Other soldiers also searched the dwellings, but not to save stragglers. Instead, they looted anything of value.

At one village, dark-haired people with iron thrall collars darted out of the huts. As the Saxons ran from Arthur's troops, the British slaves ran towards them.

"British soldiers!" they called out. "Heroes! All hail to King Arthur!" Both slave men and women, and also the children, rushed to embrace the soldiers.

Tears came to Lancelot's eyes. She joined with the other soldiers in giving the Saxons' food and farm animals to the people who were slaves no longer. She and her men took the freed slaves back to camp, where blacksmiths cut off their iron collars.

Lancelot choked at the sight of the raw necks that were revealed, but she reckoned that this day was the best of the war.

Not all villages had thralls, and then all the goods went to the army. Each day, Arthur presided over the division of the spoils, and saw to it that every warrior had his share of the gold armrings, finger rings, furs, spears, and the finer household goods. But the king kept a large share of the plunder.

They stopped by a church, and Lancelot gave her share of gold armrings and jeweled finger rings to a young, black-robed priest.

"I cannot keep for myself the jewels from Saxon bodies," she said, shuddering. "But perhaps the Church can put them to good use."

"Blessings on you, Lancelot. You're a rare man," the priest told her. She shook her head. Salvation seemed far away.

One morning, as the troops rode out seeking Saxons, Lancelot spied a mass of British peasants hurrying towards the army. Some had carts, but most were on foot. They were all women, old men, and children.

They screamed, "King Arthur!" "Thank God!" "We're saved!" "Help us!" Tears streamed down their faces as they rushed to the soldiers.

The king rode up to them. "Have the Saxons chased you from your homes, my good people?" he asked.

Many cried out, "Yes. They burned our village."

A woman carrying an infant called out, "Where can we go and be safe?"

"You should move around us, and go in the direction of Camelot. Keep as far west as you can," Arthur told them. "But first, we will give you what food we can, and a share of the Saxons' goods. We will make your country safe so that you can go back."

He then ordered the men charged with keeping his share of the plunder to give the people as many of the Saxons' tools and household goods as they could take with them, and some of the Saxons' gold, too.

The peasants cheered him.

Lancelot rushed to help distribute the goods.

Arthur smiled at her. "That is why I took such a large share of the plunder: to help our people who have lost their homes."

Lancelot's heart surged with pride, and she vowed that she would keep her share for such purposes rather than give it to the churches. Though she knew that most priests would also distribute the goods to the poor, she guessed that not all would do so.

"Send those Saxons to Woden!" cried an old peasant man who hobbled with a crutch. "Hell's too good for them," a woman said. "They killed my son."

"We will bring peace, I promise you," Arthur told them.

Lancelot was proud of his words, for she recalled that Saxon peasants fleeing to their own fighters must be in similar straits. She knew her king truly wanted peace, not the death of every last Saxon.

Pausing for breath in a battle, Lancelot saw that two British soldiers were on a hill, where they were cut off from the rest of the troops by Saxons. It was Gawaine and his brother Gaheris.

"Stay with the men. I'm going to help Gawaine," Lancelot cried to Aglovale. Before he could answer, she swerved and galloped up the hill.

A Saxon-thrown axe whirled by her head, but she paid no heed. When she had reached the summit, Lancelot saw that two Saxons were attacking Gawaine, who was trying to hold them back with his sword. Another Saxon threw himself at Gaheris.

She rushed towards Gawaine, but he motioned for her to save Gaheris first. Stifling a cry of protest, she turned to Gawaine's younger brother, who tumbled on the ground with his attacker.

The Saxon's arm was around Gaheris's throat.

Taking a moment to be sure that she hit the Saxon, not Gawaine's brother, she ran her sword into the Saxon's back.

Choking, Gaheris rolled away from the corpse's embrace.

Lancelot turned to Gawaine. Blood dripped down his face, but still he slashed at the two Saxons.

Lancelot leapt to his side and took on one of the Saxons who assaulted him.

She killed one Saxon, and Gawaine killed the other.

"You're wounded!" Lancelot exclaimed.

Gawaine wiped his face with his arm, staining his already blood-encrusted chain mail. "It's not so bad. It'll just be another scar." He gave her a broad grin. "Thanks for helping my brother and me." He turned to Gaheris, who sat on the ground.

Riding down the hill to rejoin the main battle, Lancelot realized that forcing herself to save Gaheris first was one of the most difficult things she had ever done.

One night after a battle, Arthur and Lancelot walked about, giving words of encouragement to the wounded. Most of the men with terrible cuts or shattered limbs seemed reassured to have their king clasp their hands and say that their sacrifice had no doubt saved many lives.

Arthur especially praised those who would not last the night, and Lancelot's eyes filled with tears. She, too, would have been grateful for the king's words if she had been dying.

They could hear harpers playing. After a battle, Arthur had them play songs that would lift the men's spirits, or at least help them to feel poignancy rather than bitterness.

She went off to speak with her own men — the ones who were uninjured for the moment — and tried to let the music blot out her memories of the day. Later, Gawaine stopped by her tent as he made the rounds of the camp.

He looked as grimy as she was with the dirt of the battle, and just as exhausted, but he also had to see to his men before thinking of sleep.

"How many men died today?" she asked.

"Twenty-two, including a cousin of mine from Lothian."

His voice was weary.

"I'm sorry." She patted him on the shoulder. "And my youngest fighter, that boy from Dyfed. God have mercy on us!" she exclaimed. "Filthy, hell-spawn war!"

"Filthy, hell-spawn war," Gawaine agreed, taking a drink from his flask. "It's northern liquor. Have some." He extended it to her.

She shook her head. "No, thanks. Drinking that is like being hit by a throwing axe. I'll get some ale instead."

Gawaine laughed and poured some more liquor down his throat. "Here's to another rotten day tomorrow," he said. "I hope I see you again tomorrow night."

"You will," Lancelot said, though she knew there was a chance that one or the other of them, or both, might not live through the next day. Watching him walk away, she wondered whether she was seeing him for the last time – a thought she now had whenever she parted from anyone she liked.

"A messenger with the Pendragon banner is riding up the hill," a guard told Guinevere and Cai as they sat worrying about how to send enough supplies to Arthur. They had set men to building more wagons because the Saxons had burned many that had been sent to the king's troops.

They both leapt up, almost colliding, but Cai let Guinevere precede him as they hurried to the courtyard.

Guinevere's heart pounded as it always did when Arthur's messengers came. Lancelot, Lancelot, she thought. May Lancelot be safe. And Arthur. And Bors. And all the Britons.

She met Lionors in the courtyard and they clasped hands.

Lionors, as usual, was followed by a couple of her children.

The messenger rode through the gates and called out, "The king is safe, never fear," to all the people of high stations and low who were waiting to hear him.

The small crowd cheered. Guards clapped each other on the back. The messenger handed a packet to Guinevere. She opened it in front of everyone, and hoped the rest of the news was as good as his announcement. She first looked for names.

"Gryffd, Aglovale, and Sangremore have been injured, but the king mentions no other names," she told the crowd. She heard a collective sigh of relief. She thanked God that Lancelot's name was not there.

Claudia, Aglovale's sister-in-law, groaned. Guinevere gave her a gentle smile. "The king says the wounds are not grievous," Guinevere told her.

"The king writes that our troops are making progress," Guinevere told the assembled people of Camelot, then turned to go back with Cai to his office to discuss the rest of the letter, which was not as full of optimism. Supplies were still not as plentiful as they should be, and Arthur had to requisition more from the peasants than he had wanted to do. The Saxons were killing too many horses, and farm animals were not good substitutes.

Guinevere sighed for the horses, and the men who had lost them. More could be sent from Camelot, but the court needed to keep a good number in case a retreat was necessary. Arthur assured her that the Saxons were far from Camelot, but she knew that some could have sneaked past his army.

"Are you sure we have enough men to defend Camelot?" she asked Cai.

"I believe so." Despite those words he gave her a look that said of course no one could be certain.

"Arthur left the finest archers here."

Guinevere sighed. "He could use them in combat."

"So he could. But they are our best defense."

"If they stood on the walls, the Saxons would kill them."

"At least we have a spring here, and enough food for a long siege." Cai gave her a reassuring smile.

"Ah, Cai, when there is no sarcasm in your speech everyone knows that you are anxious. Try to pepper your remarks as usual," Guinevere told him.

He scowled enough to make all the serving people cower, if they had believed that he was angry. "Very good. I shall chide everyone so much that they long to hang me from the battlements."

"Not quite that much." Guinevere tried to smile.

18 THE OTHERWORLD

One early summer day the Britons passed through a village, burned by the Saxons, where women's bodies were scattered, left naked or with their skirts up, some with parts cut off. The bodies of dead children also littered the ground.

Lancelot nearly fell from her horse at the sight.

Many of the soldiers cursed and some wept. Arthur ordered that they bury the women and children. Men rushed to dig the graves, and Arthur himself dug some shovels of earth. Lancelot insisted on being one of those who gently lifted the bodies into the graves. She found it difficult not to throw herself in after them. The stench from the bodies nearly overpowered her. A priest who traveled with the army said a Mass for the dead, and a thousand voices joined in the prayers.

A few days later they came to a Saxon village, and saw a similar sight. The village had been burned, the women had been raped and murdered, and the yellow-haired children, too.

"This is monstrous," Arthur called out in a thunderous voice to the assembled troops. "I know that some of you must have done this. If anyone knows who it was, he should tell me so the killers can be punished. You are only supposed to burn down the villages to drive away the Saxons, not kill the women and children. You must let them flee. Any man who kills a woman or child will be executed."

Arthur paused. "We must also bury these bodies," he said. "The Saxon custom is to burn their dead, but there is already enough smell of death here." But this time there were not so many volunteer gravediggers. Gawaine and Peredur were the first to call for shovels and begin the work, and then some of the men followed, as did all of the senior warriors.

Lancelot again lifted the bodies into the grave. Only a few others shared this task. She stooped to lift them, and even the smallest children seemed a weight heavier than she could bear. Her knees almost gave way.

The priest said a brief prayer for the pagan souls, and a few voices joined in. She felt even more like casting herself into the graves this time than she had before, when Saxons had been the killers.

She was not surprised that no one spoke up to tell the king who had murdered the women and children.

Riding away from the scene of the massacre, Gawaine drank from his flask. The northern liquor was not enough to settle his stomach. It had been difficult to keep from vomiting or weeping, neither of which he wanted to do in front of his men.

Agravaine rode up to him. Gawaine faced him reluctantly. It was not a time when he wanted to listen to his brother's usual complaints. "Those Saxon bitches deserved what they got," Agravaine said. He spat and his eyes narrowed.

"They were raising their little bastards to kill us someday. Why not kill them now?"

Gawaine felt as if he had been dealt a mighty blow, mightier than Agravaine had ever been able to strike in fighting practice. It was a moment before he was able to speak. "You countenance slaughtering the women and children? You saw how terribly they were mutilated."

"Why not? Only a fool is tender with his enemies." Agravaine snorted contemptuously.

"Are you calling our High King a fool?" Gawaine was so angry that he couldn't see the men riding ahead of him or the fields on the side of the road.

"Oh no, he's clever." Agravaine chuckled. "It adds to his power to be called Arthur the Just. Give me a swig of whatever you're drinking." He reached for Gawaine's flask.

For an instant, Gawaine wondered whether Agravaine had taken part in the massacre, but then he remembered that his brother had not left the camp in days, until the troops rode out that morning. "Do you know who the killers were?" Gawaine kept his voice steady, though his veins were almost bursting with rage.

"Nah, probably men from one of the lesser kings' warbands. Shit, I'm tired of riding. I wonder how long it'll be before Arthur decides to camp for the night. How about that drink?" Agravaine's arm was still extended.

"You'll have a chance to rest." Gawaine did not keep the bitterness out of his voice. He poured the contents of his flask on the ground, and Agravaine stared with disbelief. "As of this moment, you are no longer my second in command. I'm going to appoint Bors to the post."

"What!" Agravaine yelled. "You can't do that! You're my brother."

"Unfortunately, I can't expel you from that position." Gawaine trembled with anger, but he did not shout.

"Because of what I said about those Saxon bitches and whelps? I didn't kill them." Agravaine clenched his fists, as if he might try to strike Gawaine.

"You are unfit to command. I say no more. If you have any sense, you won't complain to anyone." Gawaine rode off ahead of him. All Gawaine wanted was for night to come, so that he could be alone in his tent and drink enough to weep.

Would his own brother be willing to carve women's bodies? Gawaine remembered when they were boys together, throwing food at each other at supper – only when their father was not present — and dunking each other in lochs. But as Gawaine had grown to abhor his father, Agravaine had become more like Lot with every passing year. Was there some curse in the blood that had escaped him but come out in Agravaine?

And how good was he himself? Gawaine wondered. It had occurred to him that he could have saved at least one of those girls in the town his father had taken years before. Not the one his father had, but he might have been able to command some of the warriors who held the girls down in the streets. All he had thought of at the time was getting away, but now he reckoned that if Lancelot had been there, Lancelot would have thought to save a girl or two. Lancelot – now there would be a brother worth having. If only his brothers were more like him. But how could any son raised by Lot be like Lancelot?

Could he blame Lot for everything? Gawaine was the oldest in the family. Could he have led Agravaine better?

There was little he could do to change Agravaine now. He pulled his horse beside Bors's so he could ask the pious warrior to accept a new charge.

The sun was shining, but it seemed to be a merciless light glaring on a cruel world.

Lancelot still rode with the others and fought, but she spoke only when she had to, replying to questions. The sight of the bodies of the Saxon women and children was always before her. Every field was filled with them, every standing tree seemed to hold a body.

The food she ate was shared with the men who had murdered them. She no longer wanted to eat it.

For all she knew, she might be looking into the faces of the men who had taken part in the massacre. The men whose lives she saved might have been among the murderers, but she continued saving any soldier she could rescue.

The men Lancelot had counted as friends, each in his own way, seemed to be trying to reach her, but she did not want to be reached.

Bors often rode beside Lancelot and prayed aloud, but even prayers did not touch her soul. She felt that she was just a thing for killing, no longer within the reach of God.

Aglovale would come up to her and speak of homely things, such as repairing villas and teaching children how to talk and walk. "Percy could tell stories before he was three years old. When I began a story, he would finish it for me. It's amazing how children think. You should spend some time around them."

These things seemed to her to come from some world too far away to imagine. She saw only little dead children, not live ones.

Arthur spoke about his vision for a safe, united Britain, as he always had, but this dream seemed a mockery in the midst of the great blood-letting.

Gawaine also rode with Lancelot and described the mountains in Lothian, what animals lived there and what flowers grew there, and what the Orkney Isles were like with their thousands of sea birds perching on cliffs and flying up in great clouds. This talk irritated Lancelot because it almost made her want to live.

"Sea birds are all black and white, or gray or brown. They don't have much color. Why would that be?" Gawaine asked, and Lancelot was almost interested enough to try to think of an answer, which annoyed her.

Gawaine or Aglovale would sit next to her and insist that she eat. She could no longer dream about Camelot. It was too far away now. She believed that she should join the other ghosts, and she tried to. She took every impossible risk she could, but still she could not die.

She saw a British foot soldier cut off from the troops, with Saxons surrounding him. She drove her horse wildly among the Saxons, slashed with her sword, and let the soldier climb up behind her. Saxons spears and throwing axes spun past her, but she rode off, untouched.

The soldier, who was young, mumbled, "Thanks, thanks," as she left him with his companions, but she felt thankful only for his sake, not for her own.

Guinevere sat in Cai's office studying the accounts and worrying whether the taxes were enough to keep the army well supplied. Did Arthur have enough horses yet? Enough weapons? Enough food?

Sunlight streamed in the window, but it brought her no pleasure. There were roses in the garden, but they did not matter.

Cai appeared in the doorway.

"Lady Guinevere, one of the harpers from the king's troops is here with news of the battles."

Dropping the wax tablet she had been holding, Guinevere rose from the table. Her heart beat faster.

The man who stood before her was no longer young, and his tunic was worn and tattered. There was no great sorrow in his face, so perhaps the news was not bad.

"Please speak," she said.

"The battles go well." The man's voice was sonorous, as a harper's should be. "The High King charges, ever in the lead, and the dragon banner stirs the men to victory. The Saxons have no such great leader. We cut them down like summer wheat. Their numbers dwindle."

"No doubt our numbers are diminishing also," Guinevere said, annoyed by his rhetorical flourishes.

"Brave men give their lives every day." The harper nodded, moving his hand as if he stroked a harp.

Guinevere shuddered. "What of Lancelot?" She could not hold back the question any longer.

A smile lit the harper's solemn face. "He is the greatest of heroes. Lancelot goes ever in the thick of battle. Never have I seen one warrior save so many of his companions. Whenever the Saxons have surrounded a man, there is Lancelot, standing between him and death."

Guinevere swayed and blackness spread over her. She fell into a chair, unable to speak. "Enough news. The queen is not used to the details of battle," Cai said, showing the harper out.

What would life be like if there were no Lancelot? Hope would be gone. Guinevere prayed even more fervently than before.

One dreary, drizzling morning, not long after defeating a Saxon ambush, the British warriors were resting. Lancelot and Gawaine were checking the area to be sure that no Saxons yet lingered.

A detail was off burying the British dead, and the physicians were busy with the wounded, some of whom waited patiently while others screamed.

When the war had begun, Lancelot had been horrified that the British fighting men finished off the badly wounded Saxons lying on the battlefields, but now it mattered no more than anything else. She did not kill the Saxon wounded herself, but she felt no great agonies when the British foot soldiers did, as was their assigned task. Nor did the rain that dripped over her bother her overmuch; she was too numb.

She and Gawaine passed a bush, and its branches moved, hinting that something large was behind it. The area had been so hunted out by both armies that there was little chance that it was a deer or a boar.

Lancelot slashed into the bush with her sword. She felt the familiar impact as her sword cut into a human body. There was a quick exclamation, and a collapse. She parted the branches, and the body of a girl of about thirteen years, black-haired and therefore British, fell at their feet. She had apparently hidden from the soldiers.

The warriors both stood frozen, staring at the girl's body with a gaping wound in her side. Then Lancelot turned her bloody sword to her own chest.

"No!" Grabbing her arm, Gawaine held her back.

The sword was evil. She must hide it. Lancelot thrust it back into its sheath. She felt that, in killing the girl, she had somehow killed herself. Then Arthur strode across the muddy field to them and saw the girl lying at their feet.

The king began to yell, "What have you done? This is a girl, a British girl!"

Gawaine answered him.

"We saw branches moving. It looked like another ambush, so I slashed out. It was only afterwards that we saw it was a girl. It's horrible. Forgive me."

Lancelot remained frozen and silent. Her voice had gone away. She was dead, so how could she speak?

Arthur shouted at Gawaine. "You fool, why in hell didn't you find out who you were striking? What will her family think? Her whole village will hate the king's army forever."

Lancelot wandered off in a daze. The words had no meaning.

"I regret her death greatly," Gawaine said. Beyond Arthur's angry face, he saw Bedwyr, Peredur, and Bors hurrying over to them. Bedwyr's left arm was bandaged – the physicians saw to the senior fighters' injuries first – but the others had only minor cuts.

"I killed a girl accidentally," Gawaine told his comrades. His stomach churned at the sight of the pathetic body. "I thought it was another Saxon ambush. It's awful."

"It's worse than that," the king yelled, trembling with rage. "I said that I would execute any man who killed a woman, but of course I can't do that to you, so it will look as if my orders are meaningless."

"But it was an accident," Bedwyr said, trying to calm him. "Surely you'd treat an accident differently than a murder."

Arthur's anger was not appeased. "It will look as if I favor my cousin." He glared at Gawaine.

"Therefore, you will have to wear her head around your neck for a day to show your repentance."

Gawaine shuddered, but said nothing.

He almost retched at the thought of wearing the girl's head. And who would have the gruesome task of cutting it off? He knew men who cut off their enemies' heads, but he had never done so.

How could Arthur think of such a hideous punishment? The king stalked off.

"Don't worry, Gawaine," Bedwyr said. "It was Lancelot who did this, wasn't it? You're protecting him because he's half out of his mind."

Gawaine nodded, relieved that at least some of his friends would realize that he hadn't killed the girl. "Lancelot turned his sword on himself. I fear that he'll kill himself."

"We'll talk Arthur out of this punishment," Bedwyr promised.

"Don't tell him it was Lancelot," Gawaine begged. When had he ever begged for anything? He couldn't remember such a time. "Lancelot couldn't bear anyone knowing that he'd killed a girl. He probably only half realizes it himself, and this horrible punishment would drive him completely mad. I can hardly bear the thought of it myself."

"It's disgusting. We should bury the girl at once and pray for her soul," Bors said, making the sign of the cross over her body.

"No, we should find her family," said Peredur, bending to close the girl's eyes.

"Arthur never would have given Lancelot this punishment, so he shouldn't give it to you," Bedwyr added.

"Of course we won't say that it was Lancelot," Peredur reassured Gawaine. "Everyone thinks of Lancelot as the best of us, so it would reflect on us all if people knew he had killed a girl, even by accident."

So Bedwyr, Bors, and Peredur went with Gawaine to the king's tent and asked for a word with him. Gawaine doubted that their words would move the king.

Arthur's voice and face were bitter, but after he had asked about Bedwyr's wound, he grumblingly agreed to listen to them.

"You shouldn't give Gawaine such a horrible punishment," said Bedwyr, whom they had chosen to speak first because the king could hardly fail to be sympathetic to a man who had just been wounded in his service. Bedwyr's face was drawn and pale from pain and loss of blood. "It will undermine his ability to command the men, and it will demoralize the troops to see one of their leaders treated so."

"Rather, you mustn't do this because it badly uses the poor girl's body," Peredur argued. "As the father of a girl not much older, I would be as angry at you for doing that as I would be at the one who killed her. We must find her family and return her body to them as soon as possible."

Bors nodded. "It is an ungodly way to treat her earthly remains. Besides, you should not prescribe strange and horrible punishments, because men may have strange and horrible reactions to them. It might give some men the idea of cutting off women's heads."

"Surely not," Arthur said, grimacing. "But I shall listen to what you advise. Peredur, go and find the girl's family and return her body. I'll give Gawaine a different punishment."

Arthur turned to Gawaine and spoke coldly to him. "Your companions think the punishment is not fitting, so it is lifted. Therefore, I shall only charge you with protecting and defending women for the rest of your life. Swear that you will do so."

"I swear that I will," Gawaine agreed, anxious to leave and look for Lancelot.

Lancelot had gone to the bank of the river near the camp and was about to throw herself into it. The churning waters were muddy brown from rains, and it seemed a fitting place after what she had done. But as she climbed down the bank, a woman called out to her, "Lancelot!"

She looked up and saw one of the camp followers. The young, dark-haired woman, who had been one of the ones Lancelot had spoken with months earlier, might have been pretty except that her face was bruised, and a look of weariness seemed to be frozen into her features.

She rushed up to Lancelot and grabbed her arm. "Were you goin' to throw yourself into the river?"

Lancelot looked at her and said nothing.

"Life's hard, ain't it?" the young woman said. "I was goin' to do the same myself, but then I saw you. You shouldn't do it, you got everything to live for. Everybody thinks you're the greatest and kindest warrior in the world."

"They're wrong," Lancelot groaned. "But what about you, my lady? I'm afraid I don't know your name." These were the first words, other than those necessary, that she had said in weeks. She did not see the Saxon ghosts, but only the camp follower.

"I'm Maire. I can't stand it anymore. I just have to get away." She looked beyond Lancelot at the river. "I guess you'd be too worn out yourself to rescue me now."

"No, you are rescuing me." Lancelot turned away from the river and looked into Maire's eyes. The pain she saw there was more compelling than the swirling water. She shuddered at the thought of Maire's body tossed by the currents. "If you want to get away from here, of course I'll take you." She saw that even if she had done something unchangeable and unpardonable, she still might be able to help someone else.

Lancelot was, like all the soldiers, under orders to stay in the camp, but she got her horse, helped Maire up behind her, and rode west, away from the Saxons.

"I don't know what I'll do," Maire said, "but thanks for gettin' me out of there."

Uncertain where she might find a place for Maire, Lancelot rode off across fields and into a forest. Rain drizzled on them.

As they passed through an oak grove, an old nun on a rotund horse that was gray as the sky crossed their path.

"May I be of help?" she asked, nodding a friendly greeting. Lines made a web of her face, and her smile was almost warm enough to dry their clothing.

"I need a place to stay and honest work," Maire blurted out.

The nun nodded with satisfaction. "What good fortune for me!" she exclaimed. "Our convent needs a housekeeper, and I have gone looking for one. Would you be willing to do that work? I must confess that not all nuns are tidy. I'm dreadfully messy myself."

Maire's eyes widened. Her hair was tangled and wet, her face was bruised, and her gaudy gown pretty clearly indicated what her work had been. "You'd let me do that?"

"Of course, my dear, if you don't mind the quiet. The Convent of the Holy Mother is deep in the forest, a good many miles from here. Will you come?"

"Yes, thanks," Maire said quickly, as if the old nun might disappear into the trees as suddenly as she had appeared before them.

"What a blessing it is that you will help us. Then come down from Lancelot's horse and join me on mine. She's an old mare, but she's sturdy enough to carry us both."

The whole encounter so astounded Lancelot that she only fleetingly wondered how the nun knew her name. She helped Maire descend from her horse and climb up behind the old woman.

The nun then looked into Lancelot's face. "And what can I do to help you?" she asked.

"Nothing," Lancelot said, almost too ashamed to return her look. "I am beyond help. Today I struck out blindly at a bush, for I imagined that a Saxon fighter was behind it, and I killed a girl. Nothing that I can do will ever make up for that."

The wrinkled hand reached out and touched Lancelot's cheek. "No one is beyond help," the old nun said. "It is true that nothing can bring her back, but you still have a life that you must live. When we have done wrong, we must learn from it. Having done wrong does not take from us the task of living and caring for others, and your actions have shown that you know that. You must live as well as you can. You have seen that carelessness can be cruel. Do not be careless again, but caring."

Tears mixed with rain touched the nun's hand, which lingered on Lancelot's cheek and then left it.

"Thank you, Holy Lady, I shall do as you tell me," Lancelot replied.

The old woman drew an ornament made of black feathers from her cloak. "Carry these raven feathers with you always," she said. Willing to do whatever the nun said, Lancelot nodded and put the feathers in the bag she wore around her neck. How strange that both this nun and old Creiddyled had given her such tokens.

"I am Mother Ninian. You are welcome to visit our convent at any time," the nun told Lancelot.

"Thank you," Lancelot said, thinking she would never dare to visit a holy place again.

"Don't despair," Ninian said, wagging her finger at Lancelot. "For you are Lancelot, the one all men and women love most."

Lancelot gaped at the nun, who must be wrong. Surely no one loved her.

Then the old nun and Maire parted from Lancelot, and wished her Godspeed.

Gawaine walked up to Peredur and his brother Aglovale while they were tying the girl's body on a horse. Gawaine thought that if he had truly been Christian, he would have made a sign of the cross, but instead he bowed his head.

"Aglovale will go with me to look for the girl's family." Peredur's voice was solemn; the wrinkles in his brow stood out.

"I hope you find them," Gawaine said.

Aglovale, who had been adjusting the cord that bound the body, whirled around to face him. "I'll never speak to you again unless I must." He clenched his fists.

Gawaine groaned.

"Lancelot is the one who killed her. I am sworn not to tell of it, and you must not." Peredur spoke quietly.

Aglovale's eyes widened. He steadied himself.

"If Lancelot could do a thing like this, any of us could. When we've defeated the Saxons, I'll never fight again," he vowed.

"I hope you don't have to," Gawaine told him. He wondered how many people would despise him for this act that he had not committed.

When Lancelot rode back to the camp long after dark, several soldiers rushed up to her and she found that everyone had been searching for her.

She discovered that she no longer felt like speaking when she was back with the warriors.

Gawaine pulled her aside and said, "You terrified me. I thought you had jumped into the river. Don't go off without telling anyone," he lectured, as if to a child.

"I was going to jump in the river," she said, her voice expressionless.

"Gods, don't do such a thing," he exclaimed, putting an arm out as if Lancelot were trying to jump at that moment.

"A camp follower had gone there to do the same, and I took her away. If she had been the one to drown herself, would any of you have cared?" she asked bitterly.

Gawaine looked taken aback. "Why, of course I would have rescued her from the river," he said.

"But would you have saved her from what drove her there?" Lancelot demanded.

Gawaine said only, "If you're well enough to preach to me, you're healing." He did not mention anything concerning the girl's death, but Lancelot thought of it, and said, "I am not worthy to preach to anyone."

She sought out Father Donatus, who traveled with the troops, and found him in a tent where physicians tended the wounded. Not disturbing him, she stood near until he turned to leave the tent.

"Please shrive me, Father," she asked.

"Of course. Come to my tent."

They walked to the priest's tent, in which a crucifix hung.

Lancelot slumped down on her knees. "Father, I have killed too many men. And today I did worse than that. I saw a bush moving and struck out, killing a girl who had hidden behind it. I am just a brute. I've killed an innocent girl."

The priest's voice was soothing. "Don't grieve so. Killing in a just war is no sin, and an accidental killing in these circumstances is but a venial sin at worst."

Lancelot stared at him. "Surely it is not. I could have stopped myself. I didn't have to strike before I saw who was there."

"Next time you will not. You must not be so scrupulous," he tried to reassure her. "Think of all the lives you have saved and all the British people who will be safe because you fought the Saxons."

He blessed her, but she went off feeling no better than she had before. She did not believe that her sin was truly absolved.

She withdrew into silence again.

They fought more Saxons the next day, and Lancelot returned to numbness. She no longer saw the Saxon ghosts, but the pale form of the British girl. She took more impossible risks than ever. The more men she saved, the more the warriors praised her and the more she felt ashamed. She wondered whether she was under some terrible spell that would not let her die.

After a time, she began to notice the calls of birds again, and she knew that they were not ghosts from another world, but were calling her to this one. She began to come back to it. At first, the girl listened to the birds with her, then she faded, to return in dreams. The wrens especially seemed to pour out their finest songs for Lancelot.

One day Lancelot found that she was talking again, giving more than the briefest possible replies.

A near naked berserker appeared suddenly from behind a bush, and his spear slashed into Arrow. Lancelot was down, still holding her spear, and killed the attacker. Then she turned to her horse. Seeing that he had no chance, Lancelot stroked his forehead, then dispatched him with her sword. Tears burned her eyes. Now she truly had nothing left to love. She might as well die. Loving Guinevere was only a dream that could never be fulfilled. Lancelot slipped in the mud and fell. Then a charge of her own companions rushed around her, and one horse's hoof landed by her left hand, crushing her little finger and the finger beside it.

Her hand ablaze with pain, Lancelot stayed down. Perhaps more horses would trample her. Let them. She was not needed; the battle was already won. It was as good a time as any to die. Let her last sound be the beating of hooves all around her.

"Stop, fools, it's Lancelot!" cried a voice, and strong arms were there to lift her.

Quickly, Lancelot moved to get herself up. She looked into Gawaine's face. She could see from the look of sorrow in his eyes that he knew she had tried to die.

Ashamed, she turned away. "Many thanks," Lancelot said, though she did not feel thankful.

"Our men are driving off the Saxons. You must go to the tents for the wounded," Gawaine told her.

"It's good that it's my shield hand rather than my sword hand," Lancelot replied, trying to sound as if she were too strong to suffer.

"Take this, you'll need it," he said, handing her his flask of northern liquor.

She reluctantly went to the surgeon, who said that what was left of her crushed fingers would have to be removed. She drank some northern liquor and tried not to scream when the surgeon's knife cut her. She fainted from the pain, but woke again, sorry to be alive. Her hand seemed to be on fire.

At least it was an injury that did not reveal that she was a woman, Lancelot thought. She still had enough fingers left to be able to hold her shield with her left hand. How mad it was that she had escaped every Saxon axe and spear, only to be injured by a British horse.

A camp follower bandaged Lancelot's hand. The women did much work helping the surgeons in the tents for the wounded. How strange, then, that men did not treat them with respect, Lancelot thought.

The surgeon told Lancelot to stay in the tents for the wounded, but she refused. How could she piss unless she got back to the privacy of her own tent?

Gawaine was waiting when she staggered out of the surgeon's tent. "Even you are not invulnerable, Lance," he said, sounding as if he regretted the fact. He looked at her bandaged hand.

"It's nothing," she insisted, trying to keep her voice and her feet steady, though she feared there were still tears in her eyes from the pain. "The storytellers have always claimed that I could fight with only one arm. I'm fortunate. I could have lost my entire left hand, as Bedwyr has through wound-sickness."

Her voice faltered and she permitted Gawaine to help her back to her tent.

"You still could get wound fever," he warned her.

"Losing Arrow was worse than losing my fingers. It was like losing kin," she told him. Her voice was breaking. She could not hold back her tears.

"I know. It grieved me greatly when my horse was killed last month," Gawaine said, pressing her shoulders.

He left her at her tent, and she collapsed onto her wolfskin. She thought the pain would keep her awake, but she soon fell asleep.

In the middle of the night, the pain woke her. To her astonishment, Gawaine was sitting near her.

"What are you doing here?" Lancelot asked.

"I'm worried about you, of course. So are all your friends." He extended his flask. "You might want some more liquor."

She accepted the drink. Anything that might distract her was appealing. But she needed to be alone, and drinking only made that more urgent. "Many thanks, but please leave now."

"Very well."

Gawaine left and she was able to relieve herself.

She slept, and when she woke again, Aglovale was there, sitting where Gawaine had been before.

"Am I a baby that I need watching?" Lancelot grumbled, for she again felt a great need to relieve herself.

"At least you don't seem to have a fever," Aglovale said, but he left as she wanted. When she woke to the sounds of the soldiers clattering about in the morning, Bors was in her tent watching her and praying.

Her friends' concern brought tears to her eyes, though she felt she was not worth caring about. She passed several days in like manner. But the wound did not fester.

One morning, Arthur called Lancelot to his tent. There was a low mist covering the first few feet of ground of the tent city, giving the illusion of tents in clouds, which made her think of a city of ghosts. A pretty camp follower was leaving the king's tent.

The woman smiled at Lancelot in a friendly manner, not leering. Ever since she had helped Maire get away, the camp followers had smiled at her. Of course she had told them what had become of Maire, so they would not think it was something worse.

As Lancelot walked into the tent, she noticed the meadow flowers that had been crushed, perhaps by the royal feet. Stepping around a half-crushed cornflower, she tried to smile so Arthur wouldn't guess that she was in pain.

The king was solemn. He gestured for her to sit on the pile of rugs next to his own pile. "Lance," he said, speaking in a quiet tone of command, "Gawaine has told me that you have been trying to get yourself killed."

Lancelot gasped. She wanted to avert her face, but she knew that as his sworn warrior she had no right to look away.

"That kind of behavior must stop." Arthur of course did not smile, but neither did he frown. "You are one of my finest, and I can't afford to lose you. I think one more decisive battle will drive away the invaders, but I will need you by my side for many years to come. Either you will swear that you won't try to get killed, or I shall order you to return to Camelot to lead its defenses in case of attack."

Lancelot could hardly breathe.

She felt as if she were drowning and floundered for a response. "But there are no Saxons near Camelot."

"That's true." Arthur twisted his ring. "But it would be an honorable assignment. No one but Gawaine and I would know the reason for it. I would never let you be dishonored. It is not dishonorable to be grieved by war, but you must not let the grief overwhelm you." He gestured to a wine jar. "Have some wine. You look as if you need it."

Lancelot shook. She couldn't bring herself to reach for the wine. Being forced to return to Camelot while others fought sounded as terrible to her as being put in a dungeon.

Arthur poured some wine into a cup and handed it to her, a move she had never seen the king make with anyone else.

Hand trembling, she brought the cup to her mouth and drank. "My Lord Arthur," she managed to say, "We all must risk our lives if we fight."

The king nodded. "Of course. I do not charge you to be anything other than brave, but you must not deliberately try to be killed. Will you swear to do that?"

"I swear I will try to preserve myself in battle," Lancelot stammered. That was the only choice she could make.

"Very good. Go now and rest, for we must prepare for a great battle at Badon Hill." He touched her hand briefly.

Lancelot walked back out into the mist. There was no escape from her life as a killer. She wanted to cover her face with shame because the king knew she longed to die, but she had gathered from Arthur's manner that Gawaine had not told him the reason for it. If Arthur had known she had killed the girl, surely he would not have been so gracious.

The fog had not lifted, so the army stayed where it was. Gawaine found his brother Gaheris sharpening his sword in front of the tent he shared with Agravaine. Gawaine thanked the gods he had his own tent, not shared with them.

Gaheris was a fairly tall man, but shorter than Gawaine and Agravaine, and his beard was skimpier than theirs. Gaheris never had the full measure of anything, including wits, Gawaine thought. He was not simple-minded, but neither was he clever.

Gawaine squatted on the ground beside his younger brother. The smell of roasting sheep that soldiers had procured – never mind how – permeated the camp.

"We'll have a good supper tonight."

"And none too soon," Gaheris grumbled, scraping his sword against a whetstone. The noise was not pretty, but Gawaine was used to it.

"I'd like to speak with you. It might be best if you did not follow Agravaine too closely." Gaheris had tagged after Agravaine as a child, and had never changed the habit.

Gaheris scraped the sword with a screech. His eyes, which were a duller blue than Gawaine's, glared at his oldest brother.

"You do not treat Agravaine like a brother," he charged. "I like it not that you took away his position and gave it to that fool Christian, Bors. You may not have feeling for your kin, but I do."

Gawaine rolled back on his heels. He had known that Gaheris would not be pleased at his words, but he had not expected this accusation. "You don't know the reason that I demoted Agravaine," he said, trying to keep his voice calm.

Gaheris gave a sharp, unpleasant laugh. "Of course I do. It was because of what he said about those Saxon bitches."

Gawaine reeled. His head spun as if he were falling. "He told you he said there was nothing wrong with the massacre?"

"He told me that was why you took his position away. Not a good reason, if you ask me, not that you ever do. We're supposed to be killing Saxons." Scowling, Gaheris ran his finger along his sword.

Gawaine's stomach heaved. "Not women and children."

"Why not? The Saxon whores are just raising their brats to kill us when they're grown, as Agravaine says." Gaheris's face was now as unpleasant as Agravaine's ever had been. Like their father's.

Gawaine shook with rage. "You saw the bodies, you saw how they had been raped and sliced. If we kill women and children, we're no better than the Saxons."

"They slaughtered our women and children first. Maybe we taught them a lesson, and they'll think before they do it again." Gaheris made gruesome gestures with his sword.

"No doubt that's what Agravaine told you." Gawaine could not keep the fury out of his voice.

"It is. Don't get angry at me. I didn't kill them. And don't pretend that you're so much better than the men who did. You killed a girl, too. A British girl, and that's worse, to my way of thinking." Gaheris used an insolent tone that he had never tried with Gawaine before. "Wouldn't she give you what you wanted?"

Gawaine almost fell over. He put a hand on the ground to steady himself. "Gods! You can't believe I'd do such a thing! She died by accident, and I greatly regret it." He had never imagined that his own brother could charge him with such brutality.

Gaheris snorted. "No, you're too good. You like to hang about with pious fools like Lancelot and Bors, rather than your own brothers. But the story you gave out about the girl isn't true. I can tell that you're lying. You look too nervous when you talk about it."

Gawaine wanted to strike out. Instead, he spoke as calmly as possible, trying to keep his voice from shaking. "I swear by the blood of our clan that I never touched the girl, nor tried to. Her death was accidental. There are details that I can't tell you, but they are not as bad as you imagine." The price for protecting Lancelot was higher than he had reckoned, but he couldn't tell Gaheris that Lancelot had killed the girl, for Gaheris would tell everyone. Lancelot might kill himself from shame and grief.

"For certain you're as pure as Bors," Gaheris mocked him. "That Bors has never had any woman but his wife. And you prefer such a weakling to Agravaine. And that Lancelot never even looks at a woman. Why would you want a friend like that?"

Gawaine grabbed him by the shoulders and shook him. Gaheris dropped the sword. If this had been any man other than Gaheris, Gawaine would have struck him.

"How much of a fool are you? How dare you criticize a man who saved your life! When you've saved as many lives as Lancelot has, you can perhaps criticize him. Lancelot and Bors are good men, both kind and brave. What difference does it make what god they pray to or how many women they've had?"

He let Gaheris pull out of his grasp.

"Of course I'm a fool," Gaheris said bitterly. "Everyone is better than your brothers. It's just as I've said – you care little about us."

"If I cared little about you, I'd have beaten you 'til you had to go to the tents for the wounded." Although Gawaine was more sad than angry, he shook his fist at Gaheris because the angry gesture would be more likely to gain his brother's respect than clasping his hand. "That's what our father would have done if you'd ever dared to be half this insolent to him. I am the head of this family and you should listen to me."

"Lot wouldn't have demoted Agravaine. He'd have agreed with him," Gaheris objected, but his voice was calmer.

Gawaine shuddered. "Indeed. But we are fighting for Arthur, not for Lot. Thank the gods."

320

An orderly walked up to them and said nervously, "Pardon, Lord Gawaine, but the king is asking for you."

"Then I'll come." Gawaine nodded to his brother, who sullenly returned the gesture, and walked away. Did he prefer Lancelot and Bors to his brothers? By all the gods, he did! Lancelot was worth facing his brother's insults. But Great Daghda's Cauldron, it was hard to lose authority with his brother because of taking the blame for Lancelot.

Gawaine tried to control his face so the king would not be able to see his misery. He hoped that his little brother Gareth, who was being raised just by Morgause, without Lot's influence, would become a better man than Agravaine or Gaheris. Perhaps better than Gawaine himself.

But what if he had sons? Could he guide them to be good men, or was there a curse in his blood and might they be like Agravaine and Gaheris? Or Lot?

For Lancelot, Badon was just another battle. Blood, blood, blood. Blood, death. Blood, death. But not her own. Almost numb, she lifted her sword again, and again, and yet again. She moved like one in a dream, a nightmare that would never end.

When no more Saxons attacked her, she looked about and realized that they had fled – those of them who lived, that is. Although the British bodies on the ground were many, the Saxon dead far outnumbered them.

Had her friends survived? Was Arthur alive and unhurt? That was all she could think of. Staggering through a hillside covered with as many corpses as stones and passing many soldiers as dazed as she was, Lancelot looked for the faces she most wanted to see. She steeled herself not to respond to the calls of the wounded – there were too many to help. Instead, she listened to hear whether any of the voices were her friends'.

She peered up the hill, and there, still on his white horse, was the king. Seeing Lancelot, Arthur rode to her.

She lifted her hand, "Hail, Pendragon!" she called out, as loudly as she could, though her voice faltered.

"Victory!" he cried. "The Saxons have gone to meet Woden. They won't trouble us for some time to come." His eyes glowed with triumph.

"And on our side? Who lives?" she asked. That was easier than asking who had died.

"Gawaine, Bors, Peredur, Bedwyr." He recited the names proudly. Each name made her sigh with relief. "All alive? Truly?" she choked.

"Truly." He flashed a smile at her and rode on to congratulate as many soldiers as he could. Now Lancelot could look to her own troops, count the dead and help the living. Where was Aglovale? Alive, she prayed.

Not far away, she could see Sawyl, wounded but alive. She hurried towards him. Arthur turned his horse back in Lancelot's direction. "You are the one who will carry the news of our victory back to Camelot. It will take some days for the rest of the army to follow you."

"But . . ." Lancelot began, stunned at the thought of leaving so soon.

"You have done well today, but the fighting is over," the king said firmly. "Tomorrow morning, when you've had a rest and some food, get a fresh horse and go. Everyone at Camelot will be anxious to know what has happened."

After giving his order, he rode off.

Lancelot bent over Sawyl. The young man had a chest wound, but she had seen men with similar wounds survive. "Help me," he moaned.

"I'll see that you get to a surgeon," she promised.

As she held Sawyl's hand and looked for someone to help him, she soon found Aglovale, who exchanged a weary smile with her. They joined every man who was able in carrying off the wounded –although there were far too many of them for the surgeons to care for anytime soon – and seeing that the dead were buried.

Night came, and she still was trying to estimate how many of her men had survived. Some of the badly wounded had died before anyone could take care of them. Lancelot demanded that a surgeon attend to one of her men whose leg was nearly severed.

Turning away from the tents for the wounded, she closed her eyes for a moment. She heard a voice calling "Lancelot!"

She opened her eyes and saw Gawaine, who threw his arms around her. "Lance! We've won!"

His voice was elated, and she knew it was because he was glad to see her still standing. She returned the embrace, then pulled back to look at his face, which had a new cut that would give him another scar. "It's good to see you."

"And you. Have a drink." He held out his flask of northern liquor, and she accepted it.

Pouring the liquor down her throat, she hoped it would numb her. It occurred to Lancelot that she had never hugged anyone, but she was sure Gawaine was as exhausted as she was, much too weary to notice anything.

"I've been seeing to the wounded," she told him.

"So have I," Gawaine said, not surprisingly. He took back the flask and drank.

They exchanged the flask back and forth a few times, and, inexplicably, they both laughed, perhaps in astonishment that they still lived.

"You should go get some rest." Gawaine grinned. "I hear you have a long ride tomorrow."

"I'd rather stay with the rest of you."

She wiped drops of liquor from her chin.

"We'll follow you soon. Arthur couldn't send me back first, or all the others would be worried that I'd be celebrating with their wives or sweethearts."

Gawaine guzzled a final drink, extended the flask to her, and put it away when she declined.

"Of course I wouldn't, Lance. Don't get solemn. You don't want to be sober."

"No," she agreed. "I don't." She staggered back to her tent and found oblivion for the night.

19   RETURN TO CAMELOT

With every movement of her horse's hooves in the direction of
Camelot, Lancelot felt more and more like a soul in Purgatory
being forced from death back to life. She felt no gratitude. She
was raw, going back skinless into the world. Knowing that every
sight and every word would bruise her, she feigned indifference.

The fields she passed bloomed with meadowsweet and pink
knapweed. Goldfinches pecked eagerly at thistles. The contrast
with the scenes of battle was too great. She could still see the
meadows littered with the bodies of men and horses, and smell
the rotting corpses.

There, again, was the familiar hill, and there the caer. The
farmers in the fields at the bottom of the hill called out greetings,
and she yelled "Victory!" to them. They dropped their scythes
and yelled back, echoing her.

"Victory!" she called out with a bravado she did not feel to the
guards opening the gates for her, and they cheered.

When she dismounted, they crowded around her to hear tales
of battles, but she shook her head. "We have won," she said to

them. "King Arthur is triumphant. You must wait for others to tell you the story." Men clapped her on the back, but she moved away from them as soon as she could.

How strange it was to see people who had never dwelt in the Otherworld of battle. Some of the guards and warriors seemed real, because they had fought for a time, and returned as she had.

But she did not want to look at the ladies. They were too innocent; they would despise her if they knew the terrible things she had done.

They ran up to her. Clearly, they cared more about whether their own menfolk survived than about the general victory.

Lionors, with a boy of about three running in her wake, was the first to reach Lancelot.

"Greetings, Lancelot. How is Bors?" she cried, panting.

"He has a few new scars, but he is well." Lancelot wished she were with him, not in the courtyard.

Lionors sighed with relief. "He lives, God be praised. Perhaps our many prayers have helped preserve him." She caught up the small boy in her arms. "Did you hear? Your father still lives. He'll be home soon."

Then a girl named Meleas, who was young Sawyl's sweetheart, darted up. "Is Sawyl well?"

Lancelot hesitated and the girl's eyes narrowed with fear.

"He is wounded, but I think he'll heal," she told Meleas.

Meleas gasped.

"He'll be back soon, and you can tend him," Lancelot said, trying to reassure her. She did not think it necessary to say that the wound was in the young man's chest.

Meleas bit her lips. Lionors patted her shoulder and muttered soothing phrases.

Peredur's wife Claudia, being older and more dignified, approached at a slower pace, but no less anxiously.

"And Peredur?" she asked.

"He is well, and so is his brother," Lancelot told her.

"Thank all the saints and angels," Claudia said, dabbing her eyes with a small cloth.

But as Lancelot walked towards the hall she had to face Ailsa, a pretty young woman who had been Rhun's bride only a year before.

Lancelot said quietly, "I'm sorry, Ailsa. Rhun died bravely."

Ailsa collapsed in a faint, and Lancelot caught her in her arms. Wincing from the pain in her wounded hand, she ordered a guard to carry Ailsa to the house she had shared with Rhun.

Despite the ladies' anxiety and grief, Lancelot felt that either they or she must be unreal, because they did not live in her nightmare, or she thought they did not.

She almost envied them because they had never killed anyone. Even their grief was clean and innocent.

Then she saw Guinevere, approaching across the cobblestones. The queen moved swiftly to Lancelot's side. She wore a russet gown, far less cheerful than her usual colors, but she was beautiful as ever.

"My lady, we have won a great battle. Victory is ours,"

She tried to make her voice full of rejoicing.

"Thanks be to heaven," Guinevere said simply, with relief but not delight.

Though it was the end of summer and Lancelot had last seen her in winter, Guinevere's face was paler than it had been.

"How are you?" the queen asked in a voice full of concern.

Her gaze was even warmer than it had been the first day they met.

Lancelot could not look the queen in the eye. How little she felt she deserved such warmth.

"Look at your hand! What happened?"

Guinevere stared at Lancelot's bandaged hand as if she had never seen a wounded warrior before.

"I lost two fingers when a horse stepped on it. It's nothing." Lancelot held her hand back, for the queen looked as if she wanted to take hold of it. Lancelot tried to keep her voice steady and not weep at the tenderness in the queen's face.

"That is not nothing! You must be in pain." Guinevere seemed to be forcing herself not to touch Lancelot.

"Not so much, Lady Guinevere." She tried not to see that the queen was almost in tears. "The king is well, thank God," she added, noticing that Guinevere had not asked about him.

"Good. I knew you would not be shouting about victory if he were injured." Guinevere's voice dropped so low that Lancelot could barely hear her. The queen looked at Lancelot's face as if it did not look the same as it had, and likely it did not. Lancelot wanted to cover her face with her hands.

"I'm glad you have returned."

"Have I?" Lancelot asked. Feeling that she would begin screaming if she said any more, Lancelot turned away. She was not the same Lancelot. She never would be the same again.

"I must speak with Cai." For Cai was approaching at speed much faster than his usual measured pace. He waved and beamed at Lancelot.

She was glad not to face Guinevere further. It was impossible that the queen could return her love. She must be very foolish to love another woman. No doubt she was the only woman who had ever felt this way. And even if it were not for that, Guinevere was married to the great king. Moreover, even if there had been no other obstacles, surely Guinevere could not love the killer that Lancelot had become.

Cai embraced her. "I am glad you are home. We have housed a merchant and his family who fled the Saxons in your home, but

I shall find other quarters for them. And can I now tell them that it is safe to return?"

Lancelot nodded. "I believe it should be safe. You did well to take in these people." She hoped that the people would leave soon, so she could be alone, but she knew that was selfish.

Cai found another place for them that very day.

The most soothing presence at Camelot was Catwal, who said little, but having been blinded, must know something of the kind of suffering that Lancelot now was used to seeing every day. When Lancelot did not want her finer tunics put out and insisted on continuing to don her much worn clothes from the battlefield, Catwal did not remark on it but tried to clean them as much as possible. Despite his best efforts, they were pungent and smeared with stains that were better left unexplained.

Lancelot could hardly remember that she had once thought Camelot stank because of its ditches full of wastes. The smell was mild compared with the stench of a battlefield. The scents wafting from the kitchens were so pleasant that breathing them in made her feel guilty.

Lancelot spoke mostly to the few other warriors who were there and tried to avoid the queen. She attempted to speak with Gryffyd, who had been sent back to Camelot because he kept seeing Saxons where they were not, and sometimes had to be locked in his room so he would not injure anyone. But Gryffyd did not recognize Lancelot.

Even Lancelot had to rest. She did not want to go off to her small house and sleep, because she feared dreaming of fields of rotting corpses. Or of the corpse of the girl she had killed.

The next morning, Guinevere stopped by the great hall. She hoped to see Lancelot, who was there, clenching her right hand into a fist and unclenching it while she listened to a guard who looked at her as respectfully as if she were the king himself. Guinevere hardly dared to approach, for fear that Lancelot would be unable to talk to her.

Gryffyd, sword raised in his hand, came rushing into the hall. His once handsome face was unshaven and contorted with rage.

"Saxons! The filthy Saxons are here! I saw them in the courtyard just now!"

"No, lord, those were our own men," said a guard, and Gryffyd smote him down with a blow that would have spilled his brains had he not been wearing a helmet.

Lancelot hurried to Gryffyd, apparently to prevent him from slaughtering the guards. "No, Gryffyd, there are no Saxons here. Give me your sword," she said in a calm voice.

"Filthy Sea Wolf! I'll send you to Woden!" he screamed.

"No, Gryffyd, it's Lancelot!" Guinevere cried.

Lancelot did not draw her sword. "I'm Lancelot. Put aside your weapon. You're at Camelot. There are no Saxons here." Lancelot moved towards him with her empty arms extended, but he lunged at her. Frenzied with a fear she had never known before, Guinevere rushed between them.

Lancelot gasped. "Stay back, Lady Guinevere!"

"Gryffyd, pray help me," Guinevere said, summoning her most womanly tones. "The Saxons are in the courtyard. Come out and fight them there."

Though his sword was in the air, ready to strike Lancelot, Gryffyd halted. "In the courtyard?"

Guinevere clutched his arm. "Yes. Please come, the ladies are much afraid. Make haste." She turned to the door that led to the courtyard, and gestured for Gryffyd to go before her. Lancelot quickly followed, as did several guards. A number of them grabbed Gryffyd from behind and took away his sword, subduing him without hurting him.

He groaned. "My lady! I have failed you. The Saxons have captured me."

Guinevere patted his arm. "Not so, brave Gryffyd. You have saved me, and all of us. Your display of valor frightened off the Saxons, and these good British guards will take you to rest and be given your supper, and the physician will attend you to make sure you are not wounded."

He bowed to her. "Thank you, gracious lady. I hope that I have helped."

There was a great clamor as the guards helped Gryffyd back to his room.

But Lancelot, who was trembling, took hold of Guinevere's arm and pulled her into a nearby passageway.

"My lady, you were very brave and very clever, but you should not have taken such a risk."

Lancelot's touch thrilled Guinevere. "Why not? Your life is worth more than mine."

"That is not so!" Lancelot exclaimed.

She looked at Guinevere as if she were an angel descended from heaven. "I am only a warrior. You are queen of all Britain."

"What of it? You are a better person than I am." Guinevere tried to express her love in her gaze and her tone, if not her words. For once, Lancelot had abandoned her reserve. Please kiss me, Guinevere prayed silently.

"My lady, you are finer than anyone else in the world," Lancelot said fervently. She kissed Guinevere on the mouth. Guinevere was filled with joy at the touch of those soft lips, but Lancelot pulled away.

"Pardon me," she gasped.

"I pardon you for kissing, but not for ceasing to kiss."

Cai rushed up, calling out, "Lady Guinevere! Are you well?"

Lancelot moved back several steps.

Had Cai witnessed their kiss? Surely not, for Guinevere saw nothing but concern in his face. Other warriors and ladies followed him, all of them exclaiming over Guinevere. Over and over, she assured them that she was unhurt. While Guinevere was thus surrounded, Lancelot slipped away.

It had been too good to be true. Lancelot might never kiss her again. Guinevere realized that, although the fear of dying had kept her from wanting a child, her own life was less important to her than Lancelot's. She had never imagined she could care more about someone else than she did about herself.

Lancelot hurried off to the walls to watch for the troops' return. What a reckless fool she had been! Should she ask again for Guinevere's forgiveness? No, it was better to say nothing, for she might say too much, and so might the queen.

What incredible sweetness there was in Guinevere's mouth! Brief as the kiss was, it was softer and warmer than Lancelot could have imagined. Her lips felt miraculously – no, sinfully – good. She knew she would cherish the memory – or be haunted by it – forever.

Lancelot stayed by the outer walls, peering into the distance for the first sight of the victorious army, although she knew it would take days for the men to arrive. She was the first to spot the troops, bearing the Pendragon banner, tattered but still held high.

Lancelot rode out to meet the men. In the forefront she saw Arthur, his face as proud as Julius Caesar's must have been. She rejoiced at the sight of him. The king's gaze was not on any person, but was fixed on his high caer.

Riding through the waves of warriors, she called out greetings to Bedwyr, Peredur, Gawaine, and Bors. Every face delighted her, as much as she could be delighted. Even though she had known that her comrades survived Badon, she had had lingering fears that something could have befallen them meantime.

Then she saw Aglovale on a cart with the wounded. He held a man who seemed half dead. She recognized all too well the dying young warrior. "Greetings, Sawyl," she said, trying to look just at his face, not the wound in his chest. He was covered with sweat. Aglovale mouthed the words, "Wound sickness."

Sawyl seemed to recognize Lancelot. "I'll never see Meleas again," he choked. "Tell her . . ." His eyes closed and he breathed his last.

"Oh God's angels." Lancelot reeled. "She's just a mile away at the caer. Is there no mercy?" she asked bitterly.

Aglovale shook his head.

Her eyes full of tears, Lancelot rode back with them and helped unload the wounded and do what was possible to ease their pain. Meleas was making her way among the returning men. Her brow was wrinkled, showing she was not seeing the face she sought. Lancelot went up to her. "I'm sorry, Meleas. Sawyl just died on his way here."

"No!" she cried out. "No, it can't be." Leaning forward as if she might fall, Meleas grabbed Lancelot's shoulder.

"I'm afraid it's true. Let me take you to him."

Lancelot took her by the hand to where she and Aglovale had carried Sawyl's body. Meleas threw her arms around the lifeless young man and sobbed.

Camelot was filled with wild outbursts of joy, people dancing in courtyards, ladies throwing themselves into the arms of returning warriors, and wine, beer, and mead flowing like water.

Many rejoiced over those who had come home, and some wept for those who had not.

Cai clasped his fine warrior, Dinadan, in his arms, more tightly than men generally embraced other men.

Lancelot watched them wistfully. Some men loved other men. Perhaps she was not the only woman who loved another woman? No, everyone knew about men like Cai, but she had never heard such a thing about women.

Lancelot also saw ladies exclaim with delight as the warriors opened their bags of plunder and began giving gifts of Saxon gold ornaments and cloaks.

The finest of the ornaments the king brought to the queen.

Lancelot was near when Arthur pulled some ornaments of Saxon gold from a leather bag and presented them to Guinevere.

"Surely these belong to Britain rather than to me," Guinevere said, scarcely looking at the plunder. "I care only about your safe return."

Her husband grabbed her in his arms.

Lancelot quickly turned away.

As the celebration progressed, Lancelot felt more alone than ever. She stayed with the wounded and tried to be of use.

Aglovale did the same, while others were rejoicing with song, drink, kisses, or some combination.

"The killing has come to an end, and now we can try to recover ourselves," Aglovale told Lancelot, when they had turned away from a young man they had comforted over his newly lost leg. "As for me, I'm going home to my family tomorrow and I'm never fighting again. Perhaps you might want to do the same. There are other lives besides being a warrior at Camelot."

But Lancelot shook her head. Her voice was pained. "There is no other life for me. This is my work. This is how I can help."

"There are other ways to help people besides fighting!" Aglovale insisted.

"Get a home of your own, with a wife and children, and you'll be too busy to go off and fight other people's battles."

Lancelot shook her head again. "This is the way that is open to me. I have learned this skill and I must use it. What if women died because I was not there to rescue them?"

"But does fighting all the time make you happy?" Aglovale asked, his eyes full of concern.

"Why should I be happy?" Lancelot replied. "I scarcely think that is possible. All I can do is be useful." The mere thought of happiness was too painful to bear. No matter what Aglovale said to persuade Lancelot, the response was always the same.

"I cannot leave Camelot because I am sworn to King Arthur," she insisted. And because it was the only place where she could see Queen Guinevere.

20   THE QUEEN'S MOVE

The warriors were more raucous than ever at the feast on the
night of their return, Guinevere thought, watching as they fell on
the meats and cakes that Cai had ordered the cooks to prepare
as soon as the word of victory had come. Some men could not
keep their eyes off the ladies, while others could not keep their
hands off the serving women. Every warrior who could drag himself to the table did so, but some stared off as if they could not
believe they had returned. The mead jars went around again and
again.

To man after man Guinevere said, "I am glad that you have
returned." It was true that she might not like them all greatly,
but she surely did not want them dead. Even Gawaine she
greeted cordially, and he smiled in return.

Merlin's hair had turned white. He spoke with Guinevere more
gently than he had before, but generally he seemed even more
removed from all that passed around him.

Arthur's face had new creases that made him look more dignified yet somehow more human, less like a Greek god. A scar on

his hand snaked up under his sleeve and doubtless further up his arm. It was good to see him safe in his familiar chair, Guinevere thought. If only she could keep that distance between them. If only she could be one of his friends, not his wife. She feared that after the war he would be anxious for her to bear him a son.

When the men could eat no more, Arthur rose from the table and took Guinevere by the arm. "Come along, my dear. It's been too long since I've been alone with you," he said in a voice that was audible to the warriors sitting closest to them.

Guinevere glanced at Lancelot and saw the handsome face contorted with a look of pain that made her feel like a betrayer. The hall, lit with a hundred rushlights, dimmed. Guinevere could barely refrain from shaking off Arthur's hand. Her lips could still feel the sweetness of Lancelot's kiss, though several days had passed.

Guinevere realized that she not only would have to win Lancelot to her bed, but also would have to leave off lying with Arthur. If Lancelot became her lover, she was too sensitive to endure Guinevere's lying with her husband, too. Guinevere shuddered at the fear of being finally put aside. She did not want to be sent to a convent while Lancelot was at Camelot. Nor was Guinevere eager to lose what power she had.

Guinevere thought of Lancelot's worn face and realized that she loved her enough for the risk, but she must plan as carefully as possible. Perhaps she need not leave off being queen if she plotted well enough. Whatever schemes she might devise, she dared not fail to let Arthur embrace her when he had just returned from the war.

Lancelot sobbed in her bed. She wept because, miraculously, all of her closer friends had survived the war. But the tears turned bitter at the thought of Guinevere with Arthur. Choking, Lancelot tried to think on other things. Guinevere was not for her, never would be for her. She buried her head in her pillow and cried herself to sleep.

One evening when he had been back for a few days, Arthur sat in Guinevere's room. Slowly savoring a cup of red wine, he said it was far better than any he had drunk while he pursued the Saxons.

"Many terrible things happened in the war," Arthur told her. "Gawaine killed a British girl accidentally, and . . ."

"He killed a girl! And you let him remain one of your warriors; you honor him for his fighting!" Guinevere did not try to contain her anger as she usually did. She trembled with rage.

"I told you it was an accident, and of course I was very angry," Arthur tried to explain.

But Guinevere said, "An accident, of course. How easy it would be to mistake a British girl for a Saxon warrior. Don't tell me any more. It's horrible. You may forgive him, but I never shall." When Gawaine was away at war, without the caer's women vying for his attention, he became a brute.

She dug her nails into her hands at the memory that Arthur had once wanted her to lie with that savage. And she must still speak with him, knowing he was a murderer.

Had Gawaine thought she was cool before? Now her face and her voice would show the true depths of her hatred, though her words must not.

Arthur just shook his head and observed, "It's war."

War was hard on women, Guinevere thought. She would never want to wear the gold she had been given, for she feared that it had been taken from Saxon women's bodies rather than their jewel boxes.

Arthur patted her hand.

"I can't expect you to understand how much men go through in war. I think Lancelot might have suffered the most. We really should find a wife for him. Can you think of anyone suitable?"

Guinevere stared out of the window and tried to control the tone of her voice. "No. He'll have to find one himself. He's very particular."

"But so many young women have lost husbands and sweethearts that there should be many to choose from," Arthur said.

Perhaps Lancelot would find someone else to love. The thought made Guinevere want to scream.

The woman bent over a fire and stirred the stew she was cooking for the Saxons. She had added just a tiny bit, not enough so they would notice, of the contents of their slop jar.

She averted her eyes from the drunken Saxon men, boasting as if they had won the war instead of losing it.

The smoke from the fire and the sweat on her face concealed her angry tears. Her rage was almost great enough to prompt her to burn the wooden, thatch-roofed house with herself in it.

Why didn't the thrice-cursed king send his army to every Saxon town to free all the British thralls? Why hadn't his men come to burn the wretched settlement where she was forced to live? She had hoped every day to hear their horses. She had longed to see the log lodges in flames.

Now she would always be a slave, always have to open her legs for the stinking Saxon brutes. She had strangled her first baby so he wouldn't become one of them. Now, when she gave birth, they took the babies away.

She didn't know what became of them, except that they were Saxons. She would have given herself to any British warriors who saved her and cut off the iron collar that made her neck and shoulders ache.

She now walked with a stoop, although she was not old.

No one would ever help her. If King Arthur's men had ridden into her settlement, they would have seen whose face she had.

She cursed her sister. Even as a slave of the Saxons, she had heard that spoiled, petted Guinevere had become High Queen!

Why should Guinevere have such luck? Guinevere always got what she wanted. If only they had been changed at birth, so she could have been Guinevere and Guinevere could have been Gwynhwyfach. It was Guinevere's fault that their father, the vile Leodegran, had sent her to that farm the Saxons had attacked. If only they had killed her, as they had her mother, instead of making her a thrall. Gwynhwfach tried to dismiss the memory of her mother's mutilated body.

A Saxon woman yelled at her. The woman hit Gwynhwyfach sometimes because her filthy husband forced Gwynhwyfach to lie with him.

Gwynhwyfach hated the sight of him, but not as much as his touch.

Gwynhwyfach lifted the heavy pot off the fire and carried it to the table. She imagined ordering Guinevere to carry it.

With the king and the other warriors back at Camelot, Lancelot resumed wearing her finer clothes, as they did. The ladies also put on their better gowns, and Camelot was once again a garden of bright colors.

Lancelot no longer felt discomfort when she sat with the other warriors at the table. They were her sword-brothers now. Remembering how each of them had fought beside her, she was pleased by their familiar presence. However, the prolonged drinking still made her weary. She crossed the courtyard to get away from the drinking and to cool her head by climbing the outer wall to watch the stars.

Lancelot could not forget the touch of Guinevere's lips. The sweet memory nearly crowded out thoughts about the war. But she must banish the memory – the kiss surely could never be repeated. She sinned not only against Arthur, but also against Guinevere, who likely would be repulsed if she knew that a woman had kissed her with passion.

Lancelot looked out at the bright sparks in the sky and wondered whether she was truly forgiven for her sins in the war, as Father Donatus had said. Perhaps it was a sin to doubt that a priest could give absolution, but she did. The moon was in the darkening part of its cycle, and she felt forever caught in a dark part of her soul. She no longer saw the corpses of fighting men, but the memory still festered in her heart.

Her life was filled with deception. No one knew what she really was. Her stomach heaved. She had drunk too much wine after all.

The thought of the other warriors finding out she was a woman was worse than ever now, but not because she feared they would attack her. Now they were her friends, and she would miss them if they turned away from her. She pictured them, disgust on their faces, refusing to speak with her. How could she bear to see such a look on Bors's face? And what would life be like without Gawaine? Now that she knew what friendship was, she would be sad to lose it. Truly, she was doomed to be lonelier than a soldier separated from his companions in the thick of combat. She groaned and covered her face with her hands.

Guinevere could not dismiss the thought that Gawaine had killed a girl. It was wrong to do nothing about it.

One morning she told Fencha, "Tell Gawaine that he should come to my room today."

"The Lord Gawaine, Lady Guinevere?"

Fencha raised her eyebrows, for she knew that Guinevere liked him little.

"That's what I said." Guinevere was more curt than usual, but she was too agitated to be gentle, even with her dear old serving woman.

Guinevere looked at the courtyard, where trees were beginning to shed their leaves. A misty rain drizzled on the cobblestones.

In a short while, she saw Gawaine cross the courtyard, his glance straying towards her window.

There was a knock at the door. "You may enter," she said, not softly.

Gawaine walked into her room, where he had never been before, and bowed to her. Droplets of rain clung to his red hair. He glanced about the room as if to see which of her women were there. When he saw that they were alone, his eyes widened with surprise. He bowed to her. "Good day, Lady Guinevere. I came as soon as I received your message. Is there any way that I can assist you?"

She was seated, but she did not ask him to take a chair. She looked at him as if he were a criminal on trial. "Arthur told me that you killed a girl in the war."

Gawaine pulled back like a man who had been struck. After a moment's pause, he said, "That's true, Lady Guinevere."

"I shall always hate and despise you for that." Her voice was level, but showed her contempt.

He turned pale. "So be it." His voice sounded hollow.

His meekness moved her not at all.

"If you ever plan to marry, I shall tell the girl beforehand. It is not right that she should never hear of what you have done."

Gawaine sucked in his breath.

"Please don't do that, Lady Guinevere." His brow furrowed.

"If a girl has been killed, everyone should know who has done it." The blood in her veins surged with anger.

"I should tell all of the women at Camelot the truth about you, so they might treat you accordingly."

"No!" he cried out, putting out a hand as if he would dare to stop her. "You must not let this tale be told. You don't understand the consequences."

"I understand the consequences for you well enough." He dared to protest against even a slight measure of justice. "I don't think the women who flirt with a man should be kept ignorant of the fact that he is a murderer."

"I am not a murderer," Gawaine said in a voice that was apparently striving for calm, but his hands had clenched into fists, though he kept his arms hanging by his sides. "It was an accident. I saw the branches of a bush move, and I thought there was a Saxon behind it. I struck out. But sadly, it was a girl."

"Was anyone with you when you did that?" Guinevere asked, doubting that anyone had been.

"No. I was alone." His voice had deadened.

"So I must believe you? I do not. But perhaps other women will find your account more persuasive."

"You must not let this story go any further." He wiped his forehead. "If you do, my mother will put a curse on you."

Guinevere felt a cold wave sweep over her. "Your mother's curses have more to do with poison than with magic."

Gawaine flinched, which seemed to confirm that his mother was a poisoner.

"You threaten me?"

Gawaine shook his head. "I do not threaten you, except to say that you will greatly regret what would happen if the story is made known. Heed what I say."

"If I do not tell all the women, you may still be sure that I will tell the one you want to wed, if you ever do."

"Very well." Without asking for permission to leave, he turned and left her room.

Guinevere did not fear Gawaine, but she did fear Queen Morgause. Everyone believed that Morgause had poisoned her husband, and there were rumors of other poisonings as well. Was exposing Gawaine's deed worth risking her own life?

Gawaine shivered as he walked through the rain, though it was not overly cold. He had not liked using his mother's name as a threat, and he would never tell Morgause about the girl's death or Guinevere's anger. But he could not tell Guinevere that Lancelot had killed the girl, for he believed that the queen was the last person Lancelot would want to know. He had seen how Lancelot now looked at Guinevere, and he suspected that Guinevere was the woman Lancelot longed for and could never have. If the whole court spoke of Gawaine as the girl's killer, one of his friends, probably Bedwyr, would insist on making the truth known, and poor Lancelot would commit suicide.

Gawaine had long since accepted the fact that Guinevere would always dislike him, but he was unnerved by the thought of having to face every day a woman who thought of him and hated him as someone who could murder a girl.

Guinevere sewed with the ladies who were making new clothes in celebration of the victory. A harper played discreetly in the corner of the room His songs were merrier than they had been during the war.

Guinevere looked closely at Agatha, a lady of some twenty years who was wedded to the warrior Lucius. "Come to my room, Agatha," she said. "Please help me decide what fabric to choose for my new gown."

Some of the ladies eyed Agatha as if they envied her for being chosen for that task. Guinevere knew that as soon as she left the room, the ladies would gossip about why Agatha was favored.

But Agatha herself kept her eyes cast down as she walked reluctantly behind Guinevere. When they were alone in the bedchamber, Guinevere turned to her.

"You have seemed nervous of late, looking always at the floor. When your sleeves slip down, I can see that there are bruises on your arms. Your husband has beaten you, has he not?"

Agatha gasped. "No, Lady Guinevere. I hurt myself. I am very clumsy. I fall and bump into the furniture."

"But you were not so clumsy when he was away at war," Guinevere observed. "Please don't be afraid to tell me. I want to help you. I feel sure that Lucius is beating you."

"He never did before the war, Lady Guinevere. He's been different since he came back."

"Arthur will make him stop."

Agatha wrung her hands. "Please don't tell the king, your highness. I know he doesn't want his men to do such things. I fear he'll send us away."

Guinevere took hold of the woman's agitated hands. "And then you would be alone with your husband, without any protection. No, Arthur will tell him that he mustn't never do it again, or risk being sent away. If Lucius were sent away, you wouldn't have to go with him. You could stay here always as one of my ladies."

Agatha pulled away her hands and put them over her face.

346

"Then everyone would look down on me and say I was a bad wife."

"I would not allow anyone to mistreat you. I cannot let the beating continue. I must tell Arthur. I shall do all I can to help you." Guinevere tried to sound gentle.

Agatha nodded, uncovering her face, but she still looked at the floor. Guinevere knew that Arthur would do as she said. He was not a bad man. It was perhaps a pity that she could not love him.

As the days passed, Agatha's bruises healed, and her gaze was no longer on the floor. Sometimes she smiled at Guinevere.

In the great hall, Lucius avoided looking directly at Guinevere. Lucius, so proud of his Latin, so sure that he was the most culti-vated man at Camelot, must be ashamed at having his brutality found out.

Women suffered not only during wars, but after them as well, Guinevere thought. Why did men need threats to keep them from injuring the women attached to them?

And why did Arthur tolerate far worse violence from Gawaine? Guinevere bit her lips.

Lancelot winced slightly at the boastful songs a harper sang in the great hall. After the victory over the Saxons, bards came to sing the praises of Arthur, even more than they had before. Some made it sound as if he had won the victory single-handed, or with a handful of warriors, rather than with thousands of men, a good number of whom had died. "Arthur the Saxon-Slayer," sang the harper, adding that name to his title of Arthur the Just.

"Arthur the Saxon-Slayer!" yelled the warriors in response. The select group of warriors who went to drink in Arthur's room after listening to the harper sing about him began to jest.

"Did you know that Arthur discovered Britain?" Dinadan asked. "It was an unpopulated island before."

"No, but it was he, not the Romans, who brought Christianity to Britain," Bedwyr replied, swilling his wine.

"No one knew how to write until Arthur discovered writing," Gawaine said.

"People wore only skins before Arthur discovered clothing," Dinadan countered.

"People did not know how to cook food until Arthur discovered cooking," Cai contributed. He drank his wine slowly, as if savoring it.

"Did you know that Arthur defeated Julius Caesar?" Gawaine asked, thudding his wine cup on the table for emphasis.

"First, he defeated Alexander," said Cai.

"The pharaohs feared him too much to fight him," Dinadan contributed, clinking his winecup against Cai's.

Lancelot told no such jests, but she smiled a little.

She saw that Arthur laughed merrily at the jests, and she thought it showed how little vanity he had that he could do so.

But all of these men would die for him. If jests of this nature had been composed by a bard and told around Britain, it would have been a devastating attack, and a great shame. The warriors kept the teasing at home, and she approved of that.

The warriors sparred in the practice room, as they generally did on a cold day. When most of the men had finished and gone off to drink hot ale in the great hall, Gawaine motioned Lancelot to stay.

Having little desire to drink at midday, Lancelot remained. She leaned against the cold wall, which felt good when she was sweating.

"I can hardly believe we are back at Camelot fighting only in practice," Lancelot said, shaking her head. "It's like a dream."

Gawaine grinned, as he used to before the war. "It's real enough. I still feel the hit you gave my shoulder a little while ago." He rubbed it, as if the blow had been hard, which it had not. "In past times, you used both hands to fight. Do you want to practice using your left hand again? I think you could still find a way to hold a knife."

Lancelot stared at her damaged hand. The wound had healed, although she sometimes thought she felt pain in the missing fingers, impossible though that was. "I could try," she said hesitantly. "I've never seen anyone fight holding a knife with three fingers."

"But you are Lancelot, so you could do it." He spoke her name as if he were a bard singing her praises. "Want to get your knife?"

"Indeed I do." She smiled, which she rarely did now.

Lancelot had never felt so clumsy. Holding her knife seemed so awkward, and of course it hurt. Sometimes she dropped it, and cursed when she did. But she practiced often with Gawaine, and in time she could fight left-handed with her knife and even hold her sword two-handed for sweeping blows.

One evening Arthur summoned Guinevere to his room. Old Merlin already sat there. The king had a faraway look in his eyes. "Sometimes I wonder whether we should carry our peace and justice to the continent, now that we have defeated the Saxons. No doubt the empire would welcome a good ruler."

Guinevere held back a gasp. Scowling, Merlin spoke sharply. "What do you want with a lot of foreign subjects to plot against you? Here are your people, here you are loved and needed."

Guinevere made her voice softer.

349

"The people love you because you have brought peace. Surely the spirit of King Arthur's reign is the spirit of peace and moderation. You have already shown that you are the greatest war leader in the world. There is no need to show it again."

Arthur smiled and patted her hand. "Thank you, my dear. 'The spirit of King Arthur' – I like that."

Merlin's voice was not sweet, but his words were. "In centuries to come, no one will even remember whether there was an emperor at Rome in the Age of Arthur. That is what this time will be called, the Arthurian Age."

Arthur repeated the words caressingly. "The Age of Arthur. The Arthurian Age. Too good to be true, of course. You flatter me."

Guinevere silently agreed, thinking this praise a little fulsome even for a king. But she was glad that someone else also tried to curb Arthur's ambitions. The thought of another war, an unnecessary one, made her want to scream.

Guinevere pondered how she could stop lying with her husband without angering him. She wondered through the long nights. She tried to plan while she was sewing, while she sat through endless meals at the table, while she was walking from room to room, while she was riding through forest and field – and even when she was working on the tax documents, which made her all the more severe with those who failed to pay.

Lancelot's pale face and the sad, sometimes even vacant look in Lancelot's eyes nearly drove Guinevere mad. The hollow tone in Lancelot's voice haunted Guinevere. She must act, she must save Lancelot. The need was no less urgent than when Gryffyd had his spell of madness and nearly struck down Lancelot.

On a chill winter afternoon, Guinevere asked Arthur's body servant, Tewdar, to tell her when the king was alone.

350

When the man brought her that information, she thanked him and went to the king's private chamber.

She wore a pearl gray gown of the finest material.

"My Lord Arthur, may I have a word with you?" she asked, entering the room.

Arthur sat reading a report that she had written on tax records. "Of course, my dear," he said, putting down the report. "I am pleased that you came to speak with me. This is a fine report, but I am even more interested to learn what you observed about the lesser kings' tribute that you could not put in writing."

"Thank you for your confidence in me. As you know, Uriens of Rheged never pays all that he should. He always claims to have far fewer horses than he does. But there is another matter I would like to discuss." Her voice became quieter.

"Yes?" He clearly was listening to her.

"I do every service that I can for you, but like everyone else, I am better at some things than at others," she said. She paused.

"For once, I disagree. You are excellent at everything you undertake." He smiled at her in the same way that he smiled at his favorite warriors, or even as he smiled at Merlin.

She had always hoped that he would give her that smile. "It seems certain that we shall not have a child."

Arthur's smile changed, but he had enough control to prevent it from fading too much. "I cannot forget the prophecy . . ."

"I understand. I am glad that you are always kind to me." Guinevere smiled without any hint of flirtation. "But you must perceive that I am not skilled in the way of a woman with a man."

He stretched out a hand to her. "My dear, please . . ."

"Pray let me continue." She looked him in the eye. "I so appreciate your kindness in trying to be a good husband to a cool-tempered wife, but if there is no question of a child, surely you can find more pleasure with other women. It will not hurt me if you cease visiting my bed, as long as I can serve you in other ways."

Arthur said nothing. He twisted his ring of office. Then he returned her look. "I prize you highly, my dear. You are indeed a queen. I am glad that I married you. No other woman could help me as much as you have, or could be so understanding." He took her hand and clasped it. "Please let me know if you want me to resume my duties to you as a husband. You are still beautiful, and I would deem it a pleasure. I don't want you to feel lonely or neglected."

"I know you will always do your duty to me, as you do to your kingdom." She accepted his hand and touched it lightly. "I am proud to be queen of the greatest kingdom in the world."

He rose, came over to her, and kissed her cheek. She kissed his and left the room.

Her heart beat wildly. She had been sure that he was so clever that telling as much of the truth as she could would be the best tactic.

Part III   The Queen's Warrior

21   THE QUEEN

Lancelot tried out new horses, but none suited her. Perhaps she was too particular, too unwilling to replace Arrow, she told herself. One morning she rode Whirlwind, a brown stallion that the grooms said was skittish. When Lancelot saddled him, he tried to bite her, but she gave him a dried apple to calm him.

The first buds were starting to form on the trees, but Lancelot paid them little heed. Her mind turned to the day she first saw Guinevere. Perhaps it would have been better if they had never met. How full of anticipation she had been when she first came to Camelot, how full of hopes!

She crossed a swollen stream, spilling over with silt, twigs, and dead leaves, dulled but turbulent, like her soul. Spring frogs were piping. No doubt their chances of mating were far better than hers. She came out upon a ridge overlooking a large meadow. A single horse and rider galloped across the meadow. Guinevere! If only Lancelot could join her and be joined to her.

But why did Guinevere ride so fast? Another rider was pursuing her! All thoughts of herself forgotten, Lancelot kicked Whirlwind into a gallop and rushed into a mad pursuit. Let the horse's name be true! Lancelot's heart pounded and her blood rushed through her veins as it had not in many a day. She directed her horse to go between Guinevere and the pursuer.

She could see Guinevere's horse enter the woods, but she no longer saw the pursuer. Did he want to capture the queen and hold her for ransom? Did he even recognize Guinevere as the queen, or did he simply intend the rape of a beautiful woman?

Lancelot raced into the woods, though the path was tangled. Before she could change Whirlwind's course, he dashed so close to a tree that a branch struck her chest and knocked her off.

As she fell, Lancelot thought, God protect Guinevere. Perhaps I'll die now, not suicide, so maybe not damnation.

Her foot caught in the stirrup, and the horse ran, dragging Lancelot along. Her body thudded against the ground; her head hit stones. She prayed for a quick death.

Lancelot was barely conscious, but she heard another horse gallop up to Whirlwind. Its rider somehow stopped the runaway horse. One of her fellow warriors must have seen her. But he should instead have ridden to rescue the queen.

Lancelot felt too weak to open her eyes, which were filled with dust. Someone took her foot out of the stirrup. She felt kisses on her lips – Guinevere's. The queen knelt beside her, sobbing and calling, "Lancelot, Lancelot." For a moment, all Lancelot could think was how good the kisses felt, though her head and much of her body ached.

Lancelot forced her eyes to open.

"You're alive! Thanks be to Heaven," Guinevere cried. She put her hands on Lancelot's cheeks. Guinevere's face was contorted and her eyes were wild. "Say you're all right!"

"Yes," Lancelot said, disturbed that her own voice sounded so weak. Guinevere looked at her as if Lancelot were an angel bringing a divine message. She stroked Lancelot's forehead.

"Are you the one who stopped Whirlwind? I had no idea you could stop a runaway horse."

"I've always been good with horses, thank Saint Hippolytus," Guinevere said, invoking those beasts' patron saint. "Of course I've never done anything like that before, but this time I had to." Her voice trembled.

Lancelot could barely open her eyes wide enough to see that Guinevere had tethered both horses to a nearby tree.

Lancelot recalled how she had fallen. "Where is the man who was pursuing you?"

Guinevere's eyes widened, though they had seemed as wide open as possible. "No one was pursuing me, except you. I was just letting my horse run. Then you frightened me because I didn't recognize the horse you rode. But when you fell, I looked back and saw you. I had to save you."

"But a man was pursuing you," Lancelot mumbled, taxing her aching brain.

Guinevere shook her head. "There was no one. Your eyes deceived you."

Lancelot felt a chill. Was she mad? Hadn't she seen another horse and rider? Was it perhaps a shadow? Did she fear so much for Guinevere's safety that she imagined danger where none existed?

"My horse startled a deer that ran across the meadow. That must have been what you saw." Guinevere touched Lancelot's cheek.

"Perhaps it was. Why were you riding alone?"

"I was hoping I might meet you."

Those words were sweet to hear. But Lancelot felt her face flush. "I wanted to save you, but you saved me."

The queen smiled. "It doesn't matter who saved whom, dearest. Try to raise your head. Not too fast, though."

Not wanting to worry Guinevere, Lancelot raised her aching head and sat up.

"Did that hurt? Are any bones broken?"

Guinevere ran her hands over Lancelot's arms and legs.

"I'm not seriously hurt," Lancelot reassured her.

The touch of Guinevere's hands made Lancelot's heart beat faster than ever.

Guinevere's mouth touched Lancelot's lips again. Lancelot thought she might pass out, this time from bliss.

"I love you." Guinevere's voice was so full of passion as to be almost unrecognizable. "I will love you now, I must. I won't be put off."

Lancelot wished she could die at that moment, before she had to say her next words. "You don't understand. I am a woman."

Guinevere looked in her eyes. "Of course, I know that. I always have."

Lancelot reeled as she had when falling off the horse. "But you love me despite that?"

"I love you not in spite of your being a woman, but because you are a woman." Guinevere covered her face with kisses. "You foolish dear, I've hinted so many times that I knew your secret. How could you not understand me?"

Lancelot pulled back. "Arthur . . ."

"I never loved him, I never wanted to marry him. Don't reject me for doing what I most hated! I have never loved anyone but you. Don't be uneasy. I have stopped lying with him; I never will again. I know you love me. Please say you do." The proud queen's eyes, like her voice, actually begged Lancelot to respond.

Lancelot choked. "You know I do." She herself was no doubt damned already, but Guinevere was not. "But how can I endanger your soul . . ."

"I am a grown woman. Let me be the keeper of my own soul. Surely coming near to hating my husband because I had to lie with him was a greater sin than loving you could be."

Lancelot gasped. How could anyone hate Arthur? But she too would hate if she were forced to lie with someone she did not love. Guinevere kissed her mouth again, and Lancelot returned the kiss. What Guinevere said was true. Nothing mattered but loving each other.

Guinevere's hands slipped under Lancelot's tunic, and helped her take it off. As if she were finally taking off a lifetime of chain mail, Lancelot yielded.

Guinevere unwound the cloth that flattened Lancelot's breasts. Guinevere's soft hands covered her with caresses.

Lancelot could scarcely believe that Guinevere wanted to touch her thin, hard-muscled body.

To Lancelot's astonishment, Guinevere's mouth followed her hands. Despite all the years of binding, Lancelot's breasts could feel the touch.

"Don't be afraid," Guinevere soothed her.

When Guinevere's mouth touched the parts that she had covered most carefully, Lancelot was stunned. She could scarcely believe that anyone would do such a thing. It was frighteningly good. She had heard that newborn bear cubs had no shape until they were licked, and that was how she felt, shaped into being.

Lancelot began to touch Guinevere. At first, she used her right hand only because she feared her mutilated left hand might disgust the queen.

Guinevere took both of Lancelot's hands in hers. "Touch me with both your hands, dearest. I love your hands because they are yours, as I love every part of you."

Lancelot stroked Guinevere as Guinevere had stroked her, finding all the places that were far lovelier than any gown that had ever covered them. She tasted Guinevere. When Guinevere cried out, Lancelot was overwhelmed with delight. Soon Lancelot saw the dear eyes closed, and she believed that Guinevere slept.

Am I completely mad? Lancelot wondered, lying beside Guinevere. I must be under some spell or in some other world. Nothing could be this good. It will not last. When Guinevere wakes and sees me beside her, she might scream. She cannot possibly want me as much as I want her. She will spurn me, and it will be unbearable. I'll have to run off deep into the forest and become a hermit, if I don't go entirely mad.

Guinevere opened her eyes and looked into Lancelot's. "This is the only joy I have ever known. I have never loved anyone but you. You are the dearest person on earth, dearer to me than my own self. I fear that you will shrink from me as a wicked woman who drove you to sin, and I cannot bear it." Guinevere's eyes were full of tears. Her face glowed like a Madonna's.

Or perhaps, Lancelot thought irreverently, Madonnas were made to have the look of a woman whose face was contemplating the one she loved. The look was enough to live for. Lancelot tried to return it, and knew from Guinevere's eyes that she had succeeded.

She had been wrong to turn away from Guinevere's look these past years. "You are my love and my joy," Lancelot murmured. "There really is such a thing as joy. I had scarcely believed it."

She kissed Guinevere's lips. For the first time since Lancelot's childhood, happiness seemed possible. She held Guinevere close for a long time, but it seemed only a moment before Guinevere said, "We must dress and return to Camelot."

She began pulling bits of leaves out of her hair.

Sighing, Lancelot rebound her breasts and put on her tunic, which seemed like returning to armor.

Lancelot was troubled with a new question. When would she be with Guinevere again? And could she dare to ask?

Guinevere removed some leaves from Lancelot's hair. "Will you come to my room tonight?"

"If you want me." Lancelot touched Guinevere's cheek, rubbing off a streak of dirt.

"Of course. I will always want you." Guinevere's smile was a bit shy. "Meet my serving woman Fencha near the walled garden, and she'll show you a hidden way."

Lancelot threw her arms around Guinevere and could barely manage to return to garbing herself and making the necessary departure.

Guinevere's gaze never strayed from Lancelot, who rode beside her. It seemed that every hurt and indignity her mind and body had felt was healed by Lancelot's touch. Lancelot was so tender, so loving.

She feared that Lancelot might still be overcome with guilt, go to a priest and renounce her. Let Lancelot love me, please let Lancelot love me, she repeated to herself, as if begging the saints to release their hold.

That evening, apprehension gripped Lancelot. How would it be possible to speak with Guinevere in front of the host of warriors, ladies, and servants – and the king? Lancelot wanted to run away to the forest, go on a long quest, and never face them.

She also thought she could never bear to leave the caer's walls again.

The world had changed. How could it be that the warriors in the great hall were acting much as usual, that Bors was telling her about a lad he was training? What did she care? She managed an answer.

Guinevere walked up to her . . . surely they must be enveloped in a radiant cloud. It was not possible to speak in ordinary words.

But Guinevere said, in a tone much like her usual one, "God grant you good evening, Lancelot. Are you well?"

Somehow she forced herself to reply to those precious words, "Yes, thank you, Lady Guinevere, and I hope that you are well also," without calling her dearest or saying how sweetly some strands of hair strayed across her cheek.

Unbelievably, the gold-torqued king was there, seeming to notice nothing. He kissed Guinevere on that very cheek and said, "You're looking very fair tonight, my dear."

Lancelot froze. So Arthur would still kiss her.

Smiling at her husband, Guinevere spoke calmly, "I am a trifle weary. Pray let me sit with the ladies tonight and listen to their gossip at supper."

"Of course, my dear, whenever you want. I know that the men's talk does not always interest a lady, but I like to have you sit by me sometimes."

He patted her arm absently, and Guinevere walked down the hall to join the ladies.

Bedwyr and Gawaine were discussing some newly purchased horses and Lancelot pretended to listen to them. This was how it would be, this was how it would have to be. Forever.

22   THE STOLEN NIGHTS

When Lancelot left her house that night, she feared that someone was watching her. She guarded herself more carefully than if she were sneaking up on Saxon troops. A bat fluttering by made her jump. The moon was only a sliver, but Lancelot feared there was all too much light.

Visiting the queen's bedchamber at night was likely as dangerous as fighting Saxons. She could be killed, but Guinevere was surely worth the risk.

People seldom came by the chapel to pray at night, so Lancelot thought she was safe enough near it. But she heard voices in the nearby walled garden, so she slipped into the chapel. She hated the hypocrisy of this move, but there seemed to be no other choice.

She lit a candle. Staring at a statue of the Virgin Mother holding the Infant, Lancelot prayed to her own mother.

"I love Guinevere so much, even though she is married. Help me to know what is right and to do it, Mother."

No voices sounded in the chapel. No sudden streams of light shone. Lancelot buried her head in her hands.

After a while, she felt quieter and left the chapel. Perhaps she would be forgiven for what she did. Or perhaps she was damned already and one more sin wouldn't matter.

Guinevere's serving woman met Lancelot outside the walled garden and showed her the way to a secret door. Lancelot was glad that the woman's face showed no hint of a lewd smile.

Lancelot opened the hidden door and ascended a secret staircase. At the top, there was a door that looked ordinary, but it must be enchanted because the queen was on the other side. Lancelot opened the door.

Guinevere wore an embroidered white bedgown. Her braid was undone and her black hair streamed down her back.

The sight of her reduced Lancelot to silence.

A brazier warmed the room. Beeswax candles flickered on the table, which was covered with a jumble of scrolls and even leather-bound books. No other room in the caer had so many books.

None of the hangings on the walls depicted battle scenes, nor indeed did any of them depict men. The largest hanging was of girls picking fruit, while another showed a woman reaping.

Gold-tasseled cushions rested on the chairs, and one held a sleeping gray cat.

There were more cushions on the bed, which was hung with fine green curtains.

When Lancelot glanced at the bed, Guinevere's gaze met hers.

Lancelot felt her face flush. Guinevere approached her and kissed her flaming cheeks. Lancelot felt as if she would faint as Guinevere guided her to the bed.

The Feast of the Resurrection came, and Lancelot went to Mass with everyone else, but she felt no joy. Far more candles than usual made the chapel glow with light, and incense permeated the air. Many people, Guinevere included, went to the altar, but Lancelot did not. She watched them as if she were again an outsider, dwelling in a place beyond the world. Only a few others, like Gawaine and his brothers, stayed back and did not partake of the bread and wine.

Afterwards, Lancelot busied herself at the stables until it was time to go to the day's feast. Little as she wanted to attend, she knew her presence would be missed if she did not.

The scents from the kitchens were even more fragrant than usual, but they did not rouse her appetite. Instead of entering the great hall, she hung back behind a wagon, as if she were fascinated by the barrels that were its load.

"Lance." A hand touched her shoulder.

She turned to see Arthur. Trying not to flinch at the touch of the man she was betraying, Lancelot inclined her head. "God give you a good holy day, my lord."

Arthur looked at her as if she were wounded. "My friend, I fear you are too scrupulous. Are you still troubled by the things we did in the war? If you aren't good enough to take the sacrament, none of us are. You are one of the best men I know, if not the best."

Lancelot froze. "My lord, I have my reasons." Her voice was as formal as if they were in the great hall with hundreds of listeners. "I beg you not to speak of this again."

Removing his hand from her shoulder, Arthur shook his head. "Very well, but don't be too solemn. Pray come and enjoy the feast." He clearly expected Lancelot to walk to the hall with him, and she had to do so. She thought her guilt must be written on her face.

When she chose to be Guinevere's lover, she had not pondered how difficult it would be to speak with Arthur or how little she would want to see him.

She thought how horrible it would be if Guinevere went back to him. Lancelot tried to dismiss the idea from her mind.

She did not go to Guinevere's room that night. Instead, she went to the chapel and knelt on the cold stone floor. The place which had been lighted by so many candles earlier was in darkness except for a small oil lamp on the altar.

She knelt there for some time before Father Donatus came to her and asked softly, "Lancelot, may I help you? Would you like to be shriven?"

She closed her eyes, then reluctantly opened them, turned to him, and shook her head.

She could just barely see the priest's face in the dim light. His brow furrowed. "You are a good man, Lancelot. Giving the Church and the poor your share of the plunder from the war has made you the most generous man in Britain, save only the High King. Why, with that, and your chaste temperament, people already talk of sainthood."

Lancelot groaned. She had once liked thinking of herself as good, but she had lost that feeling during the war. She also liked more than a little her reputation for being good. No doubt the reputation would continue though she deserved it no longer, if she ever had.

"I am no saint," she said. "I thank you for your concern." She rose and left the chapel, trying to keep her pace steady.

She could never again be shriven, Lancelot realized, for she did not have true repentance. She would lie with Guinevere again the next night and, she hoped, every possible night for as long as they lived. She could never be absolved of her sins again. Neither could she take any other sacrament.

Taking the sacraments without being shriven would be a sacrilege. With a sinking heart, Lancelot rose from her knees and left the chapel.

No doubt she was damned, but she could not leave Guinevere.

At supper the next evening supper she saw that the queen was pale, with circles under her eyes.

Guinevere did not look at Lancelot.

That night she returned to the queen's room.

Guinevere's white embroidered bedgown accentuated her face's pallor. "I feared you would never come to see me again." Guinevere's voice was nearly breaking. Astonished at hearing the tremor in the queen's voice, Lancelot took hold of both her hands. "I could not keep away, though you are my king's wife."

Guinevere's brow wrinkled. "Arthur does not own me. Do you believe he does?"

"Own you?" The bitterness in Guinevere's words startled Lancelot. "Of course not. But he must love you."

"Is that what you imagine? No, he does not. He merely likes me." Guinevere shook her head.

"How could he not?" Lancelot didn't believe her. "But even if he does not, my loving you is a sin."

"No, our love is not a sin!" Guinevere's small hands grasped Lancelot's stronger ones so hard that they hurt. All traces of regal aloofness had vanished from the queen's face. "I thank God for our love! I have never before loved anyone more than myself, and I am sure that's good, holy, and right."

Lancelot put her arm around Guinevere. "Right or wrong, I love you. I must believe that you will be forgiven for loving so much, but as for me, who knows? I cannot seek absolution, for I shall never give you up. So I cannot take the sacraments any more."

Guinevere tossed her head defiantly.

"I shall take them as usual. If we both held back from the sacrament, it would be like shouting out our love in the great hall. Truly, your conscience is too tender. How many people who take the sacraments are lying with whomever they please? And I have no intention of telling a priest that I love you. Failing to love you and comfort you would be a sin." Guinevere kissed her cheek and stroked her hair.

And would Guinevere always love her? Lancelot felt that she could never be whole alone again, if she ever had been.

Guinevere tried not to sing or even hum while she sewed with the ladies or worked on the accounts with Cai. It was not her custom to make music, and she feared her joy would be noticed. She held herself back when she wanted to run, on her way from the courtyard to the stables, because everyone would stare. She did let herself smile more often, though she heard ladies whisper that perhaps she was finally with child. It seemed that she could hear Lancelot's voice and feel Lancelot's touch for many hours after they had parted for the day.

She noted with pleasure that Lancelot could not refrain from smiling at her more often in public and making innocent remarks to her even in the largest gatherings.

Lancelot woke sighing. The first thing she saw was Guinevere's face, looking at her through the dark. A faint light from candles made her beloved visible.

"Why the sigh? Did you have a bad dream?" Guinevere asked, touching Lancelot's face.

"I dreamed that I was trying to protect a fox cub, but it kept disappearing. I thought that if only I were good enough, I would be able to protect it. I have such dreams often, about cats, rabbits, robins, all sorts of creatures."

She kissed Guinevere's soft hand.

"You're such a creature of the forest," Guinevere said with some surprise. "My mind lives in rooms. People, not animals, fill my dreams. I just dreamed that I was young, telling my father that I would not marry Arthur. Sometimes I dream that I am sitting through an endless meal at the round table. I want to leave, but my legs won't move; they have turned to wood. I also dream that my golden torque is strangling me to death." Her voice choked.

"What sad dreams. Let me soothe away the sadness." Lancelot took her in her arms and loved her.

Another night, Lancelot dreamed she was lost in a field full of blood-soaked corpses, and ones long past bleeding.

She woke, and there was Guinevere, putting an arm over her.

"What is it, my sweet? You moaned so in your sleep."

"I dreamed about the war." Her voice was hollow. "You can't imagine what it was like." Great, choking sobs shook her.

Guinevere took her in her arms and kissed her tear-stained cheek. "It is over. We are together. That horrible time is past."

She put a hand on Lancelot's breast, but Lancelot said, "Not now."

If Guinevere knew what a killer she was, surely Guinevere would not want her, Lancelot thought. How could the queen love her if she knew about killing the girl? No, it would never be possible to tell Guinevere about that.

"I think you knew sorrow before you ever came to Camelot," Guinevere said, stroking Lancelot's hair.

"When I was ten years old, I saw my mother raped and murdered. I put the man's eye out." Lancelot's voice trembled as she told what she had never told anyone before.

"Your poor mother! May God strike down all such evil men!"

Guinevere cried out, embracing Lancelot as tightly as possible.

Although Lancelot felt that no one who had done as much killing as she had deserved to be comforted, she let Guinevere hold her. Before the night was over, Lancelot was calmer.

Lancelot did not mind that she had to rise and leave before dawn because she liked to do so anyway. Certainly there were other warriors who were returning from assignations early in the morning, but instead of going to her own house, she went out in the woods. She was still tired, so she napped under a tree.

She knew that Guinevere generally slept a trifle late, but perhaps no one found that strange for a queen.

When Lancelot rose from her nap, she startled a woodcock that had come along the path. The bird flew up with whirring wings, and Lancelot marveled at it. She did not have to train aspiring warriors until midday, so she could spend much of the morning in the woods. She had brought Raven, a black mare she liked better than any other horse since Arrow died.

Strangely, Lancelot had not noticed that this spring was more beautiful than any other. The primroses had never been so yellow, nor the violets so purple. Last year, during the war, she had believed that green shoots would never thrill her again, but she had been mistaken. She rejoiced at the song of a thrush.

After the birds' early chorus drifted off to occasional bursts of song, Lancelot realized that she had just observed the woods with a blank mind and had not thought of Guinevere for a little while. Before Guinevere, it had been sadness that stole back into her mind when she recalled herself, but now it was joy.

This joy was like nothing else. The pleasure she had taken in winning fighting contests and hearing herself praised was meager compared with love. Why did men prize fame so greatly? It was all very well, but the delight in loving and being loved went far beyond such small victories.

At supper in the great hall, she dared to exchange brief glances with Guinevere. Lancelot then forced herself to look away for fear that their elation would make their love known to everyone.

Arthur spoke at great length about something, but Lancelot's mind was on other matters, all of which concerned Guinevere.

Lancelot rode with the others to the Pentecost contest field. The crowd seemed even larger than it had in other years, perhaps because there had been no contest the year before, when they were fighting the Saxons. How different the warriors looked, with their chain mail polished, instead of covered with grime and gore.

It seemed that the spectators screamed louder than ever. In the midst of the din, Lancelot realized that people were calling the names of the warriors, especially her own and Gawaine's.

"Lancelot!" "Gawaine!" Lancelot!" "Gawaine!" The people yelled. Ladies were pelting them with flowers.

Lancelot's head spun. She turned to Gawaine. "What is all this clamor?"

He rolled his eyes. "We're war heroes now."

"God have mercy on us!" Lancelot's hands covered her mouth to stifle any stronger exclamation.

"Be calm. This is just another contest to show off." Gawaine smiled reassuringly.

Lancelot pulled herself back to the present, looking at him rather than the cheering crowd.

"True. It matters not at all which of us bests the other, for in any real fight we'll be together."

"Indeed, it matters little. But I'll try to win anyway." His smile became a grin. "The ladies are watching."

Lancelot recalled that it would matter to Guinevere to see her win, and defeated him, though the fight was so long that she was gasping for breath afterwards.

When she rode up to the royal stand for her prize and saw how the queen beamed at her, Lancelot was glad she had won.

Gawaine took his defeat with good grace. That night he and Lancelot sat beside each other at supper and shared a goblet, as everyone did when the many guests of Pentecost descended on them. Only Arthur, Guinevere, and the lesser kings had their own goblets, while the others were shared between two people. The warriors had drinking horns of their own, but they knew that Arthur wanted to display the silver goblets.

"Very friendly of you to share a winecup although you were fighting each other earlier today," Bedwyr remarked.

"Gawaine wants to share his goblet with me only because I drink so much less than he does," Lancelot replied, eyeing the cup as if she expected Gawaine to drain it any moment. Men's humor appealed to her much more than it had in her earlier years at Camelot.

Gawaine shook his head. "I share it only so Lancelot won't drug me, as he obviously did before the fight so he could win."

Lancelot joined in the general laughter. "No, I think you lost the fight because you tarried too long with whatever woman you visited last night." She had not been with Guinevere because Camelot was so full of guests that a night-time meeting seemed more likely to be discovered.

"Last night?" Gawaine grabbed up the goblet, guzzled the wine, and gestured for a serving boy to fill it. "More likely it was because I was with a sweet lady this morning."

"Not even you would do that just before a fight," Lancelot said, laughing.

The serving boy refilled the cup.

Taking it up, Lancelot pretended to drain it, though she just sipped.

Gawaine reached out as if to snatch the goblet away from her, and she laughed so hard she almost choked. It wasn't so bad living like a man after all.

Guinevere saw Lancelot share a cup with Gawaine and laugh at his jests. Her stomach tightened and she could scarcely eat the food set before her. How could Lancelot jest with a man who had killed a girl? Surely Lancelot must know what Gawaine had done.

When Lancelot left the table and walked into the courtyard, which was brighter than usual because the king had ordered that many rushlights be placed outdoors to impress the guests, a loud voice called after her. "Lancelot! A word with you."

She turned and saw King Uriens of Rheged, a thick-jowled, massive man.

Amazed that another king would want to speak with her, she bowed to him. "Of course, my lord."

Uriens chuckled. "'My lord.' I like the sound of that, coming from you. May we talk at your house?"

"It is very modest for a king to visit." Lancelot flushed. Indeed, she still had only the simplest wooden bed, chest, table, and two chairs, which was all she wanted. It was no place to entertain a king. Indeed, Arthur had never been there.

"That does not matter. Allow me to come."

"Of course, my lord," Lancelot said again. Uriens had already congratulated her on her victory. What more could he want?

They walked to her house and she ushered him in. "Will you have some wine? Mine is not as good as what the high king is serving at the feast." She began to realize that Uriens must want her to leave Arthur's service and come to his. What a mad idea. Who would leave the greatest king in Britain, if not the world?

"I have had wine enough, and I shall return to the great hall presently," Uriens said, seating himself on one of the chairs though it was small for him. "I witnessed your heroism in the war, and now I see that, though you have lost fingers, you are as fine a fighter as ever." He beamed at Lancelot.

"Thank you, King Uriens." Lancelot bowed her head. She no longer wanted to call him my lord if he thought he might become her lord.

"You are a man of few words, so I shall not prolong mine," Uriens said. "I want you to come to my service and be my war leader. You would have far finer quarters in my caer."

"What a gracious offer. Thank you, but . . ."

"Please listen to me. I offer you more. I propose to wed you to my daughter. A tie in the flesh is better than a pledge of service." Uriens beamed as if he were offering Lancelot an empire.

Lancelot reeled. "Your daughter? But I am not of royal blood. I am merely a warrior, and my land in Lesser Britain is not extensive."

"I have considered that. But a man who can fight as you can, who is also a man of character, is what I need. My own sons cannot fight as well as you, and I want you to be their war leader, too, after I am gone. But fortunately, I am in good health." Uriens patted his stomach. "I can see that you are amazed, but I assure you that I mean all that I am saying."

"Noble king," Lancelot said, trying to sound as conciliatory as possible. "I will never leave my sworn lord, King Arthur of Britain. I have vowed to serve him, and I shall never consider serving any other man, no matter how great. I thank you for your generous offer."

Uriens shook his head. "Arthur has bewitched all the finest men in the land. I suppose your loyalty is to be commended."

"Thank you, my lord." Lancelot was not overly warm. Uriens was an ally of Arthur's and had only to ask for Arthur's help if there was any difficulty in Rheged. She did not like it that he tried to suborn one of Arthur's warriors.

"I bide you good-night, then," Uriens said, rising and leaving her house.

Lancelot sighed with relief and prepared for bed.

The morning after the feast, Lancelot's head was heavy. As usual at such times, she decided to go for a ride. To her surprise, Gawaine was also at the stables.

"You are going to ride at this hour?" she asked.

Gawaine shook his head. "No. I feared my horse had strained himself in the contest, but I see that he is fine. I'm going to the hall to see what food is left over from the feast. If nothing has been set out yet, I can get some cold meat from the kitchen."

"No doubt the kitchen servants won't mind. They seem fond of you." Lancelot grinned. What an endless appetite Gawaine had! She wasn't ready for another meal. "I had the most amazing evening last night." She went to Raven's stall, and Gawaine followed her. "King Uriens asked me to marry his daughter! He thought he could persuade me to leave Arthur's service for his." She chuckled at the idea. "I never expected to be sought as a husband for a king's daughter! But I suppose he had asked you first."

"I won't deny it. The lesser kings have been after me for years." Gawaine laughed. "Now that they know how well you can fight, of course they will want you for a war leader. But king's daughters aren't necessarily wonderful wives. I've always refused such a match. If I hadn't, who knows? I might have been married to Guinevere! What a terrible fate!" Gawaine clutched his head.

Lancelot was so taken aback that she couldn't reply quickly. The thought turned her stomach. "It's good that you aren't," she said. She would have been even more distressed at betraying Gawaine than at betraying Arthur. Eager to change the subject, she added, "Some of our companions also have urged me to marry their daughters or their sisters. Whenever a man mentions his daughter, I know what words will come next."

"Of course they all want you. You'd be a fine husband." Gawaine gave Raven a friendly pat. "If I had a sister, I'd want you to marry her. And because I'm your closest friend, no doubt she's the one you'd choose."

Lancelot choked. She finished tightening the saddle. "If you had a sister, she'd probably be too wild for me."

"That would do you good." Gawaine laughed. "Don't marry some pious girl. You need someone wilder than you are. And no insults about my sister, or I'll have to challenge you to a fight."

Helpless with laughter over this jest, he strode off to the hall, and Lancelot took Raven out of the stable. Was Guinevere wilder than she was? Yes, likely so.

Early one morning when Lancelot was pulling on her tunic, Guinevere said, "You could ride with me at times as my escort, if you would. Will you go with me today?"

"Yes!" Lancelot's heart raced. So excited was she that she ripped her tunic where the sleeve met the shoulder. For once she was not sad to leave the dear room.

It was easy to find another warrior to teach the boys in her place. Bors graciously agreed to take on the task. After all, two of the lads were his sons.

When the sun had risen and begun to warm the air, Lancelot hurried to the stable. Telling the stablehands they could continue the game of dice they attempted to hide from her, she saddled the queen's horse as well as her own.

At Guinevere's arrival, Lancelot bowed deeply, then helped the queen onto her horse. Every touch, no matter how brief, was precious.

They rode down the hill and past the farmers digging in the fields. Some raised their heads to watch the queen go by, and Guinevere waved to them. Lancelot felt a surge of pride that this great woman was her lady.

Soon after they passed the farmers, Guinevere cried out, "Let's race!"

"Agreed!" Glad that Guinevere was such a good rider that there was no fear that she couldn't keep up, Lancelot let Raven gain speed.

The two mares galloped. Sometimes one was in the lead, sometimes the other.

As unrestrained as her horse, Lancelot shouted with joy. The fields were green, the larks sang, there was nothing more to wish for. Guinevere's horse won.

The two lovers, flushed, disheveled, and laughing, looked into each other's eyes. Lancelot reached over and clasped Guinevere's hand. Life was perfect.

One night, when she and Lancelot were stretched out, resting after love, Guinevere asked, "What would your ideal world be like?"

Lancelot smiled and closed her eyes. Although she generally would rather be silent after love-making, the idea of a perfect world appealed to her. "I would ride through forests, climb mountains, and swim in lakes, the birds would always be singing, and you would always be by my side. There would be no fighting, and no one would go hungry." She sighed because that was only a dream. "But I suppose yours would be different." She looked at Guinevere inquiringly.

"It would be a city," the queen said. "I am sorry if that disappoints you." She kissed Lancelot's neck to make up for it. "You could walk through the streets and see that the goldsmiths doing fine work were women, and the blacksmiths also. The harpers would be women, and so would the priests. Women would preach and study every kind of text. The farms also would be run by women, and the accounts kept by them, and women would collect the taxes. The warriors contesting with each other cheerfully would be women, too."

"Would there be any men in this city, and what would they be doing?" Lancelot asked.

"The same work they are doing now, if they would let the women do it, too," Guinevere answered impatiently. "I knew that would be your first question. You think so much like a man."

"As I must pretend to be one, that may be necessary. I suppose the ruler would be a woman as well?" Lancelot could not refrain from asking, for she thought Guinevere might like to play that part. Guinevere sat up and replied with some irritation.

"No, women would rule themselves, and would be able to. I am not just thinking of myself."

"If you eliminate your work, can't you end mine also? I see that there would be warriors in your world, but not in mine," Lancelot nuzzled Guinevere's shoulder, but she shuddered inwardly at all the killing she had done, especially the death of the girl.

"In my ideal world, you would have no time for that, but would have to spend all your hours as a lover. And I would, too." Guinevere said, following words with action.

Lancelot wandered to the courtyard, where two girls of noble families stared at her and giggled. Tired of being seen as a potential husband, she sighed.

She saw Ailsa walk across the courtyard and stopped to greet her. The lady's pace was slow and her garb was black. "God grant you good day, Lady Ailsa. I hope you are doing well." Lancelot made her voice sympathetic because she felt sure that Ailsa still grieved over Rhun's death.

Ailsa looked at Lancelot without seeming to see her. "Good day, Lord Lancelot. Pardon me, but I am in mourning." She went on hastily.

Lancelot almost jumped back. Ailsa seemed to believe the only reason a man – or Lancelot – might speak with her was romantic interest. Well, that was what most women thought, and it was often true of men. Lancelot shook her head.

That night Lancelot sat at Guinevere's small table, which seemed still more congenial than the great round one. Lancelot ventured to ask, "What are women's lives like? Now I wonder more about what they are thinking."

Guinevere picked up her cat, which had been rubbing against her ankles, and put it in her lap, where it curled up and purred.

"Which women do you mean?"

"All of them – ladies, serving women, farm women – all." Lancelot took hold of Guinevere's hand – the one that was not petting the cat. "But truly, I can't talk to any other women. If I do, most of them flirt or imagine that I am flirting. I don't know what they are really like."

After kissing Lancelot's hand, Guinevere sat back in her chair and sipped red Gaulish wine from her silver cup. "As things are now, most think much about men, on whom their lives depend. They talk of men, with more or less discretion. Some say how much they quarrel with their husbands, while others remain silent. Some say their husbands lie with them too much, or too little. Some whisper about the looks of this man, or that one – or about yours."

"That much I could guess." Lancelot sighed. "But what else do they think about? Do any of them wish they could ride through the countryside as I can? What was it like being a girl?"

"When I was a girl, I much enjoyed my giggles and confidences with my friends." Guinevere smiled mysteriously and averted her eyes. "But once women have children, many talk of nothing else. Do many women think of living like men? Why imagine a life you can never have? It's more likely that they dream of being wealthy than of having work they might enjoy. Probably many of them imagine they would like to be a queen, and envy me rather than you. Some speak of what is fitting for women to do and are harsh with each other, saying 'How dare she speak so freely, that brazen creature?' and so forth. Some like it not that I read so much, and if I were not a queen I would hear more complaints about it." She shook her head and looked at her books, which were piled at the table's edge. Her scrolls were hanging in bags from hooks on the wall.

"No doubt it is hard to see others do what you cannot." Lancelot took a sip of wine. "Most women's lives seem so dull to me."

"Many are far worse than dull. But they can't think that, or the pain would be unbearable." Guinevere's voice was a little sharper. "You'll never understand what their lives are like because you never had to marry."

Lancelot nodded, shuddering slightly at the thought of being married, as well as at Guinevere's annoyance. How strange that Arthur had chosen to marry Guinevere without even asking Guinevere whether she wanted him. How could a man lie night after night, year after year, with a woman who did not love him? Even if his wife did not tell him that, couldn't he guess the truth? No, she must not think too much about Guinevere's suffering in her marriage, or it would be impossible to endure speaking with the king.

Lancelot thought about how easily she could have been forced to marry. And how had she escaped? Because of her mother's death. If her mother had lived, her father never would have disguised her as a boy or hired the fighting teacher. The price of her freedom was her mother's death. Perhaps it was morbid to think that, but of course as a child she had had no choice, would never have said, "Let my mother be murdered, so I can become a warrior," but her life was founded on that terrible beginning.

"It's true, I know nothing of marriage, but I hope some women – and men – love as much as we do," Lancelot said.

"No other woman is as fortunate as I am." Guinevere leaned over and kissed her mouth, and solemnity vanished. The cat jumped indignantly out of the queen's lap.

"I have devised signals we can make to communicate with each other at the round table and in other public places," Guinevere said. She made a small motion with her fingers. "This is for saying, 'I can't wait until we can be alone.'" She moved her fingers in a different way. "And this is for saying 'I won't be able to come to you tonight,' which I hope you won't use often."

Lancelot laughed with delight at the queen's ingenuity. "I surely won't."

"We must use the signals sparingly. We can't be always moving our hands. But still it is better than nothing," Guinevere said.

"Far better." Lancelot tried copying Guinevere's motions. "You are the cleverest woman on earth, as well as the dearest."

Guinevere rewarded her with a kiss.

Someone knocked on the queen's door in the middle of the night. Guinevere woke in Lancelot's arms. Opening her eyes, Guinevere saw that Lancelot was already awake and clasped her tightly. They both froze. What if it was Arthur?

"Lady Guinevere!" called a woman's voice in tones more peremptory than usually were addressed to the queen. The locked door rattled.

Lancelot leapt out of bed as quietly as possible, grabbed up her clothes, and fled into the secret passage.

Silently cursing, Guinevere pulled the wall hanging over the passage door behind her and called out in a sharp voice, "One moment, pray. Who disturbs me at this hour?"

"Claudia," came the reply. It was Peredur's wife, the senior lady at court, gray-haired, rather stern, and pious.

Guinevere flung on her white woolen bedgown and unlocked the door. In her most regal tones, she demanded, "What is it that brings you here so untimely?"

Claudia's countenance was severe and her voice dared to show displeasure. "Why lock your door when you have so many guards, my lady? Back in Dyfed, when I was a girl, the queen slept with her ladies when her husband was not with her."

"And why should I care what your queen's custom was?" Guinevere frowned. It was clear that Claudia thought only of propriety and had no idea that Guinevere might actually have a lover.

Undaunted, Claudia pursed her mouth and said, "A messenger has come from Powys. He brings an urgent message from your father and says that he cannot give it to anyone but you. They let him through the gate this late at night only because he wore the wildcat badge of Powys."

It was no time for formality. Throwing a green wool cloak over her bedgown, Guinevere bade her, "Take me to him."

"Will you not dress first, Lady Guinevere?" Although Claudia also just wore a bedgown and shawl, she looked even more scandalized than she had been.

"I will not." Guinevere was out of the door and on her way to the great hall. Claudia trailed after her.

In the hall Guinevere found her father's man-at-arms Rhys, who looked tired, grimy, and pale. Some of the king's dogs had wakened and were sniffing Rhys. The great fire that had blazed earlier that night had left only glowing embers among the ashes.

"What message from my father?" Guinevere asked, hastening to Rhys, whose face had wrinkles it had not worn when she last saw him.

"I'm sorry, Lady Guinevere. He is gone. His heart failed." Rhys looked as desolate as might be expected in a warrior who had lost his king.

"No!" Stunned, Guinevere clasped one of his large hands.

She realized that she knew almost nothing about her father. What had Leodegran really thought, what had he really loved? He had liked hunting and the food at his table, but was there more to him than that? Had he wondered whether she was happy, or just boasted that his daughter was High Queen? He had generally smiled at her, and he had brought a priest to teach her more than other girls knew. Perhaps he had been a good father to her, though not to Gwynhwyfach.

Guinevere had not seen Leodegran in years, but the knowledge that he was gone somehow made the world a lonelier place. Not weeping, she sat down on a bench and stared at Rhys's familiar face, which regarded her with sympathy. She gestured for him to sit beside her.

Arthur arrived soon and hugged her, but she remained aloof. He spoke of appointing a regent until her half-brother, Cadwallon, was grown.

Guinevere counted it part of the pain that she could not have Lancelot's comforting until the next night.

When she did see her warrior, Lancelot was of course as sympathetic as Guinevere could wish, but remembering the knock at the door made both of them nervous for weeks afterwards.

Sitting in the queen's room, Lancelot tried to ignore her sore muscles, aching from much sword practice, and to revive enough for long embraces. Unfortunately, she was sometimes too tired to make love, but they could sleep in each other's arms nevertheless.

"Tomorrow, would you accompany a lady to the Convent of the Holy Mother?" Guinevere asked. Her voice indicated that she expected Lancelot to agree. "Ailsa has refused to remarry. She says she could never lie with anyone but Rhun. When he died, she was carrying his child, but in her grief she lost it. She has begged her family to let her stay in a convent instead of marrying again, and I have persuaded them to let her. If she wants to leave it after a while, she can do so. I think you would be the most appropriate escort for her."

Lancelot paused. She wanted to avoid going to that convent because it was difficult to keep any secrets from the wonderful old nun Mother Ninian, and Lancelot didn't want to admit that she was an adulterer.

"Perhaps Bors would be more suited to the task?"

Guinevere frowned slightly, which she rarely did in Lancelot's presence. "His wife will give birth to another child any day. You are the one who should go."

"If you wish it." Lancelot tried to conceal her reluctance.

"Poor Ailsa." Guinevere sighed. "Once I offered to teach her to read. Now she says she's sorry she declined, but I told her the nuns would gladly teach her. She needs to think of something besides her loss."

The next day was warm, as was to be expected in summer. Goldfinches chirped, but few other birds were conspicuous.

If Ailsa was grieving, she did not show it, but neither did she show much pleasure in the journey. Her face and voice lacked expression.

Lancelot tried to be courteous, but she did not burden Ailsa with unnecessary conversation.

The journey was uneventful.

After she had brought Ailsa to a plump sister porter who embraced the young woman as if she were kin, Lancelot asked to see Maire.

The sister porter told Lancelot to wait in the garden, where she admired the foxglove and herbs. The place was well-tended, as she would have expected a convent garden to be.

Maire entered from the kitchen door. Her hair was bound in a veil, but she wore dark blue, rather than the nuns' black. The circles under her eyes were gone, and she looked well fed. There were traces of flour on her hands.

"Greetings. Are you content here?" Lancelot asked, inclining her head.

"Indeed I am, thank you. I'd be happy to stay here forever." Maire smiled, but she did not look Lancelot in the eye.

Thinking that Maire wanted to forget the past, Lancelot merely said, "Very good."

"It's a feast day tomorrow, so I'm making honeycakes. Let me pack some for you." Maire hurried off on that errand.

But it was Mother Ninian who brought the basket of honeycakes. "I had hoped to see you sooner, Lancelot." The slight reproach was said in a warm tone. "Would you walk in the forest with me?"

"Of course." Lancelot pretended to study the herbs in great detail. It was strange for a nun to walk alone with a warrior, but perhaps this old woman was allowed more liberties than other nuns.

Lancelot was impressed by how quickly the nun strode, like a much younger woman. When they came to a sunlit clearing in the woods, Ninian rested against a tall yew and turned to her.

"I have something to confess to you," Lancelot said, as she had known she would. Her voice faltered. "I am a woman."

"I knew that, dear." Mother Ninian looked as if she saw into Lancelot's soul, and apparently she did.

Lancelot gasped. "Truly? And you know how fearful I have been?"

The old nun nodded. "That's why I wish you had come to me earlier. Have you found love? I had thought you would." She sounded as if the answer was certain.

Lancelot felt her face become hot with blushing. "Yes, I have found a love and she loves me well." What would the nun think of the word "she"?

"And is there more that you want to tell me?" Ninian's voice was like that of kind confessor. She seemed not surprised in the least to hear that Lancelot's love was a woman.

"She is married," Lancelot admitted, scarcely daring to look at Mother Ninian.

The old nun's face did not show the dismay that Lancelot had expected, nor was there any censure in her voice. "And who is she?"

Lancelot forced herself to say the words "The queen. I am an adulterer."

Mother Ninian raised her eyebrows. "Do you think the king loves his wife?" she asked.

"Surely he must, but Guinevere says he doesn't," Lancelot said, though she remembered that the king hadn't contradicted Gawaine when he had said that Morgan was the only woman Arthur had ever loved. And Guinevere had insisted that Arthur didn't love her. But how could he fail to love such a beautiful, brilliant, desirable wife?

"He loved his sister, but he abandoned her." Ninian looked into Lancelot's eyes. "People are not always what they seem. I am a nun and not a nun; Queen Guinevere is a wife and not a wife."

"But this is adultery, and perhaps treason, too," Lancelot said, appalled that a nun, even a partial one, would take sin so lightly.

Ninian shook her head. "Not loving her might be treason against yourself and Guinevere. You love her dearly." She reached out and patted Lancelot's arm. "You had fallen into the sin of despair, and Guinevere has saved you from it."

Could it be that, instead of sinning with her, Guinevere was saving her from greater sins? It was almost too good to be true. "You are too kind to me. Much more than I deserve." Lancelot choked on the words.

"If I am kind to you, it is because I have sympathy for you, living a life always in disguise." The old woman studied her face as if it were a book. "I know what it is to wear a disguise. I have not always been a Christian nun. Once I was a holy woman at Avalon."

Lancelot stared at the old woman as if she were a shapeshifter. Of course Lancelot had known other pagans, like Gawaine, but they were not especially holy. And Merlin was so remote that he seemed to live in another world.

Ninian sat down beside her and held her hand.

Lancelot wondered how she had looked when she had not worn the black and white habit of a nun. What color had Ninian's hair been when she was young?

"Avalon is gone now. The priests have claimed it," the old woman said, nevertheless smiling so that her wrinkles seemed like works of beauty.

"When I was young, I believed that the old ways would last forever, that people would always invoke the gods and goddesses under the names I knew." Ninian sighed. "My friend Merlin thought so, too."

"Merlin? You know him? I don't understand him at all," Lancelot said, trying not to show the fear she always felt when she thought of the king's old adviser.

"To be sure I know him. How not?" The nun's voice sounded far away, not unlike Merlin's. "We learned together – perhaps too much. We have lost our world. He has pledged himself to save Britain with Arthur, for Arthur is all we have. It is hard for those of us who grieve for the past, the present, and what is to come." She stared off into the trees as if she could see the future in them.

"You know the future?" Lancelot whispered, awed by one who had that gift. "What will happen to us all?"

"Do you think I would tell you?" cried the old nun, throwing up her hands. "No one can bear to know what will be. If you look at Merlin's face, you can see what a burden he bears. Do you imagine that mine is less? No, I shall tell you about the past, if you wish, but not a word about the future."

"That is very wise, no doubt," Lancelot admitted. What if Guinevere would stop loving her someday? It was better not to know now. She sat listening to the nun and shredding bits of bark that had fallen on the ground.

"Do you remember the feathers I gave you?" Ninian asked.

"Of course. I have kept them," Lancelot said. Her hand touched her chest where the hidden bag of her small treasures pressed.

"And I suspect that someone else has given you a similar feather."

Lancelot gasped. "Indeed. A crone who taught me much about the forest gave me such a feather when I left Lesser Britain."

"They are the feathers of ravens." Ninian's voice was low and solemn, as if she spoke of the holy saints. "The raven is the one who bears us away in death. When you carry these raven feathers that have been blessed, it knows you for one of its own and will not take you too soon. That may be why you have not found death in battle, even when you hoped to find it."

Lancelot shuddered. "That sounds like a gift from the devil."

Ninian grasped her wrist, hard.

Lancelot's hand shook under her grasp.

"I do not traffic with devils, and indeed there are no such beings, as far as I know. These are gifts of life, for you must live. You have much work to do."

"I have come to you with the sin of adultery on my soul. Must I add to it the sin of heresy?" Lancelot shook her head. She loved the old nun and wanted to believe her every word, yet she was unsure.

Ninian put an arm around her with more open affection than might be expected from a nun. "Do not let me hurt your conscience. I do not want to tell you more than you can hear. Be easy in your heart."

Lancelot returned the old woman's embrace.

She wondered whether she could ever be easy in her heart again. "I'm not sure I want to know about the past or the future," she said. "The present is difficult enough for me."

The old woman looked in her eyes. "I want to give you the gift of understanding, though it is a difficult gift to receive. Blessed are they who can understand life and do not reject it."

"I shall ponder your words," Lancelot said, puzzling over them.

As they walked away, she heard the song of a wren. Like Guinevere's love, it warmed her.

She accompanied the old nun back to the convent, thinking how difficult it must be to be shut in those four walls.

387

What would it be like to think only of divine love, not human?

Still thinking of Lancelot, Ninian made her way through the convent gate, but she was deterred on her way past the vegetable garden by her good friend, Sister Darerca. Ninian smiled at tall Darerca and admired her bright blue eyes, framed by thick eyebrows.

"So, what witch medicines were you out gathering today, my pretty pagan? Or were you communing with one of your animal deities?" said the tall nun, shaking her head.

"I was meeting Lancelot properly. We scarcely had a chance to talk when I met her before."

"The one who delivered our good housekeeper from the army? No doubt she's worth your trouble. A good thing it is that I came from across the sea to save you from spending your whole life worrying about people." Sister Darerca wagged her finger, as if in mild scolding.

"You did nothing of the sort, Darerca." Ninian laughed and wagged her finger in imitation of her friend.

"Don't mock me. You believe only in your pagan visions. But didn't I picture you from far across the sea, and leave Ireland, the fairest land that ever was, just to gladden your heart?" Darerca gave her a look that was much fonder than nuns generally gave one another.

"You did no such thing." Ninian chortled, nevertheless moving closer to her. "You came to this convent years before I did."

"And didn't I know that you were in the future? And didn't you call me from there? And didn't I leave the holy land where I learned all I know at the knees of the great Saint Brigid of Kildare, when I had been just a wild girl, scarcely more pious than you are, and the darling of both the great warrior Cuchulain and the great Queen Maeve whom he fought?"

This boast was too much for Ninian.

She sank down into the turnip patch in a fit of giggles.

"Perhaps you weren't so fond of Brigid's convent, and she hasn't been canonized yet. You are many years too late for Maeve and Cuchulain. But no doubt they would have wanted to know you if they could have."

"You with all your lies about the future, with your tales about poor Britain someday conquering all of Ireland, you dare object to my true stories about the past!" cried Darerca, scowling in an exaggerated way. A bell summoned them to prayer.

Breathless from racing her horse against Lancelot's, Guinevere clasped her beloved's hand. A pity they could do no more when they were in the open air. It would be foolhardy to risk another lovemaking in the sunlight like their first embraces. Lancelot's horse had won, which was good, because Guinevere had feared that her handsome warrior sometimes held Raven back.

Lancelot's usually sun-browned cheeks were red and her dark hair was ruffled by the wind. Her dear brown eyes regarded Guinevere as if she were the only woman in the world.

The yellow autumn leaves made the forest very fine to look upon. Guinevere thought she would be happy to remain forever in the glade where they rested.

A motion in the trees caught her attention. There was a man on horseback nearby. It was Arthur. He stared at them and then, to Guinevere's astonishment, he laughed.

Guinevere continued smiling. She did not let Lancelot know what she had seen. Since Arthur looked so calm, it seemed best not to alarm Lancelot and to avoid a confrontation. Turning her horse towards a trail that led away from Arthur, she said, "Let us ride a little further," and Lancelot readily agreed.

Guinevere tried not to think on what might happen. Arthur's holding back in the shadows and laughing suggested that he realized that Lancelot was not simply escorting the queen as a guard. Guinevere was sure that it would be fatal to act frightened, and worse to flee.

If Lancelot and Arthur fought, Lancelot would surely be pursued and face death. And if Arthur found the love affair amusing, Lancelot would be offended, even humiliated.

Arthur did not attempt to follow them.

When dark clouds appeared in the sky, Guinevere suggested that they return to Camelot.

That afternoon, rain poured past Guinevere's window, splashed across the cobbled courtyard, and ran into the ditches. Gently touching the scroll she was reading, she wondered whether the damp air would damage her fragile books. She tried to keep her mind off more serious worries.

Fencha was mending a hem that Guinevere had torn. The gray cat played with a stylus that Guinevere had dropped on the floor.

The door creaked. Guinevere looked up and saw Arthur enter her room. He gestured to Fencha to leave.

Of course Guinevere had to smile at him, but she was careful not to smile too warmly. He grinned, slightly boyish but insinuating. "My dear, I have an idea. Don't say no too hastily. I know that you are a devoted wife, but I can see that Lancelot is exceedingly fond of you. I have never seen such a look on his face as I saw this morning. Would you consider encouraging him? That way, you might have a child, and he is a fine man, whose son I wouldn't mind calling my own. You wouldn't hear of doing anything with Gawaine, but I think you like Lancelot much better."

Guinevere's mouth dropped open. She let her scroll fall to the table. A thunder clap sounded in the sky beyond the window, but it was no more startling than Arthur's words. The cat ran under the bed.

Patting Guinevere on the shoulder, Arthur spoke as calmly as if he were discussing the fare at supper. "You know how fond I am of Lance. And how could I be jealous of an innocent like him?"

Lightning blazed in the distance, but it did not betoken danger. Guinevere didn't know whether to be angry or amused that Arthur was so certain he was a better lover than Lancelot. Appalled as she was that he would again ask her to lie with someone else, she was even more astonished that he hadn't guessed that she and Lancelot already were lovers. She was speechless.

"You don't reject the idea? Good." He gave her what was no doubt supposed to be a reassuring smile. "You will consider what I have said, Gwen dear?" Arthur asked her solicitously.

"I will." Guinevere was careful not to say more. She found his cynicism disgusting, but of course he did not love her.

"I thought you'd be sensible." He kissed her lightly on the cheek. "If only the child doesn't look too much like Lancelot. Well, if it did it could be fostered somewhere and people could be told that it had not survived. I still dream that a son of mine would slay me, but I cannot imagine that a child of Lancelot's would."

Guinevere turned away, as if in embarrassment, so he departed discreetly. The thought that Arthur imagined he could arrange her intimacy with Lancelot nauseated Guinevere, but perhaps it was better that he knew. She had no mind to have him come knocking at the door while Lancelot was there. Lancelot would be so horrified that she might never come back.

It was absurd that her husband thought her adultery was his idea and did not realize that the love affair had already gone on for months, but Guinevere did not laugh. It was like one of Gawaine's stories, and she did not want to be a character in such a tale.

Must she tell Lancelot? Would Lancelot be more distressed about their love than ever? Would it be harder than ever for her to face the king?

Guinevere struggled with herself and decided it was more important to keep Lancelot from fearing a knock at the door than to save her from embarrassment. But there was no need to tell that Arthur was so base as to actually be pleased about their love.

That night when Lancelot came to her room, Guinevere asked her to sit down at the little table. Guinevere poured red wine for her warrior.

After Lancelot had taken a few sips of wine and set her goblet back on the table, Guinevere spoke. "There is no more need to fear that Arthur will discover our love, for he knows that we are together and he will make no complaint. I did not tell him, but he was clever enough to see it."

Lancelot gasped. She reddened and put her hands to her face. "How can we ever face him again?"

"I knew you would be distressed, but please try not to be." Guinevere put her hand on Lancelot's arm.

"He does not have the same feelings you do. Of course he would be dishonored and have to take action if anyone else found out, but otherwise it does not matter to him."

Lancelot shook her head. "That seems impossible. If you told me you loved someone else, I could not bear it. How could he?"

"You love me. He does not, as I have told you. He respects me, and that is all I want. I knew I would embarrass you, but I had to let you know that you need not fear him greatly."

She took Lancelot's hand.

"How can he be so kind? I cannot comprehend." Lancelot clasped her hand.

"I don't know how we can live this way, with him knowing that we love each other."

"There is no other choice. I am not ashamed, and you must not be ashamed either." Guinevere made her voice sound much calmer than she felt.

"He can never have you back." Lancelot leaned over and kissed Guinevere's lips.

"Never," Guinevere affirmed. "We belong to each other now."

The next time Arthur came to Guinevere's room, he flourished a scroll. "Take a look at this letter from Maelgon of Gwynedd. Do you think there's something insolent in the tone?" he asked.

Proud that he asked her opinion, she read the scroll and pondered. "It's not insolent enough to require a response, but he bears watching," she told him.

He nodded. "Exactly what I thought. I like to have your judgment sometimes. It seems that I hardly see you anymore."

A few afternoons later, he was at her door again.

Believing that he wanted to consult her again, she smiled in welcome. He sat in a chair by her table.

"I have heard that Marcus of Dumnonia is settling his disputes with the Irish. Do you think that bodes ill for us? Might he then seek more independence from us?"

Guinevere paused. "He might. On the other hand, if the Irish make fewer raids on the coast, surely that would be good for the people, Lord Arthur."

She was pleased at being his counselor or friend, not his mate.

23 THE RAVEN AND THE HAWK

Lancelot and Gawaine rode through a forest in Gwynned, returning from a visit to that land's king, Maelgon. Arthur did not want to leave Camelot, so he sent his cousin on purely ceremonial visits. Gawaine had chosen Lancelot as his companion, which flattered her. But now she was tired of endless feasting at the marriage of Maelgon's son.

"I am glad that Maelgon has no more sons to marry," she said. "Many more such feasts and I'd be too heavy to fight."

"Ah, but he has daughters, as we know too well." Gawaine laughed, for Maelgon had tried to match him with the older girl and Lancelot with the younger. "But we managed to escape without offending him too much."

Lancelot groaned. "If I wanted to be betrothed to anyone, it surely would not be a six-year-old child. Ugh."

"You're out of danger now," Gawaine said.

Something heavy fell from the branches over Lancelot's head, knocking her off her horse. Whoever it was tumbled with her. His body pinned her down. His hands tightened on her throat. The fall had stunned her, and it was hard to fight. Gasping for breath, she struggled to break his grip.

But the man's grip loosened and he slumped over. She was able to turn her head enough to see that he was dead, and Gawaine's sword stuck out of his back. Gawaine stood over them. He lifted the man's body off Lancelot.

She saw a man with a cudgel running towards Gawaine. She yelled, "Behind you!"

He pulled out his gore-covered sword, turned to the other brigand, dodged the cudgel, and slashed at him.

The brigand dropped the cudgel and fell to the ground. He grabbed Gawaine's leg and tripped him.

Lancelot could scarcely move her right arm, which had been twisted when she fell. She used her left to pull out her knife and throw it, cutting the brigand in the neck. He collapsed.

Gawaine rose, still panting. "I knew that teaching you how to fight with your left hand would save my life someday." He extracted Lancelot's knife from the dead man's neck. "So much for safety," he said. "A man also tried to land on me, but he missed and fell to the ground. I leapt off my horse and killed him. That's why it took me so long to help you."

Lancelot shook. "I might never have seen Guinevere again," she gasped.

Gawaine stared at her. "Guinevere? Do you mean that the two of you . . ."

"Oh no," Lancelot said hastily, realizing her mistake, but she felt her face turn red.

"Great hounds of Annwyn, you don't mean Guinevere's human enough to take a lover!" Gawaine laughed. "Of course I've noticed that you've always stared at her like a starving puppy, but I had no idea she'd give you a chance."

"Hush!" Lancelot gasped, moving away from the brigand's body, as if even in this desolate place they might be overheard. "You must never tell anyone. Swear you won't, as you are my friend," Lancelot demanded, horrified that she had let her secret out so easily, after being with Guinevere for only a year. Do I protect Guinevere so much less than I protect the secret of my sex? She chided herself.

"No one will ever hear of your love through me," Gawaine promised. "Don't worry yourself. Perhaps she'll have a child, and that should please Arthur."

Lancelot choked. She had expected to hear some condemnation of her lying with Arthur's wife.

"The war is over, but yet we've killed again," she said. She shuddered. "How many more times will I have to kill?"

"Who knows?" Gawaine said. "It seems that there are no more brigands. Let's leave these by the roadside."

She nodded, and avoided looking further at the corpses.

Lancelot realized that she had changed much since the war. Her life was precious to her now, mostly because of Guinevere.

They rode through glens and across mountains.

Lancelot eyed Gawaine more carefully. Would he tell that she and Guinevere were lovers? Would it slip out when he drank? The thought that she had betrayed Guinevere by telling him shamed her. She feared to tell Guinevere and face her anger.

But the journey was difficult enough to demand her full attention. At times their horses had to cross streams rushing high with snowmelt, and the warriors' legs were soaked. Shivering, she wondered if she would catch the ague.

When they had climbed a hill and were resting their horses, they looked down on a tapestry of green woodlands and lapis lakes. Their beauty made Lancelot's heart ache. It was her first journey away from Guinevere since they had been together. Did

Guinevere miss her as much as she missed Guinevere? "If only Guinevere were here." Lancelot sighed.

Gawaine laughed. "Why should a woman come on such a difficult journey? You're worse than I am, Lance. Even I don't think of bedding women all the time."

She felt herself flush. "That's not what I was thinking of. I meant that I would like her to see this land," she said, sweeping her hand over the wild places they saw both near and far.

But Gawaine only laughed, and a raven dipping in the sky and calling seemed to echo him.

They camped under a grove of ash trees. A drizzling rain that began after midnight disturbed Lancelot only a little. It woke her, but she fell back to sleep.

Then she saw fields of corpses and woke screaming.

"Are you all right, Lance?" Gawaine asked from under the next tree. "Nightmares about the war?"

"Yes." She tried to stop shuddering.

"We all have them. Want to talk about it?" His voice was gentler than usual.

"No, thanks. You know what it was like." She stared at the tree above her to remind herself that she was no longer at war. The rain had stopped, but she brushed water from her face.

"I hope you can rest now."

"I think I can. Sorry I woke you."

"That doesn't matter. I can go back to sleep."

She stretched out again. So men, too, had such nightmares. Well, of course they did.

Guinevere read her scrolls late into the night, until she began to worry that the dim light might hurt her eyes. Every night she feared there would be a knock at the door, though it seemed that

Arthur had plenty of mistresses. She asked Fencha to sleep on a pallet in her room.

One afternoon when she was discussing tax reports with Arthur in her room, he looked up from a wax tablet.

"Happy with Lancelot, are you?" he asked. The way he glanced at her was too familiar.

"Yes." She answered as briefly as possible, and did not meet his gaze. She understood that he was asking whether she wanted him to come to her. She had not guessed that knowing she was with someone else might make him want her again, but she could see that it did, at least a little. She must discourage him. "I fear that Maelgon of Gwynned is cheating on his taxes, my lord, even as Lancelot and Gawaine are paying him a visit in your stead."

"The ungrateful wretch!" Arthur exclaimed, pounding on the table. But after he had done exclaiming about Maelgon, Arthur asked, "Is there any sign of a child?"

"No, my lord. I'll tell you if there is." Guinevere looked out of the window, as if to say that was a painful subject.

When her husband left the room, Guinevere sighed with relief. She would never lie with him again, but she hoped not to have to fight over it. And perhaps such a fight was most likely when Lancelot was on a journey, which happened all too frequently.

Lancelot was not at war, but there was always a chance that she might not come back. Guinevere could never forget that. She hoarded her moments with Lancelot as treasures that she could go over in her mind every night, like a miser counting his gold.

As Lancelot and Gawaine rode on, their food was depleted. They tried their luck at hunting, but the deer were hidden from them, and the hares also. Even the grouse seemed to have vanished from the earth.

"Why isn't Arthur here with us? Perhaps some hand would come out of a lake and offer him food," grumbled Gawaine one night as they camped on the side of a mountain, low enough so they could have shelter under the scraggly mountain oaks and rowan trees and high enough so they could enjoy a view.

Lancelot laughed at his reference to the tale that Arthur liked to tell. "It may be Merlin that you want, then. Pray a little, and you might get such powers yourself."

Gawaine shook his head. "No, prayer would produce only bread, and that's the one thing we have already. Besides, your god would more likely turn my bread to stones than these stones to bread."

"Surely not. There is no doubt compassion for the hungry, even for a miserable sinner like you."

"Look, that sparrowhawk is harrying a raven."

So it was, and the raven harried it in turn, but neither injured the other. "They're just jousting, not battling," Lancelot said.

"As they always do."

"Like us, Hawk of May." Lancelot referred to Gawaine's childhood name, Gwalchmai. She knew the name because Arthur and the other warriors often made jests about it.

"Indeed, Raven," he said, grinning, looking at Lancelot's black hair. Raven was her mare's name, so it seemed that he mocked her. "Although surely if I were a hawk I would be larger than a sparrowhawk."

"No doubt a goshawk at least," she agreed. They watched the sky warriors' contest until the two dipped out of sight. Then the sky began to redden.

"If only some woman, witch or enchantress, would appear in the sunset," Gawaine said, peering into the rosy sky as if he might be able to discern one. Lancelot stiffened.

"If there is one, I hope she can create supper out of nothing. I would rather have hot food than the aging oat cakes in my bag."

Gawaine pretended to sigh. "How shallow of you, to want her only for such mundane things. I want her for herself alone."

"I can guess what part of herself, too. Don't bother to tell me," Lancelot replied irritably, moving to a slightly more distant rock.

Gawaine grinned. "So you finally have a woman," he began.

"That's no concern of yours," she grumbled, getting out her oat cakes.

But he continued talking as he took off his boot and shook a stone out of it. The colors in the sky were fading. "When you decide to sin, you certainly make no small foray, but charge right in. You might have made a more prudent choice. Remember, there are many others."

"There are no others," Lancelot asserted, trying to hold her temper.

Gawaine put his boot back on and took his wine flask from his saddlebag. "Now that you're lying with a woman, I should give you some advice," he said.

"I don't need any," Lancelot insisted hastily, also refusing his proffered flask.

Gawaine laughed. "That's not the kind of advice I mean. All I can say is that women like a man to take a long time and pay them every attention." He leaned back against a rock. "What I meant to say is that women are different from each other," he advised. "There's more to it than face, form, and coloring."

"What?" Was this actually information that he thought had to be imparted? Hadn't he always known that? She tried to keep from expressing even more astonishment.

"I was just eighteen, visiting home after Arthur's war of succession, when I married my first wife, Keri." He averted his eyes.

"I loved her dearly. She was very fair and laughed all the time. We were happy together. When she died in childbed after nine months, I couldn't believe it. Then, a year later, I met a girl who looked something like Keri, and I married her." He swallowed a great gulp of wine.

Now Lancelot looked away, for the sky was not yet dark enough to hide her face.

"I realized as soon as I married her that she was nothing like Keri. She was nice enough, but very different. I was so unhappy that she could see it, and I soon saw that she was unhappy too. So I tried to be pleasant to her all the time, to make it bearable for her, and she also pretended to be happy to cheer me up. Then I began to realize that most marriages were like that, or worse.

"For me, she was only Not Keri. The prospect of spending my whole life with Not Keri was terrifying. But of course I could go off with other women, and live at Arthur's court. She could not turn to other men, and I didn't want her to, but I was sorry for her.

"I returned when she was going to bear a child, but she died in childbed, too. I hate to admit it, but though I grieved over the death of the baby girl, I was relieved that I didn't have to spend my life married to Not Keri."

"I suppose she had a name," Lancelot said, trying not to sound too harsh.

"Of course. It was Anna," he replied.

Lancelot shivered, pitying that other Anna.

"So, when I saw that women are different, I decided to try them all," Gawaine added, resuming his usual jesting tone and drinking more wine. "Don't believe that a pretty face and form are enough to make you happy."

"I certainly won't. I never have imagined that," said Lancelot, thinking it was already clear how miserable she would be with any Not Guinevere.

"Good. Even if a woman is beautiful, you won't be happy unless she's warm-hearted and can laugh a little."

Lancelot again found this obvious, and made no reply. Could he possibly be suggesting that he thought Guinevere was cold and could not jest?

"It's too bad you don't like to hear me tell tales about women. Stories about imagined women are much more amusing than the truth about real ones." Gawaine moved closer and elbowed her in the ribs. "By the way, it was wise of you to choose the only woman in Britain who doesn't want me."

"I think there might be a few others," she observed.

They both laughed.

In the night, Lancelot woke to the sound of moans.

Gawaine was crying, "Not the women and children! No, no!"

"Gawaine! Wake up, you're having a nightmare," Lancelot called out gently.

He made some unintelligible sounds. "What? Oh, Lance. Thanks, the nightmares about the war go on and on, but they don't always wake me up. I wish they did."

"Are you well now?"

"Yes, thanks. I'm fine." However, his voice was not hearty as usual. "Go back to sleep."

Lancelot rolled on her side and tried to dismiss the memories of war that his groans had brought back to her. Perhaps women and men weren't so different after all.

Guinevere stretched out on Lancelot's side of the bed.

Lancelot had been gone too long – none of her scent was left on the coverings.

There was a chance of danger in any long journey. Even in a skirmish with brigands, it was possible to be killed. How long would it be before she knew Lancelot was unhurt?

Some women claimed they would know immediately if the men they loved died a hundred miles away, but Guinevere didn't believe that.

However bad a man Gawaine might be, at least he was such a good fighter that Lancelot was probably safer traveling with him.

But it infuriated Guinevere that he had so much time to be with Lancelot, when she, who loved Lancelot so much, had so little time. Just snatched hours at night, never whole days.

Guinevere sighed and tried to force herself to sleep.

After weeks of rain, the sun shone on Camelot. Guinevere burned with desire to course through the fields and the woods. She decided to ride alone, though Arthur didn't want her to do so. Bors had the ague and there were no other warriors she wanted as escorts. Perhaps Dinadan might be acceptable, but he had gone away for a few days. She went to the stables early, at a time when most of Camelot would be breaking their fast, and told Cuall, "I shall ride unaccompanied this morning."

The old stablemaster frowned at her as few dared to frown at the queen. "If you say so, Lady Guinevere. I and all my stable-hands will be drawn and quartered if you meet with any trouble, but do not worry your head about such small things."

Knowing that what he said was only a little exaggerated, Guinevere said, "Just one day only. I promise to take care. I value your lives as well as my own."

She rode down the hill and out of sight as quickly as possible. She enjoyed the feeling of being alone. Somehow she felt free, as if she could travel to Rome or Constantinoplis if she wished. Or if she could wander as Lancelot did. She especially liked seeing the leaves, which shone with spring green, but she wished that Lancelot were there to see them with her. Spring smelled fresher as she put distance between herself and the caer.

All manner of birds were singing. Lancelot would have been able to identify every song, but Guinevere knew only the most common ones. Sparrows flew up as her horse passed by.

Coming to a field where new grasses shot up among the brown sedges of winter, she let her horse gallop. As soon as she did, she heard another horse behind her. Turning her head, she saw a warrior in chain mail on a brown horse – an ordinary enough sight – but although he was far away, he seemed to be pursuing her.

Nonsense, Guinevere told herself, there is no danger. There's likely some good explanation for his behavior. But she headed into the nearest woods.

When she looked again, the man was gone. Probably he hadn't been pursuing her after all.

Or perhaps Lancelot really had seen someone that day a year earlier? No, that thought was foolish, Guinevere chided herself. Why would someone pursue her one day, and then not again for more than a year? She wouldn't mention the incident to anyone, for perhaps there was no incident at all. And of course she should not have been riding alone. She knew that it was a foolish risk for a queen to take.

Lancelot and Gawaine came to a small mountain town and had all the bannock and yellow cheese, and also trout, that they could eat, and were content. They thanked the old peasant woman who had cooked for them, and went outside to sit, watching children and dogs play in the dust. White blossoms grew on the hawthorne trees and scented the air.

"The people are kind here. I would be well pleased to rest here tonight," Lancelot said. She wondered whether it would be better to ask to stay in one of the thatched huts, which smelled strongly of the animals that lived there, with only a few lathes between them and the people, or to sleep in the open.

Gawaine smirked. "Ah, yes, we should stay here, but rest is not on my mind. It's Beltane tonight."

Lancelot groaned. "I never remember it. Very well, go off to your pagan fires. I'll get a good rest and stay with the horses. I don't want mine driven between flames."

"If we tell them that our horses are too high-strung and we don't want them driven through the fires, they may think we're odd, but they'll let them be." Gawaine slapped Lancelot's shoulder.

"But they'll never forgive you if you stay away, a handsome man like you. You would be insulting them. These mountain girls are pleasant and sweet. They weave flowers in their hair and sing like angels."

"Chanting pagan prayers."

"Chanting the tunes their people have sung for centuries, dancing in the firelight. You don't dance much at Camelot, but perhaps you would like it better under the stars."

"If it were only a matter of dancing," she said, and sighed. She would like to try dancing in a place where no ladies had matrimonial designs on her. She avoided the feast day reels at Camelot as much as possible.

"Don't be a fool, Lance, you won't live forever. Just come and dance if you want to do no more." He grinned as if he could see that Lancelot was weakening. "But you likely will want to do more."

Lancelot shook her head. "I cannot. I am vowed to Guinevere."

"What, never to kiss another woman? Only you would make such a vow to a married woman." Gawaine rolled his eyes. "But you know such vows are made to be broken."

"Mine are not," Lancelot insisted. "Still, I did not vow never to dance."

As twilight came, a procession of villagers formed, young women and men, and older ones, too. The young women, who were more numerous than the young men, had woven flowers in their hair. All were singing.

Lancelot blotted out the words to the songs. Going to a Beltane celebration was quite against her principles, but the evening was mild and full of the scent of the first grasses. Little frogs were piping like woodland sprites.

She went along with the procession, though she did not sing. Men lit the fires and drove the cattle between them. The cows lowed, but they were unhurt. It was the same with the sturdy mountain ponies – they were frightened but not injured. Lancelot watched to see that her horse was not among them. The men drank heather beer. Lancelot did not. She felt intoxicated already.

Men put branches into the fire, then waved them around, sparks flying. Some of the men with branches drove the cattle and horses back to their byres. An old man played pipes.

Men and women began to dance in lines, weaving back and forth. Lancelot grabbed an old farmer's rough hand and joined in. Then the dancers paired off. Gawaine danced with a pretty, giggling young woman who surely was too old to be unmarried. Lancelot was thinking about slipping away when a young woman of about eighteen or nineteen with violets woven into her thick brown hair began to dance with her.

Knowing but little of dancing, Lancelot let her set the pace and whirled around with her. Soon both were laughing.

The girl threw her arms around Lancelot's neck. Lancelot drank in the perfume of her flowered hair.

"Let's go off. All of the others are," Violet Hair said.

Some of the couples were slipping off into the trees, and others were falling down without going too far.

"Will you mind if I do no more than dance and walk with you, fair one?" Lancelot asked. "I will leave the dancing now, but if you want lovemaking, you should choose someone else." She was surprised at how reluctantly she said those words and thought of the woman going off with one of the men.

Violet Hair's eyes widened. She laughed. "Let's go off, then. There's no one else here I want." Lancelot felt a surge of warmth toward her, and said, "Let's be off, down into the dell," and they whirled off like sparks from the fire, into the darkness.

Lancelot caught her hand and they ran downhill until they were breathless, beyond the shouts and laughter by the fires, then collapsed by the side of a brook that laughed as much as they did.

Violet Hair threw her arms around Lancelot's neck and kissed her mouth joyfully.

Lancelot pulled back, lying on her side. She felt herself flush with shame for letting the girl come so close. "Please don't be disappointed. You are sweet, but I'll not lie with you tonight. I love another."

"But this is Beltane." The girl laughed again. "She'd understand. She's probably at some Beltane fire herself."

Lancelot shook her head. Surely that was the last place that Guinevere ever would be. "No, she's a pious Christian." She was sorry for the lie about Guinevere's piety. "And so should I be."

"Holding back at such times goes against nature," Violet Hair said. "What's your name, Handsome? I'm Teleri."

"I am Antonius." Lancelot rose from the ground. "Let's walk some more. Are you married?"

Teleri shook her head. "My lad died fighting the Saxons."

Lancelot sighed and thought how many men had lost their lives. She pressed Teleri's hand.

They walked by the brook and saw the moon sparkling on the water and stars in the heavens. Lancelot wished that Guinevere was there, but she smiled at Teleri, who reached over and tousled Lancelot's hair. She ruffled Teleri's in return.

They saw the fire on the hill above, and answering fires on much more distant hills. Lancelot took Teleri's hands and danced with her again, whirling over the fields, stumbling over rocks, and laughing giddily.

They sank down exhausted, and Teleri tried to kiss Lancelot again. Lancelot pulled away.

"You're sweet, Teleri," she said again. "Are you happy?"

"Happy tonight." She smiled tenderly at Lancelot, who could see a little of her face in the bright moonlight.

"Do you have trouble rising? I could help you."

Holding back laughter, Lancelot said, "Thank you, no. I can make love, but I love someone dearly and have vowed never to lie with another, not even on Beltane. I hope I am not hurting you."

"No, Handsome, you're not. You told me you wouldn't."

She stroked Lancelot's hair.

"You're very gentle. But I think you're a little shier than you say."

"No, let's just look at the stars," Lancelot said, lying back on the ground and surveying the heavens.

A moment later, Teleri leaned over her and pressed her body to Lancelot's. She pulled back slightly and, still leaning over her, asked, "Are you a woman?"

"I am," Lancelot said gravely. She moved further away.

"Is that why you don't want to kiss me? Have you been laughing at me? That was not how it seemed."

Teleri put her hand on one of Lancelot's.

"No." Lancelot shook her head. "What I said was true. I love another woman, and I am promised to her. I do like you."

"Can women like each other so? Why, I think I can." She pressed Lancelot's hand.

Lancelot returned the pressure. "Perhaps you can, with someone else."

"You said 'Antonius' as if it wasn't really your name. Now I know why." She touched Lancelot's cheek tentatively. "That man who travels with you, does he know?"

Lancelot choked. "No, what a thought! Of course he doesn't."

Teleri giggled, and the laugh spread to Lancelot. As they shook with laughter, Teleri put her arms around Lancelot. "Please show me."

Lancelot shook her head and gently disentangled herself from Teleri's arms. "I'm sorry. If I were not pledged, I might. But I cannot. Can't we just look up at these stars and be happy?"

The fires on the hills were burning lower. They talked about many things, and walked more, holding hands.

As dawn came, Lancelot escorted Teleri back to the village. After they had parted, Lancelot went to look after her horse. She fed the mare, but was not hungry herself.

Teleri had given Lancelot food to take with her, cheese and dried pork, which she packed in her saddlebags. She was feeding Gawaine's horse, so it should not suffer if he were delayed, when he strode whistling to the trees where the horses were tied.

His voice showed no trace of the previous night's drink. "So, Lance, how are you?" he called out cheerfully.

"Very well indeed. Are you ready to depart, or do you need to go off and sleep?"

"No, let's go, it's time to leave. All good things must end."

As their horses trod a winding mountain path, he said, "So Lancelot celebrated Beltane after all." He grinned broadly.

Lancelot shook her head. "Not so. I celebrated no pagan feasts. I only danced. And a girl kissed me, I must admit."

"Only a kiss? That's very foolish, if true. But I'm afraid it is." He gave a mock groan.

"Yes, it is. But I enjoyed meeting her," she said, ignoring the groan. "I'm glad you persuaded me to go. You're very persuasive." She burst out laughing at the idea of Gawaine trying to persuade her to lie with women. Larks were singing in the nearby fields, adding to Lancelot's feeling of contentment.

"How could I have lain with her? I'm such a good lover that she might have been spoiled for anything else," Lancelot said, choking with laughter.

"No doubt." Gawaine chuckled. "You're certainly full of cheer from that kiss. But I suppose you don't want me to tell anyone that you went to the Beltane fires."

She gasped and stared at him in horror. "Lancelot at the Beltane fires! No, please don't!" Even if her reputation for holiness was not entirely true, it pleased her a great deal and she didn't want to lose it.

"Everyone at Camelot would enjoy that," he said. "But of course I won't tell, for you. Men keep secrets for each other."

Lancelot said, "No doubt." St. Agnes's maidenhead, she was more a man than she had reckoned!

A little later, as they were riding through a mountain pass, a few small rocks fell from a cliff, showing how inhospitable the terrain could be. Patting her mare's neck to calm her, Lancelot wondered what it would be like to live in a tiny place that was scarcely a village, cut off by the mountains from the rest of the world, for all of one's life.

"What will her life be like? I'll never know."

Gawaine shook his head. "Plenty of hard work and many children, most likely."

Lancelot sighed. "I hope not."

"Just remember how pleasant the night was. Don't wonder about what their lives will be like. That would spoil it all"

"So that's the key to womanizing," Lancelot replied in a bitter tone. "Well, I cannot do that." Tears formed in her eyes. "I hope she'll be happy, though I doubt it."

"You care too much, Lance," Gawaine told her.

"That is far better than caring too little," she retorted, riding off ahead of him. Thoughts crowded her tired brain. Did she want to become more like a man? She answered herself with a resounding no.

Guinevere smiled with pleasure when Lancelot came to her room the first night after she returned. Lancelot's presence made it seem that sunlight streamed into the room, although they had only the light of a few candles.

But Lancelot hung down her head and blushed. "I must admit that I went to the Beltane fires with Gawaine."

"What!" Guinevere grabbed the edge of her table.

Unspeakable thoughts crowded her mind.

"I did dance with a girl and walk off with her, but I did not kiss her though she kissed me. I know that I should not have danced with her so long, when you have no chance to do such things. But she discovered that I was a woman, and she did not mind. I hope she finds some happiness herself. Please forgive me.

I'll never do such a thing again." Her head had been bowed the whole time and she had not looked at Guinevere's face.

"Of course I forgive you." Although Guinevere's muscles relaxed with relief, she did not touch Lancelot.

"Perhaps the woman's life will be changed for the better, but it would be dangerous if she told your secret."

"I didn't tell her my true name," Lancelot admitted.

"No doubt that is not so unusual," Guinevere snapped. "Men probably do that all the time."

Lancelot winced. "No doubt."

Rage made Guinevere's head feel as if it would burst. She wanted to yell, "How can you bear to be around Gawaine? Do you condone his killing a girl in the war?" But fear, even stronger than the rage, gripped her. How could she bear it if Lancelot, like Arthur, just accepted this killing as some minor fault? No, she was not ready to hear the answer.

Then Lancelot took her hand. "Would that we could dance in the fields and under the moon."

Guinevere saw the love in her face, buried her qualms, and put her arms around her. "Would that we could."

Guinevere clung to Lancelot and prayed with all her heart that Lancelot would never leave her for someone else, or for any other reason.

24   THE FISHER KING

One evening Lancelot sat at the small table in Arthur's room with the king, Gawaine, and Peredur. Though she felt honored to be one of those invited to come to this smaller table after supping at the great round one, she wondered how soon she could leave and go to Guinevere. No, she remembered, Guinevere was sitting up with Fencha, who had the ague. Guinevere's care for the old serving woman made Lancelot think even more highly of her beloved than she had before.

Arthur's room was lit by bronze oil lamps adorned with dragons. Several braziers kept the room hot though it was summer and there was little chill. And the wine that his man, Tewdar, poured in the king's room was even finer than usual. Lancelot enjoyed the taste so much that she had difficulty keeping herself to her usual single goblet.

The talk had drifted to the war, as it so often did. The men liked to discuss the details of battles, but Lancelot would have preferred to forget.

"Aglovale served you well, did he not?" Arthur asked Lancelot.

"Indeed," she said, smiling at the thought of her friend, whom she had not seen since the war. "He was not only brave, but wise as well."

"A fine man," Gawaine added, downing his wine.

"Such a man should be here at Camelot," the king suggested. Even when slouching slightly, Arthur had a regal air. "I want him in my service. Would you visit him and ask him to join us?"

"Surely Peredur should be the one to ask," Lancelot replied, looking at that warrior, who did not slouch a little in his chair as the others did. His military bearing belied the social nature of the evening.

Peredur shook his head. "Aglovale is not overly fond of advice from his older brother. I think he would listen more readily to you."

"Very well. I surely would like to see him," Lancelot agreed. If only all missions the king sent her on could be as pleasant.

Slumping in her chair from exhaustion, Guinevere could barely keep her eyes open, but of course she wanted to see Lancelot. She had spent the previous night watching over Fencha, who had had a high fever. Finally, at midday, the fever had broken. The worry that Fencha might die, as so many people did from fevers, left Guinevere drained, almost too tired to stand.

Lancelot entered, and Guinevere summoned a smile. She looked forward to Lancelot's tender embraces and soothing voice.

Lancelot's eyes sparkled. "Wonderful news. Arthur is sending me to call on my friend Aglovale and invite him to become one of the king's men. I'm so glad to have the chance to see him."

Guinevere frowned. "Wonderful, indeed. You'll have a chance to get away from Camelot for a safe and pleasant journey, while I must wait here and long for you."

Lancelot flinched, as if she had been slapped. She paused, then hurried to clasp Guinevere's hands. "Dearest, I wish you could come with me. Of course I'll miss you. I don't want you to be lonely."

Guinevere tried to hold back her resentment. "Come with you? Oh yes, of course. Travel around the country with you. That can never be." Tears welled up in her eyes, and she could see that Lancelot also was on the verge of weeping.

"I know it's not your fault, my love." Guinevere put her head on Lancelot's shoulder. Though she believed that Lancelot would take her along if she could, Guinevere knew that Lancelot would enjoy the journey anyway, even without her.

Lancelot traveled to Dyfed, where Aglovale's family lived. She crossed the Severn River on a ferry and found a partly restored Roman villa made of stone. A thatched roof in good repair replaced the original one, which likely had been tile. Two boys came running as soon as Lancelot and her horse appeared within sight of the villa. They stared openly at Lancelot.

"Are you an angel?" the older one asked.

Lancelot laughed. "No."

Aglovale came out of the villa and embraced Lancelot. A few hairs in his beard had begun turning gray, though he was young for that.

"I'm glad you've come. These imps are my children, Percy and Illtud. Boys, this is Lancelot, King Arthur's famous warrior."

"Will you teach us how to fight?"

Percy, the tallest, asked eagerly. "I've heard that you're the greatest warrior in the world, and I want to become a great warrior, too."

"You'll learn to fight in time, Percy," his father said with little enthusiasm.

"Lancelot also knows the forest better than anyone else, and he can teach you many things about that."

"Yes, the forest!" Illtud shrieked.

A gentle-faced woman with straying brown hair emerged from the villa.

"This is my wife, Olwen," Aglovale said. "My dear, this is Lancelot, my old commander from the war."

Olwen smiled graciously. "You are well come."

The boys' eyes grew wide when they rode into the forest with Lancelot. For them, the world was full of wings and paws and crawling things, and it all enchanted them. They wanted to hold every insect and follow every bird and butterfly.

In the evenings, they came home exhausted, but not too tired to tell their mother everything they had seen, and their father, too, if he had not come with them, as he sometimes did.

Lancelot learned that going about in the forest with children needed its own rhythms. They moved about in great bursts of energy that exceeded hers, then suddenly became exhausted. Sometimes a particular rock or tree caught their attention for reasons that were not apparent to her, and she had to wait while they explored it.

Lancelot told the children stories about the creatures that lived in the forest. In the evening, sitting by the fire with Aglovale, Lancelot drank the barley beer that Olwen had brewed. Wandering in the forest was all very well, but it was time to broach the reason for her visit.

"The king would like you to live at Camelot and serve him there. It is a great honor that he asks this of you."

She smiled, pleased at giving Aglovale honor.

He shook his head. "I do not like being put in a position where I must refuse the king. My life is here, with my family."

"You could bring your family to Camelot. I should have made that clear," Lancelot said, a little surprised at how quickly he refused. Who could turn down the High King's own request? She never had.

Aglovale did not hesitate. "Then my sons would doubtless become warriors and spend their whole lives fighting. Percy probably will anyway, but Illtud might not if he remains here. And Olwen is fond of running her own house. I would far rather sit at the head of my own modest table than at the king's great one. And I have vowed never to fight again. This is the life for me."

Lancelot stared in disbelief. "That is what you said at the end of the war, but now you have had a chance to rest. Your home is a pleasant one, but do you know what an honor it is to have the king ask you to serve him?"

A smile crept over Aglovale's face. "An honor that you think I should accept. Thank him graciously for me, of course.

"Nothing is more important than family, Lancelot. You would know that if you had one yourself. My wife has a younger sister, a sweet girl . . ."

"Not you, too! Everyone tries to find me a wife," Lancelot exclaimed, jumping up from her bench, then flushing because she feared she had been rude.

"And why not? You'd make a fine husband. It would take only a day's ride to meet her, if you'd come with me."

"I came here to persuade you to change your life, not to have you persuade me to change mine!" Lancelot said, still standing.

Aglovale laughed. "If you will stop trying to persuade me, perhaps I'll stop trying to persuade you. Seeing how happy my life is here should be all the persuasion you need. Sit down and have some more beer."

"It's getting late. I should retire," Lancelot replied.

After retreating to the room where she slept, she thought for a long time on what it might be like to live in a place of her own with Guinevere, but she could not picture taking Guinevere to Lesser Britain, nor indeed Arthur permitting it.

The next day when Lancelot walked in the woods with Aglovale and his sons, they came upon a pond that was still, except for the occasional squawk of a heron or quack of a duck.

"Let's go swimming!" Illtud cried. "Won't you swim with us, Lord Lancelot?"

"No," Lancelot said, inwardly sighing.

How often she had to decline swimming.

"Oh, please, it's so hot!" Illtud begged, and Percy chimed in.

"No," Aglovale chided them. "Don't argue with Lancelot, who is kind enough to take you into the forest and teach you many things. Lancelot does not want to swim."

Lancelot walked on ahead of them.

A moment later she heard Illtud say, "But, father, I've heard him say he likes swimming very much."

"Don't question him about it," Aglovale told the boys. "Perhaps he only swims alone. Perhaps he has battle scars that he doesn't want anyone to see."

Lancelot pointed out the tracks of an otter.

"Good!" said Percy. "Let's hunt it and get an otter skin."

"No," Lancelot said, for she was particularly fond of otters. "You'll be doing enough hunting later. Now you need to watch the creatures, and imagine how it would be to live in their skins. I'll help you find an otter, if you'll promise me that you'll just watch for now."

Of course the boys promised, and she found an otter – actually three of them – and they watched them diving and chasing, and were as full of joy as the otters themselves. The otters sometimes noticed them, then dove, stuck their heads out of the water, and watched the people before resuming their play.

"I do feel as if I've lived in the skins of the animals," Percival said, bouncing like an otter.

The next day Lancelot said Aglovale might take the boys swimming as they wanted to go so much. Meanwhile, she would rest. Aglovale said he would take them to the pond where they had found the otters.

But as soon as they had gone Lancelot went to the woods by another path and headed to a different pond, where she stripped off her clothes. Hiding them behind a bush, she slipped into the water. Swallows dipped around her, and she was glad. She did not believe the tales that said they visited the devil in hell.

Cooled from the day's heat, she rose from the waters and stepped to the shore. She put on her breeches, but just as she was putting on her tunic, she heard a gasp, looked up and saw Aglovale, fully clothed, walking on the path by the pond.

He stared at her as if she were a dragon emerged from the waters. Then he quickly turned and called out, "Not this way, boys. I know a shortcut," and hurried away.

Shaking, Lancelot pulled on her clothes. Her heart was heavy. She had no fear of Aglovale, but wondered whether he would still be her friend. She walked reluctantly back along the path without enjoying flowers or trees. She had no idea how welcome a guest she would be at his villa now, but she had to return to it.

It was dusk when she arrived.

Tentatively, she entered. "Supper is almost ready," Aglovale said in a tone much like his usual one. "The boys and I had a fine swim today."

She forced herself to look him in the eye and saw the same friendly smile that she had seen many a time in the war. He shook his head as if perplexed, but still he smiled.

The supper was ordinary enough.

When the children had gone off to bed, Lancelot sat near the firepit with Aglovale and Olwen as she had on other evenings. She marveled that a man sat in the evening with his wife rather than with other men.

Taking up her embroidery, Olwen smiled at Lancelot. "It is good that you go out in the forest with our sons. But, dear husband, why don't I go out into the forest with Lancelot and our children? You can see that the cows are milked, the straw on the floor is clean, the mead is fermenting as it should, the bread rises, the clothes are mended, and the supper is prepared, and watch that the serving woman does not sleep all day or go off to visit her young man."

"Oh, no, my dear," Aglovale said hastily. "I could never do your tasks as well as you do them."

"No doubt it would be harder for you to learn them than for Lancelot to learn how to fight," Olwen replied, casting a baleful glance at him. She smiled again at Lancelot.

Lancelot tried to return the smile. So Aglovale had told his wife. "Be assured that neither of us will reveal your secret," Aglovale said, proffering Lancelot a cup of mead. "How did you ever manage to keep hidden during the Saxon War?"

"With great difficulty. I didn't bathe during the whole course of the war. I must have smelled rank," she said, looking to see whether he would agree.

"No worse than the rest of us, I'm sure, though we plunged into streams a few times. Our smell alone would have been enough to make the Saxons faint, if they hadn't smelled still worse." Aglovale downed some mead and Olwen wrinkled her nose.

The next morning, they all ate bread and cold meats. Percy looked with puppy eyes at Lancelot.

"Lord Lancelot, could I have an adventure with you alone?" he begged.

"Very well, if your parents agree," Lancelot said.

"A dangerous adventure," Percival insisted.

"Yes, dangerous enough for a boy of ten years," Aglovale said, smiling.

"I understand," Lancelot agreed. "Shall we go on the river in a boat?" she asked the boy. "Will that be a great enough adventure?"

"Will we have to fight anyone?"

"Probably not," Lancelot admitted.

"Well, I suppose a boat ride would be interesting," the boy acknowledged.

Lancelot took him to the river, and they found a dilapidated mud-daub hut with a small boat nearby. No one came to the door when Lancelot knocked, but they heard a weak sound from within.

"We should go in," Lancelot said, leading Percy inside.

The hut was only moderately clean, and smelled strongly of fish. They found an old man moaning on a pallet. His face was pale and gaunt.

"Are you very ill?" Lancelot asked him. "How can we help you?"

"Please bring me some water," he begged.

"Get him some water, Percy," Lancelot said as she bent over the old man. Percival found an old tin bucket and left the hut.

Can that really be an old fisherman? Percy pondered as he looked for a stream. A stream would surely have purer, more life-giving water than the nearby river. No, the man's face was too noble. Many of the apostles were fishermen, so no one should be fooled if a saint took on a fisherman's garb as a disguise. After

423

all, this was an adventure with Lancelot of the Lake, the magical warrior, so things were not as they seemed.

This was no ordinary fisherman, but a king in disguise. A fisher king. That look of suffering on his face was too profound to come from mere physical pain. No, the king suffered from some great spiritual wound, and if he was not healed, the land around them would be laid waste. The waters would dry up and the trees would shrivel. If the fisher king was ill, all of his people would sicken.

Percy found a glistening brook, darting merrily over rocks. It must come from an enchanted fountain. This surely was the very water that would heal the king. And what he carried was no ordinary bucket. Any fool could see that it must be a magical vessel, enchanted to look like a bucket so no one would steal it. He lowered it reverently into the water and filled it. It was a holy vessel, blessed by a saint.

Percy carried the brimming vessel back to the caer, for of course this was no mud-and-wattle hut, but a stone caer that was under a spell. No, not mere stone – it was gold and silver, but only the eyes of faith could see. To prove his worth, he must bring the water to the fisher king without spilling a drop.

He entered the caer, knelt before the fisher king, and offered him the waters of life.

"Thank you. You're a good lad," the old fisherman said, and Lancelot smiled at Percy with approval. That looked to be a heavy bucket, and the boy had brought it brimming full. But why was he kneeling to the fisherman?

Lancelot talked a while with the man, learned that he had frequent pains in his thigh, and promised to find a wise woman who would know what herbs would be good for him.

"I can't take you out in the boat," the old man said. "But you can take it out yourselves."

Lancelot didn't know much about boats, but she managed to row the little coracle out onto the water for a short distance, and Percy's brown eyes shown with delight.

The day had been fair, and Lancelot was not greatly alarmed when clouds appeared in the sky. Then the clouds darkened, so she decided to row back to the shore from which they had come.

But sooner than seemed possible, rain began to fall, driven by a sudden wind. Percival laughed at the rain, but Lancelot did not. She had let the boat flow with the current, and found that rowing back against the current was far harder. The waters would not take her where she wanted to go, but pulled her onward. A surging current smashed the little leather boat against a rock, catching Lancelot's mutilated left hand against the stone. She dropped the oar.

"God's mercy!" she cried out. How could she steer the boat back to safety with only one oar? The task had been difficult enough with two. She tried to row in the direction of the lost oar, but the water dashed it far away, carrying it down the river. The little boat spun out of her control. Rain pelted down on them, filling the boat.

"Bail out the boat!" Lancelot cried to the boy.

"Don't fear, I brought the holy vessel," Percy said, scooping the water out with the old tin bucket. "This boat moves by itself," the boy exclaimed. "The Lord is taking us on an enchanted journey, perhaps as far as the Holy Land." He seemed wild with delight.

Shuddering, Lancelot tried vainly to guide the boat towards the riverbank. It was unlikely that Percy could swim well enough to navigate the surging river. She could imagine the boy's young head sinking beneath the waters.

If the boat sank, was her swimming strong enough to save both of them?

She would rather die than tell Aglovale and Olwen that she had caused the death of their beloved son.

The boat dashed onto a rock. A great hole was torn in its side. Water rushed in, and the boat began to sink.

"If the boat capsizes, hold onto me," Lancelot ordered, trying to keep her voice calm. "I'll help you get to shore."

"The Lord will save us," said Percy, still apparently unafraid.

The current brought them a little closer to the bank.

Lancelot stretched out the oar, trying to dig it into the bank. The boat was swept along, and she dropped the second oar.

"No!" she gasped. Her heart seemed to stop beating. Blessed Mother, if you do not care about saving me, at least save this innocent child, she prayed.

A massive sycamore, the largest Lancelot had ever seen, hung over the riverbank. She reached up, grabbing for a branch, and held on. "Hold me, Percy!" she yelled.

The boy grabbed hold of her, and the boat spun on without them. Percy held her fast, and the bucket was slung over his arm.

"The bough will break! Jump to shore!" Lancelot cried.

The boy jumped. She saw him land on the bank, grasping at roots to keep from slipping into the waters. She jumped, and heard the branch crack just as she let go. She thudded against the bank, but she managed to get hold of roots and pull herself up. Percy still hung from the roots, but she grasped his arms and dragged him to safety.

The rain stopped as suddenly as it had started.

"I saved the holy vessel!" Percy said, picking up the bucket, which had spun onto the bank when he jumped. "The enchanted boat may go as far as the Holy Land. I wish we could go with it, but I suppose I wouldn't want to leave my family without saying farewell."

The boat was carried out of their sight.

Lancelot thought it would soon sink, but she kept her thoughts to herself. She pulled herself up on the bank, gasping with relief.

"The Lord has cared for us." Percy still seemed unafraid.

Lancelot nodded, wondering whether he was saintly or just foolish. She staggered to her feet.

"Now we shall have to walk back. And pay someone to make a new boat for the fisherman. He may be too weak to build another himself," she said, feeling wretched at losing the man's source of livelihood.

"I must return the holy vessel to the fisher king," Percy said, smiling. "He must have known that the enchanted boat would leave him."

Keeping near the riverbank, they made their way through brush and bracken back to the simple hut.

They passed the hut of a crone, and Lancelot asked her to visit the old fisherman and bring him her best medicines. She promised to do so.

The sun shone again, and their clothes were half dry by the time they had visited the old fisherman, paid him for the boat, returned the bucket, and made their way back to Aglovale's villa.

Percival's words spilled out before Lancelot say anything.

"It was a great adventure," he told his brother and his parents. "We went to the caer of the fisher king, who was very sick. He needed a drink from a holy vessel, and I got it for him. Then we rode in an enchanted boat that moved by itself."

"But there was a storm!" Olwen protested, putting her hand out to feel his damp clothing. "Were you out on the river then?"

Lancelot nodded and sighed. "But we are safe now, thank St. Peter and all the apostles who were fishermen." She collapsed onto a chair.

"Change your clothes, Percy," his mother said.

"And you should, too, Lancelot," she added.

Guinevere asked Luned to bring her honeycakes, and the serving woman went off to get some. Fencha raised her eyebrows. She did not say that Guinevere had eaten very well at the round table only a little while before.

Guinevere ignored the implied criticism. She knew that she ate more, especially more sweets, when Lancelot was gone. They filled an empty place in her, and Lancelot never smiled the less if Guinevere grew plumper.

Nevertheless, Guinevere wanted exercise, and she preferred that to be on horseback. She had been riding with Bors every day, and, much as she liked him, she was tired of his pious remarks. So she was not much grieved when he asked to be excused the next day to help his oldest son buy a horse. She decided not to ask any other warrior to accompany her.

Guinevere rose early and went to the stables. She smiled at the young stablehands on duty.

"Today I shall ride alone," she said.

They stared at her.

"Will you be safe, your highness?" one of them asked.

"I shall not go far." She smiled even more warmly. "And I shall be sure to praise you to the king. I think you also need a new roof."

"Thank you, highness," the men said. They beamed at her.

She rode off alone, though she knew she could not do it often. She hoped that Arthur would not hear about it.

In a meadow, she paused to watch two fawns that frolicked while their mother munched on tall grasses.

But the doe soon ran off and the fawns bounded after her.

Guinevere let her mare run, but even as she did, she heard another horse galloping. Turning her head slightly, she saw a warrior on a brown horse.

Guinevere shivered, and swerved to the right, directing her horse into the forest.

As before, the warrior did not follow her there.

Guinevere caught her breath, but she still shook. It must be the same warrior who had pursued her before – also when Lancelot was away on a journey. The man just wanted to frighten her, she hoped. But who would want to do that?

Her thoughts turned to Gawaine, who seemed to be her only enemy at Camelot. If she had really been pursued the day that Lancelot fell from her horse, that had been not many months after Guinevere had confronted Gawaine. The man couldn't be Gawaine himself, because the last time she had been pursued, Gawaine had been traveling with Lancelot. But Gawaine could easily have persuaded or paid some other man to follow her. True, she had never heard of Gawaine doing anything by stealth, but a man who could kill a girl must be capable of anything.

She couldn't tell anyone. There was no proof that the pursuer was not imaginary.

And if Arthur learned that she was riding alone, his solution would be to put a stop to it.

True, it was a great risk for a queen to ride alone, but she longed to do so once or twice a year. And the strange man had followed her two or three times, but done nothing more.

One evening when Lancelot and the boys returned, Aglovale had another guest, a beefy old man named Cadwy, who was introduced as Olwen's father. Olwen and Aglovale both smiled, but their eyes looked weary.

"I'm honored to meet the great Lancelot," Cadwy boomed. His voice and his breath showed signs of mead consumed. "Why can't you go out on quests as he does, Aglovale, instead of hanging around your home with your wife and children? Don't you have the courage to go out looking for fights?"

Aglovale sighed, as if he had already answered the question a dozen times that day. "I would rather be with my family."

"Aglovale was very brave in the war with the Saxons," Lancelot protested. "Surely that is more than enough fighting to last a lifetime."

"But you still fight," Cadwy insisted. "It is a great shame for a man to be so fond of sparring with his wife that he no longer wants to fight like a man."

"I don't know which is worse, your view of love or your view of fighting," Olwen told her father.

But Cadwy would not leave off. "If only Aglovale were as manly as Lancelot."

Olwen laughed, and the laughter spread to Aglovale and Lancelot. "Truly, I think Aglovale is a better father than a man like Lancelot would be," Olwen said.

"I agree," Lancelot added. She saw that she would never persuade Aglovale to go to Camelot. It was time for her to leave.

Lancelot came back full of stories about the wonders of Aglovale's children and full of praise of Aglovale.

"Imagine," she told Guinevere, "a man who is always teaching his children things and telling them stories. And when the children are not there, he speaks mostly about them."

Guinevere's brow creased. "And if you could find such a man, would you go off and have children?"

She did not look at Lancelot, but stared out of her window into the dark. Lancelot burst out laughing and grabbed one of Guinevere's clenched hands. "Why, I have never had such a thought in my life! Don't worry yourself." She pulled Guinevere to her and pressed their lips together.

Guinevere sighed and relaxed.

"But still it would be good to help orphan children, if only we could," Lancelot ventured, holding her tight. For she had begun to imagine what life might be like if she could have married Guinevere, though she tried to keep such thoughts out of her mind. How could they give up Camelot, the best and noblest place in the world? The land that embodied justice? The place where nearly all her friends lived?

One afternoon, after telling Arthur about some particularly fine horses the tax collectors had taken from a reluctant lord, Guinevere said, "I recall that poor mad Gryffyd has a daughter. His wife died in childbed during the war. I have sent to Dyfed for the girl to be raised as a fosterling here."

Arthur smiled, but did not put down the tablet on taxes that he had been scanning. "Very thoughtful of you. Perhaps the sight of her will rouse her father to his senses."

Guinevere nodded, though she thought that was unlikely.

Some weeks later, a girl of about ten years with flyaway brown hair was brought to Guinevere's room. "This is the Lord Gryffyd's daughter, Talwyn, Lady Guinevere," said a lady stern of voice and face. "I am Clarissa, daughter of Claudius, who traveled with her. Bow to the queen, child."

The girl's bow had a bounce to it, and her brown eyes looked up questioningly.

"That's not a proper bow!" the lady reprimanded her.

"The queen won't like you if you're so undisciplined."

"Oh, but I shall," Guinevere said, touching the girl's shoulder. "Thank you so much for bringing her here. Please leave us," she said with courtesy but little warmth, for what she had seen of the lady was enough to inspire dislike.

The lady gave Talwyn a look that was none too kind. "Mind the queen," she said sternly. She bowed far more deeply than necessary, and took her leave.

"She must have been awful to travel with," Guinevere said.

"She is awful." Talwyn nodded.

"Please sit down. Or would you rather look around the room first?"

"Could I look at the room? I never saw anything so pretty."

Guinevere showed her wall hangings, gowns, and jewels, then bade her sit down at the table. She sent Fencha to bring the child some wheaten bread and honey.

"The clothes and jewels are all very well," Guinevere told her, "but here are my true treasures." She indicated her scrolls and books. "Have you learned to read?"

Talwyn shook her head. "No, lady queen."

Guinevere was amused. "Lady Guinevere will do. We both know that I am queen, so we don't need to keep reminding ourselves of it. I shall teach you how to read."

The little brow wrinkled. "But, Lady Guinevere, everyone says that I am stupid and slow. I don't sew or spin at all well."

"Do they say that?" Guinevere frowned. "You don't seem stupid or slow to me. I don't sew or spin well, either, so perhaps they would say that I am stupid and slow as well."

The little mouth opened wide. "No one would say that, Lady Guinevere."

"Indeed not, even if I were. Do you like to sew or spin?"

The little head shook. "No, Lady Guinevere."

"Well, everyone must do some work, and you must do that, but I shall teach you other things as well."

Fencha appeared bearing the bread and honey.

"Now have some food, child," Guinevere told her.

She watched intently while the girl ate. Her manners were none too dainty. Guinevere smiled at that.

When Talwyn finished, she licked the last of the honey from her lips and looked up.

"I'm a bad girl, Lady Guinevere," she confessed.

"How so? Why do you say that, child?" Guinevere felt as if she were falling under a spell that was not unlike falling in love.

"My mother died and my father is mad. Nurse said it's because I'm bad and unruly. What's mad, Lady Guinevere?"

Guinevere felt her blood race with anger, but she concealed it so the child would not think she was angry at her. "What dreadful things to tell you. Your mother died because she was trying to give birth to another child. Many women die in childbed."

"I know. I was there." The girl's voice trembled. "But Nurse said that if I had prayed better, she wouldn't have died."

"Nonsense, that had nothing to do with it." Guinevere, speaking in a voice of authority, pressed the girl's hand. "Why would God punish your mother because of a little girl's prayers? I saw my mother die in childbed, too, so I can understand how you feel. And your father was much grieved by fighting in the war and cannot find his way out of it. He cannot believe that the war has ended. Neither of these things has anything to do with you. None of it is your fault. Never listen to anyone who tells you such cruel lies."

Talwyn just looked up at her. The girl's wide brown eyes reminded Guinevere of Lancelot's, though they did not have the hint of sorrow that still lingered in her lover's eyes at times.

"Tell me if anyone here is cruel to you. I shall not allow it."

Guinevere rose. "I shall have Fencha show you to the room where the girls sleep. Is there anything else you want, Talwyn?"

The girl nodded. "I want to see my father."

Guinevere scrutinized the girl's face to see whether she could bear it. "So you shall. I'll take you to see him. But it will be difficult. He was so often attacked by Saxons that he tends to think that every man he sees is a Saxon, come again to attack, although the king has subdued all of them. Your father generally realizes that women are not Saxons, so I hope that he will recognize you, but I don't know whether he will. Try to be brave, because he has suffered a great deal." She put her hand on Talwyn's shoulder. The girl nodded solemnly.

Guinevere took Talwyn to the locked room where Gryffyd was kept. He had serving men – ones who passed the test of not looking like Saxons to him – attending him, so he looked presentable enough. They entered the room, which was small and dark and rather pungent.

Guinevere and Talwyn were not accompanied by guards because around Gryffyd it was safer not to be. Huw, the serving man who was his chief warder, let them in. Tending a madman was no great joy, Guinevere supposed.

"It's Queen Guinevere," Huw told Gryffyd in a voice that held a hint of anxiety.

Gryffyd liked Guinevere but was unpredictable.

He raised his weary face and moaned. "My poor queen, still a captive like me!"

"Yes, but I am well treated and fed well," she replied, thinking there was more truth to what she said than anyone might guess. "Do they still feed you well?"

He moaned again. "Oh, they feed me like a king, the devils, but a man wants more." She smiled in an attempt to warm him.

"You do have more. Your daughter is living with me now, and she cheers me greatly. She is safe and well, and wants to see you." She pulled the girl up beside her.

"Talwyn!" her father howled. "Better you should be dead than a captive of the foul Saxons. Where is my sword?" He thrashed out his arms, and Guinevere grabbed one of them. He ceased struggling.

"No, no, my good Gryffyd. We are well treated in this caer. No one will harm her. I give you my word. Guinevere's word."

He faltered. "Truly?"

"I'm safe, Da," Talwyn told him. "I just wanted to see you."

"My poor little girl." He reached out and patted her head. "But where's your mother? Did the Saxons . . .?"

"No, Da, she died in childbed. I saw her." Talwyn's voice quaked.

"In childbed, to be sure. My poor Gwen. You know that she was named like you, my lady," he said to Guinevere, lucidly enough. It was true; Guinevere had been his wife's name.

"My poor little girl. What can I do for you?" He lifted the little face and looked into it.

"I shall care for her myself, never fear. She'll grow to be a fine woman," Guinevere assured him.

"But the Saxons," he moaned. "But a captive."

"I swear that no Saxon will ever touch her," Guinevere replied. "She'll be no more a captive than any other woman. Less, if I can manage it."

"You are such a great queen that even the Saxons heed your word," Gryffyd said, kissing her hand.

"Be brave, my child," he told Talwyn. "Listen to the queen."

"Yes, Father," she promised solemnly.

"Rest you calm, Gryffyd," the queen said, and took the girl from the room.

When the door closed behind them, she pressed Talwyn into her arms. "You're a brave girl." Talwyn wept on her shoulder.

Lancelot crossed Talwyn's path in a passageway when the girl was carrying some vellum to the queen. She was pleased that her dear Guinevere had a fosterling to care for. "It is well that Lady Guinevere is teaching you to read. Perhaps you'll be as clever as she is."

Talwyn grinned. Her hair was as unruly as usual. Lancelot smoothed it. "I'll never be that, my lord," the girl said. "I like the reading, but the Latin grammar makes little sense to me. It's so silly to say that things like tables and farms are male or female that I can never remember which is which."

Lancelot laughed louder than she usually did. "Yes, it can be hard to remember."

"I watch the boys in the courtyard with their wooden swords. They look to be having such fun. I wish I could have one." She looked up at Lancelot as if imploring her.

"Do you indeed?"

The next day, Lancelot appeared at the queen's room in the afternoon, an unusual hour for her, and through the commonly used door, not the hidden one. She bore a wooden practice sword.

"The young lady wants one. It can do no harm." Lancelot said, but her voice made it a question, addressed of course to Guinevere. Talwyn, who had been bending over a wax tablet, also turned to the queen.

Guinevere merely shrugged and said, "Why not, child? You can keep it in my room. But don't tell anyone."

Talwyn pressed her hand to her heart and swore that she would not.

Guinevere watched with pleasure while Lancelot and Talwyn, brandishing wooden swords, jumped around the room. Talwyn had been brought in after Lancelot so she would not see that

Lancelot came through the hidden entrance. Fencha had cleared away as many things as she could. It was late, but Talwyn was allowed to stay up at times for these secret lessons.

"Have at you, wicked warrior," cried Talwyn, knocking her sword against the wooden one that Lancelot held.

"Do not scream," Guinevere warned her.

"Beware, Long-Haired Warrior, and watch your footwork. Watch your left, watch your left!" cried Lancelot, attacking on her right as soon as the girl turned to the left. "Don't trust your enemy!"

They knocked over a chair, but Guinevere only smiled.

Lancelot leapt up on the table to attack from above, eliciting delighted shrieks from Talwyn.

"Hush, children, you're too loud," Guinevere scolded them.

"Sorry, my lady. I can scarcely control myself when I face such a formidable foe," Lancelot said, jumping down from the table.

Talwyn's hair was one great tangle. She gasped for breath, and Fencha brought her water to drink. Lancelot and Guinevere exchanged a warm glance over the girl's head.

25 THE FATHERS

Arthur and Gawaine rode through the forest in early autumn, reminiscing about the details of past battles and laughing over old adventures with women. Sunlight dappled the dark forest and they were full of cheer.

Gawaine was glad to spend some time with his royal cousin. It was rare that he could ride out alone with Arthur, as he had more often when they were young. He reached in his pack. "These are the finest of apples," he said. "I go to Avalon every year to pick them. It's sad to see the place overridden with monks and priests, but it still has the best fruit."

"You old pagan!" Arthur chuckled.

"Don't pretend you care," Gawaine teased him. "You would pray to Lugh or any other god for victory."

"I have no problem with the Christian God," Arthur said. "He's clearly stronger than the Saxon gods. Merlin did well to see that I was raised as a Christian."

Gawaine gave a fruit to Arthur, and kept one for himself.

They munched while they rode, savoring the tart, juicy apples.

In a glade, they came upon a plump old nun, who gave them a broad smile. "Greetings, King Arthur, greetings, Gawaine of the Matchless Strength," she said. "Stop a while and refresh yourselves at the brook."

They stopped and greeted her, and drank from the brook that raced through the woods, carrying small fish on great quests. Gawaine smiled at a frog that leapt away with a croak when it saw them.

"It is nearly harvest time," the old nun said. "What you have sowed you shall reap. Look for your children."

Arthur gave her a pitying look. "Your prophecies are wrong. I have none," he said. "More's the pity."

"Yes, you do," she told him, her gray eyes reproachful. Then she regarded Gawaine. "You have a daughter whom you must find someday."

Gawaine felt a momentary surge of joy, but then told himself it was foolish to believe the old woman's ranting. "I had a daughter who died the day she was born."

"You have another, who knows nothing about you. You should find her."

Perhaps the old nun was right. He had been with so many women. Of course there might be children, especially from the time when he was so young that he never tried to prevent them. Why did he think so little about that? Didn't he want to see such children, if they existed? Gawaine realized that indeed he did want to see any child of his.

Perhaps the nun did know of a daughter. "Where is she? Do you know?"

"She's in a place with many other women, I can't tell you where," the old nun said solemnly, a stern look on her wrinkled face. She now seemed as cheerless as her black robes.

The old woman appeared to be so certain. A place with many other women? That sounded bad. Perhaps that was why the nun's face was grim. "Oh Gods, I must find her." He groaned. "The poor girl must be in a bawdy house." His feeling of elation vanished. His stomach heaved. He realized what he had never admitted before: Many whores – he did not know how many – must be forced by panderers to do what they did.

"How can I find her? Does she look like me?"

"Only around the eyes," the nun told him. "Blessed are they who try to right every wrong, especially their own."

Then she turned to Arthur. "You also have children. If you don't find them, it will lead to their destruction and yours."

"A girl?" Arthur asked. "In some low house, like Gawaine's daughter?"

"Yes to the girl. And, yes, one child is in a low house."

"I have no great interest in a bastard daughter, and certainly not one like that. That's no child fit for a king. How could I take her to the court?" Arthur shook his head. "She would disgrace me."

"But surely many men would be glad to marry a king's daughter, even a bastard," Gawaine said, stunned by Arthur's response. "You might make another ally by such a marriage."

"Not with a girl who has been raised as a whore." Arthur shook his head. The nun cried out in anger at his words and, turning away from them, stalked off into the trees.

They did not try to detain her.

Arthur looked not sorry to see her go. "The old woman was raving. It's clear that I cannot father any child. Would you really look for a girl who's ruined just because that madwoman told you to?" he asked Gawaine.

"What does ruined mean in a daughter?" Gawaine asked. "She would still be my child." He was already imagining what he would do if he found her. It wouldn't be possible to get her the kind of husband he'd want. No nobleman would wed her. "I could get some old Roman villa for her, and provide for her, so she could take only what lovers she likes."

Arthur raised his eyebrows. "Are you truly going to search bawdy houses for a daughter you've never seen? It's an impossible task – you'll never find her. And if you did, what do you think she'd be like? Glad to have a rich father, no doubt, but not likely to be fond of you."

Gawaine grunted, not pleased at the thought of being seen only as a source of wealth. "That's not the point. Of course she might be numb, hardened, or embittered, but she'd be free."

Perhaps the nun was mad, but she had seemed sane. She reminded Gawaine of the holy men and women of the old faith he had encountered as a child. She did not hide away in tremulous modesty, but issued orders. That was how a holy woman acted.

Would he search for this daughter, who might be only a phantom? Why, it was better to search and be mistaken than to refrain and always fear that he had a daughter living in misery. He knew that he could never forget the nun's words. If only she had told him who the mother was, so he would know where to start looking.

The joy between men and women was fleeting, Gawaine thought. But the bond between parent and child, that was far stronger. At least his bond with his mother was, though he never thought of his long-dead father with much affection. But some children must love their fathers, even if he had not.

Of course if he wanted children, he did not need to search for this girl. All he had to do was marry. But the thought of marriage made him recoil as it always did. He imagined being tied to a woman whose face he was tired of, whose voice made him weary.

442

Of course he probably would marry again someday, but only if he found a woman who would always interest him, or if his longing for sons became stronger. A man of almost any age could have sons.

So they rode on. Arthur mused, "In the unlikely event that this tale is true, and there is a girl in a brothel who is identifiably my daughter, no doubt you'll find her and help her discreetly. There is no need for the king to be involved."

"Of course I shall look for her as I search for my own daughter," Gawaine agreed, amazed that Arthur cared so little about this possible child. Any child of Arthur's would be Gawaine's kin, too, so he wanted to find her, though not with the same passion he felt at the thought of finding his own child.

Passion? Yes, he felt more stirred by this daughter than he had been by anything in years. Though he knew she might not care about him, he hoped she would.

He pictured a girl who looked rather like his mother, only with bluer eyes like his own, throwing her arms about him and sobbing on his shoulder that she was glad he had come to rescue her. Although he couldn't imagine most of the whores he had known acting in such a way, he nonetheless thought his daughter might.

Gawaine took on many small quests looking for his child. He first went to all of the bawdy houses anywhere near Camelot, to see whether any of the girls had his eyes. In the first brothel, he looked at the girls, whose eyes were all kohl-darkened. Only two had blue eyes, and one was a woman too old to be his daughter. The other had eyes of a pale, watery blue, nothing like his. Seeing him look at her, she winked in an attempt at flirtation that was clearly half-hearted. She seemed too young to be a whore, only about thirteen. Gods, the girls seemed so much younger than they had before he had begun looking for a daughter.

An older redhead with large breasts whom he had been with before said, "Stay back, girls, he's come to see me. Haven't you, Gawaine?"

He nodded and went with her. But once in her room, he told her that he was tired, and just sat on her bed and rested. He paid her anyway, of course.

At the next bawdy house, most of the girls looked too young for whoring. His gorge rose and he chose none of them. He realized that he would never again want to lie with a woman he had bought.

The panderers and the customers gave him sneering smiles because he did not choose any women. He could bear their disdain only because he was so used to having men envy him for all the women who flocked to him.

Then he searched out women he had been with, at least the lowborn ones, because it was their daughters who might find themselves in brothels. He knew it was an impossible search. He had no idea how to find them all, but the thought of the daughter, perhaps with his mother's face, impelled him to try. He imagined a girl like his mother being pawed by drunken men.

He rode to a dusty farm and wandered through the pigs and fowl to the thatch-roofed farmhouse.

A dark-haired woman heavy with child was weeding a vegetable garden. "What do you want here?" she demanded.

"I came to learn whether you ever bore a child of mine," he asked, as courteously as possible.

She put her hands on her hips. "What do you care? No, I never did, and a good thing, too. Now, get off before my husband sees you talking to me. You warriors are all worthless louts, taking all you can get."

"Good day," he said, making a circle around a pig and swinging back onto his horse.

He hadn't remembered her name. He hoped that not all the women would curse him. Would a daughter curse him, too?

He rode to a goldsmith's shop in a nearby town. Dogs and children played in the muck of the street. The clatter from a blacksmith's shop filled the air.

At the goldsmith's, a young sandy-haired apprentice sat at a bench.

"Is your master's daughter Erith about?" Gawaine asked, though he feared that she had long since married and moved away.

A large, buxom woman with a neat brown braid hurried in from a room at the rear of the shop. She called out, "Gawaine! I'd know your voice anywhere. Go off, lad, and let me talk with the noble warrior."

The apprentice darted out into the bustling street.

"It's good to see you, Erith. You're still as pretty as ever." She was not. He wondered how much banter would be needed.

"Still the same flatterer you always were. Well, I'm no young thing to listen to it now," she said, but she grinned at him.

"I know this is a strange question to ask after all these years, but did you ever bear a child of mine?" he asked, feeling like a fool.

Erith's smile faded and tears came into her eyes. "I did indeed, a fine strong lad. He died in a Saxon raid."

Gawaine shook and put an arm out to her. "Oh, Erith, I'm sorry."

"I wish you had seen him." She dabbed her eyes with a cloth.

"So do I," Gawaine replied, realizing that he was telling the truth. "I wish you had sent me a message about him."

Tears dripped down her cheeks. "I should have. But my father urged me to because he believed you would give me money, and I couldn't bear for you to think that's what I wanted."

He took hold of her hand. "I wouldn't have thought that of you, but I owed it to the boy to provide for him. Do you have other children?"

"Aye. I married my father's apprentice, who was good to me, but him and my father both died of a fever. He left me with a boy and two girls. I have the shop, and a fine apprentice, but I'm so lonely."

She gave him a look that he knew well. Though she was no longer as pretty as he had recalled, he spent the night with her. He knew she wanted him to visit again, and so he would. He realized that it was unlikely that any daughter of Erith's would be in a brothel; perhaps he had just been drawn to see her again. Some of the women who were too lowborn for a king's son to wed were more pleasant than the women he could have married.

In another town, Gawaine went to a tavern, and found a thin woman who frowned at him. Only one customer sat at a table near the fire.

"Greetings, Senara," he said cordially. "So you still own this tavern."

"I do. The ale's good, if you want to buy some. You wouldn't much like the wine." Senara, whose fair hair was bundled in an untidy braid, seemed indifferent to him.

"Ale, then."

She poured him some ale. It didn't taste too bad.

"I have been thinking about my life and wondering whether I have any children. Did I leave you with child?"

Her eyes narrowed. "I had a daughter. I suppose she was yours."

"And where is she?" he asked. Perhaps she might be the girl in the brothel.

"She died in childbed at thirteen." Senara's face was blank.

446

"I'm sorry." He tried to imagine what it must be like to die at thirteen.

She stared at him with cold gray eyes. "If you're so sorry, you might give me a little for the cost of raising her."

"Of course." Gawaine pulled off a gold armring, one taken from a Saxon he had killed, and gave it to her. He had many others.

She fingered the gold.

He was just as glad that Senara's daughter wasn't the girl he was seeking. He was hoping for a girl who was much warmer-hearted than Senara. But why should Senara be warm to him? He had simply used her and ridden away.

Gawaine kept on searching, but there was no sign of a living daughter. He would go back to court, or on his more usual missions for the king. Then, after a while, thoughts about her nagged him. He could imagine that being required to see many men in a night was not pleasant, so he searched some more.

Lancelot's muscles ached from teaching riding maneuvers to aspiring warriors. As she walked across the courtyard, she thought only of the pleasures of rest. A whirlwind threw itself at her. Talwyn, hair tangled as usual though she grew taller and taller, grabbed her arm.

"Lord Lancelot! Look at my essay." She thrust a wax tablet in Lancelot's hands.

"You're writing essays now! Splendid!" Lancelot smiled at her.

"Do you like it?" Talwyn looked at her with imploring eyes.

"I haven't had a chance to read it yet." Clearly Talwyn expected her to read it while standing in the courtyard. Lancelot obliged. The essay, which touched on farmers and weather, seemed charming to Lancelot, although she was not certain whether all the verb tenses were correct.

447

"It's wonderful," she proclaimed, beaming at Talwyn, who took a little leap, presumably of joy.

"Oh, thank you! Queen Guinevere said I shouldn't use the expression 'mirabile dictu' three times in such a short essay. But it sounds so grand."

It was an expression that Talwyn used frequently in speaking as well. "Probably the queen is correct, but it's a pretty expression, and I don't mind hearing it often." Lancelot returned the tablet. The girl darted off.

When Lancelot visited the queen's room that night, Guinevere's greeting was more restrained than usual. She bade Lancelot sit and poured her some wine.

"I am sorry to say this," Guinevere said, taking hold of Lancelot's hand, "but Talwyn is growing up, and you will have to be more formal with her to preserve her reputation."

Lancelot pulled away, knocking over her winecup. "What! She's still a child."

She grabbed a cloth and mopped up the wine she had spilled.

"Yes, she's an innocent girl, but some of the ladies complained about her earnest talk with you in the courtyard. They thought it improper for her to be so familiar with an unrelated man." Guinevere made a face as if she were tasting something bitter.

"She's like a daughter to me!"

"I know, dearest, but no one else will see it that way." Guinevere took her hand again. "You seem to be a man, and young girls cannot be too friendly with men or gossips will say they are loose. I had to tell Talwyn she must be more distant with you."

"That's awful." Tears formed in Lancelot's eyes.

"Yes, it is." Guinevere kissed her, but the kiss did not soothe away the hurt.

After the king had played a board game with Lancelot and defeated her as usual, Merlin walked in without knocking.

Although Lancelot usually was not especially glad to see Merlin, she was not sorry to see him at the moment. She preferred to have other company around when she was with the king. Impatient to visit Guinevere, she stared out of the window at the moon, only half of which was visible that night.

Arthur greeted Merlin warmly. "How good to see you. Please join us."

But the old sage declined a chair. "I worry about the young men who have been coming to you since the war," he said, his voice even more somber than usual. "It is not enough to teach them to fight. A teacher must love his students and show them how to live."

"As you taught me." Arthur looked up at Merlin, for all the world as if he were still the old man's pupil.

Lancelot put away the game pieces in a carved wooden box that belong to Arthur.

"Now that we have vanquished the Saxons for some time, how can we give the young men a goal, so they don't just rush around the countryside testing their prowess in needless fights?" Merlin asked.

Lancelot seldom said much around Merlin, but now she felt moved to speak. "I have been thinking about that problem. Perhaps we could hold a religious ceremony when a young man vows to join the king's service, so that he might be inspired to do good deeds. The young men could hold a vigil in the chapel the night before the ceremony."

Arthur nodded. "A religious ceremony. Yes, I like that idea. We must foster the young men carefully."

"That will do for a beginning," Merlin said. "But I fear the next generation. I fear them." Then Merlin left the room in his usual abrupt manner.

Perhaps the old always fear the young, Lancelot thought.

The owner of this brothel didn't even take care to hide the whores' bruises. Most of them had at least one eye blackened. Thank the gods none of them looked in the least like himself or Arthur, Gawaine thought, turning away, only glancing briefly at the proprietor's mocking look because he didn't choose any.

There had been a widow in the next town who had liked him. Perhaps she still did, and had not remarried. He went on his way.

The boy in the kitchen watched the proprietor, Dunaut, who was well enough dressed to pass for nobility, come laughing to the back room. As a servant, the boy needed to watch every movement, for he never knew when the panderers might strike.

"These great warriors from Camelot are nothing as men. We just had one here: Gawaine, who's supposed to be famous for womanizing, but all he wanted to do was look! And only at their faces! All talk and no action! So you can see you're better off with us," Dunaut said, kicking the boy, who was carrying food to the other panderers.

"Don't drop that, or I'll take your hide off!" Tudy, a heavier panderer, yelled at him, but the boy had learned how to carry things without dropping them while receiving a moderately hard kick. He drew on all his strength, for he knew that as soon as he put down the food he would get a harder blow. And, just as he anticipated, Tudy gave him a shove that would have knocked him helpless onto the floor just a year ago. He was stronger now, but he pretended to be unable to keep from falling, as they wanted to see him do.

"Hey, king's boy, pretty face! Come here and beg, and I'll give you a fine crown," jeered Coan, the youngest panderer, holding up a plate covered with gravy.

The boy lifted himself up gradually. He would be hit if he rose either too slowly or too fast.

"Don't dirty his pretty red hair," said Dunaut. "Let's not spoil his looks. He's not bad when all of the girls are busy . . . you pleased me last night, Mordred, so I'll reward you. You can have one of the girls for a while. Aelmena has been sullen today, so she needs to be beaten. You punish her, then you can have her for a little while."

He turned to the other panderers and said, "You know I don't like boys usually, but who could pass up a chance to have a king's son? Pity we can't get money from the king for you, Mordred, but by the time we could tell you looked like him, we had beaten you too much for you to be worth much."

Mordred had heard those words many times. He tried not to show how eager he was for the girl, because if they knew he really wanted something, it would be taken away.

"Thank me prettily, now, Mordred."

"Thank you, noble sir," said Mordred, giving the deep bow they wanted, and calculating for the thousandth time which kitchen knife was the sharpest and which of them it would be most prudent to kill first. Probably Dunaut.

"If only King Arthur could see him now!" laughed Coan.

"He doesn't want to see you, he'll never want to see you," Dunaut jeered. "Your mother was nothing, just another whore, and your father knows nothing about you and cares less. We're your only family, and never forget it. Who knows what would have happened if Gawaine had asked to see the boys? He might have killed you because you'd be a rival heir to the throne."

451

"Or he might have killed us all for keeping you here," Tudy said, taking a swig of ale.

"Or he might have fucked you for a jest and ridden away," Coen said, laughing his ugly laugh.

"Well, he didn't see you," Dunaut said. "Here's a stick to beat the girl."

Mordred took the young whore off and beat her as hard as he could, thinking only of the day when he was strong and skilled enough to kill the panderers, and the more distant day when he could wield a sword at Camelot. He was bitterly ashamed of his mother, a dead whore he couldn't remember.

His father had vanquished the forces of the Saxons, so surely Mordred could defeat three panderers. When he killed them, he planned to own the brothel himself. Then he would pay to learn sword fighting and noble speech and manners. The next vengeance would have to be much slower.

26   THE SEDUCERS

Gawaine woke beside a pretty lady whose brown hair spread across his arm. Dawn's rays had barely begun to sneak through his window, so he wondered whether he could detain her a little longer. She was unmarried, though she was old for it, and he did not want to destroy her reputation, though she had not been a virgin. Strange that she was not better guarded at Camelot.

She opened her eyes, which were hazel. "I suppose you'll be off to a Mass soon," she jested.

"Not likely," he mumbled, stroking her hair.

"How can you bear to attend them?" she asked, sitting up and moving away from him. Her breasts were small but shapely. "A man like you, who was raised in the old faith?"

"Often I stay away, and when I attend, I pay little heed to the words, Cigfa." His voice was slightly cross. A discussion of religion was not what he had in mind.

"How sad it is that the priests' prayers are the only ones at Camelot." Cigfa cast a sad-eyed glance at him.

"The people must long for a ruler who listens to the old gods."

"What?" He sat up abruptly. Cigfa had not been long at Camelot, but even the newest lady should know that her words verged on treason. "The people love Arthur. You must know that." He tried to keep his voice from sounding too harsh, but it was a struggle.

"The people love you, too, Gawaine." Smiling, she put her hand on his arm.

"If so, it is because I am loyal to Arthur." Her touch did not thrill him any longer.

"You are too modest." Her glance was warm. "All the world knows of Gawaine, the great warrior from the North. And all the world knows that he is not truly a Christian, but believes in the old gods. And they would rejoice if you were the one who had the sword of power."

"My cousin's sword?" Gawaine cried. "Can you imagine I would try to take it? If all the world knows so well what is in my heart, they must know that I love Arthur." He left the bed and began pulling on his breeches.

"But don't you love the gods more?" Cigfa also rose from the bed and again put her hand on his arm.

Even the dawn's glow could not make her scheme pretty. Gawaine shook his head. "Do you think the gods can't hear our prayers if we use other names for them? Does it matter so greatly if we say Lugh or Christ? I can pray in a chapel as well as an oak grove." He gently removed her hand from his arm.

"Gawaine!" she cried out, as if in pain. "Think what it would be like to restore Avalon! You are the only one who could do that."

Gawaine put on his tunic, then looked into her eyes.

"I cannot restore the past. No one can."

"But you are the greatest fighter in Britain! Think what you could do if you had the sword of power as well. No one could challenge you."

"The sword has no great power. That is only a tale Arthur created to embellish his legend. Who gave you these ideas? Who sent you to speak with me?" He tried to keep the anger out of his voice. She was too young to remember Avalon.

Her face paled. "Many want you to lead."

He snorted. "I doubt that. Could it have been my cousin Morgan?"

Cigfa raised her head with pride. "I have the honor of knowing the Lady Morgan."

Yellow light was replacing the rays of dawn. Starlings were squawking outside his window. Gawaine sighed. Last night seemed far away. "And this was how she thought to persuade me? It would have been more flattering if she had sent for me herself."

"I am sure she would be glad to speak with you," Cigfa said hastily, but she looked at the floor as if he had insulted her, and perhaps he had.

He touched her hand gently. "I have nothing to say to her. I thank you for your generosity last night, Lady Cigfa, but I wish it had not been because someone asked you to do it."

"It was not for any mortal!" she exclaimed, reddening.

He was ashamed of what he had just said, true though it was. He had as good as called her a whore. She had believed in what she was doing.

Gawaine tried to make his voice gentle. "Pardon my crude speech. I meant no insult. I understand that you were doing all that you did for the goddess. I remember when such things were considered sacred, and Beltane was a ceremony, not a place where people thought only of finding pleasure. I merely doubt that the lady Morgan is as pious as you are." He kissed her forehead, then went to his clothing chest and pulled out a huge cloak.

"This cloak should hide you if anyone sees you leaving my rooms."

She dressed quickly and pulled the cloak over her shoulders. Her face was well hidden in the deep hood.

Left alone, he poured himself some ale, sighing as he did so. He seldom felt sad after lying with a woman, but this time he did. How could anyone imagine that a pretty woman's flattery was enough to make him change his loyalties? How could Morgan tell a girl to lie with him as a way to serve the goddess, when it seemed that Morgan wanted only to serve her own plans, which sounded unsavory? He had difficulty believing that religion was her chief concern. And he was stung that, if she thought bedding was the way to persuade him, she had not tried it herself. He had been pleased with their long ago interlude and had believed that she was also.

Riding through a forest on a fine autumn day, Lancelot enjoyed the yellow leaves, which seemed to promise that life would be eternal, or at least glorious. She hoped to glow as brightly before she fell. She heard geese flying south, calling far above her, and she wondered whether she would ever journey to warmer lands. No, she could not bear to be so far from Guinevere. Her meditations were interrupted when a lady by the side of the road called out to her. The lady was standing beside three horses, no doubt her own and two others.

The lady was about twenty years old, fair of face and elegant of gown. Her embroidered traveling cloak was rather fine for riding.

"You are Lancelot, aren't you? Help me! My husband is fighting another man," she called out. Lancelot rode over to her.

"If you want me to help your husband, you must explain a little more, my lady. Did this man attack him?"

"No," she exclaimed, her voice nearly breaking, "I want you to help the other man. My husband attacked him and he can't fight as well as my husband can."

"Were you running off with him, my lady?"

She shook her head and sighed. "Oh, no. I wouldn't run off with him, because my husband is rich and he is poor. But I do like him and I don't want my husband to kill him. Won't you help?" She stretched out her hands in an imploring gesture.

Lancelot hardly knew where to place her sympathies. "I don't know, my lady. Where are they?"

"In yonder clearing," the lady said, pointing in the direction from which yelling and clattering resounded.

Lancelot dismounted and walked to a clearing where a tall man wearing chain mail was pressing a fierce attack on a slender man in a green tunic. The man without armor had a short sword and was agile, but clearly did not have the same kind of training in fighting as the larger man. Nor was a short sword much protection against a long one.

"What is happening here?" Lancelot called out.

The man in chain mail looked up. His face was red and his eyes glinted like a boar's. "You're Lancelot! I've seen you in fighting contests," he cried.

"Help me punish this cur who tried to seduce my wife. I'm going to kill him."

The one in the green tunic turned slightly. Lancelot saw the seducer's handsome face and rushed into the fight. There was something about the lines of that face, the smooth cheeks, the slim build.

Lancelot threw herself between them and stumbled, so the husband tripped over her. Then she flourished her sword uselessly at the seducer, who ran away. As the husband tried to get up, Lancelot fell into him, making him stumble again.

"What in Annwyn is the matter with you? Are you drunk?" yelled the enraged man.

"Only a little," Lancelot mumbled, using a voice that pretended to be the worse for wine.

They heard the sound of a horse galloping.

"He escaped!" cried the infuriated man, his face redder than ever. "I must follow him."

Then the lady rushed up and flung herself on him. "Oh, dearest, you are safe, thank the holy angels. When I saw that ruffian ride away, I was so afraid that he had killed you." She kissed his cheek and clung to him.

"Yes, yes, I'm safe," he said, shaking her off. "But I must pursue him."

"No, don't give him another chance to kill you!" she moaned, trying again to cling.

"Nonsense, that whoreson can't fight half as well as I can," the man said. "If it hadn't been for Lancelot's blundering, I would have killed him." He stalked off towards the horses. Lancelot and the lady followed.

"But who knows, even you could have an accident and be hurt," his wife said solicitously, as she hurried after him.

"Which way did he go?" her husband asked.

"Oh, I don't remember, it was all a blur. I was so terrified when I saw him run out alone, as if he had hurt you." The lady's voice sounded helpless.

Her husband scowled at her. "Think."

"Oh, I suppose it was that way," she said, pointing. "But it's hard to be sure."

"Why don't you go that way, then, and I'll go the other," Lancelot said helpfully. "If I find him, I can fight him."

"Much good that will do." The man snorted. "You're a disgrace to King Arthur."

"Oh, sir, you have wounded me," Lancelot moaned. "Say anything but that. Surely my disgrace is mine alone."

The man had mounted his horse. "Yes, your disgrace is yours. Go on your way. I don't want you with me."

"Godspeed, my noble husband," his wife said in a tone of stirring devotion.

"Godspeed," Lancelot also called out to him.

He rode off and Lancelot mounted her horse.

"Oh thank you, kind lord," the lady said, smiling warmly.

"Be more careful next time, my lady," Lancelot replied and rode off in the other direction.

After a while, Lancelot saw tracks leave the road and go deeper into the forest. She followed them for a distance. Then she called out, "You can come out now, the man has gone."

Laughing, the seducer appeared from behind an oak tree and strode up to her. Yes, Lancelot had been right, she was another woman dressed as a man.

Lancelot stared. She saw a woman of about her own age, with dark hair, gray eyes, and a slender body. Her green tunic was good but old, as were her cowhide breeches.

"So you're Lancelot. I should have known no man could be as good as the tales say you are. Glad to meet you, Lance. I'm Drian." A man's name, of course. Drian's voice had an accent that was neither a noble's nor a laborer's, and it was not clear where she hailed from. Perhaps from Dyfed. She extended her hand.

Lancelot smiled and clasped it.

"You should be more careful. That lady wanted to stay with her husband, so she surely wasn't worth the risk."

Drian hooted. "How do you know she wasn't? Haven't you ever lain with any married women?"

Lancelot felt herself blush. "Perhaps I have."

"Why not?" Drian patted her on the shoulder. "It's a good jest on the husbands."

"I have never thought of it that way," Lancelot replied stiffly, moving away from her. "So you take advantage of many women? You shouldn't."

Drian laughed again and shook her head. Her gray eyes were full of merriment. "You could say they take advantage of me, couldn't you? Haven't you loved many women?"

"Only one woman. I want no other," Lancelot said in her most formal tone.

"Who is she?"

"I cannot say." Lancelot sealed her mouth in a firm line.

Drian grinned. "Come on, Lancelot of the Lightning Arm. Let me give you something to drink."

"No, well, perhaps a little." Drian was not exactly respectable, but Lancelot did not want to leave the company of the first woman like herself she had ever met.

Drian pulled out a flask from the pack on her horse. She brushed some acorns from a place on the ground and seated herself.

After getting some wheaten bread from her pack, Lancelot joined Drian sitting on the mossy ground. She looked appreciatively at the silver birches and gold-leafed oaks surrounding them. A red squirrel carried acorns to some caer of its own.

Drian offered Lancelot mead, and Lancelot offered her bread.

"For a warrior, you have a kind face," Drian said, drinking some mead.

Lancelot sighed and cut herself a slice of bread. "Perhaps I shouldn't have been a warrior, but it's too late to change my life to a gentler one."

"I'm a harper." Drian gestured to a small harp that was tied to her horse. "Music is the most gentle of all arts."

Lancelot knew that not all music was gentle, but she made no comment about that. "After we have finished our meal, would you play something?"

"For you, gladly." Drian made a sweeping bow, as if to a large audience.

"I would expect to find a harper at some lord's dun, not in the forest."

Drian chuckled. "Sometimes I have to leave those lords very quickly, so it's good to know places in the woods where I can retreat. I can hunt for food. I'm good with a bow and arrow. Sometimes I have to leave before the lords pay me. But if I do -" Drian put her hand in a small bag at her waist, pulled out a silver medallion with an amber stone, and pinned it to her green cloak.

"Why, the man who attacked you was wearing that!" Lancelot exclaimed, horrified.

"Yes, he was, but he wanted to give it to me. Didn't you hear him say so?" Drian's voice was earnest. She buffed the medallion.

"You stole it!" Lancelot felt her face grow hot with anger. She leaned forward.

"Say, rather, that he owed it to me for attacking me, as well as for some days of harping at his holding. I only made his wife happy, which is more than he'll do. No doubt she'll be more content to stay." Drian's voice was not entirely soft now.

"That doesn't make stealing right!" Lancelot argued.

"You've never been in need, I reckon?" Drian's tone held no trace of apology.

"No, I have not," Lancelot admitted, wondering not for the first time what her life would have been like if her parents had not been nobles.

"You can do as you please. One like us who was born poor must make her way however she can and be prepared to leave any place as quickly as possible."

Drian's tone was harsher now. "I never know when someone might guess that I am a woman."

Drian tore her slice of bread to bits. "I've had some close calls when men have suspected I was a woman. I can run fast and I have a fast horse. But you can't always count on having the swiftest horse. You shouldn't live around so many men, Lance. They're dangerous." Drian looked her in the eyes, very seriously.

Lancelot almost jumped, as if she had been stung. "My friends would never turn on me."

"Oh, of course not," said Drian with considerable sarcasm. "Warriors never attack women."

Lancelot studied her bread. "I suppose there aren't many men I could trust to befriend me if they knew I was a woman," she admitted.

"Are there any?"

"At least one knows and is trustworthy," Lancelot said, thinking of Aglovale.

"That's more than I'd have guessed." Drian pressed her shoulder. "Don't think about them. Let me play some music for you." She took up her harp and sang some love songs.

Drian's voice was good, and her playing was spirited but unschooled. Nonetheless, Lancelot much enjoyed hearing her.

"Very pleasant," she said when Drian paused.

Drian shook her head. "I know it's not what you're used to at Camelot. I taught myself. I couldn't risk asking any bard to teach me."

"Of course," Lancelot said, wondering what Drian's playing would have been like if she had been trained.

Drian leapt up. "There's a sport I can beat you in."

Doubting her, Lancelot tried to hide a smile. "What is that?"

"Running."

Lancelot shook her head. "I can run faster than many men."

Drian snorted. "I don't doubt that, nor do I doubt why you'd want to. But I know much less of fighting than you do, so I've had to learn to run faster than anyone. Race me, and I'll show you."

Seeing that she would offend Drian if she refused, Lancelot said, "Very well. The forest is not the best place to run."

"But I'm used to it. Come on, I dare you."

Drian dashed off among the trees, and Lancelot rushed after her. Drian had told the truth. She ran like the wind, and darted around the trees like a hare.

They came to a clearing, and Lancelot almost caught up with her, but not quite. Lancelot felt a surge of exhilaration in her blood as she tried to run as she had never run before, just for the joy of it.

They were among the trees again, and Lancelot tried not to lose speed as she made her way through them, but that seemed impossible. She lost sight of Drian.

Lancelot kept on running as best she could. When she passed a large oak, arms grabbed her. Drian held her and kissed her lips.

Lancelot gasped in astonishment.

"I've won, and you must forfeit a kiss!" Drian cried.

Lancelot simply stared at her.

"What, have you never played catch and kiss?" Drian asked, embracing her.

"No." Drian's touch was far from unpleasant, but remembering Guinevere, Lancelot pulled away.

"How can you have lived so much and still be so innocent?" Shaking her head, Drian laughed. Lancelot flushed.

"I have not met an abundance of women like you."

"That's a pity."

They dropped to the ground and sat a while.

Lancelot had much to say. "How long have you known that you loved women, if I may ask? When did you first . . . ?"

Chuckling, Drian shook her head. "Always, of course. The first time I held a girl in my arms, I was fourteen. And you?"

Lancelot felt her face flush again. "I didn't realize until I was past twenty, and met the woman I love. And I was closer to thirty than to twenty when we first embraced."

"Pity the poor girls who missed you." Drian patted her shoulder. The pat turned into a stroke. "I could be very fond of you."

Lancelot looked her in the eye. "Drian, I have loved only one woman and I always will."

"What!" Drian laughed. "Lance, nobody is that pure."

"I'm not pure, just faithful."

"Perhaps I could change your mind?" She touched Lancelot's cheek.

"No, Drian," Lancelot said gently, removing the hand. "No one can change my mind."

Drian sighed, but changed the subject, and they talked about many things. Then the afternoon light began to fade, but Lancelot was reluctant to leave. "How can I just go off and never see you again?" Lancelot sighed. "Can we meet some time?"

"That could be arranged." Drian grinned.

"Just to talk."

"Oh, of course. Meet me in this clearing, a week from today, then."

So Lancelot rode off, hoping that she might see this friend at times, for after all there was no one else like her.

Lancelot returned to the clearing in the forest on the appointed day. The trees were bare and Drian was not there.

Lancelot sat on the cold ground, waiting.

Early snow flurries came and stung her cheeks, but still she waited until well past dark. Then she departed, worrying that some angry man whose wife or jewels had attracted Drian might have injured her.

One morning at an early hour, Guinevere heard a knock at her door. Bors's wife Lionors entered.

"Lady Guinevere, may I see you privately?" she asked, giving Fencha an apologetic look that nobles did not often use with serving people. Lionors's voice was anxious and her forehead showed more wrinkles than usual.

"Of course you may." Stifling a yawn, Guinevere smiled at Fencha, who bowed her head and left. It was good to see gentle Lionors, but why did she seem upset?

"Lady Guinevere, is everything well with you?"

"Quite well, thank you. Come and have a sip of wine with me," Guinevere said, gesturing for the lady to join her at her table, where she was breaking her fast with wheaten bread and fruit.

Lionors seated herself. Her brown hair was somewhat disarranged, showing its first gray strands. "Please forgive me for repeating this filth, but you should know that malicious people are whispering about you and Lancelot because you like one another."

She blushed. "I never heard anything so outrageous! How could anyone imagine anything ill of Lancelot, much less of you?"

Guinevere's stomach muscles tightened. She had heard of such rumors before, and they always chilled her.

How many rumors there must be if Lionors had heard them! But it was necessary to maintain her usual calm, so Guinevere did. She shook her head.

"How disgusting. It is sad that anyone is so low minded. I hope no one disturbs Arthur with such gossip. Go ahead, have a little wine. It is already watered."

465

Lionors poured wine into a silver cup. "Thank you, Lady Guinevere. Forgive me if I am bold, and say things I would never have dared to say before." She picked at the skirt of her pale green gown. Apprehension showed in her eyes.

"I am strong enough to bear a great deal. What is it?" Guinevere patted her hand to put her at ease.

"My lady, some people whisper that the king has not come to your room at night in years." Blushing, Lionors looked at the floor. "If that is true, it must grieve you so much. I shouldn't speak, but I know what it is to love a husband. I am so fortunate that Bors never looks at other women.

"Father Donatus is a kind man," Lionors continued. "You could ask him to speak with the king about his duties to his wife. Sometimes a marriage needs help to mend it. Don't be afraid to seek assistance from a priest, my lady."

After speaking so boldly Lionors gulped down the rest of the wine, in a manner far different from her usual modest sips.

Guinevere repressed her desire to laugh. Maintaining her gravity, she patted Lionors's hand again. "Thank you for your concern, but my husband does all that I could wish."

A smile broke out on Lionors's face. "Oh, Lady Guinevere, I am so glad to hear it."

Thinking it was time to change the subject, Guinevere said, "Now tell me, how is your son – is it your youngest? – recovering from his broken ankle?"

Lionors took a smaller sip of wine. "No, it's not my youngest. It's Matthew, my ten-year-old. His ankle is mending nicely, thank you, but he is vexed that it delays his sword practice."

Not for the first time, Guinevere regretted that she could not confide in anyone but Fencha. She was surrounded by women, some of whom she liked, but none could understand or approve of her life.

As the company of warriors feasted at the round table, a harper told of a love so powerful that all the birds in the forest sang to celebrate the lovers' joy. Guinevere noticed how others were or were not affected by the music.

Paying no heed to the words, Arthur was engaged in conversation with Gawaine. Old Merlin rose from the table, as he so often did before anyone else had finished eating and drinking, and walked away muttering as if love were an idea he wanted to escape. Lancelot could hardly conceal her pleasure in the song, but stared smiling at her mead horn.

Guinevere thought of the verses that she could never compose, or never tell about if she did. She would not write of birds and flowers, giants or dragons, but of a woman who was more daring than any man. These harpers could sing what they pleased, and Gawaine could devise any tale he wanted, but she, the queen, could not say what was in her heart. Of course, she could not praise her woman warrior, but neither could she write about an old woman like Fencha, the lines formed on her face from a life of toil, the legs now aching from a life of serving others. No one would want to hear such a tale.

But, glad that the music had brought such a smile to Lancelot's face, Guinevere beckoned the harper. The song was a little too honeyed for her taste, but she told him that she would send him a gift the next day.

"Thank you, your highness." He bowed deeply. In a voice far softer than the one he used to fill the great hall, he said, "I have a message for you as well."

"Give it to my old woman, Fencha," Guinevere said.

She still felt a slight thrill at receiving a message from Morgan, but far less than she had before she had known Lancelot's love. It pleased Guinevere to have harmless secrets from Arthur.

467

Guinevere sighed. If only she could write little notes to Lancelot. That would have been much more enjoyable than writing to Morgan. But that would have been too dangerous for Lancelot. Do I care more about protecting Lancelot than Morgan? Guinevere asked and easily answered that question.

That night she was with Lancelot, but Fencha brought her the letter in the morning. There was a chill in the room, but Guinevere sat close to the brazier. She glanced at snow that drifted past her window. Drinking hot ale, she opened the letter.

My dear sister,
Perhaps the day is drawing nearer when you could wear a larger torque. Don't you want to wear the gold before your hair turns gray? Your letters show that your judgments are as wise as anyone's. Everyone knows that you are the most learned person at Camelot. Why must you defer and take second place?
Of course you would need a war leader, but I have heard rumors that you might have a good one, the greatest in the land.
It is no virtue to be too modest about your abilities. No doubt you are as brave as you are clever.
You are surely clever and brave enough to find a way to take the famed sword. Who knows what would follow from that?
Your sister

Choking on her ale, Guinevere stared at the letter as if it were written in some language that she did not know. She read it again. It truly said what she thought it did. She shivered. The snow seemed to be falling in her room instead of the courtyard.

The idea of lifting her hand against the man who had snored beside her for a decade turned Guinevere's stomach, even though she did not love him. Perhaps if he had been cruel, she might have been able to strike at him. But she liked Arthur well enough,

468

especially when she did not have to lie with him. And certainly she believed he was a good king.

Morgan had once loved Arthur. How could she think of injuring him, or even rising against him? But Morgan had little to lose, and Guinevere had a great deal. And the thought that Lancelot would turn traitor was mad. Such an idea would be the surest way to lose Lancelot's love. But Morgan did not know Lancelot, Guinevere reminded herself.

Guinevere still wanted to rule someday, but now that she had love, she was far less anxious about the prospect. Her heart was too full to spend much time lusting for the throne. And she had no desire for the sword, either.

She thrust the letter over the flame of one of her beeswax candles. She could not burn it quickly enough. The ashes that fell on the table she swept onto the floor.

The snow outside the window was falling harder, but she thought it was not as cold as Morgan's heart had become. Yet why not? Arthur had cast her off.

Guinevere thought of making no answer to the letter, but she feared that Morgan might mistake silence for consent.

The letter that she was wrote was as brief as possible:

My dear sister,
I am content as I am.
Your sister

Morgan flung the letter on the ground. Guinevere must love someone else, probably the warrior Lancelot whose name was often mentioned as the queen's champion.

It had been foolish to appeal only to Guinevere's pride. When Guinevere was a girl, she had clearly been smitten with Morgan.

469

She should have pretended to desire Guinevere and written letters full of love. That way she could have bound Guinevere to her more closely.

Guinevere had just finished dressing and Fencha was fastening a lapis brooch on her gown. There was a knock at the door, and Guinevere called out, "Come in." She didn't want Fencha to go to open it because she could see that walking was becoming painful for the aging woman, although Fencha wouldn't admit it.

Enid, a pretty girl whom Guinevere had never liked – who had, in fact, giggled when the queen quoted long-dead poets – asked to come in. Her eyes were red and her mass of light brown hair looked scarcely combed.

"It's a trifle early for a visit," Guinevere said, but her voice was not harsh.

"Your highness, I beg you, could I speak with you alone?" Enid could scarcely keep the anguish out of her voice.

Guinevere could not refuse that tone. "Of course. Fencha, please leave us alone for a time."

Fencha eyed the young lady carefully, and left.

"Please be seated."

Enid sat down and began to weep. "Your highness, I have been very foolish, and I am with child. But that is not the worst. A warrior I am fond of, Gereint, has asked for my hand, and my father has agreed to a betrothal. Gereint believes that I am a virgin, and I'll lose him if he learns that I'm not." She let out a loud sob and wiped her face with her sleeve.

"I have heard that there are ways to escape bearing a child, but I don't know what they are. Do you know any wise women who have such remedies? Will you help me?"

Guinevere felt a moment's hesitation because she had never liked Enid or thought that Enid liked her.

470

She went over to her and took Enid's hands in hers.

"I know one who can help. Don't be afraid. I'll send for you as soon as I have the remedy. You can take it here in my room and rest."

Enid, like other unmarried girls at the caer, shared a bed with another girl. She wept and kissed Guinevere's hand.

"Thank you. You are so good. I really want to marry Gereint." Guinevere patted her cheek.

"He's not too bad, as men go. Don't worry, all will be well." Guinevere spoke with Fencha.

The next morning, Enid returned to Guinevere's room.

"You'll have some pain and nausea," Fencha told her. "But I'll be here with you."

"I shall think about you and come to see how you are doing," Guinevere said, squeezing her hand.

"I can never thank you enough." Enid clung to the hand that was offered.

Fencha, who was well schooled in all of these matters, seemed calm, but Guinevere worried about Enid all day.

Hearing that Enid did not feel well by evening, Guinevere insisted that she stay in her room for the night. Enid slept on a pallet that Fencha sometimes used when Lancelot was not at Camelot.

The next day Enid was better, though still a little weak. Guinevere said that she could stay another night if she wanted.

Enid looked at her fondly, but there was fear in her look, too. "Thank you so much for everything, Lady Guinevere, but I can't do that. No one must ever suspect what I've done. It was the king who got me with child, and he would be angry."

Guinevere felt as if the breath had been knocked out of her. She was more frightened than she had ever been. "He would be. You must never, never tell anyone about what we have done. It would be much worse for me than for you. It would look as if I had made you do it."

Tears formed in Enid's eyes. "I know. I won't tell. I'm sorry to put you in this position, but I thought that you were the only one who would help me."

Guinevere touched her hand.

"Well, if neither of us tells, and I know Fencha won't, there's no harm done. But you had better go back to your own quarters now."

After Enid left, Guinevere trembled. Her heart raced. She did not think she could have helped Enid if she had known that the child Enid had carried could have been a rival heir to the throne. Arthur would never forgive Guinevere if he believed that she, out of envy, had prevented another woman from bearing his child. If there were an actual child, he probably would have tried to dismiss his nightmares and rear it proudly. Surely Arthur could have persuaded Gereint, or someone else Enid could like, to marry her afterwards. Surely Arthur would not have put Guinevere aside and married Enid.

Guinevere was sitting at her table with her head propped in her hands when Fencha returned.

"Oh Fencha, it was the king's," she said in a shaking voice.

Fencha touched her shoulder. "Yes, but we prevented it, my lady. I have managed to give potions to all of his mistresses for years now, but I didn't know she was one. I'm glad that she came to you." The old woman chuckled.

A shiver ran up Guinevere's spine. "How could you do such a thing to women without their knowing it?" Fencha's eyes widened as if she were surprised that Guinevere did not approve.

"Why, I've done it ever since he sent the Lady Morgan away. He deserves it after what he did to her."

Guinevere now trembled with anger rather than fear.

"But the women do not. Let them decide whether they want to bear children. Morgan should have no say in it."

"But, my lady, of course they can still have children by other men. They all marry someday, if they aren't married already," Fencha explained patiently, trying to touch her shoulder again

Guinevere pulled away from her. Had she been foolish to imagine that she had any friend? "And if I had wanted to bear a child, would you have secretly prevented me from having one, too, for Morgan's sake?"

"My lady, how can you think it?" Fencha's voice was grief-stricken. "You must know that I love you. I thought it was better for you also if he had no children by other women."

Guinevere was touched by the imploring look in Fencha's eyes, but did not soften entirely. "Did Morgan order you to give a potion to the women?"

There was a look of confusion, true or feigned, in the aging face. The old woman's hand flew to her mouth, a gesture that seemed to show she was concealing something. "I thought she would have wanted it, but no, she didn't tell me in so many words."

Not knowing what to believe, Guinevere pressed on. "Are you my woman, or Morgan's? How can I spend my days with you if I don't know? Should I tell you to leave my service and go to hers?"

Tears dripped down Fencha's cheeks. "I don't want to leave you, Lady Guinevere." Her voice shook.

Guinevere still held back. "I have trusted you. It is as if my mother betrayed me. How shall I ever trust you again?"

Fencha cringed.

"My lady, I have sat by you when you were ill, and you have sat by me when I was ill. How could I not love you? You have cared more about me than the Lady Morgan ever did. She left me here to be her eyes and ears at court. She cared more about that than about having me with her."

Guinevere studied her face but was not convinced. The woman had shown how underhanded she could be. "You must prove that your allegiance to me is greater than your loyalty to Morgan."

"Trust me, please, Lady Guinevere," the old woman begged. "I thought the Lady Morgan told you all, but perhaps she does not. I know her messengers. She sends messages to others besides you. Do you want to see such of them as I can get?"

Guinevere closed her eyes for a moment. What, after all, had she known of Morgan? That she was beautiful and clever, and had at least one woman at Camelot. Were those reasons enough to trust her? Did Morgan care about other women, or just about her own power? Her last letter had been frightening. It might be well to know what she was writing to others.

Guinevere opened her eyes, and was determined to keep them open. "Take no risks for yourself," she told Fencha, "but if there are any such messages that I might see, perhaps it is well that I do."

Then she embraced the old woman. "Oh Fencha, I would have been sad to lose you," she said at last.

After Fencha left the room, Guinevere stared unseeing out of the window. Even her old serving woman was full of secrets. Could anyone ever truly know anyone else? Could she trust anyone?

Lancelot rode through the forest near Camelot. It was midsummer, so there were more flowers in the fields than among the trees. Although some birds did not sing as much as they had a month earlier, thrushes and wrens still burst out in song, and a careful listener could hear the chirps of nestlings calling for food.

But Lancelot heard something else. Someone was behind her – no very strange occurrence – but whenever she stopped, the other horse stopped also. She was being followed.

Her every muscle tensed, she directed Raven behind a tree and waited to see what would happen.

In a moment, a rider came into view.

"Lance? Where are you? Don't hide from me. I just wanted to surprise you."

"Drian!" she called out with delight and rode up to greet her. Lancelot pulled beside her and threw her arms around her.

Drian grinned, returning the embrace. "It's not easy to do much when we're both on horses, Lance. Let's get down on the moss."

Choking with laughter, Lancelot slapped her lightly on the shoulder and moved away. "It's good to see you. I feared we might never meet again. I didn't know how to find you."

"But I knew where to find you. How could I stay away from such a beauty?" Drian made a face like a love-struck swain, greatly exaggerated.

"You managed to stay away from our appointed meeting last fall." But Lancelot was too glad to see her to be much annoyed. "I thought something had happened to you."

"It did. It's a long story I can tell you sometime. But now I've come to visit you and see whether the people here like my music." She patted her harp, which was tied to her horse.

"You are well come, but I don't think your playing will be quite to the king's taste," Lancelot said, for only the most skilled of harpers played before the king.

"I don't care about his taste. I think my playing will be to your taste." Grinning, Drian ran her fingers in the air as if she was stroking an imaginary harp – or something else.

Lancelot felt herself blush. "I am still true to my love, as I've told you. But you can stay at my house. I wouldn't want you to have to sleep in the hall."

"I'd much rather sleep, or not sleep, at your house," Drian told her.

"I'll likely be with my sweetheart at night," Lancelot warned her.

"I can't believe you'd be so discourteous to a guest," Drian chided. "Not even to please the queen."

"It would be very strange if I didn't come to her tonight. And I'd miss her," Lancelot said.

"It is the queen!" Drian crowed. "I trapped you! The songs say you worship her."

Lancelot was angry at herself for letting out her secret. "Don't sing those songs. You must never tell anyone about us."

"I never would," Drian promised. "So that's what Queen Guinevere is like. I'm eager to see her."

They talked ceaselessly, both on their ride to Camelot and when they arrived at Lancelot's house. Catwal found a great deal of bedding for the comfort of the guest, the first Lancelot had ever had.

Lancelot went to Guinevere's room as usual that night.

"I've heard that a man is staying at your house," Guinevere said, her expression puzzled rather than chastening.

"Can that be so?"

"No, of course not. Don't worry. It's another woman who pretends to be a man," Lancelot told her.

"Oh, a woman. Then of course nothing could happen." Guinevere's voice was rich with sarcasm.

Lancelot's face reddened but she stood her ground.

"It could not, because I love you only.

"Drian is a friend and a harper. She doesn't play well enough to appear in the great hall before the king, though."

"I would like it very much if she would play for me," Guinevere said too sweetly. "She can come tomorrow morning to the room where the ladies do their needlework."

"Very well. I hope you like her," Lancelot said, feeling that that was not to be.

The next morning, she told Drian she was to play the harp for the queen. "But remember, she's mine," Lancelot jested.

"She's not the one I'm aiming for." Drian grinned at her.

Lancelot brought Drian to the ladies' sewing room. Many ladies looked at Lancelot as if she were the one who had come to entertain them, and some batted their eyelashes. But some of them looked Drian over with more or less modesty.

"You honor us with your presence, Lord Lancelot," simpered one young married lady.

"How kind of you," said Lionors, apparently oblivious to any undercurrents.

"Lancelot is always kind," Guinevere said. "Come, harper, let us hear how you play." The queen wore a rust-colored morning gown and no jewels, but she was fairer than ever, with heightened color in her cheeks.

Drian made a sweeping bow to the queen and less grand bows to the other ladies. "I am honored," she said, and commenced playing.

The music was spirited, but that was the best that could be said for it. Nonetheless, Lancelot was glad to hear Drian play in a warm room rather than a forest glade. Yet it was more pleasant when there were only the two of them. Drian looked at her frequently, which made Lancelot blush.

After a couple of songs, both of which told of the delights of infidelity, Drian paused.

"Is my playing to your liking, your highness?" she asked Guinevere.

"I thank you for your efforts," Guinevere said, not smiling. "You play with enthusiasm if not great skill."

"But I think I can play better than you can," Drian said in an undertone, so only Lancelot and Guinevere could hear her.

"I doubt it," Guinevere said, narrowing her eyes. "You had best just play your own instrument."

Lancelot broke into a fit of coughing.

Drian patted her on the back, which did not help matters.

"Are you well, Lancelot? Perhaps you need to be out riding with the men instead of resting with the ladies," Guinevere said, with a smile that was not one of her warmest. "The harper may stay here and continue to play for us. No doubt he will soon have to leave to play at another caer."

"Yes, it is best if I return to my duties. Thank you, Lady Guinevere." Lancelot bowed to her and to the other ladies, and retreated.

That evening, when Lancelot returned to her house to change her clothes before supper, she saw that Drian was drinking freely from some fine wine that Catwal must have procured for her.

Holding up a goblet as if in a toast, Drian said, "I was not a great success today."

"You didn't try to be," Lancelot accused her.

"I was courteous to a fault." Drian shook her head. "I didn't steal a single jewel from the queen."

"I should hope not!" Lancelot cried. Then she paused. "But Drian, she wasn't wearing any."

Drian shrugged. "None except her wedding ring, and I don't suppose you'd mind overmuch if I took that."

"You must not take anything of hers!"

"I would, but you won't let me." Drian put down the goblet, dipped her finger in the wine, and licked it.

Groaning, Lancelot put her hand over her face. "You didn't have to flirt with me so much. Now she'll never like you."

"You don't seem to worry about whether I'll like her," Drian complained, staring at the candle on the small table. "I'll take her hint and go tomorrow. There are too many men here. Every time I walk out of your house, there are mobs of them."

"I'll miss you, but perhaps that's best," Lancelot said, trying not to show how relieved she was. "I hope we meet again."

"Away from the watchful eyes of the queen."

"That won't make any difference!" Lancelot cried, raising her voice.

"We'll see." Drian reached out to her harp and moved her fingers over the strings.

Later, in Guinevere's room, Lancelot said, "Drian will leave tomorrow."

Guinevere nodded. "Very good. She is annoying, but the true reason I wanted her to leave is that when people see the two of you together, it would be much easier to guess that you are women. How could there be two men with such smooth cheeks?"

"Oh. That's a good point," Lancelot admitted. "Is that truly your reason for wanting her gone?"

"I trust you," Guinevere said, kissing her.

Guinevere fretted over the tax records. Cai was so busy managing the caer that the figures were more often left to her. It was time to train more people to do the task, she thought. But where could she find them?

Arthur entered the small room, which he seldom graced with his presence. Guinevere inclined her head to him. "I am glad to see you. I wonder whether you might have lessened your objections to asking a monk to help with the tax records."

He grimaced. "I have not." Sitting on Cai's chair, he glanced at the pile of vellum on the desk. "Clerics are well enough for copying proclamations and so forth, but I don't want them too involved in governing. If you need more help, perhaps one of the men who was injured in the war could be trained."

"Very well." She smiled. At least he had listened to her.

"I came to speak with you about another matter. This is a quiet room when Cai isn't here complaining." He paused. "Still no sign of a child?"

"No, my lord." She averted her gaze.

"It seems we both are unable to bring forth new life." Arthur sighed. "Perhaps our blood goes too much to our brains, and cannot find its way to help us breed." He looked her in the eye. "You may do as you please, but you are smiling too much at Lancelot."

She tensed, but tried to keep her expression from changing. "Indeed?"

"Yes." Arthur twisted his amethyst ring. "Everyone can see that he is smitten with you, but you must be careful to appear aloof."

He didn't have to explain that this was an order. She knew it. "Yes, my Lord Arthur. I shall take care not to smile at him too much." She hardened her heart, but not to Lancelot.

"I know I can count on you, my dear." Arthur's voice held the same amount of warmth it did when anyone at Camelot acquiesced to his wishes. He rose and clasped her hand.

She smiled at him, but not more affectionately than she would smile at Bors or Cai. "You can always depend on me."

He kissed her cheek. "I have other business to attend to. You may look for an assistant if you wish."

480

"Thank you, my lord Arthur."

Her husband departed. Husband. How she detested that word. That man even owned her smiles. She looked with disfavor at the ring on her finger. Then she closed her eyes for a moment and thought of Lancelot.

27 THE GREEN WARRIOR

One winter evening the company was seated at the round table. Even the great firepits were not enough to warm the hall, but hot spiced wine sufficed to provide cheer. Lancelot drank more than usual, just to keep out the chill, and noticed that she was not the only one who did so.

Guards at the door cried out, and a man on horseback rode into the hall.

Cai jumped up. "Out!" he cried. "How dare you insult the High King by bringing a horse into his hall!"

"I bring a message to Gawaine ap Lot," called out the rider, who was dressed all in green. "He's to come as soon as he can to the hall of Bertilak, the Green Warrior, whose lands lie to the north of Kledyr of Dyfed's lands."

There was a great clamor from all the warriors.

Gawaine rose from his seat at the table. "I am Gawaine. I know where Kledyr's lands are. Your lord's message sounds like a challenge, so I must accept it," he announced.

"Very good. I'll tell my lord Bertilak." The man rode out of the hall.

"Your reply was a bit hasty, Gawaine," Arthur admonished his cousin.

"Not so. We all must be ready to face challenges," Gawaine replied, grinning.

Lancelot groaned and wished Gawaine were less eager to prove how bold he was.

Gawaine journeyed through a forest in the chill of winter. It was not the usual season for travel, and he wished the invitation, or challenge, had been issued in milder weather.

His plaid wool cloak did not spare him from the howling wind. His fingers felt frozen, but he could still move them. Patches of snow covered the ground and the sky was gray.

Gawaine tried to cheer himself by thinking on happier moments – the surge in the blood that came from a tumble in the hay or a good fight. When those were lacking, a good tale or jest about them was nearly as pleasing.

He came upon a place that, strangely for the season, was all green. Pine and fir trees there were, laurel, and holly, growing in unusual profusion and proximity, but no trees that were bare.

A small caer appeared, jutting out of a hillside among the green trees. The thought of a warm hall cheered him, and the prospect of a hot meal pleased him no less. Gawaine wondered greatly at all the green, but approached the caer.

A man in mail all of green rode out to meet him. Gawaine had never before seen any man taller than himself, except for Saxons, but this dark-haired man was no Saxon. "Who are you?" the man boomed in a voice as deep as he was tall.

"I am Gawaine ap Lot of Lothian and Orkney, one of King Arthur's warriors."

Gawaine bowed his head, but even as he did, his neck felt strangely sore.

"I am the Lord Bertilak, the Green Warrior," said the man in verdant mail, appropriately enough. "You are welcome to stay at my caer. There is only one condition. You may not lie with my wife. I will cut off your head if you do."

Gawaine grimaced at this grisly suggestion, but he said, "Of course I wouldn't try such a thing. That would be an insult to your hospitality. It's true that I have no great reputation for purity, but even I don't go around seducing other men's wives."

"You are well come, then," the Green Warrior said, beckoning him to enter the caer.

Bertilak's great hall was well appointed, mostly in green, and a great feast was set on the table. Venison, hares, and a roasted boar were almost enough to make the great oaken boards groan. The aromas were so enticing that Gawaine wanted to pounce on the meats.

"Thank you," he said, bowing his head. "This feast is fit for a king." He drew near to a blazing fire and gladly received a cup of hot mead from a serving man. He savored the taste.

Then the Green Warrior's wife entered the hall, and Gawaine saw that she was beautiful. And even more familiar than beautiful, for she was Alais, a lady with whom he had had a very pleasant interlude a few years earlier, when she was unmarried and he had stayed at the holding of her father, Kledyr.

She nodded to him, but only politely. Her eyes did not meet his. Her glossy black hair shone in the light from the torches.

He bowed to her and greeted her formally, asking her how her father was.

"I have not seen my family in years," she sighed, regarding the rushes on the floor. Gawaine found her words strange, for her family lived not many miles away.

After supper, the Green Warrior showed Gawaine to a fine sleeping room that, like the rest of the caer, was decked in green.

The next morning, just as Gawaine was waking, his host knocked on his door and entered.

"We finished the venison last night. I'm going out to hunt for another deer," he told Gawaine.

"Very good, I'll hunt with you," Gawaine said, stretching.

But Bertilak shook his head. "No, you'll stay here and rest. I insist." And he went on his way.

Dawn had scarcely appeared in the sky and Gawaine was not fond of waking early, so he went back to sleep.

When he awakened, he found that the sun was streaming in the window, and Alais was sitting on a chair beside his bed.

"Dear Gawaine," she said, and sighed.

He remembered what his host had said about beheading, so his voice was less warm than it might otherwise have been. "How good to see you," he said to her. "Are you well?"

"No," she replied, shivering, which was not so strange in the middle of winter. "My husband is a hard, cold man, although he acts polite enough to other men."

She leaned towards Gawaine, but he leaned away from her.

"Indeed." He tried to be cool himself. He could well believe that the Green Warrior was cold, but it was no concern of his.

"Oh, Gawaine, if even you are cold, what shall I do?" Alais exclaimed, her lip trembling as if she was about to weep.

"He learned after we married that I wasn't a virgin, and he has hated me ever since. I'm so miserable." Her voice broke.

Gawaine felt a knot in his stomach at the idea that some of Bertilak's coldness was his fault. "I'm sorry, but what can I do to repair the past?"

Alais sat on the bed.

"I'm afraid of my husband," she whispered. Her eyes looked like those of an ill-treated dog. "He's jealous of me, but he cares nothing about me. I was distressed when you went away, but now it seems to me that the time with you was golden. I've never had any pleasure except with you. I want to be in your arms again." She put her face close to his.

He kissed her, and she snuggled up to him.

"You'll feel pleasure now," Gawaine murmured. He decided not to keep his promise to the Green Warrior.

After they had lain together, she clung to him.

"Please take me away with you," Alais begged.

Gawaine guessed from the tone of her voice that she wanted to be with him always. He did not feel the same about her, but he hated to deny her anything at the moment. Still, he could not make false promises.

"Where could I take you?" He could not carry off a noble's wife to Camelot. Arthur would be furious and would not want her to stay, and no one would befriend her. Lancelot might be able to get away with rescuing an unhappy wife, but if Gawaine did, everyone would know that the woman was his mistress.

She sighed as if she knew that he did not mean to keep her with him. "You could take me back to my father's dun."

He stroked her dark hair. "I am willing, but your father might send you back to your husband. If your father does not receive you well, I could take you to Lothian. My mother, Queen Morgause, would let you stay as one of her ladies." He knew that his mother would do anything he asked, and would think no less of a woman for preferring him to her husband.

"When my mother sees the scars on my back, she'll persuade my father to let me stay," Alais whispered, looking down as if she were ashamed.

"Scars on your back!" Gawaine had not looked at her back.

He did, and saw a tracery of scars, some old, some newer. His heart felt heavy at the thought that beatings might have come because she had not been a virgin when she married. He trembled with rage.

"I'll kill the whoreson!" he exclaimed, holding her tighter. "How dare he treat you so! When he returns, I'll challenge him and fight him."

Alais grabbed his shoulders. "No! He might kill you instead. He is very strong." Her dark eyes showed more fear than they had before.

"But I am a fine fighter. I'm almost certain to defeat him." Gawaine pressed her tight, though he thought no more about love-making. Pity had replaced desire.

"Almost! That is not certain enough. And you must not fight him here, surrounded by his men. Please, let us go away as quickly as possible," she begged him.

"If that is your wish," he said reluctantly, for his arms already ached to strike at the brutal husband. "Do you want to go pack your things?"

"No, let us flee," she gasped, leaping from the bed and pulling on her clothes.

Gawaine dressed quickly also. They left the caer through a side entrance and went to the stables.

The moment Gawaine opened the stable door, a great crowd of men leapt out, surrounding him and pushing him back into the stableyard. He tried to draw his sword, but two men grabbed his right arm and another tore his scabbard from his side.

Others held his left arm.

The Green Warrior stood before him.

"You've broken your promise, Gawaine," he thundered. "I did not hunt – except for you. I'll cut your head off – or hers."

"I have not broken my promise," Gawaine asserted, struggling against the men who held him.

"You have! Whose head shall I cut off? Yours or hers?"

"If you must be cutting off any, it should be mine, not the lady's," Gawaine insisted, glancing at Alais, who had been seized by two men.

"No, mine," cried Alais.

"You have had her, or you would not be so eager to protect each other. Bind him," growled the Green Warrior.

Gawaine struggled mightily, but there were too many of them. The men flung him on the earth, amongst the green trees, and tied him with rope. His helplessness enraged him. What a fool he had been not to guess that the husband would trap him! Why had he listened to Alais and tried to sneak away, instead of challenging Bertilak to a fight?

The Green Warrior seized a great axe and hovered over Gawaine. He fought against the ropes that bound him. After so many fights, it was bitter to die helpless. Mother! Morgause! He silently called. If you have any magical powers, help me now!

Alais screamed, "No, don't kill him, it's all my fault!" Her husband's men still restrained her.

Gawaine was sure her husband would kill her, but he feared that her display of affection for him would prompt the brutal man to make her death even worse. Bertilak might tell his men to rape her.

Gawaine heard the sound of hoofbeats, but he thought it was only more of the Green Warrior's men.

Thinking that he was about to die anyway, Gawaine said, "Don't hurt the lady. I forced her."

"He did no such thing," Alais insisted.

Gawaine let his eyes rest on a pine tree's green, the last color he would see.

A familiar voice called out, "What cowardly murder is this?"

Gawaine strained to turn his head slightly, and he saw that it was Lancelot. Perhaps the gods still favored him.

"Stay back!" the man in strange green mail yelled. "This cur has sworn that he would not seduce my wife, but he did."

"Even so, you have no right to bind and slaughter him." Stunned by the sight of a man about to kill Gawaine, Lancelot leapt off her horse and advanced on them.

Lancelot knew that the husband did in fact have the legal right to kill a man who had lain with his wife, but that did not matter. Under the law, one could not even avenge the death of a man found in adultery with another man's wife, but this law meant little to Lancelot compared with her friend's life. "Don't you dare to meet him in a fair fight? Who are you?"

"I am Bertilak, the Green Warrior. Who are you?"

"I am Lancelot of the Lake," she replied, "He is my friend, and if you won't fight him, you must fight me."

"Please save him, Great Lancelot!" cried Alais, whose eyes were wide with terror. Two men held her arms.

"I'm sure this foul man is the one who took my wife's maidenhead, and I have waited years for revenge," the Green Warrior said, shaking his fist. "My honor demands it."

"Why should you care what she did before she married you? Men think too much about virginity," Lancelot said with disgust. "What would be honorable is treating your wife with respect."

"I thought that Lancelot was a man of honor, but you don't sound like one. You're as shameless as Gawaine," the Green Warrior yelled. Two of Bertilak's men attacked Lancelot, but she quickly dealt them blows that knocked them to the ground.

"Put aside that axe. If you try to behead him, I'll do the same to you," she cried, lunging at Bertilak.

490

The Green Warrior seemed about to drop the axe on Gawaine even as Lancelot attacked, but as he pulled back he let it fall too late, and it barely scratched Gawaine's neck.

Bertilak grabbed the axe again, swinging it towards Lancelot, but she killed him before he could strike, and the axe fell where it split only a few inches of earth.

Most of Bertilak's men backed off, but one still held the lady.

"Release the lady and unbind my friend, or more of you will follow your master," Lancelot ordered, so they did as she bade them.

The lady rushed to Gawaine and dabbed his neck with her handkerchief, but there were only a few drops of blood on it.

"Thank all the gods, you're safe," she said.

"Rather, thank Lancelot," Gawaine replied, somewhat abashed. He nodded to Lancelot, then put his hand on his neck.

"I followed you because the adventure sounded risky," Lancelot told him. "But it seems that I should not have traveled a full day behind you, as I was almost too late." Turning to the lady, she asked, "Do you want to leave, my lady? Or is this caer yours now?"

"My husband's brother will inherit it. I am only too eager to leave," the lady said, shivering.

The three of them made haste to depart. Bertilak's men offered no obstacle.

Lancelot rode ahead to give Gawaine and the lady, whom Gawaine introduced as Alais, daughter of Kledyr, a chance to talk. Perhaps this time Gawaine would do the honorable thing and marry the lady. Alais regarded him with worshipful eyes, as if he were her savior. They rode beyond the green, and Lancelot found bare branches more appealing than she ever had before.

She had had enough of green for the moment.

After a time, Alais and Gawaine caught up with Lancelot.

Alais's eyes were red. "I shall go to my family," she told Lancelot. "They live not far from here. My husband would not let me see them, and I miss them sorely."

Lancelot nodded. "Whatever you say, my lady."

They proceeded mostly in silence after that. Lancelot assumed that Gawaine and Alais could think only of each other, so she did not try to speak with them.

They came to a villa that looked as it must have when the Romans first built it, with even a fine roof of tile. An elderly lord and lady exclaimed in delight at the sight of their daughter.

"My husband is dead," she told them as her mother embraced her. "He foolishly started a fight with the lords Gawaine and Lancelot."

"I'll shed no tears for him. I like it little that he never let you visit us," her mother exclaimed, clutching her daughter as if to say that she would never again let her go.

Her father was more restrained. "Greetings, Gawaine," he said, eyeing the tall warrior skeptically, as if he wondered what Gawaine's part in Bertilak's death had been. "And I am honored to meet you, Lord Lancelot. You will be welcome guests."

But Gawaine said, "We cannot stay for even one night. We must return to Camelot. The High King needs us."

Lancelot found those words odd, but she said nothing.

Lancelot and Gawaine rode back in the direction of Camelot. The winter afternoon light made patches of snow gleam. A flurry fell on the warriors. Lancelot wrapped her crimson cloak around her. Her nose and ears were chilled. Why hadn't Gawaine wanted to stay in the warm villa despite the threat of snow? Brushing the snowflakes out of her eyes, Lancelot was the first to break the silence. She was chagrined that Gawaine had not spoken with Alais's father. Wasn't he planning to marry her, then?

"That was awful," she said rather sharply. "I am not so pleased at killing a man because you committed adultery."

"You're a fine one to complain about adultery," he grumbled, not looking at Lancelot. "Not all husbands are as complaisant as Arthur. Are you still with Guinevere?"

Lancelot flinched. "Of course I'm still with her. We love each other." How dare he compare her love with his endless womanizing! She would be only too glad to wed Guinevere, if she could.

"Such arrangements don't last forever, Lance."

"Don't call my life an arrangement! My love will last forever!" Lancelot exclaimed, tightening her hands on the reins.

He nodded. "Yes, you might always love her. I was not just speaking of your feelings . . ."

Stung, Lancelot interrupted him.

"Say no more about my life. Did you offer to marry Alais?"

"No," Gawaine replied, not sounding as abashed as she thought he should. "But I shall devise a tale about this adventure that says I did not lie with her. She gave me this sash, and I'll make up a story to go with it." He pulled a woodland green sash out of his pack and showed it to his friend.

Rooks calling out in the trees seemed to be saying that women were fools.

Lancelot fumed. Did Gawaine never think what it must be like to be a woman, embraced, fought over, and abandoned within a single day? "Don't you see that the life you lead generally has worse consequences for the women than it does for you? This is surely not the only one whose husband was angered when he discovered that she wasn't a virgin. Why can't you love one woman, and stay by her? And why not Alais, who did not try to save herself but shared the blame to try to save you?"

To her surprise, Gawaine actually shuddered. He looked off into the white-covered forest.

"After what I have been through, can you imagine that I need your preaching to make me think of such things? I no longer desire her. All I feel is pity. I didn't dare stay around her because I feared that I would marry her out of pity and regret it for the rest of my life. You should have no compunction about killing Bertilak. If you had seen the scars he gave her, you would have done it gladly."

Lancelot gasped. She had not guessed that Bertilak had injured his wife.

"I have discovered that it isn't good for killing and loving to be too close together," Gawaine said. "I don't want to look at a pretty woman and see the Green Warrior. I used to go to a tavern after a fight, but now I go off in the woods by myself."

Lancelot felt more sympathy than she had expected. "I do the same," she exclaimed. "So you have that problem, too. It is not what one thinks of when one becomes a warrior. I haven't talked about this, not even with Guinevere. She couldn't understand because she has never killed anyone."

"How could you talk about it with a woman? No one could," Gawaine said. He paused and slowed his already slow horse. "Once again, I owe my life to you. What a good friend you are, following me because you thought my journey would be dangerous. No one but you would have done that. Many thanks."

Lancelot remembered how horrible it had been to see that axe hanging over Gawaine. She disapproved of his womanizing, but he had been a good friend to her. Her voice was a little gentler. "He didn't injure you, did he?" she asked.

"No, but it was humiliating being tied up like a boar and nearly slaughtered like a sheep. I have never been captured before." He still wasn't looking at Lancelot. His head hung as if he were ashamed.

"I won't tell anyone," she assured him.

She thought he had no need for shame, at least not for being captured. Abandoning the lady might be a better ground for it.

"I'll tell, then," he exclaimed loudly. "You shall have all the honor you deserve."

"I don't care," Lancelot insisted, frowning.

What honor was there in killing an angry husband?

"I care," Gawaine replied, then turned and regarded Lancelot. His red hair and beard sparkled with snowflakes and beads of water from melting snow. "I'm sorry that I got you involved in such an episode. And if you don't want your name to be used in this rather sordid tale, I'll leave it out." He smiled. "I can see why you wouldn't want it known that you have killed an outraged husband."

Lancelot was not so pleased that he still referred to her adultery, but after all she was glad that he was alive. She looked at the scars on his face and remembered the battles that had put them there. "I'm glad that I arrived in time. I would have grieved if he had killed you," she admitted.

"I am in your debt," Gawaine said, in voice that seemed too solemn for him.

Lancelot shook her head. She was too grateful for the many times he had helped her to want much of his gratitude now. "You are not. You certainly have saved my life before, but I am most grateful for your help in the Saxon War, when I could hardly speak after we saw the bodies of the Saxon women. You were one of those who kept talking to me to keep me going."

The memory made her want to tell him a secret that she had told only to Guinevere. Gawaine spoke of his mother more than most men did, so he might understand. In a voice so low that she wasn't sure Gawaine could hear her, she said, "When I was ten years old, I saw my mother raped and murdered. I put the man's eye out."

"Gods! What a terrible thing for a boy to see!" he exclaimed, jerking his horse's reins and stopping it.

And even worse for a girl, she thought. Unable to face Gawaine after this revelation, she rode off ahead of him.

Later, when it was nearly twilight, and they were riding slowly to rest their horses, an owl started hooting. The snow cloaked their shoulders in white before it melted.

Despite his mantle of snow, Gawaine was smiling more than he had earlier in the day. He brushed snow from his face. "As a token of my thanks, I want to tell you the secret of my success with women."

"I don't need . . ." Lancelot interrupted, not wanting to hear the details of whatever he did.

He continued regardless of her wishes. "I would not tell other men, for they would foolishly believe that it is low and disgusting, but you would want the woman to be as pleased as you are. Use your tongue. Many women like that best."

Lancelot almost fell off her horse with astonishment. She mumbled, "I know."

"Good for you." Gawaine laughed and clapped her on the back. "I'm surprised that you know that much about women."

Amazed that he did, again she rode off ahead. She had heard some men say that women had done a similar thing to them – not women they cared anything about, for the men believed it was filthy and degrading. But she had never heard a man say he had done such a thing to a woman. How strangely contradictory Gawaine was, so concerned about women's pleasure, yet so heedless of what might befall them afterwards.

Nevertheless she realized how much she would regret losing Gawaine's friendship if he ever learned that she was a woman.

Guinevere returned to the stables earlier than she had planned. Though years had passed, the man on horseback still pursued her. Since nothing ever happened, she shouldn't be afraid. But the pursuit still unnerved her.

Even when Gawaine went off on some quest, he nonetheless sent his minion to distress her. It must be Gawaine. She had never seen him lurk or spy, but who else could it be? No one else had any reason to dislike her. But it was impossible to tell Lancelot, because Lancelot would never believe that Gawaine could do such a thing. Guinevere hoped that one of the red-bearded warrior's adventures would be his last.

When Lancelot and Gawaine had returned to Camelot and left their horses at the stables, they walked to the great hall.

A gray-haired serving woman strode, boldly as a man, towards them. Her face had few lines, but her hands were those of a woman who had scrubbed all her life. She was buxom and pleasant-faced, but no beauty.

"Come to welcome me, Ragnal?" Gawaine grabbed her and kissed her cheek. "This time I almost came home carrying my head."

"It's a good thing you didn't." She wagged her finger at him as if scolding. "How could you kiss me then? And it would be sad if you lost your beard."

"Lost my beard!" he cried, touching that object protectively. "No. No one would dare try to shave my beard. That would have been tragic indeed."

"I'm glad there was no serious danger," Ragnal said, sighing in relief.

He kissed her again. "I'll see you tonight."

"If I'm not too tired, Lord Gawaine." Her expression said that she would have been glad to go off to a secluded corner that moment.

"Very well, Ragnal. If you're not too tired." Laughing, he watched her walk away.

In an aside to Lancelot, Gawaine said, "She's the woman I like best."

"Best? A serving woman?" Lancelot said before she could stop herself.

Gawaine frowned. "Yes, a serving woman. I suppose you've never thought of wanting a serving woman."

"No, in fact I haven't," Lancelot replied, not sure whether that was good or bad.

"The great Lancelot could never want a woman who was lower born than he, only one who is higher born."

Lancelot flinched. As the years passed, she had thought less about Guinevere's station being higher than her own. And Gawaine was as highborn as Guinevere, much more so than Lancelot, but he had never said so before.

He must be fond indeed of this Ragnal.

In the practice room, Bors said to Lancelot, "I suppose you've heard about Gawaine and the Green Warrior."

"Yes," Lancelot said noncommittally, putting down her practice sword after defeating Bors as usual. She was curious to learn what tale Gawaine had told.

Bors rubbed his face with a towel. "It was noble of him to stick out his neck for the Green Warrior to chop off because he had broken his promise and not told him about accepting the kiss from the lady, wasn't it?"

"Why should he let someone chop off his head, no matter what he had done?" Lancelot asked, almost choking over the idea that

Gawaine had voluntarily stuck out his neck for the blade. "That would be foolish, not noble." Keeping her face averted, she poured water from a jar into a cup and drank it. The practice room was cold, but she was sweating from the exercise.

"I see that you haven't heard the whole story," said Bors, a little offended. "At least the lady's virtue was preserved. Perhaps the Green Warrior was some holy spirit testing Gawaine."

"Don't ask me," Lancelot said, holding back laughter. "You can see that I know nothing about it." Clearly Gawaine had made up some fantastic tale, as he liked to do.

"I see that you don't." Bors nodded. "It's an edifying tale, and no one should make dirty stories of it, although some people are already. Gawaine and the lady exchanged only a kiss, and she gave him a magical green sash that protected him from the Green Warrior's blow. So a woman saved Gawaine's life! Can you imagine that?"

"I can," Lancelot replied, smiling at how Gawaine unwittingly had told the truth. Then the thought struck her that he might be displeased if he ever learned that his life truly had been saved by a woman, and she stopped smiling.

Lancelot decided to tell Guinevere the true story of saving Gawaine. In the flickering candlelight of the queen's room, she could see Guinevere frown.

"I wouldn't much care if the Green Warrior had swung that axe," Guinevere muttered.

Feeling as if she had been slapped, Lancelot stared at her. How could such a beautiful, tender woman speak such cold words?

"How can you say such a thing? He is my friend and is a brave man who has saved many lives, mine among them."

"No doubt because he likes fighting as much as he likes whoring." Guinevere's voice was sharp. "He's just a killer."

"Why, so am I, then!" Lancelot cried out, leaping up from her chair. "How is it that you can bear to be around me?"

Guinevere reached for her arm, but Lancelot pulled away.

"Nonsense. You fight only to help others."

"So does Gawaine. If you hate my friends, you must hate me, too." She turned to the hidden door.

"Not so! Calm yourself," Guinevere appealed to her, but Lancelot left, slamming the door to the secret passage.

Lancelot practically fell down the narrow stairs. Angry though she was at Guinevere, her greatest anger was at herself. She was worse than Gawaine, if Guinevere only knew. She trembled at the thought of Guinevere turning away from her if she learned that Lancelot had killed a girl. Perhaps she should just go away and become a hermit. She did not deserve a woman's love and a life full of praise as a great warrior.

She went to her room, but there was no sleep for her that night. As dawn's first rays lit the sky, she went to the stables to saddle her glossy black mare and ride in the woods.

While she saddled Raven, she heard a rustling in the straw near her stall. Ever alert for the slightest sound, she turned and saw Guinevere, standing there red-eyed.

"Please forgive me. I didn't mean to hurt or insult you." Guinevere said in a humble tone that she had never used before.

"I know." Then tears started in Lancelot's eyes and she turned back to her horse. "We must not be seen talking like this."

"Tonight, then?" Guinevere clasped Lancelot's hand for just an instant.

"Very well." Lancelot sighed. Unworthy though she was of Guinevere's love, she could not bear to give it up. Guinevere could never love her if she knew the truth.

"I told the stable guard I was afraid that Shining Star might not be well. I suppose I should go to her stall," Guinevere said, and slipped away.

Lancelot decided to ask the king to send her on a mission. There had been recent reports of a band of brigands in Cornwall, which was far enough away to help her hide her fears from Guinevere.

Lancelot mounted her horse and rode out as usual. There was little snow in the forest near Camelot, but icicles jutted from some branches. A crow cawed at Lancelot.

On the ground in front of her, she saw the body of the girl she had killed.

Lancelot jerked the reins, stopping her horse. What she had thought were logs were the bodies of dead soldiers. Streaks of blood ran through the snow.

She covered her eyes with her hands. If a Saxon wanted to strike her, let him.

Gradually, she lowered her hands. The snow was white. The logs were logs. There were no corpses.

Her whole body shook. She would never be at peace.

28 THE LADY OF TINTAGEL

Lancelot stretched out to sleep under a sycamore in a Cornish forest. The sycamore was a sacred tree in Cornwall, so it might protect her. She had seen no sign of brigands.

The night was not cold for winter, but still it was not so pleasant for sleeping under a tree. She told herself that she should have stayed at the last farmhouse she had passed.

A fox barking in the night made her smile. In her dreams, the fox came up and sniffed her, then bit her neck.

She woke to find a knife at her throat. Every muscle in her body prepared to strike. If she must die, she would not be slaughtered like a sheep. She kicked the brigand who was attacking her, so his knife slipped and cut her shoulder instead. Then another brigand lifted a cudgel over her head.

When she woke again, it was daylight. Her head ached more than it ever had and her shoulder bled profusely. Her sword and purse had been stolen. She felt for the bag of small treasures that she wore around her neck. It was still there.

Her pearl from Guinevere was safe.

Her horse was nowhere in sight.

She tried to bind up her own wound as she usually did with cuts. However, this one was the worst she had ever received when she was alone. The blood was not easily staunched. The pain and loss of blood made her almost unable to rise. The throbbing in her head from the cudgel's blow made thinking difficult, and when she tried to walk she staggered. She called her mare and, miraculously, Raven soon trotted up to her. Raven must have run from the brigands.

When Lancelot tried to mount her horse, she swayed and almost fell. Finally, she rode off through the forest to look for help.

As the sun grew brighter in the sky, she barely clung to Raven's reins. She prayed for deliverance, though she thought God had little reason to save an adulterer. She would not promise to give up Guinevere, nevertheless. The thought of never seeing Guinevere again made tears pour down her cheeks. If she died there in the forest, Guinevere would never know what had happened to her. The bare trees seemed to be portents of death. There might never be another spring for her.

Too weak to keep riding, she almost fell off Raven, landing under an oak tree that was covered with lichens. She told herself that a rest was all she needed. However, she said some prayers before she lost consciousness. She feared to join the souls of the men she had killed. It seemed too much to hope that she could join her mother instead.

Guinevere fretted over her scrolls. How many times could she read Ovid? And she did not care to read about Aeneas and all the dangers he faced. She knew that Lancelot had gone off to fight brigands because she was angry at Guinevere for criticizing Gawaine. Cursed red-bearded lecher! Guinevere was tired of

Lancelot risking her life to save him. Indeed, she was weary of Lancelot risking her life for any reason. And if this was Lancelot's way of punishing Guinevere, well, Guinevere did not like that either. She reached for another honeycake, though she was careful not to let any crumbs fall on the scroll or to handle it with sticky fingers. Why could she not protect Lancelot better? If that meant her own words should always be more honeyed than the cakes, she should speak thus, Guinevere thought. She wished she could have followed her lover and guarded her.

Lancelot dreamed that she was carried off by a lady she had never seen before to a caer, and held there. The lady was stroking her, but Lancelot kept saying, "I must be true to Guinevere."

"Be true to Guinevere – I'm only dressing your wound. Hold still," a commanding but sonorous female voice said, and a lady was indeed rubbing some smelly herbal substance onto Lancelot's wounded shoulder. The touch made her wince, though the lady was not ungentle.

Lancelot's eyes dimly saw a long and elegant face and flaming red-gold hair. The lady wore a fine russet gown, a string of amber beads, and a large garnet ring.

Lancelot could gradually see that she was in a bed covered with embroidered coverlets. A tapestry depicting a warrior and a lady kissing decorated the wall facing her.

"Let me out of your caer," Lancelot demanded, appalled at how feeble her voice was.

"You can leave any time you wish, but I don't advise it, if you want your shoulder to heal. You are welcome to stay after you are healed, but you should not travel at the moment."

"My lady, I must not linger," Lancelot said solemnly.

"A little pompous, aren't you, but rather sweet," the lady said.

Lancelot drifted off to sleep.

When she woke again, the lady was still there, accompanied by a hare-lipped serving woman. The lady motioned for the serving woman to leave them.

"How are you, Lancelot of the Lake?" the lady asked, rising from her chair.

"You know who I am?" Her voice was distraught. Who was this lady who knew about her, and how discreet was she? Would she tell that Lancelot was a woman?

The lady looked rather like a forest creature, reminding Lancelot of many she had seen. Not a deer – something wilder.

"Are you surprised that a witch knows about you?" the lady said, with an ironic smile. "No, I'm not a witch, unless praying to the goddess Cerridwen makes me one. Or knowing the healing arts. I have heard it prophesied that someday every woman who knows them will be called a witch."

"Surely not," Lancelot said, beginning to guess who the lady was.

"I am Morgan of Cornwall, Arthur's sister. He it was who let me be called a witch. But I am a friend to Guinevere. She and I have exchanged messages for many years, so do not fear me. You kept calling her name, so I guessed that you must be one of Arthur's warriors. Lancelot is reputed to be the handsomest, and to be very fond of the queen. I had never imagined that you were a woman. Now rest. My serving woman is bringing you some food."

"Thank you, Lady Morgan," Lancelot replied, wondering whether the lady was truly a friend of Guinevere's and could be trusted.

The lady laughed in return, and her serving woman brought delicacies including fish and oysters, and Lancelot realized that she could hear the sound of the sea and smell its salt breath. She was hungry and ate eagerly, hoping that these were not magic viands that would change her into a dog or some other creature, but they did not appear to do so.

She slept again, and the next time she woke she felt much better. She heard shrieks and thought that they might be coming from prisoners tortured in the caer, then realized that they were the calls of gulls. Morgan again sat beside her.

"Thank you for healing me, Lady Morgan," Lancelot said, bowing her head as much as she could while lying in bed.

"I am glad to help you," Morgan replied, but her look appraised Lancelot coldly. "Are you my brother's lover?" she asked in a bitter tone.

Lancelot gasped and pulled the coverings even further over her than they were already. "No! I have never thought of him, or any other man, in that way. He does not know that I am a woman."

Morgan shook her head and smiled differently. "Have you never been with a man? What a strange woman you are."

"Why must a woman lie with a man?" Lancelot asked, just as cold as the lady had been.

Morgan smirked. "So, do you think you are one of them? I must say that's not how you look to me."

Lancelot felt her face grow hot because this lady had seen her undressed. "I am not a man, and I do not want to be one, but only to seem to be one."

"And what is it like to love a woman? Is Guinevere still beautiful?"

Lancelot stiffened. "She is more beautiful than a meadow in the dawn. But I cannot discuss these things with you or anyone."

"Now you must rest," Morgan told her, and went away.

Lancelot felt anything but rested after this discussion.

When Morgan left, Lancelot tried to get out of bed and walk, but her body was not ready. Tomorrow, she told herself.

The next day when she woke, Morgan was there again, looking at her closely. Her green eyes seemed to see completely through the bed coverings to Lancelot's body.

Unwilling to lie there and be watched, Lancelot tried to stand, and found that she could, a little. As she was wearing only a woolen bedgown, she asked the lady to leave while she dressed.

"You want to fly away," Morgan said in a soft voice. "But why? We have barely met."

"My lady," Lancelot said, "I am not sure I want to know you better."

Morgan only laughed. "As you are not comfortable with me here, come out and join me on the rocks."

As soon as Morgan left, Lancelot dressed in her customary clothes, which were lying on a nearby stool. They had been cleaned considerably since she last wore them. In addition to a tunic, she put on her mail, and even her crimson cloak.

Reminding herself that Morgan was her king's enemy, Lancelot left the caer and found it surrounded with rocks. Green waves, with white caps gleaming like soldiers' helmets, assaulted the rocks, leaving strands of seaweed in their wake.

Morgan sat on a rock with gulls swirling around, screaming like charging Saxons. Further down, a regiment of sandpipers rushed by the edge of the water, then flew up in a cloud. A cormorant's snaky head emerged from the sea. On rocks further out, a seal basked like a warrior guarding his hill fort. At the base of a cliff, a pied oystercatcher battered oysters.

It all looked rather sinister to Lancelot. There were no decent trees for cover in case any danger appeared. There was only a long, steep causeway joining the caer to the mainland. Morgan rose and offered her a hand to help her footing on the rocks.

Lancelot did not take it. She sat on a rock at some distance from the lady's.

"Isn't the sea beautiful, like a woman who might enfold you in her arms?" Morgan teased.

"I have never been fond of the sea," Lancelot said, dismissing Morgan's flirtatious tone.

Morgan sighed with exasperation. "You should love all things from the gods. The sea is the domain of the god Mannawydden."

"I do not believe in these gods and goddesses of yours," Lancelot replied.

Morgan sat up straight on her throne of stones. "But your ancestors did. How can the Christians banish all the gods and goddesses? They live, no matter what the Christians say. Your fellow Christians call me a witch and say that our religion is evil. And my brother allows them to stamp out the old ways. What do you think of that?"

Lancelot shook her head. "Christians do as they think right, my lady. Do I agree with everything any Christian does? No."

Morgan's flaming hair rippled in the sea breeze. She smiled an enticing smile. "We need not talk of the gods of our ancestors. Let me be your friend." She extended her hand.

Lancelot remained seated and again ignored the hand.

"I don't trust you. You are no friend to my king."

Morgan's brows knitted and her glance became fiercer. "Your king, my brother, who exiled his own sister. Can you, who are supposed to befriend all women, support that?"

Lancelot frowned. "Are you are hinting at treason to the king? I would oppose that, make no mistake."

Morgan's voice was sickly sweet. "I did not speak of treason. How terrible to think of betraying the brother who betrayed me. How fortunate Arthur is to have such a devoted friend. But if Arthur were no longer High King, you could go off and live with Guinevere, if that's what you want. If you love her so much, surely you must mind that she is his wife."

"So who would you replace him with, my lady?" Lancelot eyed her suspiciously. Surely Morgan had no reason to care whether she would like to go off with Guinevere. "Yourself?"

"Wouldn't a woman warrior rather serve a queen than a king?" Morgan asked.

"I do serve a queen as well as a king," Lancelot retorted.

Morgan raised her eyebrows. "Indeed you do. Many would say that loving the king's wife is treason, but of course that cannot be so because you would never be disloyal."

Lancelot felt her face flush with anger that was all the fiercer because her guilt was pricked. "Do not speak of her."

"You don't understand." Morgan smiled but her green eyes did not. "I know that you are a woman. If you don't help me, I could send word to Arthur. He does not want to hear from me, but he would pay attention to such amazing news."

"You wouldn't!" Lancelot's heart beat louder than the gulls' screams.

"How do you know that?" Morgan drawled. Her gaze was fixed on Lancelot.

"I don't ask you to wound Arthur. All I ask is that you steal his sword and take it to King Uriens of Rheged."

"Steal his sword! I could never do such a thing." Lancelot almost fell off her stone.

"The loss would only wound his pride and lessen his power. Many people believe that the sword is magic, so its loss would weaken him. If Uriens had it, his prestige would be increased." The seal slid off its rock and was replaced by another seal. "He is the most powerful king who still follows the old gods, so I wish to strengthen him. That isn't so dreadful, is it?"

Lancelot leapt up. "Betraying my king is dreadful." Her hand went to the place where her sword would be if she still had it.

"You trust him."

Morgan also rose and picked up a mussel shell, which she turned over in her hands. "Then you trust that he will treat you no differently if he learns that you are a woman? Wise, kind King Arthur would not expel you from his service. He would never cast you aside as he did me." She tossed the shell into the sea.

Lancelot's heart constricted. "No matter what he would do, I cannot injure him for my own selfish reasons."

"I am not asking you to injure him, just to help me lessen his power a trifle." Morgan spoke calmly, as if she were discussing the waves that were breaking on the shore. "He has a large warband. No one else could defeat him in combat. But I can't believe that even he, proud though he is, would start a war over a sword."

"My lady, I will not help you." Lancelot trembled with anger, not unmixed with a touch of fear of discovery. "How do you know I won't tell him about your plan?"

"If you do, he would learn more quickly that you are a woman."

Morgan grabbed another shell and tossed it after the other one. "I shall give you until next autumn to decide. If you do not help me, perhaps Arthur will learn the truth about you. You would never know when the message would come or who would bring it, but your life would be changed forever."

The gulls' shrieks seemed louder, as if the birds might descend and tear at Lancelot's flesh.

"I have done you no harm, so you have no reason to do me harm," Lancelot said. "You may give me time, but I will not change my mind. I thank you for healing me, my lady, but I must leave now."

Morgan nodded with queenly grace. "Yes, you may leave, strange woman. Don't tell my brother that you saw me, or you may discover the limits of his friendship. He is jealous of anyone who comes near me. You will find your horse in the stable, and my armorer will give you a sword. Farewell."

Lancelot bowed slightly to her, retrieved her horse from the stable, accepted the sword, and rode over the steep causeway back to the cliffs of the mainland.

The waves lashing at the black rocks below confirmed her belief that Tintagel was a dangerous place. She knew that Morgan spoke truly that Arthur would not be pleased to hear that Lancelot had been healed by his sister. She would tell only Guinevere that Morgan had healed her.

Her heart was heavy with the fear that Morgan would reveal the truth about her sex.

What would Arthur do if he knew? Would the knowledge that he had relied on a woman to lead troops anger him? Would he be enraged at her deception, and never trust her again? Would he send her off so no one would ever learn that his famous warrior had been a woman?

If she had to leave, would Guinevere run away with her?

Would Arthur say Lancelot could stay, but demand that she give up fighting? What would she do if she could not fight, or even train others to fight? Would the king want her to dress in different clothes, change her walk and her speech? Would he order her to give up her very name?

She would not. She would go somewhere, anywhere, where she did not have to dress in skirts and gaze away modestly when men looked at her.

How many of men's beliefs had she shared? How often had she thought that a woman who looked her in the eye was too bold? She regretted those judgments now.

Would Guinevere still love her if she wore women's clothes?

Lancelot's heart constricted with the thought that Guinevere might not.

Guinevere had difficulty concentrating on her reading.

Lancelot had been gone so long. Arthur should not let his great warrior face risks so often.

Guinevere heard a sound at the door hidden behind her tapestry. Her heart beat faster. The tapestry waved, and Lancelot entered the room. This was the first time she had ever come to visit Guinevere before returning more formally to Arthur.

Lancelot's face was pale in the candlelight. Guinevere rose to greet her but was struck by the pain in Lancelot's brown eyes.

"You look much worn from your journey."

"I was wounded by brigands and left for dead, but the Lady Morgan found me and saved me."

Guinevere felt a pain in her chest as if she had been wounded herself. She kissed Lancelot ardently and held her.

"I almost lost you! Thank the Virgin that Morgan saved you! Let me see where you were wounded." She pulled at the tunic, not waiting for Lancelot to take it off. A moan escaped from Lancelot's lips. A large bandage covered her shoulder. The sight tore at Guinevere's heart.

"It must pain you a great deal. How did you ever manage to ride here?"

"It doesn't hurt so much."

"Oh, don't talk so much like a man. Of course it does."

"Not enough to keep me from kissing you." Lancelot kissed her lips and nuzzled her neck.

Guinevere sighed with contentment.

Pressing her close, Lancelot said, "Morgan has no good will toward Arthur."

"How could she?" asked Guinevere sharply.

"If a man you trusted let you be called a witch and sent you to a remote place of exile, would you have much love for him?"

"No, but she seemed to think that because I love you I might betray him," Lancelot replied. "I cannot be pleased by that."

"No doubt she was just trying to learn what you truly think," Guinevere said, nuzzling her in return. She had no desire to talk about Arthur or Morgan or to do anything but kiss Lancelot. "Sit down and rest. You must be tired."

Lancelot sunk into a chair. "I am."

Guinevere poured wine for her and cut a slice from a cheese that stood on the table.

"You are so good and sweet," she said. "There is nothing in you but gentleness. It's true what they say, that you're the best and kindest warrior in the world."

Lancelot pulled away. She ignored the wine and cheese.

"I'm not. But I'm not what Morgan thinks, either. She asked me to steal Arthur's sword and give it to Uriens of Rheged, and said she would tell Arthur I'm a woman if I did not."

"No! I can't believe that Morgan would harm you!" Guinevere recoiled, feeling as if someone had hit her in the stomach. "I thought she was a friend. Surely she wouldn't tell."

"She said she would if I did not steal the sword, and of course I cannot." Lancelot's face had new lines in it.

"Of course you can't. Why would she want to promote old Uriens? He's just an ordinary chieftain who drinks too much when he comes here at Pentecost." Feeling weak, Guinevere sank down in a chair.

"He's pagan, as she is," Lancelot explained, frowning. She rose and paced about the room. "She said she wanted just to weaken Arthur, not destroy him. Perhaps I should tell him all the truth, even that I am a woman, so that I need not fear what Morgan would say."

"You cannot!" Putting out a hand to restrain Lancelot, Guinevere felt as if the breeze that blew into her room was a bitter wind. "Arthur would never understand. You could not be his warrior anymore, and we might be parted." She felt sure that Arthur would no longer stay away from her if he knew that her lover was not a man. Guinevere shuddered.

"We will never be parted," Lancelot said, taking her hand. "I fear you are right that I cannot tell Arthur. Yet I worry that I betray him by not informing him of Morgan's plot."

"It will never succeed. No one who is close to him would steal his sword. We must find some other evidence of this plot that does not implicate you." Guinevere's voice was grim. "Or me. She approached me a year or two ago with a suggestion for a plot, but I refused her."

Lancelot gasped. Guinevere took a deep breath. "I was a fool not to realize that she would also approach others. But I never could have imagined that she would try to involve you, much less threaten you." She tightened her grip on Lancelot's hand.

The beeswax candles still glowed on her table, but it seemed as if the room had darkened.

"Would you still love me if I were forced to wear a woman's gown?" Lancelot asked.

Guinevere's eyes opened wide with astonishment. "You would be my beauty in any clothes, but we need to be as we are now. And I like you best in no clothes at all." She stroked Lancelot's hair, and the room began to lighten again.

When Fencha brought wheaten bread for Guinevere's breakfast, Guinevere put it aside and took hold of the old woman's hands. "It is more urgent that I learn about Morgan's letters." She looked deep into Fencha's eyes.

"I must know if she sends messages to King Uriens of Rheged. Indeed, I must see any such message. If not, harm may come to me."

"Oh, my lady, she would never harm you!" Fencha exclaimed, her eyes widening.

"She might harm Lancelot, which amounts to the same thing." Guinevere could hear the anxiety in her own voice. There was no need to feign queenly serenity with Fencha. "Please help me."

"Of course, my lady." The old woman returned Guinevere's pressure on her hands.

Lancelot sat in Arthur's room, where she and Gawaine drank with the king after supper. As usual, she drank one cup of wine for every two or three of Arthur's and Gawaine's. Her eyes strayed to the sword hanging on the wall. The candlelight made the great amethyst on the pommel sparkle.

Of course swords were not magical. Would it injure the king so much to lose it? He could easily have another made that was as good or better. She bit her lip. How could she even think such a thing? Perhaps she should tell him the truth. Guinevere might be wrong in her belief that he would not understand.

"I have such a weakness for pretty women," Gawaine said, quaffing some of the king's best wine. "No doubt that will be my undoing."

"If you don't watch out, it might be." Arthur chuckled. "Don't let them weaken you. You always have to keep the upper hand. Women are foolish and tricky unless they have a man to guide them."

"Oh, I'll guide them — right to bed," Gawaine retorted, stretching.

Lancelot sighed inwardly. No, neither her king nor her good friend could ever understand her. They would no longer be her friends if they knew the truth.

She eyed the sword again. Was a blade worth more than her life, her happiness?

Perhaps not, but her honor was worth more than her life. What honor would she have left if the king learned she was a woman? Would he simply laugh at her, see her as a little fool pretending to be a warrior? Would he tell Gawaine, and would Gawaine also laugh? Would they never respect her again?

If Arthur didn't respect her, would Guinevere be able to love her? Why was Guinevere so distressed at the thought of Arthur knowing? Would Guinevere not let herself love a woman if her husband knew their love for what it was?

Lancelot choked on her wine.

"Isn't the wine good? Should I call for another jar?" Arthur asked.

"No, it's very good," she managed to say. Indeed, she was tempted to drink until her worries were drowned. Why did Morgan leave her so many months to wait? Her fears grew and the anticipation of – she knew not what – was nearly unbearable.

On her way to train the lads learning to be warriors, Lancelot shivered. She could see her breath. The morning frost gave the practice yard a silvery glow as if it had been enchanted overnight.

The king's body servant, Tewdar, hurried across the courtyard to her. Even though he limped, he could manage a run.

"The king bids you come to his room without delay, my lord." The man's voice had an edge to it.

"Of course."

What could the trouble be? A Saxon invasion? An uprising? Lancelot's stride carried her quickly back across the courtyard and through the caer to the king.

Arthur was pacing about his room. Deep wrinkles creased his brow, making him look years older than he had the night before.

"Lance! My sword is gone!" he exclaimed, putting his hands to his head. "Someone has stolen Excalibur."

"It cannot be!" She shuddered. Morgan had given her until autumn to steal the sword, but autumn was nearly over and Lancelot had not. Now someone else had. She had not warned the king. The pit of her stomach sank. Perhaps it was her fault. "How could anyone have taken it from your room?"

"I was in a lady's room, and the guards must have been careless about watching my door. I must have that sword!" His hands made fists. "I let everyone think that the sword was magical, had been given me by a mysterious lady's hand emerging from a lake. That made it too tempting for someone who wishes me ill to steal. Now people will believe that I've lost power. Whoever did this will be drawn and quartered." His gray eyes showed as much distress as if he had lost his best friend. "If anyone asks where it is, I shall say that the amethyst was coming loose and had to be reset. You must find the sword for me. I can trust you to keep this secret for as long as possible."

"Of course I shall keep this loss secret. Do you have any idea who could have taken it or where they could have gone?" She thought she knew the answer to the latter question.

"No." He shook his head. "But I have asked the guards who has left the caer since yesterday. Two of the young warriors, Cynlas and Beric, left after dark. It could be either of them, or of course someone else."

"I'll track them down and find who did it," Lancelot promised. She would set off on the road to Rheged. Cynlas, conspicuous because of his brilliant red hair, was from Rheged, so she thought he was the likely thief. "I'll follow Cynlas."

"I knew I could depend on you. I'll send Gawaine, the only other man I trust as much as you, after Beric."

The king put his hand on her shoulder. It was all she could do to keep from flinching. She felt that she did not deserve his trust.

Gawaine's chest almost burst with rage when he heard about the stealing of Arthur's sword. If he caught the man who did it, the traitor would wish he had never been born.

Gawaine and Lancelot rode north as fast as they could, until they would reach a crossroad where he would go on to Eburacum, where Beric's family lived, and Lancelot would go towards Rheged. Bent on their task, they were much more silent than usual. Gawaine could see that Lancelot was as anxious as he was. Indeed, Lancelot's face was pale, though Gawaine thought his own must be red, as it was likely to be in the cold.

The trees had lost their leaves, and Gawaine was not eager to sleep under them and feel the whistling wind all night. But not long after dark, he spied the welcome light of a tavern he had visited in previous travels.

"A tavern! Good, we'll have a bed for the night."

"I'd rather sleep in the open air," Lancelot replied in a strange voice.

"Whatever for? I think it will rain by midnight. It's a good night to be under a roof." Gawaine stared at Lancelot.

"If we slept at the tavern, we might get lice," Lancelot objected, not returning Gawaine's look.

"What, have you never had lice before?" Gawaine jeered.

"Of course, but . . ."

"Time enough to worry about cleanliness when we get back to Camelot. I've stayed at this tavern. It was reasonably clean and had passable food. Come on." Taking no more time for talk, he advanced to the stableyard and handed over his horse to a stablehand.

A pleasing fire blazed in the tavern's firepit.

The tavernkeeper, who had wrinkles almost as deep as his tankards of ale, greeted Gawaine with a sweeping gesture.

"My lord Gawaine! You're in luck. We have a bed for you and your friend, even a room of your own!"

"Very good!" Gawaine flashed the man a smile.

"I don't suppose there might be two rooms?" Lancelot asked.

"No, my lord. I have only one other room, and there are already three men in that bed," said the tavernkeeper, pouring hot mead for them.

When the tavernkeeper went off to get them some stew, Lancelot said, "Perhaps I'll sleep in the stable."

Gawaine groaned. Why was Lancelot so odd at times?

"Don't worry, they'll take good care of your horse. You would look like a fool."

"Very well." But Lancelot sounded far from pleased.

Steaming bowls of stew arrived at their table, and Gawaine turned his attention to the food. The meat was tough mutton, not so strange at this time of year. Even as they ate, a pelting rain almost drowned out their talk. Thank the gods they could sleep indoors.

They went to the room, and it was so small that there was barely room for the bed, but Gawaine cared not at all. There was a candle, but he didn't light it. He sat on the bed and pulled off his boots.

The room was cold, so he laid down without taking off his clothes, pulled up the blanket, and closed his eyes.

"I think I'll sleep on the floor," Lancelot said.

"What!" Gawaine started up. "Are you mad? Why should you want to sleep on the floor? There's scarcely room to lie down."

"I don't mind. It will be fine."

"Are you afraid I'll give you lice? I don't have any at the moment." He could hardly keep his voice below a shout.

"No, there's nothing the matter with you. I just want to sleep on the floor."

"That's the most foolish thing I've ever heard."

Gawaine was angry, and even more so because he wanted to go to sleep and not be distracted by nonsense. "I've never been so insulted. No man would refuse to share a bed with any of his friends, or indeed, with a stranger who wasn't completely filthy."

"It's just my fancy. Don't let it bother you. Goodnight."

Gawaine grumbled to himself. He had never heard of a man doing such a thing. Clapping his hand over his mouth, he held back a gasp. Indeed, no man would have refused to share a bed with him. Lancelot was a woman! The modesty, the smooth cheeks, the endless sympathy with women! What a fool he was, never to have realized! Gawaine tried to make no noise. He didn't want to talk to Lancelot.

If Lancelot had not made such a fuss about sleeping in the bed, they could have both slept in it and he'd likely have been none the wiser. But she was too embarrassed. Ridiculous, since she was almost as close to him on the floor as she would have been in the bed. And they had often slept a few yards from each other under the trees.

A woman had defeated him in fighting, many times! True, he had often defeated her, too, but he never would have fought her in the first place if he'd known she was a woman. How could it be that she fought so well? His own pride had kept him from seeing what should have been obvious. Her cheeks were only a little raw, with never any stubble. She could have rubbed them with something to make them look raw.

Lancelot was false. His best friend – but was she truly his friend? – had deceived him for some dozen years. If Lancelot was false, likely no one was true. The only people he had trusted as much were his mother and Arthur.

They both would do questionable things for their kingdoms, and for their own power. Bors was good enough, but he would do whatever a priest told him to do, whether it made sense or not. Lancelot had seemed better than anyone else. Except for Lancelot's love for Guinevere.

Guinevere! Was Lancelot's love for her just a pretense, an excuse for not having a wife? Could she really be Arthur's mistress, not Guinevere's lover? No, for then Arthur would never have sent Lancelot off on so many dangerous missions. Lancelot's passion for Guinevere – the strangest thing of all –was real enough.

If Lancelot was a woman, why would she love another woman? The thought came to him forcefully that Lancelot had seen her mother raped and murdered. That must be why she was as she was.

The war! Lancelot was a woman, but she had gone through everything, she had seen every horror. Gods! He shuddered. She had saved his life, she had risked herself to save so many lives. Thank the gods he had said he had killed the girl, so Lancelot would not have to bear the shame.

Gawaine could not sleep, but he was not eager for the day. He didn't plan to let Lancelot know that he knew. She had deceived him, so let him deceive her for a while. Of course he would never tell anyone else. But how could he bear to speak with Lancelot, how could he be around her?

He had said so many things to Lancelot that he never would have told a woman. She had let him make a fool of himself.

Before dawn came, Gawaine decided to leave. Lancelot usually rose at dawn – all he wanted was to be gone.

It was difficult to open the door and get out of the tiny room without stepping over Lancelot. He carried his boots downstairs and put them on at one of the benches. He didn't wake anyone to give him food.

On his way to the stable, Gawaine laughed. He had always thought it rather callous for a man to leave a woman before she woke! The circumstances now were a little different, but he might as well have a laugh at her expense. She surely had had many at his.

As he rode off, Gawaine thought of jests he could make to Lancelot. He favored, "Couldn't you trust yourself in bed with me?" That would make her furious. He wasn't sure he wanted to anger her that much.

The thought that he had lain in bed, frozen and speechless, because the person in the room with him was a woman rather than a man, made Gawaine laugh.

But, though he didn't want to be with Lancelot at the moment, he was sorry that she was going off into possible danger alone, and he vowed that he would go with her on such missions even more often than he had in the past.

When Lancelot woke, she saw that Gawaine was gone. No doubt she had offended him, but she couldn't worry about that. All she could think of was leaving as quickly as possible to get Arthur's sword, and hoping that she wouldn't be banished when Morgan told Arthur that she was a woman.

Clutching something under her cloak, Fencha burst into the queen's room. She closed the door behind her carefully.

"My lady, I have a letter from the Lady Morgan to King Uriens!" She thrust a leather packet at Guinevere.

Guinevere grasped the packet, extracted a sealed vellum letter, and broke the seal.

"Poor Irion! He will never be able to carry messages again," Fencha said, shaking her head.

Caring little about the messenger, Guinevere sat down and pored over the missive.

The honeyed words were all too familiar. Guinevere recognized the style at once. How could Morgan address sixty-year-old

Uriens, whom she must not have seen in many years, in such tender terms? Unless these terms were a code for something else.

Yes, there was something different from her letters to Guinevere. Even if Morgan truly did intend to marry the aged king, who had never had a handsome face, would she need to tell him how many men-at-arms she could summon, or to find out how many Rheged had available? Another kind of alliance was planned.

This intimate letter to Uriens would make it clear that Morgan had been part of the plot to steal Arthur's sword – indeed, that she was the instigator.

The thought of siding with Arthur, whom she had never wanted, against Morgan, whom she once had wanted so much, seemed ironic. But Morgan had threatened to reveal Lancelot's sex, which would ruin their lives. Neither did Guinevere want Uriens for a ruler. Arthur was more far-sighted and concerned with the welfare of Britain as a whole.

Guinevere had no wish to harm Morgan. Arthur would imprison his sister if he knew that she plotted with Uriens. Her pleasant exile at Tintagel would be at an end. A warning should be enough to keep her from further plots, and from disclosing Lancelot's secret. Guinevere sent a message to Morgan.

Dearest sister,
I hope as always that you are well. I so appreciate your letters.
But the ones that come across my path that are not addressed to
me are sometimes less pleasant.
Rheged is very far from Cornwall, too far for a convenient ally.
Are you truly considering marrying the ancient Uriens? You have
my congratulations if you are. Perhaps you simply want to see
the forests and lakes of Rheged.

Yet your words about your dower said rather too much about the number of your fighting men for my taste. As always, I cherish our friendship and I appreciate your noble ideals.

As you have wanted a women's council, I give you a woman's counsel. In me, you have an ally. And it is this alliance that you should trust. I shall let no one harm you, nor will you be obscure if it is ever in my power to bring you from Cornwall.

But you know as well as I who holds the heart of Britain, and who has the skill to bring men together. Do not set the dogs against the bear, or imagine that they would serve you if they could harry him.

Nor should you reveal my friend's secret, for if you do Arthur will see your letter to Uriens and will know what you intended. Be my friend. You are not the only one who has spies. My silence concerning this matter, if it goes no further, is a proof of my fondness.

Your sister

Morgan should learn that the girl who had once hung on her words had grown up, Guinevere thought. Now that she knew what love was, there was no need to play at it with one who toyed with her, as she suspected Morgan had.

Brooding over her troubles, Lancelot rode across a meadow of brown grasses.

Wind kept pushing her cloak away from her body, but the cold air seemed only a small matter. A kestrel flew from a tree branch to catch an unlucky mouse, and Lancelot felt that she could be trapped just as easily.

She scarcely noticed a beautiful lady ride up to her until the lady almost hovered like a kestrel over her.

The lady, whose golden hair shimmered in the sun, said, "Greetings, noble lord. Who are you?"

"I am but a poor warrior," Lancelot said, bowing. Even on such an important mission, one should always be courteous. She thought to avoid the usual clamor and adulation that came when she gave the name of Lancelot.

"Mysteries are always exciting, especially when the Unknown is so handsome," the lady exclaimed with delight. "I am the Lady Lydia, a poor widow," Her cloak was fit for a queen – snowy wool, embroidered with gold, which did not seem prudent in the deserted meadow. "My villa is near, poor wayfarer, and I would be honored if you would be my guest for supper and rest there tonight."

Lancelot hesitated, but a rumbling in her stomach convinced her. She had no food with her, because she had been too preoccupied to bother with it. The sun would soon set and the wind would likely be stronger that night. Raven needed a night's rest, and Lancelot could do with one as well.

"Thank you for your kind offer. It has been some days since I have had a proper meal, so I'll gladly accept. But I'm on an important mission and will have to leave by dawn."

Lancelot's feet felt frozen. She was eager to warm them beside a fire. She was just as glad that she did not have to sleep on the bare ground. The villa was small, but well restored, with even the tile floors in good repair. But the servants moved about uneasily, as if they were accustomed to frequent reprimands.

Lancelot was pleased to sit in a chair, not on a bench, while she dined. The roasted partridge was so succulent that she ate more than usual.

Lydia had changed into a red gown embroidered with gold thread and wore a good many jewels.

After they had eaten, the servants left them alone.

The lady said, "You are so handsome. I hope that you will come to my room tonight." She tried to take hold of Lancelot's hand.

Why didn't I see this coming, Lancelot sighed inwardly, ignoring the proffered hand. "Thank you for your kind offer, my lady, but I am pledged to another and cannot accept it."

"You are married?" asked Lydia, pouting.

"Not exactly, but I am pledged." Perhaps she should have said she was married, Lancelot thought as soon as she spoke the words.

"She would never know." Lydia batted her eyelashes.

"But I am true to the lady I love." Lancelot's voice was testy, for she was irked at the lady's presumption. She rose, prepared to spend the night under a tree.

"Don't go. I long for you." Lydia grasped Lancelot's hand.

Lancelot wanted to say how little she longed for Lydia, but the habit of courtesy was ingrained in her. "Forgive me, my lady, but I cannot stay here if you continue pressing me to break my pledge."

Lydia dropped her hand and sighed. "You grieve me, but you may stay here anyway. I wouldn't send you out on this cold night just because you are vowed to another."

"Thank you, my lady." Lancelot was relieved, for she longed for a bed, though not the lady's.

"Have some more wine," Lydia urged.

The wine in the goblet of rare green glass tasted strange, almost biting, but Lancelot was thirsty and drank it nevertheless.

When Lancelot had retired to her chamber, she found that her head was heavy and throbbing. She slumped onto the bed and fell asleep immediately.

In the middle of the night, Lancelot felt someone get in the bed beside her. Her heart pounded.

She was so groggy that she could scarcely move. Terror seized her. Where was she? What man was this? A fellow warrior? A brigand? A Saxon?

She struggled to fight back, but her limbs would not obey her. A mouth kissed hers, and she managed to turn her head away. Hands touched her. It was a woman!

Lancelot's heart ceased thumping wildly. She would not be raped. She recognized the smell of Lydia's perfume. She must stop Lydia without hurting her. "Stop! Don't!" Lancelot cried in a too weak voice. Lydia kissed her neck. "No!" Lancelot gasped, pulling away. "Please, leave!"

Lydia's hand groped Lancelot's crotch, trying to caress what was not there. It pulled back at finding what was.

"You're not a man!" Lydia shrieked.

"You're not a lady!" Lancelot replied angrily, moving away from her.

"You horrible creature! I kissed and touched a woman! How disgusting!" Lydia cried out.

"I did everything I could to keep you from it. I certainly didn't want you to." Lancelot glared at her indignantly through the dark.

"Posing as a man. You shameless thing! How could you be so deceitful?"

"I am the shameless, deceitful one?" Lancelot almost laughed.

"You drugged me and got into my bed without my consent."

"Don't you dare talk to me like that, you monster!" Lydia snarled. "Leave my home at once. I despise you! I never want to see your hideous face again,"

Lancelot suddenly felt sober. "I never want to see you again either."

Lancelot hurried to the stables and saddled her horse. How glad she was that she had not told her name! Was this how people would treat her if they learned she was a woman? Perhaps she would soon know the answer.

Forcing Raven to travel on through the night, Lancelot struggled against yielding to whatever drug Lydia had given her. Lancelot's vision blurred and her ears rang. A Saxon berserker lunged at her horse, and Lancelot swung her sword against him, but felt it hit the wood of a tree stump. Hoping she had not damaged her sword, she sheathed it and moved on. The war is over, she reminded herself. The war is over.

The forest of Rheged was darker and denser than the forest near Camelot. Day was little different from night. The black muck of the forest floor sucked at her mare's hooves, slowing Raven's progress. Fearing that the sword would arrive at Uriens's hall before she could retrieve it, Lancelot urged the mare on.

Riding as if pursued, she felt little desire for sleep, but Raven needed rest. She would not kill her horse, even for Arthur's sake.

No birds sang at this time of year, but wolves howled at night. These wolves might be hungrier than those she had encountered in the past. But for their mournful sound, the forest seemed deserted. She tried to calm Raven, who was unnerved by the howls.

Some said that spirits walked in such a forest, but Lancelot tried not to think of that. She stayed awake cheerlessly, rising often to put more branches on her fire to keep the wolves away. But she feared Morgan more than the wolves. Regardless of whether Lancelot found the king's sword, Morgan surely would denounce her as a woman because she had not been the one to steal it.

Little of dawn could penetrate through the thick woods, but Lancelot knew it was no longer night.

Patting Raven, she mounted and rode on.

Soon she could smell a cooking fire.

There might be a peasant's hut nearby, but what peasant would want to live in this deep forest?

She approached cautiously. There was only a small open fire, with a red-haired man tending it.

It was Cynlas, the young warrior she sought. Filled with anger at the sight of him, she charged up to the fire and swung down from her horse.

"Traitor! You have stolen the king's sword! Hand it over!" Flourishing her sword, she lunged at him.

"Lancelot!" Cynlas almost toppled into the fire.

Before he could recover, she grabbed him by the collar of his tunic and shook him. "Don't resist, or you forfeit your life."

He kicked her, and she fell onto the ground beside him. She had dropped her sword, and Cynlas threw himself on her back, holding her down. His hands grasped her neck in an attempt to strangle her.

Summoning all her strength, she forced herself up and twisted free of his grasp. Cynlas leapt up and ran to his horse, but as he swung up she grabbed his leg and pulled him off. He jerked free and ran.

Something long wrapped in leather hung from his saddle. More concerned about retrieving the king's sword than taking Cynlas back for punishment, she grabbed it from the horse and began to unwrap it. A large amethyst gleamed up at her. Excalibur!

A score of riders emerged from the path.

"Lancelot! You've brought me my sword as I knew you would." Thick-jowled, gray-bearded Uriens, followed by some twenty of his men, called out to her. The men surrounded her before she could take more than a few steps towards Raven.

"I did not!" she exclaimed. "It is King Arthur's sword, and I am returning it to him." She pulled the leather covering off the sword and held it poised for battle.

"My friend said you would not steal the sword yourself, but you would be the one Arthur sent to retrieve it," Uriens said, not naming Morgan though it was certainly her whom he meant. "And you will yield it to me," he demanded.

She flourished the heavy Excalibur. "I won't give this sword to anyone but the High King."

Uriens remained calm. Despite his bulk, he sat his horse well. His hand reached out for the sword. "I am a king, so you may give it to me. You're a great warrior and I don't want to harm you. I would treat you as an honored guest. And I would be right glad if you chose to become one of my warriors.

"Even you cannot defeat a score of men," Uriens continued. "Would you kill some of them in a hopeless cause? I want the sword, but it is not worth men's lives, certainly not yours. Yield it to me."

Lancelot hesitated. None of the men advanced on her. She would have to attack them if she wanted to try to escape with the sword. Of course Uriens was right that she could not defeat all twenty of them. He had made the most telling argument: She did not want to kill or injure men needlessly, when she could not possibly win. Much as she wanted to return the sword to Arthur, she would have to yield it up.

Cynlas had returned to the clearing. He grinned, gloating at Lancelot's predicament.

She relaxed her sword arm. "You are correct. I cannot succeed against so many. But you should let me return the sword to its rightful owner. The High King will be vexed if you do not."

Uriens smiled and moved his horse a little closer to Lancelot.

"Vexed? No doubt. But not angered enough to make war on me, I'll wager. Hand over the sword."

Thinking that there was little choice, she handed up the sword, hilt extended.

She groaned when she saw the amethyst covered by Uriens's large palm. Uriens held up the sword and his men cheered.

"I shall hold a feast in celebration." His eyes gleamed with triumph. "Come and be my guest, Lancelot."

Her pulse beat fast with anger. "I am no guest of yours. I shall never rest until I retrieve the sword."

Uriens scowled. "Be a guest in my dungeon, then. That might cool your ardor. Take him," he commanded, and several men leapt off their horses and grabbed her.

Her own sword she had left on the ground, and one of the men took it. She struck at the men with her fists, but they quickly subdued her.

"What you're doing is wrong, Father," protested a clean-shaven young man with light brown hair. He wore a gold torque that was nearly as fine as the one on Uriens's neck. "King Arthur is your sovereign. You should return his sword, and you should not imprison Lancelot."

"Be silent, Uwaine!" Uriens shouted, turning a red face to the young man. "I am sovereign here, and you are my subject."

Uwaine glowered, but he ceased speaking.

Lancelot was forced to mount Raven and ride with them. She looked around for a chance to dart off through the trees, but men were guarding her on all sides and the forest was too thick to get through on horseback.

They brought her to a huge stone and timber hall, surrounded by stables, sheds, and thatch-roofed huts. She dismounted with some dignity, but guards grabbed her arms and pulled her along.

"So you're the great Lancelot," a foul-breathed guard said contemptuously. "Not willing to die for King Arthur's sword, were you? Perhaps after you've had some time in the dungeon you'll be sorry you didn't."

She was taken to a pit with a barred grate over it.

Guards pulled back the grate and thrust down a ladder for her to climb. She climbed down, saw the ladder withdrawn, and heard the grate close over her.

She stood in a dark pit with filthy straw on the floor. The smell of wastes of the men who had been here before her was almost overwhelming, but at least she was alone.

How long would it take before they found out she was a woman? Uriens had made no sign that he knew, so perhaps Morgan hadn't told him – yet. But how could she keep her secret as a prisoner? Perhaps she should have accepted the offer to be a guest after all. Yet she could not, for it would then seem as if she gave up the sword willingly. Unnerved by the darkness, she paced about the small cell. She heard a scratching sound in a corner. Rats, no doubt. She shuddered at the thought of lying down and trying to sleep on the filthy straw with rats molesting her.

Time passed, but still she remained upright. To keep calm, she counted the number of times that she paced the cell, but she stopped counting after one thousand. She feared that she would start seeing the corpses from the war again.

How long would she be away from the trees and the grass, the birds and the smell of flowers? She needed them as she needed water.

"Lancelot!" a voice called down to her.

It did not sound menacing.

"Yes?"

"I am Uwaine, King Uriens's youngest son. I've come to get you out of the dungeon. The king is holding his feast and I've sent the guards off to get their share of meat and ale."

The grate creaked open and a ladder appeared.

Though her limbs were stiff, she scrambled up the ladder.

"Many thanks," she exclaimed, as Uwaine caught hold of her arm and helped her out.

"My father pays no heed to me. I knew he was wrong. All my life I have wanted to become one of King Arthur's warriors. Will you put in a good word for me?" he pleaded.

"Indeed!" She would put in many, if Arthur would ever listen to her again.

But Arthur's name reminded her of the sword.

"I can't leave without King Arthur's sword." She sighed.

"A friend of yours has taken it from my father's quarters. I think my father will be too drunk when the feast is over to notice that it's gone, if he doesn't just collapse where he sits, as he often does." Uwaine's voice was bitter, as if his father had disappointed him many times.

"A friend of mine?" Who could that be?

"Which of your friends is good at taking things?" said a familiar voice.

"Drian!" Lancelot exclaimed with delight.

"I was complaining at the feast about my father's imprisoning you," Uwaine said, "and, after most of the men were drunk, this harper came up to me and suggested that we help you escape and get the sword."

"Look." Drian handed Lancelot a long object in leather.

"Can it be?" Lancelot eagerly tore at the wrapping and opened it enough to see a purple gleam on the end. Lancelot clutched the sword. "But Uwaine, won't your father blame and punish you?"

"He might, but I can take it. What can he do? I am his son, after all."

"He might disinherit you."

"He might." Uwaine nodded.

"But I am only his third son, and would not get much anyway. If I don't help you now, I lose my chance to ever be one of King Arthur's men."

Drian snorted with impatience. "Come, we must get away as soon as possible. Everyone will be looking for Lancelot, so you should wear a disguise. While I was in the family's quarters, I found a gown and a veil. You can be my wife."

"Your wife? I don't want to disguise myself as a woman," Lancelot complained.

"You should, it's a clever idea," Uwaine urged. "That way you can ride pillion on your horse. If two horses were missing, they'd know you were both gone. If you take one, everyone will be too busy to notice that the harper has gone, too, or to connect him with your escape. They'll be looking for a lone rider."

"You can change clothes when we get in the woods," Drian said, casting a wary glance around her. "Let's make haste."

They moved through the dark courtyard to a stable.

"Who goes there?" called out a guard.

"Uwaine," the young man said.

"Aye, my lord," the guard replied, moving on.

They entered the stable, found Raven, and Lancelot saddled her. She patted the mare to reassure her about taking a strange rider. Then Lancelot swung up on the saddle and Drian got up behind her.

"You will commend me to King Arthur?" Uwaine whispered.

"I shall praise you as you deserve. I hope your father does not punish you severely." Lancelot was anxious to be gone.

Uwaine pointed out the road and they pounded off through the night forest. They must get as far away as possible before morning. Raven seemed rested and ready to go as fast as she could, though the road was not a good one and she was carrying two riders.

For once, Lancelot regretted that there was a full moon and a cloudless sky.

They paused only for Lancelot to put on the gown and veil, with Drian helping her. Then Drian was the one to swing up onto the saddle, and Lancelot to sit behind.

At dawn, they hid among the trees. Exhausted, Lancelot slumped onto the ground and drifted off to sleep, but Drian seemed wide awake.

Lancelot woke to the sound of horses' hooves. Uriens's men were searching for her, but they passed by. She was glad that the soil was dry, so Raven's tracks were not easy to find.

In the light, Lancelot could see that the gown she was wearing was yellow, and of costly material. The lady who had lost it would miss it. She wished Drian had stolen a gown that was not so fine.

"I also brought some ladies' gloves," Drian said. "There aren't many ladies with three fingers on their left hand. We can fill the extra fingers with dirt."

"I can't get dirt on my hands," Lancelot whined in a fake baby voice. "Very clever." She took the glove, stuffed dirt in the two fingers that would have been empty, and put it on.

"What name do you want me to call you?" Drian asked. "Pick something pretty."

Lancelot smiled. "Anna, I think. I like that name very well."

"Anna," Drian sighed in tones of great passion. "Anna, my beauty."

Lancelot tapped her on the shoulder. "Let's cover your harp." Fortunately, the harp was small. "Harpers don't usually ride across the country with their wives."

"If only I could," Drian sighed. "If only I had a wife in the first place."

They covered the harp with Lancelot's cloak, but the shape was unmistakable if anyone looked closely. They tried even more carefully to conceal the king's sword. Drian offered to wear it, but Lancelot shook her head. The two proceeded on their journey.

"Thank you for everything, but we should have taken two horses," Lancelot complained. "We could have ridden faster, and it's uncomfortable perching on the back of the horse."

"Remember, it was my horse that we left. But I like having your arms around me," Drian said, turning to grin at her.

"We can steal a new horse when we have a chance."

"We can buy one!" Lancelot was stirred, and not by passion.

"What, they put you in a dungeon but they let you keep your purse?"

"Yes."

"Ah, you nobles lead a different life." Drian shook her head.

More men in chain mail thudded up behind them. Lancelot hadn't expected a second search party. The warriors paused.

"Have you seen a man in chain mail fleeing in this direction?" one of the warriors asked. "A handsome man with black hair?"

"He rushed past us earlier," Drian said, scratching her head as if trying to remember when that had happened. "Very rude he was, too. His horse stirred up a lot of dust."

"We're on the right track," the warrior cried to the others, and they went on.

"See, the disguise was a good idea," Drian said, patting Lancelot's right hand, which was holding on to her. "Now, be a good little wife and do what I say."

"Don't carry the pretense too far," Lancelot warned her.

"I'm a hero," Drian boasted.

"I stole back the king's sword. Do you think he'd miss the amethyst if it happened to come loose? He could get another one."

"Drian!" Lancelot shouted. "Don't you dare!"

"I was just jesting. I knew you wouldn't let me take it."

Lancelot had a chance to think during the ride. She felt little pleasure at the thought of returning to Camelot. Morgan surely would send Arthur a message revealing her secret. Even bringing

Arthur's sword back might not convince him to allow a woman to be one of his warriors.

But she would give her life for him. She would have rotted in Uriens's dungeon if need be. If the king was worth this fealty, could he turn away one who had sworn an oath to him and never broken it?

29 A DOUBLE DISGUISE

After the moon had risen, Lancelot and Drian came to a tavern. This time, Lancelot was glad to share a room, and pleased that they had one to themselves. The noise from the men drinking in the tavern didn't bother her much, nor did a few spider webs in the corners. The room was warm, compared with the ride, and especially with the dungeon.

"I'm longing to change out of this gown, but I suppose I can't go to bed a woman and leave as a man in the morning, even in this out of the way tavern." Lancelot rolled up the gown's sleeves, which were too sweeping for her taste. "But I'll change when we're back on the road."

"Are you sure of that?" Drian looked out of the window. "Some men wearing Uriens's colors are riding up to the tavern."

Groaning, Lancelot looked through the window and confirmed the sighting. "I suppose we had better not leave in the morning until after they've gone."

"Don't worry. We have a whole night 'til then." Drian looked at the bed meaningfully.

"I can't sleep with you," Lancelot said.

"But you're my wife." Drian pulled down the blanket.

Lancelot shook her head. "I'm not."

"We could just sleep together and do no more."

Lancelot found that a pleasant idea. She relented. "I suppose we could, just for one night."

They kept their clothes on – Lancelot didn't care whether she wrinkled the gown – and slept spoon-fashion.

In the morning, Lancelot slept later than usual. When she woke, Drian had left, but the harp was still there.

The sun climbed high in the heavens, and Lancelot tired of waiting. No matter how strange it looked for a woman in a gown, she went to the stable, determined to saddle Raven and tie on all their things, including Drian's harp and the king's sword. Of course the sword was still covered with leather.

"Your husband makes you saddle your own horse!" exclaimed a stablehand, staring at Lancelot as if she had three heads.

Lancelot sighed. "He's a bit of a tyrant, I fear. Would you help me, kind sir?"

"Tsk, it's a shame. To be sure I will."

She let him put on the saddle, but she tied on the harp and the sword herself, though she felt clumsy with one hand in the partially dirt-filled glove. She whispered in Raven's ear to reassure her that she wouldn't have to carry two riders for long.

The white-bearded tavern keeper came to the stable door and watched her. "Poor lady, it's a good thing you can fend for yourself. Your husband got in a quarrel this morning, and he's in a fight now, I'm afraid, and with a famous fighter, too."

"What!" Lancelot wheeled about to face him. "How could that be? Who's he fighting?"

The man sighed and gazed at the stable floor. "I'm afraid it's Gawaine ap Lot himself. You might be a widow this day."

"No! Where are they?" Lancelot vaulted onto the horse as well as she could in a gown. The skirt ripped.

"In the meadow about a mile south of here." Both the tavern-keeper and the stable hand stared at her, now as if she had ten heads.

Lancelot rode as fast as she could, the stable yard's chickens squawking and fluttering as she went. Would she be soon enough to keep one of her friends from killing the other? Gawaine could not know that Drian was her friend, and certainly not that Drian was a woman.

She rode to a field where a crowd was watching a fight.

That is, Gawaine was fighting and Drian, still unhurt, was flourishing a sword with determination but little skill.

"Stop!" Lancelot yelled, riding through the crowd and into the center of the field. Men scurried aside to avoid her horse. Some yelled and shook their fists at her. There were too many people around for explanations. "Jump up behind me!" she cried to Drian, and extended her hand.

Drian quickly obliged. "My fine wife!" she exclaimed.

Gawaine froze, staring at Lancelot. He stood there holding his sword in the air.

"I'll explain later," Lancelot shouted to him as she rode off with Drian.

When they had gone about a mile, Drian said, "Thanks. I'm glad I got away from that son of a witch."

"Thanks!" Lancelot all but shouted. "That's all you have to say? Don't call Gawaine that. He's my friend, or he was. How did you make him so angry? He's no brawler, and it's unlike him to fight anyone who is . . . not highborn," she said, not wanting to say lowborn.

Drian clung to her a little too much.

"Not that high up! You won't distract me," Lancelot complained. "No, not that low either. What did you do to anger Gawaine?"

"He just saw me and demanded that I fight. It could be because three years ago I ran away with a girl who was supposed to marry Agravaine ap Lot."

Lancelot groaned. Gawaine had good cause. But she could see why a girl would prefer Drian to Agravaine, reckless though that might be.

"What happened to the girl?"

"She left me for someone else."

"Did he marry her?"

"No."

Lancelot groaned again. "But he might have abandoned her by now. What will happen to her? Perhaps she is starving and desperate. Even marriage to Agravaine would have been better."

"I don't think she's starving. She left me for a rich widow," Drian said ruefully.

"Oh. That will be easy to explain to Gawaine," Lancelot said with sarcasm. And Gawaine had seen her in this miserable gown and likely realized that she was a woman. Lancelot did not look forward to meeting him again.

"You can't go back to Camelot now. He must know that you're a woman."

"He's probably the least of my problems," Lancelot said, wondering if that were true. "I have to get out of this gown. I must have looked like a madwoman dressed like this when I rescued you. I can hardly move in the foolish thing."

"Best not change out of the gown 'til we see whether Uriens's warriors are still about," Drian warned. "And we'd better switch places, my dear."

"No doubt you're right," Lancelot grumbled. Grudgingly, she went back to riding behind Drian. They spotted some grouse, but it seemed best not to stop to hunt them.

A peregrine falcon, needing a meal more than the travelers did, swept down and carried off a grouse. Lancelot was reminded of the hawk on Gawaine's shield.

At midday, they came to a village where they were able to buy a horse for Drian. Lancelot insisted on giving Drian the money to pay for it.

"You saved me from the dungeon and left your horse, so I must give you this one," Lancelot said, as they purchased a fine chestnut gelding.

"If you wish, but I could pay for it myself. You don't think I took only the sword and the gown, do you?" Drian winked. "Remember, I left Uriens's keep before I was paid."

"Drian!" Lancelot moaned, putting her hands to her head. "Is there any holding where you are welcome to return?"

"I don't steal from all of them," Drian said, patting her new horse.

"Such restraint." Lancelot's voice was full of sarcasm.

"Hurry up," called the horse trader, who had been too far away to overhear the conversation. "King Uriens's men want to buy horses, too, and I can charge them a handsome price."

Only a little alarmed, Lancelot and Drian went to a tavern and were munching on meat pies when a tall, red-bearded man strode up to their table.

"Lady, you look beautiful in yellow," Gawaine said, bowing to Lancelot.

"You look pretty in plaid," she said, glancing at his cloak. "It has almost as many lines as the scars on your face."

Drian tensed, but Lancelot put her hand on Drian's arm.

"Don't disturb my wife," Drian said.

"I only want to compliment your lovely wife," Gawaine said, sitting down at their table, taking out his mead horn, and pouring some of their mead in it. "I have never seen such a delicate lady."

"I have never heard a man whose talk was so empty," Lancelot replied, narrowing her eyes. She lifted her left hand, still gloved, to show that she was pretending to be a lady who had all five fingers. Gawaine regarded the hand.

"The last time I encountered your beloved husband, dear lady, was just before 'he'" (Gawaine emphasized the word to show that he knew it was false) "ran away with a cousin of mine who was betrothed to my brother. And when I encountered your husband this morning, I asked 'him'" (emphasized again) "about her, but 'he' refused to tell me." Gawaine looked none too kindly at Drian. He spoke in a falsely polite tone. "Might I ask you again what happened to my cousin Catra?"

"I have heard that she is safe," Lancelot interjected, "and living with a rich widow."

Gawaine scowled. "No man will ever marry her now."

"I believe that was the lady's intention," Lancelot said, hailing the tavern-keeper to bring more mead.

Gawaine's deepened frown showed that he understood her meaning. He exhaled.

"The meat pies here are really good. Have some," Lancelot urged. "You must be hungry after the ride from the last tavern. We were. Were you fond of your cousin, or did you know her only slightly?"

Gawaine poured himself more mead and drank it. "I never met her before Agravaine's betrothal, and neither had Agravaine. It is a matter of family honor."

"Ah, yes, honor is always a good reason for killing, even for slaughtering harpers who cannot possibly defeat you."

Lancelot put on a falsely sympathetic smile.

"I gave him the dignity of trying to fight, which is more than any of my kinsmen would have done." Gawaine glared at Drian. "Harpers are very well in their place, but they cannot rise from their station. Indeed, some cannot rise at all."

"There's no need to rise to fill a place well," Drian retorted. "For a harper, it's all a matter of the hands."

Lancelot choked back laughter. "It is a matter of having the tongue to sing sweetly," she said.

"How fond you are of your dear husband, lady. You must have known him long." Gawaine spread his arms over the table, crowding Drian's, but Drian did not retreat.

"Very fond," Lancelot said. "My life was dark as a prison cell until he came to me. And he gave me this beautiful gown to cover me." She stroked the sleeve as if delighted with its fine texture.

Gawaine raised his eyebrows and dropped his voice. "What? Have you been imprisoned? And are you fleeing in disguise?"

"Even so."

"What a pity that my friend Lancelot isn't here," Gawaine said in a more normal tone, "for he no doubt knows a great deal about the matters we have been discussing. He never misses a chance for a bawdy jest." He ate a bite of the meat pie.

"Lancelot is well known for his feats in the bedchamber."

"Indeed, he must be much more skilled than that braggart, Gawaine ap Lot," Lancelot said, sipping her mead and gesturing to Drian to let her do the talking.

"Have you had the pleasure of comparing their skills, my lady?" Gawaine asked, stroking his beard. "That would no doubt be fascinating."

"Fascinating to you, perhaps, but for me as dull as Gawaine's blade," Lancelot replied, fussing with her veil.

"True, Gawaine's blade is not sharp but gentle, my lady," he said, finishing the meat pie.

"Gentle because like unleavened bread it cannot rise," Lancelot said. She thought perhaps it was better not to drink any more. She saw that Drian was clutching her cup as if it were someone's throat, and she could guess whose.

"Doubtless my friend Lancelot is a better swordsman," Gawaine replied. "But do you know that Lancelot prefers men to women?"

"He does not!" Lancelot was unable to control her irritation.

"Did someone speak of Lancelot of the Lake?" asked a warrior who had just come in the tavern with four companions. They wore the badge of King Uriens.

"I did," Gawaine said.

Lancelot looked down, as if in modesty, at her mead cup. She was glad that the tavern was dark.

"We're looking for him. He stole something from King Uriens, and we mean to get it back. Have you seen him?"

"I haven't seen Lancelot the warrior in many days," Gawaine told them.

"What about you?" The leader, a graying man perhaps as old as Gawaine, stared at Drian. "Weren't you the harper who played at Uriens's caer the other day?"

"Impossible. He's come from Eburacum with me," Gawaine told the man.

"What do you mean to do with Lancelot if you find him?" Drian asked, frowning.

"We'll do whatever we have to do to get back what he stole," said the man grimly, going off with his companions to drink.

Lancelot spoke in a whisper. "What I took from Uriens was Arthur's sword."

"Uriens stole it?"

Gawaine also tried to speak quietly, no easy thing for his loud voice. "And now they're trying to steal it back?"

Lancelot nodded.

"We could take them, or should we try to settle this without fighting?" Gawaine asked Lancelot.

"Without fighting. They're only doing what their king ordered. I don't want to risk killing any of them unless we have to."

"Agreed." Gawaine finished his mead in one gulp.

"Let me buy you a drink, noble warriors," Gawaine said to the men, moving to their table. His voice was loud enough for Lancelot to hear easily.

Uriens's warriors smiled and thanked him.

"If you want to find Lancelot, you're going the wrong way." Gawaine put his hand on the leader's shoulder. "I saw him heading towards Eburacum."

The leader pulled back. "Why would he go there? Surely he's headed to Camelot."

"But if Lancelot has stolen something from King Uriens, perhaps he wants it for himself," Gawaine said. "Then he might not go to Camelot."

The man scrutinized him.

"You're a tall man with a red beard," he said, as if he had just noticed. "Aren't you Gawaine ap Lot, and a friend of Lancelot's?"

Gawaine shook his head. "No, I'm his brother Agravaine ap Lot, and I'm not overly fond of Lancelot of the Lake. It bothers me that people say Lancelot is as good a fighter as Gawaine, which isn't at all true. Gawaine seems to like Lancelot even better than his own brothers, and that's not right."

Lancelot smiled. No doubt Gawaine described Agravaine's feelings pretty well.

"Are you certain you saw Lancelot on the road to Eburacum, Lord Agravaine?" the man asked.

"It's important to King Uriens that we find him, and the king will be angry if we don't."

Gawaine shrugged. "Then I am sorry for you, because King Arthur will be very angry if any harm comes to Lancelot. For some reason that I don't understand, Lancelot is a favorite with my cousin, the High King. I think Arthur would draw and quarter anyone who injured Lancelot."

Uriens's men were watching Gawaine closely. One of them choked on his mead. Another squirmed.

"And that's not to speak of what my brother would do," Gawaine continued, taking a swig of the mead that he was sharing with them. "Gawaine would surely pursue to ends of the earth any man who injured Lancelot, and would kill him as painfully as possible. Not in a fight, mind you, but something much worse. But, of course, all you care about is doing your duty," he said with a smile. "You would not pay heed to any words that might distract you from it."

He nodded to them and went to rejoin Lancelot and Drian.

Grinning at Drian, Gawaine said cheerfully, "Your wife is a notorious wanton. She's slept near hundreds of soldiers."

Lancelot restrained her laughter.

Drian glowered. "I'd like to fight you."

"Ah, but now I won't fight you," Gawaine replied, gloating, and finished his mead. He gestured to get more.

"We've had enough to drink," Lancelot said, gesturing to the tavern-keeper not to bring any more. "We should leave now."

"Whatever the lady wants." Gawaine bowed his head to her.

The three rode away together, though Drian and Gawaine avoided looking at each other. Lancelot told how she had been captured and Drian had helped her escape. They lingered behind some trees on the road to see what direction Uriens's men would take, and were pleased to see they took the road to Eburacum.

"They believed what you told them," Drian said to Gawaine. "How gullible."

"Not at all. The leader knew exactly who I was – probably, who we all were – and heeded my warning." Gawaine grinned. "He just wanted to be able to halt the search without letting his men know that's what he was doing. He too carefully avoided looking at Lancelot. Men don't try so hard to keep from looking at a handsome woman. The answer is that he thought you were a handsome man posing as a woman."

Lancelot made a disgusted sound. "Perhaps he never was eager to carry out Uriens's bidding. There could be loyalty to King Arthur even in Rheged."

The three then turned south, towards Camelot. The afternoon was warmer than the morning had promised.

Lancelot eyed a patch of trees.

"I think we've avoided Uriens's men, so I'll go and get out of this wretched gown. It's hard to ride properly in it."

"I'll guard you," Drian said, casting a wary glance at Gawaine.

Gawaine's face reddened. "Oh, guard her by all means. I've been Lance's friend for a dozen years. How long have you known her?"

"Thank you for your concern, Drian, but I have no need to be guarded from Gawaine," Lancelot told her. She went behind the trees and changed her clothes as quickly as possible so as not to leave the hostile two alone together for long.

She rejoined them, and they rode mostly in silence.

After a short time, Gawaine turned to Drian. "Now will you tell me where I can find my cousin Catra so I can be certain that all is well with her?"

Drian appeared to freeze to statue-like rigidity. "No."

Gawaine sighed with exasperation. "I thought not. Don't you see that I challenged you to fight because you wouldn't tell me what happened to her? When you chose to face death rather than tell me, I thought you had done something terrible to her. Will you tell Lancelot where she is? Lancelot, if Drian will tell you how to find my cousin, would you please go sometime in the next few months and see if she is in a good place?"

"Willingly," Lancelot said, thinking Drian was wrong not to trust Gawaine, but concerned about the girl.

"Of course, I'll tell Lancelot." Drian did not smile. The two of them rode aside and Drian told her where Catra was.

"Swear you won't tell him."

"I won't, but such a promise is unnecessary."

Drian's hands were fists clutching her horse's reins.

"If Gawaine was going to kill me for running away with Catra, how can I know what he'd do to her?"

Lancelot gasped, so shaken that she lurched in her saddle. "He'd never hurt her."

"Men have killed their kinswomen for less," Drian insisted.

"I know that well, but he would not. Neither would he tell Agravaine," Lancelot said, though she knew she protested in vain.

"He won't have the chance."

"Do you think he was going to kill you because you ran away with her, or, as he says, because you refused to tell him what had happened to her? It's not so strange that he assumed the worst. You could have abandoned her, or even sold her." Lancelot hated to say those words, but she thought they were necessary.

"Of course, because I'm so lowborn, it's likely that I'd have done something awful." Drian sounded no warmer to Gawaine than she had been before.

"I suppose we have to rejoin him now." She grimaced.

Riding with her two friends posed difficulties for Lancelot, who didn't want to offend either of them. She tried to keep her horse equidistant from both, but on a crumbling Roman road, that was not an easy task.

When the three had ridden only a little further, Drian stopped. She asked Lancelot, "Are you riding with him or with me?"

Lancelot gave her a warm glance, though perhaps not as warm as if Gawaine had not been present.

"Gawaine and I are headed to Camelot."

Drian frowned. "You could give him the sword to return to the king."

"But I want to be with Guinevere," Lancelot said, sorry to pain Drian, as she knew she did.

"You should have a reward for retrieving King Arthur's sword," said Gawaine. He took the gold armrings off his wrists and handed them to Drian. Drian hesitated to take them.

"The reward is not from me, but from the High King," Gawaine told her. "He would surely give you one."

"True, he would," Lancelot agreed.

Drian accepted the armrings and put them on. Her wrists were much slimmer than Gawaine's.

For that reason, and perhaps to conceal the armrings, she pushed them up under her sleeves.

"I bid you farewell," Drian said, with a brief nod to Gawaine and a long look at Lancelot.

"Farewell," Lancelot said warmly, "until we meet again."

"Farewell," Gawaine said, "and may we not meet too soon."

"For the first time, I agree with you," Drian told him. She rode over a hill and was soon out of sight.

When Drian had gone, Gawaine said, "I fear your marriage didn't last long." Lancelot laughed.

"I have no husband, and no desire to have one."

"Won't he marry you? Has he left you with child?" Gawaine's voice pretended concern. He stroked his red beard, which gleamed in the winter sun.

. "Drian is my friend, though a very attractive one," Lancelot replied, frowning to show that the jest was wearing thin. "But I have never embraced anyone but Guinevere and never will."

"No doubt that would please Guinevere." Gawaine looked at Lancelot as if he was seeing her for the first time, and his gaze made her uncomfortable. They let their horses relax their pace as they went around a boggy patch of ground.

The afternoon sun warmed the air. Flocks of starlings gathered in the bushes. There was no reason to pretend Gawaine didn't know her secret.

"Did you guess that night at the tavern that I was a woman?"

He snorted. "I didn't guess, I knew. There was no other reason for you to be so reluctant to sleep in a bed."

Lancelot sighed. He had helped her just now, but what did he think of her? "Do you think I'm a monster?"

"A what?" Gawaine started as if a hare had run in front of his horse. "Why should you imagine that?"

"A lady called me that just the other night," Lancelot admitted, casting her gaze on the ground.

"What a sweet lady!" Gawaine's voice was heavy with sarcasm. "How did she find out about you?"

"She gave me something strong to drink and then she came uninvited to my bed. I was terrified when I woke. Everything was an awful blur. She kissed me and I tried to stop her but . . . never mind!"

"It isn't difficult to guess." He put his hand over his mouth.

Lancelot gave him a baleful look and grumbled under her breath. "Well, don't think about it. Whoever would have imagined that a woman would do such a thing!"

"She wouldn't be the first woman in history to get into a man's bed though he hadn't asked her," Gawaine smiled as if to indicate some such thing had happened to him. "But, though I've heard

of men trying to get women to drink too much, I've never heard
of a woman drugging a man. If you had kept that gown on, few .
ladies would have molested you. But, of course, some men might
have tried, not guessing that would shorten their lives."

"Didn't you talk enough nonsense for today at the tavern?"
Lancelot was tired of hearing comments about her sex.

"You can think up a lie quicker than you can lift your mead
horn."

"I have never lied to you," Gawaine exclaimed, his laughter
finished."You always know when I am telling a tale, but you have
deceived me every day for many years." His tone was not jesting.
He actually glared at her. "How can I trust you?"

"Gawaine!" Lancelot reeled from the blow. It seemed that the
day had grown colder, as if snow had started to fall. She could
barely speak. "Is it a lie that I have saved your life as often as
you have saved mine?"

"No, that is true," Gawaine admitted. "But I don't know who
or what you are." He had stopped glaring, but he did not smile.
He stared at her as if she were a stranger.

"How can I tell you what I don't know myself?" Lancelot cried.
She spoke as if trying to convince herself as well as Gawaine. "My
father raised me like a boy so I could defend myself. How can I
know what I would be like otherwise? I have to lie for my own
protection. Who am I? I am Arthur's warrior, Guinevere's lover,
and your friend. I have never let you down."

Gawaine now looked at her as he had when her hand was
wounded. His voice was subdued. "Neither have I let you down."

"Not yet," she said with a catch in her voice.

"Is it likely that I will, then?" But he now looked away from
her, which was not reassuring.

His terseness unnerved her. Gawaine was not a man of few
words. She fixed her gaze on the muddy path ahead. "What am

I? I am like Drian," she said, encouraging her mare to move a little faster. "Drian's the only person I have ever met who is like me. Call me a woman, a man, or what you will."

Gawaine finally looked Lancelot in the eye and grinned. "You truly are a woman. When I asked who you were and what you were, you did not say, 'How dare you ask me such a question. I am Lancelot of the Lake, Lancelot of the Lightning Arm, the greatest fighter in the world.' No, you said who you are to other people – to Arthur, to Guinevere, to me. Just like a woman."

"Many warriors would say what lord they are sworn to serve," Lancelot objected.

"Exactly," Gawaine said triumphantly. "A man might say, 'I am the foremost warrior of Arthur, High King of All Britain.' He would not have said who his lady is, or reminded the man challenging him that they were friends. I repeat – you are just like a woman."

"If I'm just like a woman, it took you a long time to discover it," Lancelot said, irked but relieved that he grinned.

"Yes, it took me years to uncover your secret." Gawaine smirked and brought his horse up next to hers. He put a little too much emphasis on the word "uncover."

"You haven't uncovered anything, and you aren't going to." Lancelot frowned at him. "Don't think you can talk to me that way."

He chuckled. "Don't worry, I can't do anything. A woman who apparently knows me better than I thought she did said I am like unleavened bread that cannot rise. If you can say such things, I can, too."

Lancelot felt her face flush. "No, in fact you can't." She urged her mare to ride ahead of him.

After they had ridden a short distance, Gawaine asked, "And does Arthur know about you?"

She halted her horse at that.

"No, and don't tell him. I'm afraid he would send me away."

"Of course I won't. He'd let you stay, but he might impose conditions that you would not like." Gawaine sucked in his breath. "As his wife's lover, you are in a difficult position. He shouldn't know that you are a woman."

"I wouldn't tell him," she said. "He might treat me differently."

Gawaine raised his eyebrows. "He might." He gave her a strange look. "I'll never tell anyone your secret." His voice was quieter than usual.

"I have no wish to tell Arthur, but I fear his sister will tell him." Lancelot sighed. "When I was wounded by brigands in Cornwall, she saved my life and discovered that I am a woman. She threatened to tell him if I did not steal his sword . . ."

"Morgan is behind the stealing of his sword!" Gawaine cried out, his eyes almost bulging out of his head. "I can't believe she would do such a thing. Did she want that old fool Uriens to be High King? Thank all the gods you retrieved the sword."

Gawaine reached out and nearly clapped her on the back, then pulled back as if he could not do that to a woman. "A while ago, Morgan approached me to conspire against Arthur, but I didn't take it seriously. I am not clever about such intrigue. How could Morgan have hatched such a mad plot?" He shook his head. "Never fear, I shall ask her not to reveal your secret. She used to be fond of me, so I suppose she still is."

"Thank you," Lancelot said, not at all sure that this possible fondness would be enough to silence Morgan.

"I hope you won't tell Arthur about her part in this plot." Gawaine's voice held an unusual note of anxiety. "He exiled her for no good reason, so I fear what he would do if he had cause. He might put her in a dungeon."

Lancelot shuddered.

"I spent an afternoon and evening in Uriens's dungeon. If I had had to spend much time there, I would have gone mad." She looked gratefully at the pink-gold winter sky, so different from the dark hole where she had been imprisoned. "Whatever else she might have done, the Lady Morgan saved my life when I was wounded. I would never want her to be in a prison. Of course I won't tell."

Gawaine smiled at her.

Then he looked at Lancelot intensely, as if he were a teacher trying to instruct a slow pupil. "Women are not always kind, Lance. I fear that loving a married woman so much will lead you to suffer," he said gently.

Shaking her head, Lancelot smiled. "Some other married woman might hurt me, but Guinevere would not. And when did you start worrying about women getting hurt by love?"

"Today," he admitted, shrugging his shoulders.

"I thought so." She tried to frown, but couldn't help laughing. "Loving a woman will never be safe for me. But it's worth the risk."

She wondered whether she was returning to Guinevere's love, or was she going to lose all that she valued, that love most of all, when Morgan told Arthur her secret?

As they rode on, they passed through hills and fields covered with a few inches of snow. Lancelot hoped that Uriens's men were nowhere near to see their tracks.

When they were riding through the hills, Gawaine stopped his horse, dismounted and went behind some rocks.

Realizing why he did, Lancelot laughed.

Gawaine emerged and glowered at her.

"There is a slight change in your behavior," she said, grinning.

He glared at her, but it was a mock glare.

"I had thought I wasn't going to tell you that I knew your secret, but you would have guessed quickly enough."

"If you suddenly started going behind rocks and trees, I surely would have known." Lancelot couldn't restrain her laughter at the thought. "I've never understood why men aren't more modest with each other."

"If we guessed there were women disguised as men among us, we would be. You could have warned me." He still frowned.

"Told the greatest secret of my life just to protect your doubtful modesty? Not likely."

She finally succeeded in subduing her mirth.

"I thought you were a converted Jew," Gawaine said as he remounted his horse.

"Why?" Dropping her horse's reins, Lancelot stared at him.

"Soon after you came to Camelot, Cai told Arthur and me that you must be a Jew and didn't want to show that you were circumcised."

Lancelot laughed with astonishment. "Circumcised! What an ingenious explanation! So Cai always saw through my disguise. I thought he might have. He must have been certain that you and Arthur wouldn't tell others you believed I was a Jew. I've heard there are places where Jews are treated badly." She felt a little ashamed because she hadn't thought much about that ill treatment. But it was far away.

"Cai also said that Jews have difficulty growing beards," Gawaine said.

Lancelot laughed again. "I saw Jewish merchants in Lesser Britain, and they all had beards. Cai can tell a tale as well as you can."

After a short pause, Lancelot speculated.

"You thought I didn't tell you I was a Jew, and you didn't mind that. So why should you care that I didn't tell you I was a woman?"

Gawaine looked at her as if she had made a particularly foolish jest. "It made no difference to me if you were a Jew."

"Then why should it make a difference that I am a woman?"

Gawaine snorted, as if the comment was too ridiculous to merit a response.

Not long before the sun would start to set, they came to a crossroads. "Someone has been following us," Lancelot said. "Only one rider, I think."

Gawaine nodded. "I've known that for a while. I think it's your friend. I doubt that a lone warrior of Uriens's would dare to take us on."

"I wondered about that, too, but why would Drian follow us?"

Gawaine rolled his eyes. "Can't you guess the answer? Do you want me to leave for a while so you can speak with Drian?"

Amazed at his tact, Lancelot said, "Why yes, in fact, that might be best. You can meet up with me again later."

"Don't be surprised if the harper takes some time to join you. When I leave, she'll follow me."

"Why should he?" Lancelot asked, emphasizing the "he" because that's how she thought Gawaine should refer to Drian.

"Because he doesn't trust me." When Gawaine called Drian "he," he rolled his eyes. "I'll bet you a drink that's what he does."

"Surely not." Lancelot shook her head, but she admitted to herself that Gawaine might be right.

"I don't like the idea of going off too far when it's still possible that you might encounter Uriens's men. But I'll keep far enough away to not worry your friend. If he knows so much about tracking people, he would know if he was being followed."

"I'll be safe. We can meet again tomorrow, near the next set of hills."

"If I don't catch up with you by noon, I'll go searching."

"Fair enough. Thank you." She nodded, pleasantly surprised at his thoughtfulness.

"You might be more careful about the women you like," Gawaine said, adjusting his cloak. "Your so very attractive Drian stole some of Agravaine's jewels as well as his betrothed."

Lancelot suppressed a laugh.

"You are not surprised." Gawaine raised his eyebrows more than seemed possible. "You don't mind that he's a thief?"

"Of course I do," Lancelot muttered. Her face was hot with embarrassment. Then she glanced at Gawaine's wrists, where the armrings had been. "You took those gold armrings from Saxons you killed."

Gawaine's face reddened. "I took them. I did not steal them." He raised his voice. "They are trophies of war. The Saxons would have taken my jewels if they had killed me."

"Of course," Lancelot said. "They are trophies. Perhaps Drian takes trophies, too. Would it be better if she killed the men she had taken them from?"

"You defend him! You really are smitten. It does no good to warn you," Gawaine grumbled. "At least you should realize that when you are side by side, it is more obvious that you both are women."

"Guinevere has said the same," Lancelot admitted. If Guinevere and Gawaine for once told her the same thing, it likely was true. "I'll see you tomorrow."

Gawaine directed his horse onto the other rode. "Find a nice girl and get married!" he called over his shoulder.

She wasn't sure whether he was jesting.

Lancelot's mind was unquiet. Even the golden winter light illuminating the meadow did not soothe her, nor did the magpies charm her. Gawaine would not betray her, but was he still as much a friend as he had been? How angry was he at her deception? Why did he refrain from clapping her on the back? Would they ever again have peaceful evenings jesting beside a campfire?

It was dark and Lancelot had camped for the night in a thicket near a stream and made a bed of broken branches. Apparently Drian had not been following after all, for Lancelot had seen no sign of the harper. A fire warmed Lancelot somewhat and she was beginning to drowse off to sleep when she heard a rider approach. She leapt up.

"Lance?" a voice called.

"What are you doing here?" Lancelot asked, thinking it better not to let Drian know they had realized she had followed them. "I thought you were many miles away by now."

Drian dismounted and darted over to squeeze her shoulder. "And leave you to the mercy of that man? I followed you both. When Gawaine went off, I followed him to make sure he wasn't going to double back and attack you. When I figured he wouldn't, I came on."

Lancelot hugged her and tousled her hair. "Gawaine backtrack and attack me? Not likely. You didn't need to worry about me. Surely you can see by now that he's a friend. And even if he had not been, I can fight at least as well, if not better."

"And you think there's nothing I could have done to help," Drian grumbled. "I have a bow and arrows. He may have a thick hide, but I doubt that arrows bounce off it."

Lancelot backed away from her. "Say no more. Gawaine is the last person who would ever hurt me."

"I'm thinking that when the last person who would ever hurt you, does hurt you, it pains you worse than anything." Drian's eyes were fixed on the campfire.

Suspecting that Drian spoke from experience, Lancelot touched her hand.

Drian turned to her and grinned. "There are some good things about your friend, I admit. He wears very fine gold." She pulled up her sleeve and looked at an armring, "And jewels, far more jewels than he needs."

"Drian!" Lancelot exclaimed, dropping her hand. "You mustn't try to steal anything of his."

"Don't frown at me – I can't bear it," Drian said, lowering her face in mock contrition. "I'll be content to have his gold."

"You'd better be." Shaking her head, Lancelot sighed. There was no chance of reforming Drian.

"But if he thought that gold was going to buy me off so I'd leave you to him, he was wrong. Not all the gold in the world would be enough for that." Drian put her hand on her knife.

"Drian!" Lancelot gasped. "That's not what he meant at all. The gold really was a reward for retrieving Arthur's sword."

Drian took her hand off the knife. "Maybe. But you'd better not talk to a man about his cock. Since Gawaine knows you're a woman, it sounds like a challenge."

"I'm sure he knows that's not how I meant it," Lancelot said. "I'm just relearning how to talk to him."

"Better learn quickly," Drian warned. "Any mistakes could be dangerous."

"Yes, he's very dangerous." Lancelot bristled at the implication that she was a poor judge of people. "He's told me to find a nice girl and get married."

Drian shrugged.

"Probably because he thinks anyone else would be better than I am."

"Very likely."

"You don't believe he's dangerous, but you didn't see the look on his face this morning when he meant to kill me." Drian's voice shook.

Lancelot put an arm around her. "I have seen him kill, many times. Always enemies and brigands. Always when I was killing them, too. When he challenged you to fight, why didn't you send a message to me to come and help you?"

"And risk your life? I wouldn't."

"Oh, Drian." Lancelot held her close for just a moment. Then, afraid she was going to be untrue to Guinevere, she pulled away.

"Have you had any food?" Lancelot asked, going over to her bag and getting out some barley bannock she had bought in the last town. She certainly wouldn't tell Drian that she was meeting up with Gawaine again the next day.

"Thanks." Drian took a piece and munched. "And perhaps we might sleep together again?"

Lancelot looked away. "No, I'm too tired."

"Too tired to sleep?"

"Too tired to do anything else. Besides, I really love Guinevere and I don't want anyone else." She let her voice show she was a little weary of saying so.

"You shouldn't love a married woman that much, Lance," Drian protested.

"You don't know Guinevere." Lancelot bent to stir up the fire.

"True." Drian paused. "Please, let's just sleep in each other's arms again."

The light from the campfire made Drian handsomer than ever.

"Very well. But just one more night and that's all."

"Is it so difficult to resist me?"

Drian cast an appealing look her way.

"Perhaps."

They both laughed. Then they stretched out their cloaks and curled up spoon fashion, both clothed, and did nothing more. But, remembering that Gawaine could have killed Drian, Lancelot held her tighter than she otherwise might have.

The stars in the winter sky were so low that they seemed not much higher than a roof. Lancelot stayed awake for a long time. She sensed Drian was awake, too, but feared to say anything.

Finally, she asked, "Drian, who betrayed you?"

"My father." Drian's voice choked. "And my brother. Both of them."

"Oh, Drian." Lancelot held her tight.

"I told you I was able to outrun all the men who've pursued me, but that wasn't true."

"I was afraid that was so." Lancelot stroked her hair. Tears streamed down both of their faces. Being true to Guinevere felt like being false to Drian. But no, it would be even worse to make love to Drian and then leave her. Lancelot wished she could heal every wound. Why was there so little that she could do?

After a long time, Lancelot heard Drian breathe the breath of sleep.

The next morning, Drian kissed her cheek in parting and said, "When we next meet, will I save you, or will you save me? Or will we just entertain each other?"

Lancelot was not so pleased at seeing her go off alone, for it was uncertain when their paths would cross again. And saddest of all, Drian might never meet someone who loved her as Lancelot and Guinevere loved each other.

Was it ever difficult for Guinevere to love? Lancelot wondered. Did Guinevere, living a life of luxury and safety, understand what it was to be fond of someone else and forgo that for love?

Lancelot decided she might tell Guinevere that Drian had helped her escape from the dungeon, but thought it would be better to leave out the part about spending two nights in Drian's arms, and not to mention anything about encountering Gawaine. Guinevere would not be pleased that Gawaine knew Lancelot was a woman. How strange it was that Guinevere distrusted him so much.

Guinevere tried to read one of her books, but the words blurred on the page. What if Morgan, before she received her letter, had already sent Arthur a message saying that Lancelot was a woman?

Nothing would ever be the same. Arthur would treat Lancelot very differently, and he would treat Guinevere very differently.

Likely they would have to leave. Where would they go? Probably to Lancelot's home in Lesser Britain. What would it be like?

They would probably have to leave in haste. Would Arthur pursue them? Even though he would know Lancelot was a woman, it would appear that a man was running away with his wife, and Arthur might feel he had to pursue them to avenge his honor. Would Arthur or his men kill Lancelot?

She dismissed that thought as too terrible. She should make a plan in case one was needed. She would not be able to take her books, nor would she be able to buy many others, because books were costly and she would be much less wealthy than she had ever been. She would take the jewels she had inherited from her mother, but should she take any that Arthur had given her? She didn't want to, but Lancelot was not rich, and they might need to sell the jewels.

Guinevere's Grayse rubbed at her ankles. She would not be able to take the aging cat.

In the corner, Fencha was humming while she worked on a new cloak for Guinevere. Fencha was too old to flee with them. Guinevere sighed. She would miss Fencha, and Fencha would miss her. What would it be like to no longer be queen? And worse than not a queen. Everyone would see her as Lancelot's whore. Men would leer at Guinevere when Lancelot wasn't looking, and no woman would befriend her.

What would she do? There would be no girls to find husbands for, no ladies to comfort in sickness and chat with. There would be no tax records to study – yes, she would actually miss that. No Cai sitting across the room to make witticisms. No one would ask Guinevere's advice about policy, or about anything.

"Lady Guinevere, I didn't finish the chapter you assigned me," Talwyn said, bouncing into the room. She pretended to hang her head, but her voice had a lilt to it.

Talwyn could not come with them! Guinevere sucked in her breath. She would have to leave Talwyn. She couldn't bring herself to look at the girl, and could barely speak to her.

"That's good. Sit down and work on the chapter now."

How would Talwyn bear such desertion? Who would comfort the girl? Who would see to it that Talwyn was not married off to a man she did not want? Guinevere wished she could call on Lionors to look after the girl, but she could not tell anyone there was a chance she would have to flee. Lancelot's sex would still be a secret, so Lionors would never know why they had run away. Talwyn would never know why she had been abandoned.

Forgive me, Talwyn, but I love Lancelot more, Guinevere thought. Her hand tore the vellum she was holding.

Lancelot would miss Camelot so much. She was used to having many companions. Lancelot would be lonely. Would she be bored if she had only Guinevere? Would Lancelot tire of their love?

If Lancelot had to leave, was it possible that she would not want to take Guinevere? The thought brought a stab of pain through Guinevere's whole body. No, if Lancelot left her, that would be too much to bear.

Guinevere jumped up from her chair.

"It's nearly mid-day, so the morning's chill must have dissipated. We should get some exercise. Come, Talwyn, let's go to the stables and ride."

"It's still cold, Lady Guinevere," Talwyn whined. "And you said I should work on this chapter."

"A sound mind needs a sound body. Come." Guinevere swept across the room. She could sit and think no longer.

As they rode out, the wind blew through their hair. Guinevere rode into it, pleased at any distraction.

"My face will be red, and I'll get the ague," Talwyn complained as she tried to make her horse keep up with Guinevere's.

"Nonsense, a little fresh air will improve your health."

Someone was riding far behind Talwyn. Guinevere saw the horseman who had long followed her. How dare he pursue her when Talwyn was with her! Guinevere wished she had a spear and was able to cast it at him. Without letting Talwyn know what she had seen, Guinevere said they could enter the woods to escape the howling wind. As usual, the horseman did not follow her into the woods.

As promised, Gawaine appeared around noon. "The harper did follow me," he proclaimed. "You owe me a round at the next tavern."

"With as much you drink, that will probably cost me all the money I have," Lancelot answered.

"The harper . . ."

"Don't say another word about Drian!" Lancelot cried.

"I shall be silent." This time, Gawaine moved his horse ahead of hers and urged it to go faster than Raven.

He said nothing about Drian, and not much about anything else, for the rest of the day. Lancelot felt less than cheerful.

That night they camped by a stream, but they did not jest while they ate what little food they had left.

"Will you tell Guinevere that I know you're a woman?" Gawaine asked, wiping crumbs from his beard.

"I have no plans to do so," Lancelot replied, annoyed that he had asked.

"Very wise, O Lancelot of the shining honesty." Gawaine burst out laughing, which irritated her still more. She said little the rest of the evening.

Lancelot prepared to sleep about thirty feet from him, rather than her usual distance of about fifteen feet.

"It's much safer to sleep thirty feet from a man than fifteen feet from him," Gawaine said, his voice heavy with sarcasm. "You could put a sword between us. That's what they do in tales."

"If I didn't trust you, I wouldn't travel with you," Lancelot grumbled, sure that he knew well that the distance was symbolic only. Obviously it would make no difference in safety while she slept.

"Of course not," he agreed. "Stay as far away as you like in summer, but in this season you should sleep nearer to the fire. Or would you like me to help you build another fire? If so, we should start collecting more wood, because it's getting late."

Building two fires for two people sounded foolish. Lancelot moved her things to the side of the fire opposite Gawaine.

Over the next few days they talked a little more, but far less than they had on previous journeys. When they drew near to Camelot, Gawaine said, "I'll take the road to Cornwall so I can ask Morgan to keep your secret."

"Thank you," Lancelot said, though she doubted that his request would help much. The mere thought of what Morgan might say made her shudder.

30   THE SWORD

When she returned to Camelot, Lancelot hastened to Arthur's chamber. Her scabbard held a sword that was far more precious than her own. She kept her hand on the pummel so none should see the tell-tale amethyst.

The king sat reading a wax tablet, one of his hounds at his feet. Fires in several braziers burned to keep away the winter chill. Arthur leapt up at the sight of Lancelot. "Did you find it?"

"Yes." She pulled the sword from the scabbard.

"Victory!" he cried. In an instant, he was across the room. He took the sword and held it high, as if he were a priest elevating a chalice. "It is Excalibur! I knew you wouldn't fail me. I knew you would bring back the sword to preserve my honor." He ran his finger along the blade and caressed the purple stone. Then he hung the sword in its accustomed place on the wall. Turning to Lancelot, he embraced her.

Lancelot squirmed under his embrace, pulling away as soon as she could. "Cynlas took the sword to Uriens. Uriens captured it, and me, for a time, but his son Uwaine retrieved the sword and freed me."

"Uriens dared to steal my sword!" Arthur yelled. "So all his oaths to me were false." His face reddened and his eyes blazed with rage. "And he dared to imprison you?" His hands formed fists.

"I am well, nevertheless," Lancelot assured him. "What will you do?" Not war, she prayed, not war.

The king laughed without mirth. His hands relaxed. "Let him worry about what I might do. And if the Irish raiders come to his coast, he can fight them by himself. No doubt he will beg off the Pentecost celebration next year. When he finally does come to Camelot, he will try to act as if nothing had happened. I shall just be cold, very cold."

"That's wise," she said with relief. Her good king would not wage war without great cause.

Arthur took hold of her arm. "So you were captured! Sit down, rest, have some wine, and tell me about it." He led her to a chair as if she had difficulty walking.

The king's dog padded over to Lancelot and wagged his tail. She ruffled the dog's fur.

She looked about the familiar room, with its hangings of a battle and a hunt. How often would she be allowed here, if Morgan told the king that Lancelot was a woman?

She accepted the wine that Arthur poured with his own royal hands and told the story of her fortunately brief captivity.

Morgan gritted her teeth as she read Guinevere's message.

She sank back into a chair and looked out of the window at the pounding surf. She had just received a message from Uriens —written by some scribe because he could not write – saying the sword had been stolen but Lancelot had retrieved it for Arthur. She had more than enough letters.

If only Guinevere had remained under her influence! How irritating that the queen had found Lancelot and they cared only about each other.

Morgan took up a fresh sheet of vellum and began to write.

My dearest sister,
I never intended to wed old Uriens. How could you imagine that I would?
Nor did I ever intend to reveal your friend's secret. I said only that I might, but your friend was too agitated to hear me. Have no fear.
Your devoted sister

She ran her fingers through her red-gold hair. Of course she would never have told that Lancelot was a woman. She had her own reasons not to tell.

Gazing through a west-facing window, Morgan watched the sun drop before its evening plunge into the sea. The gulls' cries were like songs from the spirits, daring mortals to try to understand them.

A knock at the door interrupted her reverie.

"Come in," she said with irritation.

"Lady Morgan, the Lord Gawaine ap Lot is here to see you," a serving man announced.

Morgan was glad that she hadn't turned around. The servant couldn't see the surprised look that must be on her face. She tried to keep the astonishment out of her voice.

"Show him in."

It had been so many years since she had seen Gawaine – long enough for the daughter he knew nothing about to be nearly grown.

Fortunately, the girl was far away and none of the servants would dare to tell him about her. Morgan remembered how well he had made love – although of course he was not Arthur – and was not displeased that he had come to visit her.

Certain of her beauty, Morgan did nothing to adjust her hair or her gown, but remained as she was.

"Greetings, Cousin." Gawaine strode into the room.

"Greetings, Cousin," she echoed, studying him. The boyish look was gone and his face, now battle-scarred, hinted at so many different dispositions that she was not sure which predominated. The warrior, the lover, the man who liked jests? He was somewhat thicker, but there was no trace of gray in his hair.

"It's true that you're an enchantress, for you've stayed as beautiful as ever," he said, bowing to her, but there was little warmth in his voice.

"If so, that's no doubt because I am a witch," Morgan replied. She wondered fleetingly whether the sunset at the window was the best frame for her beauty, then decided it was. "You look the seasoned warrior, and perhaps seasoned at other things as well."

"Perhaps too seasoned." Gawaine did not smile. "I know about the sword. Lancelot has returned it to Arthur. But you must not tell her secret."

"You've come too late to persuade me." She was annoyed that his flattery had been so brief, and at the reason for his visit. "I've already sent a letter to Camelot."

"No!" He put out a hand as if to stop her. "Who was the messenger? I must catch up with him."

Unfortunately, Gawaine seemed so determined to act that she couldn't play with him for long.

"The letter was to Guinevere, who demanded that I not tell, and I have told her that I will not."

Gawaine exhaled with relief. "The gods be praised, and the goddesses, too." His eyes narrowed. "Why did you have to suggest otherwise? I have come here in vain, but I am glad that is so."

If he thought she would let him go easily, he was much mistaken. "But I could change my mind, Gawaine. I want you to persuade me to keep Lancelot's secret." She touched his arm. "Why do you care so much? Is that strange woman warrior your mistress?"

"No," he said more forcefully than seemed necessary. "But she is my friend and has saved my life many times."

"So she is a virgin still," Morgan purred. "How very nice."

Gawaine frowned. "She is much too kind to tell your secret, so you should be kind enough not to tell hers."

"Oh, I won't, especially if you are good to me." She looked him up and down. "I've missed you."

His face became unreadable. "I might have believed that if you hadn't sent Cigfa to me. I don't believe you want me particularly."

"I thought you might prefer a young girl. Or listen to her more."

"You were mistaken. It was wrong to send the girl on such a mission." Gawaine looked her in the eye, not as affectionately as Morgan thought he should have. "So now you want me to lie with you to keep you from disclosing that Lancelot is a woman?"

"You put that so baldly, Gawaine. Let us say instead that I want your company. Wouldn't that please you?"

"Of course, my lady. I am honored." His voice was mocking, but he approached her and took her in his arms.

Knowing he would be better in bed than any man she had been with in a long time, Morgan relaxed. Gawaine would never know that he had given her a daughter, because that girl was being groomed to appear someday as King Arthur's son. And that was why Morgan would never dream of telling that Lancelot was a woman. If one woman's disguise was revealed, another's would be also. Morgan smiled to herself and wondered what she would do with Arthur's daughter.

Lancelot came to the queen's room, and saw that far more candles were blazing than she had ever seen there before.

Guinevere's face glowed more than the tapers. In an instant, she rushed across the room into Lancelot's arms.

"Morgan will not tell! She never intended to tell!" She waved a piece of vellum at Lancelot.

Holding Guinevere with one arm, Lancelot snatched the letter from her and stared at it.

The words made little sense. It was too good to be true. Her heart beat fast, but she shook her head.

"Can this be true? She threatened me! Can we believe her words now?" Tears formed in her eyes. She desperately wanted to believe that her secret would not be revealed.

"It's true, of course it's true. She was only toying with you. She is not kind, but not vicious either." Guinevere held Lancelot's face between her hands and kissed it. "Be glad, be glad. No one else will ever know your secret."

Lancelot collapsed into a chair and sobbed. Guinevere stood beside her and put a hand on her shoulder.

She would still be Lancelot, warrior sworn to King Arthur. She would always be Lancelot. No one would take her life away from her. No one would take her love away from her. She buried her head in Guinevere's breast. Never could she bear to lose this love.

Never could she tell Guinevere that she was unworthy of it, that she had killed an innocent girl.

The sister porter told Ninian that Lancelot had come to see her. They sat in the room for visitors, where the chairs were none too comfortable. A tapestry of the angel appearing to the Virgin Mary spread across one wall.

When she heard that Morgan had threatened Lancelot, Ninian gripped the arms of her chair. "Why didn't you come to me and tell me about Morgan?" she exclaimed, letting anger show in her voice as she seldom did. "I would have ordered her to give up her foolish plans and stop tormenting you. I was more advanced in the Old Ways than she was and she would have had to obey me."

"I didn't know that," Lancelot said, looking at her with wonder. "I wish I had told you."

Poor Lancelot turned so pale when speaking of Morgan that Ninian didn't have the heart to scold her more. "Trying to replace Arthur as High King is nonsense. It would only hasten the death of the Old Ways, not preserve them." Ninian shook her head. "Morgan has lived in exile too long. The isolation has dimmed her wits. And she was always too willful for her own good. How did you escape from Uriens's dungeon?"

Lancelot told the rest of her tale, and Ninian was much amused. "I would not try dressing as a woman too often," she cautioned.

"I have no intention of doing so," Lancelot vowed fervently.

When Lancelot said that Gawaine had promised to persuade Morgan to keep silent, Ninian suppressed laughter. Lancelot did not seem to guess what means of persuasion Gawaine would use, but Ninian did. Well, such things would not harm either Morgan or Gawaine.

As Lancelot was riding away, Ninian saw a slender red-haired youth dressed in breeches and tunic almost hanging out of an upstairs convent window. Ninian darted inside the convent and hurried up the narrow stairs to gently pull back her charge.

"It's not yet time for you to meet Lancelot," she scolded, panting from her rush upstairs.

"Why not?" the youth demanded, nevertheless obeying her command and backing away from the window. "I can't wait."

"Not until you go to Camelot, your mother says. Settle down, Galahad. Would you like to play a board game?" Ninian's tone was conciliatory.

Galahad laughed, merry blue eyes sparkling. "Nah, that's too foolish. All of those people just letting someone put them in squares and move them around. Why would they? It makes me laugh."

Ninian chuckled. "You'd make a terrible soldier." She patted Galahad's shoulder approvingly.

"Does that mean I won't have a place at the round table after all?" Galahad asked, suddenly anxious. "I want to be at court with King Arthur the Just and Lancelot of the Lightning Arm."

"To be sure you will. You'll be one of Arthur's warriors, but you will never fight in a war. Remember, there are others at Camelot besides the king and Lancelot," Ninian said in an admonishing tone, "such as Gawaine of the Matchless Strength, who is nearly as great as Lancelot."

"Oh, yes, he's a cousin of the king's." Galahad nodded. "My mother never speaks much of anyone except King Arthur."

"No doubt," said Ninian with a hint of disapproval. "Do you want your fighting lesson now?" She smiled indulgently.

"Oh, yes, please." Galahad rushed to get a wooden sword.

In only a few moments, Galahad stood in an empty room with the large Sister Darerca, who had rolled up her sleeves and tucked her black skirt in her belt and was menacing Galahad with a wooden practice sword.

"Step lively, now, Galahad. I may be old and I may be a bit heavy, but didn't I fight for Queen Maeve herself, and don't I have Maeve's own fighting spirit in me? And didn't I learn to fight from the great woman warrior Scathach? And wasn't Cucuchlain himself a student with me? A bit of a bully in class, he was, but I showed him that he had to respect me."

Galahad choked with laughter.

Ninian, who sat on a stool in a corner, laughed also. "Never mind her patter about legendary heroes, Galahad. Her father's holding was often under attack, so all of the girls were taught to fight, very sensibly so."

Darerca flourished her sword in Ninian's direction, then turned to the youth. Pushing back her black veil, she yelled, "Dare to defy me! I, who have the spirit of Maeve herself, will make you regret it!" She lunged at Galahad, who dodged, then parried her attack.

After the sparring was done and Galahad left for dinner in the refectory, the two nuns lingered. Darerca wiped the sweat from her face and let down her skirt.

Ninian fidgeted with her own veil, which made it looser than it had been. "It's wrong to deceive Galahad as Morgan does. She should know her true father," Ninian said.

"Have you such great sympathy for men? I never noticed it before," Darerca replied, moving to fix her friend's veil.

Ninian submitted to Darerca's efforts. "I don't think a woman needs to say who helped the goddess give her a child. But if she tells the child a name, it should be the true one." She smiled. "It pleased me to hear that Gawaine acted well on learning that Lancelot is a woman. Perhaps he will be worthy someday to learn who his daughter is."

"You were not overly kind to let him think she was in a brothel," Darerca reminded her.

Ninian shook her head. "Why not? I told him that she was in a place with many women, and if he thought immediately of a brothel, not a convent, that showed that he had much to learn, and perhaps he is learning it. I hope that Galahad will discover one day who her father is and be proud of him, but it must not happen until he is wise enough to be proud of her."

The room was darkening as the day's last light faded, but they did not light a lamp.

"Well, I've heard it said that Gawaine's a reincarnation of the great Cuchulain, so he can't be all bad." Darerca adjusted her own veil, which was askew from sparring. "Cuchulain wasn't that much of a bully in the fighting class."

Ninian laughed, but her laughter soon ended. She bowed her head. "Gawaine at least wanted to find a daughter he thought was in a brothel, but Arthur did not. I was so angry when Arthur said he did not want a daughter who was in a brothel that I left. In the heat of my rage, I did not tell him that it was his son, rather than his daughter, who was in one. No matter how angered I was, I should have told him. I should have thought more about the boy's need to be saved and less about whether Arthur deserved to find him.

I saw the boy only dimly, in a vision at the bottom of our well, but I am sure he was the king's son. I have tried to summon the sight again so I could learn where the boy is, but I cannot. If only I could find him. The poor boy was suffering so terribly." Her voice broke and she covered her eyes with her hands.

Darerca put an arm around her for comfort.

It was raining not a little, but Gawaine had been walking about on the rocks.

Morgan was sitting comfortably by the fire in her great hall when he burst in on her. He shook himself like a dog, and droplets of water flew everywhere. She didn't mind. She was used to dampness.

The perpetual cries of the gulls flying around the caer were so loud that even the rain didn't drown them out. But she was fond of the gulls and their calls.

"You wanted me to stay here so that if Arthur ever heard about your plot, it would seem that I was part of it," Gawaine accused, taking off his cloak and setting it near the fire.

"How perceptive you are, dear Gawaine." Smiling, Morgan gestured for him to be seated in a chair close to hers. "But your riding here in the first place, while Lancelot was bringing the sword back, was enough to give that appearance. I wanted there to be as many reasons as possible for people to keep silent about my role. The thought that you could be suspected should help ensure your silence, and no doubt your dear friend Lancelot's, too."

"Guinevere is not my dear friend. I wouldn't want her to know I was here." He looked into the flames, not at Morgan.

"It grieves me that you don't always find women easy to manage." Morgan teased him. She took his hand. "I do like you."

"Am I better off for that?" Gawaine sighed.

"We're both many good nights better off." She smiled to herself. This time he had been careful to make certain she wouldn't become with child. Little did he know it was years too late to worry about that. And she took her own measures to prevent bearing another child.

Morgan pressed his hand. "I've been so lonely here. You have comforted me."

Finally looking at her, he returned the pressure. "I'm glad for that. I know it's quiet here, but it's beautiful in its way. There are far worse places. Take care that you aren't sent to one of them."

She took hold of his other hand, too.

"If Arthur ever imprisons me, you'll come and rescue me, won't you?" Her tone was pleading, not one she often used.

Gawaine paused, as if measuring what he was being asked to do. Indeed, Arthur would count it treason. "I'll rescue you, if you never tell anyone about Lancelot. If you tell, I'll let you stay wherever Arthur puts you."

With a cry, Morgan dropped his hands. "I am doubly the flesh of your flesh! Your cousin and your lover. Yet you care more about that strange woman." She shook with rage. "How is it that she has such a hold on people?"

"She is good and kind, and never hesitates to risk her life for anyone else's." His voice was quiet, as if Morgan's anger didn't move him in the least.

"And she's beautiful, too. My kinsmen all betray me!" Morgan cried, rising from her chair. Gawaine must be punished. "Oh Arthur, faithless Arthur! He forgets me, but I think of him every moment of my life."

"Even in bed with me, you mean?" Gawaine's voice was low.

"Yes!" That wasn't true, and he probably knew it wasn't, but it was an insult he couldn't ignore. She was determined to wound him.

"Then I shall leave this moment. The rain is not so bad, and there's no lightning. Thank you for your hospitality, my lady." He bowed, picked up his cloak, and turned away.

Any other man would have struck her, but she had known Gawaine would not. Morgan said nothing. She felt sure that he still would rescue her if Arthur imprisoned her, and she had her own reasons never to tell Lancelot's secret. If Gawaine stayed too long, there was a risk that he might somehow learn about their daughter, and make it difficult for her to present the girl, in time, as Arthur's son.

And she had other secrets, other reasons she wanted him to leave. But when he had gone, she went out in the rain, sat on a rock, and wept. Why had she driven away the only man who was kind to her? Why had she risked losing Guinevere's friendship, for that matter? Why was she angry at Lancelot, just because Lancelot could live at Camelot and she could not?

Her whole plot had been foolhardy. But she couldn't bear to do nothing, to believe that there was nothing she could do, to be helpless. She howled into the wind.

Tintagel loomed before Ninian as her old mare slowly traversed the rocky causeway. Ninian drank in the salt air, which she had not smelled for long and long, and eyed the waves appreciatively. The wind blew so hard that she could hardly keep her veil from blowing off, but Ninian did not mind the cold as much as some people did. She enjoyed the contrast with the calm breezes near her convent. It was nearly nightfall: time for a nun, even the boldest, to be within doors.

When she arrived, the servants stared at the sight of an unaccompanied nun in that isolated place. Declining rest and refreshment, she demanded to see their mistress.

She was shown to Morgan's private chamber. Although the room was darkening, no lamp had been lit.

Morgan's face paled.

"How did you come to be here tonight of all nights? Oh, go away, Lady Ninian! You must leave."

Had Morgan gone mad? Ninian refused to show alarm.

"A fine welcome for a traveler who has come a long way because she worried about you. Word of your doings has reached me, and I came to give you counsel."

Morgan wrung her hands. "Not tonight. Please leave, or at least let my servants show you to your room, and stay there until dawn." Ninian seized hold of Morgan's trembling arms.

"What madness is this? Tonight is no different from any other."

"It is." Morgan pulled away. "I can speak with you tomorrow."

"You will speak with me now, and tell me what is so important about tonight. I won't leave this room otherwise." Ninian sat in a chair to show that she meant what she said.

Morgan shook violently. "Arthur is coming tonight. You must leave me alone."

Ninian stood up and reached for her again, but Morgan eluded her grasp. "I don't believe Arthur is riding all the way from Camelot to see you."

"Not coming that way." Morgan looked at the door, as if to make sure it was closed. "Once a year, Merlin transports him here, as he brought Arthur's father to my mother, in this very room."

"By the holy currents of the air!" Ninian exclaimed. "There is no such enchantment."

"There is! Leave me, leave me please. You can listen at the door long enough to hear his voice, then go to your room for the night. Please, I must see him." Morgan lunged at Ninian to drive her out of the door.

Morgan was so desperate that it seemed better to do as she wanted. "Poor dear!" Ninian said. "I'll wait outside your door. And in the morning we'll talk further."

Ninian found a chair for herself and sat outside the door. She prayed more anxiously than she had in a good while.

But the wait was long, and she had nearly fallen asleep, when she heard Morgan say in a barely audible voice, "You have come."

"I have come to you. You are mine forever."

582

The voice actually sounded like Arthur's.

"Please," Morgan begged, "let me see you in the flesh, not as a specter. Please let me come to Camelot and live beside you. I'll do only what you want, I swear."

"You'll do what I want, but you'll never come to Camelot. You'll never leave Tintagel for long. You are mine, now and always." The voice was no kinder than the words were.

Ninian shivered.

"Yes, I am yours, now and always," Morgan whispered.

"So you have discovered our secret."

Merlin stood beside Ninian. Trying to keep her face calm, she turned to him. He motioned to her to follow him down the hallway, and she did.

"I thought Uther had merely been disguised, not transported, when he came to Arthur's mother while she was still another man's wife. This enchantment is dreadful. You did not learn this in Avalon." Ninian confronted him, accusation in her voice.

Merlin sighed. The wrinkles on his face were much deeper than they had been when she last saw him, years before.

"Many years ago, King Uther threatened to kill me unless I made a spell to bring him to Igraine here in Tintagel. Under that threat, I manage to devise the spell. He came to her at night, and Arthur was conceived, as you know.

"Then after Arthur sent Morgan to exile here, he demanded that I make a similar spell for him because he could not give her up."

"He surely did not threaten to kill you!" Ninian exclaimed in anger. "Why did you do it?"

Merlin looked away from her. "I could never refuse Arthur anything. If you had seen how anxious he was a child, because he did not know who his parents were . . . He comes here once a year to lie with Morgan. I know no other such powerful spells, only this one for Arthur, to the place where he was conceived. The spell would not aid anyone else."

Ninian shook her head. "You do wrong," she said in her gravest voice. "I would never have thought it of you. At Avalon we learned to revere the laws of the earth, air, and water, not to bend them."

"That's true," Merlin admitted. Slowly he began to fade away, escaping her wrath.

When Ninian saw dawn come through a window and heard the morning cries of the birds, she knocked on Morgan's door. There was no answer, but she entered.

Morgan was naked on the bed. Her eyes were open, but she seemed barely conscious.

Ninian pulled the covers over her. "How are you?" She felt Morgan's forehead, which was cold, though not with the cold of death.

Morgan moaned. "Arthur, Arthur."

Ninian tried to soothe her. "I never dreamed he could be so cruel. We must find a way to prevent his coming again in this way." She rubbed Morgan's hands to make the blood circulate more vigorously.

"The sword," Morgan murmured. "Merlin's spell is on the sword to transport them. Arthur hints to clever people that the sword has no magic, which they believe readily, as I did at first. But there truly is an enchantment on the sword. That's why I tried to steal it. I would have persuaded Uriens to give it to me after he had displayed it."

"By all that's holy! Arthur calls you a witch, but it is he who uses enchantments on you! What a reversal!" Ninian made the sign of the cross, not a usual gesture for her when she was away from the convent, but she knew it was a solemn one. "Lancelot would never have retrieved the sword if she had known. We must get it back, but don't use Lancelot, who has so much to lose. You should tell Gawaine what Arthur is doing to you. Gawaine will get the sword away from him."

"No!" Suddenly stronger, Morgan sat up. "No one must know, especially not Gawaine. I wanted the sword so Arthur would have to come to me in the flesh, not as a specter, not in this hidden way. I sent a girl to tempt Gawaine to steal the sword to enhance his own power, but he couldn't be tempted. And neither could Guinevere. I tried with her also. But if Gawaine stole the sword without using it for his power, if he took it to help me, Arthur would know I have been with Gawaine and would never forgive me. Arthur would never come to me again," she moaned.

"And that would be a good thing," Ninian responded.

"No, no. I love Arthur, I must be with him. And he must be with me."

Morgan stared into space, as if she still saw him in the room. "We are bound together forever."

"What a terrible tie!" Ninian cried out. "You must break it, to preserve yourself. If only you had loved Gawaine instead."

Morgan shook her head. "Impossible. I could never love a man who gladly lets another man rule over him. Gawaine pleases me, but Arthur possesses me. It is very different."

"Indeed it is," Ninian said, not thinking the difference was in Arthur's favor.

"Arthur will never be bound to anyone else as he is to me," Morgan said, clutching the blanket as if it were a lover. "He always told me that Guinevere was like a block of wood, that no one could ever possess her."

"Very good for Guinevere." Though Ninian had met the queen only once, she liked her well. "Think on what I have said. I will do all I can for you. I will seek out Gawaine and speak with him if you say the word, but you must decide for yourself."

"I decided long ago." Morgan stared out of the window at the tossing sea, which was no more tumultuous than her face. "When I cursed Arthur, I knew the curse would bind me, too. Better bound in a curse than separated forever."

"Not better. Arthur should find a way for you to live near him, or give you up."

"You are a nun now. You don't understand."

"Believe me, I do." Ninian held Morgan's hands to warm them, although Morgan seemed far removed from her.

31   TRUTHS AND UNTRUTHS

Lancelot wanted to ride alone in the forest, but as she was making her way down the hill, away from Arthur's caer, a voice hailed her. Turning her head, she saw that Gawaine was riding after her, so she waited for him.

"Could I ride with you? There's a matter that I need to discuss." The cold air made Gawaine's breath visible.

Gawaine generally did not ride for pleasure just after dawn on cold mornings. Lancelot was not eager for a companion, but she nodded.

When they entered the bare-branched forest, Lancelot asked, "What did you want?"

Gawaine didn't look at her. "You won't be pleased to hear this. The men often play pranks on each other, but seldom on you. When you first came to Camelot, I told them you would not stand for such things, and I have often repeated that warning. But now there is a jest that I can't prevent, so I must let you know about it."

Lancelot exhaled. True, what the men thought was amusing, she often did not. "And what is it?"

Gawaine hesitated. "The men often place wagers on whether you and Guinevere lie together . . ."

"What! How dare they!" Lancelot yelled, startling a woodpecker that flew from a nearby tree.

"I knew you wouldn't like to hear that. Don't be angry at me; I am merely telling you what they do." Gawaine moved his horse away from a fallen log that was in his path. "No one has ever won such a bet, because no one knows for certain whether you are lovers."

"I suppose you don't tell them?" Lancelot asked indignantly.

"Of course not. Now there is a new bet. Some of the men plan to get you drunk – that is, to give you drugged wine because it's impossible to make you drink too much."

"Who is it? I'll fight them," Lancelot cried, digging her heels into her mare's flanks more fiercely than she had intended.

"Will you please listen? I'm trying to help you. Then, they intend to send you to a woman who will pretend to be Guinevere."

"Infamous!" Lancelot pulled on the reins, making Raven stop. "How can you speak so calmly?"

Gawaine halted his horse beside hers. "The idea is that you would lie with her because you thought she was Guinevere."

Lancelot trembled with rage. "That's the most disgusting idea I've ever heard. And these men claim to be my friends! Why haven't you put a stop to this scheme?"

"Because I think you should go along with it."

"Have you taken leave of your senses? Did you just meet me for the first time, that you think I would do anything so vile?"

"Control your indignation and listen to me, why don't you?"

Gawaine's face reddened.

Lancelot suspected that her own was much redder.

"Of course, you wouldn't really lie with her. You would slip away before you entered the room, and I'd do it for you."

"You're completely mad."

Lancelot was almost too stunned to be angry. "Why would you ever think I'd agree?"

"Because it would prove that you're a man."

Gawaine spoke as if what he said was obvious.

For a moment, Lancelot could not say anything, almost could not breathe. "No one has doubted that, have they?"

"No, but they might someday. And there's another point to be gained. The scheme would show that you've never lain with Guinevere. We could act as if you were greatly surprised by the honor, and you – that is, I – wouldn't recognize that it's not Guinevere. After all, it's likely that a man would know how his lover acts in bed. So the men who are betting that you aren't lovers would win their bet. You don't want people to believe that you and she are lovers, do you?"

"Of course I don't. I try mightily to prevent that. I don't speak with her much in public."

"But your face shows your true feelings."

A couple of crows began arguing with one another.

Lancelot shook her head. "I can't believe that even you would agree to such a revolting plan. And who would the woman be? She would certainly know that you weren't me. I don't suppose you'd shave your beard to make that less immediately obvious."

Gawaine put his hand to his beard. "Shave my beard? Never! There's a limit to what I'd do to help you."

"Help me! You talk about lying with a woman to help me! What arrant nonsense."

"Stranger things have happened." Gawaine moved his shoulders as if he were laughing.

"What about the woman?" Lancelot clenched her fists. "Again, I ask who would this poor woman be?"

"All I've heard is that she's never been to Camelot, or even seen you. So I'm betting that she doesn't know whether you have a beard or not."

"So she's some poor whore they're paying to do this?" Lancelot shook with anger. "You know what I think about buying women."

"Indeed. And I now agree with you about that." Gawaine's voice was much calmer than hers. "But surely they couldn't pick some downtrodden girl or girl with who acted whorish to pretend to be Guinevere. That would never work."

"And what if I just refuse to go along with their little plot?" Lancelot patted her horse, but her hand was not as gentle as usual.

"Then they'll know I warned you, and they'll come up with some other scheme and won't tell me. I think you should go along with this one, distasteful though it might be to you," Gawaine advised.

Lancelot wondered whether he might be right, or whether she was losing her mind. "What if Guinevere learned about it?"

Gawaine laughed. "She never will. You will do it."

"I don't know . . ." Lancelot shook her head, but she would think more about the idea.

Lancelot rode with several other warriors, Gawaine among them, to a fighting contest at a caer that was two days' journey from Camelot.

It was still early in the year, but the weather was mild enough to fight without freezing. As usual, Lancelot won.

The evening after the contest, Camlach, the lord of the dun, held a feast. But after they had finished eating, Bedwyr proposed that the warriors from Camelot go off and drink together.

Saying, "I'll stay in the hall," Gawaine nodded to Lancelot. That was the sign – her companions would give her the drugged wine that night.

She went with them to the house where they were staying. Lancelot had a bed of her own, so all she had to do was keep her clothes on, and no one knew that she was a woman.

"I have some excellent wine, better than anything they served us in the hall," Bedwyr said. "Lancelot, you're the victor. You try it first."

"Thank you," she said graciously, inclining her head. "I believe I shall." She pretended to drink deeply from the goblet he handed her, but she wore long, flowing sleeves, and was able to pour some in the sleeve.

Even the little bit she drank made her a trifle sleepy. It was not long before she said, "It seems that the contest tired me. I'll go to the other room and lie down."

Everyone bade her goodnight.

She went to the other room and rested on the bed. Soon, a pebble came through the window, which was close to the ground.

Lancelot looked up. A serving man was at the window.

"My lord," he said, "Queen Guinevere is here and has sent for you. Come through the window and I'll take you to her."

"What?" Lancelot mumbled, trying to sound as if she were drugged. "That cannot be. But I'll come." She climbed clumsily out of the window and staggered as she followed him to another house.

"She's here, waiting for you," the man said, indicating the door.

Lancelot stared blearily at it. "What can she want? I can't believe it." She hesitated. "Can it be true? Does she truly want to see me?"

"Yes, my lord."

591

"Go on, I'll enter soon enough," Lancelot said, pretending to be reluctant to open the door while the servant was watching.

He left, and a man appeared from the shadows.

"It isn't really Guinevere?" Lancelot asked Gawaine.

"If it was, she'd kill me before I got anywhere near the bed, so I certainly hope it isn't." He entered the house, and Lancelot wandered off to find some hidden place to sleep.

The next morning, she met Gawaine by the stables.

He grinned at her.

"The woman believed that I was you and thought I was with Guinevere for the first time. I kept saying how honored I was, how I couldn't believe she wanted me . . ."

"That's enough," Lancelot said, interrupting him. "I don't need to hear any more."

He chuckled. "Except that, toward morning, she spoke some sweet words to me. I gasped and cried, 'That's not Guinevere's voice! You aren't Lady Guinevere!' Then I jumped up, threw on my clothes, and ran out of the house."

Lancelot shook her head. "What madness. So you don't even know what the lady looked like."

"More to the point, she didn't know what I looked like, so she'll say I was you."

When they rejoined their fine companions, Lancelot put on a dejected look, said little, and sighed a great deal, so they would believe she was miserable because she had lain with the wrong woman. She continued acting in this manner for a number of days.

Lancelot and Gawaine were summoned to Arthur's chamber.

Arthur did not invite them to drink as usual, or even to be seated. He shook his head. "This is a strange matter, Lancelot. Not so strange for other men, but it is for you. I asked Gawaine, too, because I thought you might want his advice, but you can ask him to leave at any time if you'd like."

"Very well." Since she was not fond of speaking with Arthur alone, Lancelot thought that, whatever the matter was, she'd be glad enough to have Gawaine there.

"A lady has asked a boon of me," the king said. "Bring her in, Tewdar," he told his manservant.

In a moment, a lady entered the door. She was young, but not overly so, and pretty, with long brown hair and a heart-shaped face. She was well but modestly dressed, in a becoming gray gown. Her gray eyes were pleading, and she trembled slightly.

"Pray repeat your request," Arthur told her.

"My name is Etaine, daughter of the late Lord Menw of Dyfed," she said. "My lord, I beg you to ask your man Lancelot to marry me, for he is the father of my child." Etaine's eyes were watching Arthur, not Lancelot.

"I am not!" Lancelot cried, all courtesy forgotten. "I never saw this lady before in my life."

The lady turned to Lancelot. "I know you have not, but you made love to me in the dark that night at Camlach's dun."

Lancelot gasped and drew away from her.

This lady was nothing like the woman she had thought the men would have chosen for their jest. "I did no such thing."

"I know you had had too much to drink, but you did come to me," Etaine said. "Now I am with child, and I beg you to marry me."

"It is strange for Lancelot to lie with a woman whose face he had never seen." Arthur eyed her skeptically.

"Why would he do that?"

Etaine bowed her head.

"Forgive me, Lord Arthur, but I pretended that I was Queen Guinevere."

Arthur turned purple. "How dare you do such a thing! And how dare you come to me and ask me to help you, after you defamed my wife and struck a blow against my honor."

Etaine went down on her knees to him. "I beg your forgiveness, Lord Arthur. I am punished for my sin. Please be gracious and hear my plea."

Arthur's voice strove for calm. "If Lancelot did not even know who you were, why should he marry you? And if the room was so dark, how do you know it was he?"

"It was Lancelot," the lady insisted. "He kept saying that he was overwhelmed at the honor of lying with me – that is, with Queen Guinevere. Those who claim they are lovers slander them, for they surely are not. He seemed so shy at first, but then . . . not at all." She blushed.

"It was not I, my lady," Lancelot said, beginning to be sorry for her, but unyielding on the main point.

"Of course it was you. The only difference is that you've shaved your beard," Etaine said, looking at Lancelot's face as if to drink in every feature.

Arthur had begun to smile at her account of the night, especially when she said that Lancelot and Guinevere were not lovers, but now his eyes widened. "Lancelot has never had a beard."

The lady gasped. "That cannot be."

"My lady, it was I, Gawaine ap Lot," Gawaine said quietly, bowing his head to her.

"That is the voice!" Etaine cried. Her hands flew to her mouth. "I am ruined! You deceived me."

"But my lady," Gawaine said, keeping his voice gentle, "you were trying to deceive Lancelot."

Tears streamed down the lady's cheeks. "I had hoped he would marry me. Now he never will."

Lancelot felt pity, but not enough to approach the lady. "What a terrible way for a child to be conceived," she said, giving Gawaine a reproachful look.

"But why did you go along with the scheme to deceive Lancelot?" Gawaine asked, touching Etaine's shoulder. She did not flinch at his touch. "Surely you would not have accepted money from the men who devised it."

"No!" Etaine cried, sobbing more bitterly.

"My lady," Gawaine said softly, "I think you knew you already were with child. One of the men who devised this plan was the father, but he was not in a position to marry you. He thought of this as a way to press Lancelot to do it, and you went along because you wanted a good husband, and Lancelot has such a fine reputation."

The lady, so astonished that she stopped crying, stared at him. "That's true," she admitted. "I wanted Lancelot to be a father to my child. Oh, all is lost, lost!" She wrung her hands.

"We will see that you and your child are always supported well and have everything you want," Gawaine told her.

"You never have to lie with another man again, or you can choose any man you please. Perhaps someday you will find a husband. And you can say that Lancelot is your child's father, which is not as disgraceful as if some other man were."

But Lancelot's sympathy did not go that far. "If it's so fine to say that someone is the father, you can say that Gawaine is."

"No, I can't," Etaine objected, shaking her head vigorously. "I've already told everyone that it's Lancelot."

"Don't deny paternity, Lancelot," Gawaine admonished. "How does it harm you to let the lady say you are the father?"

"I won't go along with this plan unless you tell the child I am not its father," Lancelot demanded. "You must not deceive the child. I don't want it thinking that I am its father, but care nothing about it."

"If you insist," Etaine said with evident reluctance.

"A good solution, a kind solution," Arthur said. "Poor lady, desperation drove you almost to madness." He gave her a warmer look than he had heretofore. Then, as he glanced at Lancelot and Gawaine, he raised his eyebrows. "What I don't understand is how and why Gawaine became involved in this strange situation."

"Of course I was concerned about protecting the queen's honor, and therefore yours. I'll explain it sometime," Gawaine said, shrugging.

Lancelot thought he meant that he would obfuscate the matter as much as possible. And Arthur would be pleased to think that his honor had been preserved.

"It would have better preserved my honor to simply say that there is no reason to imagine that my wife would lie with anyone but me," Arthur said stiffly.

When Lancelot and Gawaine had left the room and were halfway across the dark and empty courtyard, Gawaine said, "This is wonderful! Better than I could have hoped."

"What's so wonderful about it?" Lancelot seethed.

"Why this proves beyond doubt that you are a man." Gawaine grinned at her.

Lancelot groaned. "So this is what it means to be a man! But what about the outcome for the poor lady?" Lancelot could be sorry for Etaine – at a distance.

Gawaine reached down and scratched the ears of a dog that had run up to them. "Didn't you hear me say I'd support her whatever she did?"

"No, I will." Lancelot's voice was firm, though she had just made up her mind. "That is more decent. Who's the father? Bedwyr, do you suppose?"

Gawaine shook his head. "Nah, Bedwyr wouldn't hide a dozen bastards, and his wife's too meek to complain. Don't worry about who the father is. Someone who cares more about what his wife thinks, I suppose. Bedwyr's the one who bet the most on your virtue, or on Guinevere's. He thought you would fall if tempted, but she wouldn't."

Lancelot grabbed his arm. "Bedwyr told you about the plan so he could win his bet."

Gawaine shrugged. "That's true. He wanted to be sure of the outcome. He didn't want you stumbling into the lady's room and saying, 'You're different than you were the other night, dear.' Yes, he probably guessed that I would substitute myself and speak in a way that showed you had never been with Guinevere. But whatever his motives were, it's all gone as well as it could have for you."

Lancelot winced. "None of the men cared if I was hurt. Do I have any friends?"

"Obviously, you do," Gawaine grumbled.

"Of course." Lancelot nodded, glancing at him. "I mean other friends."

"Peredur wasn't involved, I'm sure, and of course Bors wasn't. And Bedwyr would bet on his own death. He can't help betting on everything." Gawaine moved his hand as if he were throwing dice. "I've never seen a day when he didn't make some wager."

Lancelot turned away. "Will you make excuses for all the others, too? I have saved some of these men's lives. How could they try to do such a thing to me?"

"They do like you, Lance. But they also envy you because you are too perfect."

She sighed. "Far from it, if they only knew."

"Not so far. Ah, here are some of our companions. Perhaps they'll congratulate you on your impending fatherhood." Gawaine hailed a group of their fellow warriors who, full of drink and talking loudly, were crossing the courtyard. "I'm going on a mission to Londinium tomorrow, so let's drink with them."

Not eager to speak with them, Lancelot went off to her house.

Not long afterwards, there was a knock at her door.

Lancelot groaned inwardly. She wanted to go for a long ride, not to speak with anyone. If it was one of the men involved in the bedding scheme, she would have difficulty containing her ire.

When she opened the door, she saw one of Arthur's guards. "The king wishes to see you in his chamber, Lord Lancelot," he said, inclining his head.

"Thank you." Never had she been less eager to see Arthur, but she made haste to his room.

Of course Arthur was alone. She had known that he would be. He had been looking out of the window, and turned when Lancelot entered. His face was unusually lacking in expression. He neither smiled nor frowned. His movements were stiff and formal.

"You undoubtedly realize that this incident disgraces you," Arthur said, speaking in the voice in which he gave orders. "You must show yourself to be abashed. You should be ashamed to speak with Guinevere, so you should not address her or come close to her in public."

Lancelot's heart constricted. She could not bring herself to say yes, my lord.

"Indeed, you should go away. Not too hastily, but you should be gone for at least a month. I shall send you on a mission to Maelgon."

Lancelot looked at the floor. She had to admit that Arthur was within his rights in asking her to go.

"Now, don't sulk, Lance." The king's tone was milder. "I am angry at this situation, not at you. Remember that discretion is of the greatest importance. Do have some wine." He gestured to the wine jar on his table. "And pour me some as well."

"Yes, thank you, my lord Arthur." She hated to thank him, but she knew that no other king – indeed, no other husband – would be as kind to her as he was. Perhaps she was wrong-headed to feel ungrateful, but his power over her made her feel like a prisoner. She poured the wine.

Lancelot shook slightly as she climbed the hidden staircase. Etaine had been spreading the tale that she was going to have Lancelot's baby. Would Guinevere have heard the gossip yet?

When she entered the room, she saw from the queen's narrowed eyes and tight mouth that she had.

"Everyone is saying that you laid with a woman because you thought she was me, and that she is with child." Guinevere's tone was harsh. "Why haven't you denied it?"

More cowed by Guinevere than by any enemy, Lancelot sighed.

"Some of the men thought they had drugged me, but I really didn't drink much of their wine. They sent me to this woman. But Gawaine is the one who laid with her. Now, she is with child, but not by him. She already had been. And I am not denying that I am the father because the tale makes it seem that I am a man."

Guinevere glared at her. The queen's face was as red as her gown. "I suppose it was that wretched Gawaine who persuaded you not to tell that you aren't the father. You actually let him lie with a woman who thought it was you? I can't believe you would go along with such a repulsive scheme. I've never heard of anything so disgusting. You've spent so much time with him that you're beginning to think as he does."

It was just as well that Gawaine would be away for a while, Lancelot thought, hanging her head. "I know it's awful, but Gawaine meant no harm."

"No harm!" Guinevere's voice was bitter. "And have you told that man that we are lovers?"

"I have," she admitted, still determined not to worry Guinevere further by telling that he also knew she was a woman. "Forgive me. I let it slip out after he had just saved my life from a brigand in Gwynedd. But Gawaine is a true friend and will never tell."

"A fine friend!" Guinevere spat out the words. "He's just a brute."

The word struck like a blow. So Guinevere was going to attack Gawaine again. How could she dislike him so? Lancelot shook her head. "You don't understand. There are many good things about him. I know you hate for me to say it, and I sound just like a man when I do, but going through a war together makes a kind of bond."

"The war, indeed!" Guinevere voice was almost a scream. "Arthur told me that Gawaine killed a girl during the Saxon War. Arthur claimed it was just an 'accident of war,' but how can a man kill a girl by accident? Despite all the jests, he's just a murderer."

Lancelot felt as if she had been kicked in the stomach. She could hardly breathe. "Is that why you hate him?" She turned away and stared blankly at the wall. She had no right to keep silent anymore, even if she lost Guinevere's love.

"There was a day," both Lancelot's body and her voice trembled, "when we saw something moving in the bushes, and thought it was another Saxon ambush, such as we had been through before. I struck out. But it was a girl, about thirteen or fourteen, a British girl."

600

Her voice sounded strange to her, almost expressionless.

"And she was dead, and I had killed her. I just stared at her and couldn't move." She saw again the bleeding body in the bushes and the stricken look on the dead girl's face.

Guinevere gasped. "No!" she cried.

Feeling as if she were facing her own death, Lancelot forced herself to continue. "Then Arthur came by and was angry, and Gawaine said that he had done it, but he hadn't. I said nothing. Nothing much happened. Arthur yelled at him.

"No one would imagine that Lancelot could have done anything like that."

"Yes, Lancelot's the kindest warrior in the world." Her voice was bitter. "Lancelot would never kill a woman."

Guinevere took her hand. "I can hardly believe you could have done such a thing." Her voice shook. "Why did Gawaine say that he had done it?"

Lancelot turned to her and saw Guinevere shudder slightly, but she gratefully accepted Guinevere's hand. The queen's face was pale as snow. "Because he was afraid that I was suffering some kind of distress and was on the verge of madness. And he knew how much I would hate for anyone to know. But of course he didn't want anyone to think that he had killed a girl, either."

"But you were mad at the time, weren't you?" Guinevere said, her voice quavering. "Doesn't doing such a thing prove it?"

Lancelot sighed and shook her head. "I still knew what I was doing. I didn't have to slash into the bushes without seeing who was there."

"The poor girl. Did her family recover the body?" Guinevere slumped into a chair as if her legs could no longer support her.

"I don't know," Lancelot admitted. "I never asked. I've never spoken of it since I walked away, except to confess the sin, not even with Gawaine. And he has never mentioned it, either."

Guinevere shuddered again. "And that is why you believe he's a friend? Men's friendships are built on such terrible things. A dead girl. That's grisly."

Lancelot closed her eyes for a moment, then opened them. "You're right. It's not good. But there it is. To imagine that one can slaughter people left and right and come out pure and noble is just a dream for those who have never been to war.

"There are nicer war stories, of course, about Gawaine coaxing me to eat when I would not. This one is no doubt the worst. I hope you won't hate me?" She scrutinized Guinevere's face, trying to discern its expression through the candlelight. As usual, affection was there, if a little mixed with other things.

"Of course not, dearest! I know how good you are. I wonder how you ever recovered from that war."

Lancelot let herself relax a little. "You know very well. The best thing in my life happened not many months after the war." She looked into Guinevere's eyes to remind her just what that had been. She was not going to lose Guinevere after all. It was a miracle.

Guinevere rose from her chair and put her arms around Lancelot. They both wept. They rested on the bed, but they neither slept nor made love.

"Arthur says I must not speak with you in public now, and I must go away for at least a month." Lancelot sighed. "I will go on a mission to Gwynedd the day after tomorrow."

"Oh, my poor dear." Guinevere put Lancelot's head on her shoulder and stroked her hair. "I will be so sorry to see you go. Try to bear it."

Toward morning, Lancelot began talking almost as cautiously as if she were tracking some creature in the wilds.

"I think I should tell the other warriors that I was the one who killed that girl during the war. When I heard that you knew about her death and still thought ill of Gawaine because of it, I saw that it was wrong for me to keep silent." She listened for Guinevere's response, expecting her to be annoyed that Lancelot was concerned about the injury she had done to Gawaine.

But Guinevere held her a little closer. "Of course you should tell. If people know that it was Lancelot who did it, they will see it for what it was, slashing out unthinkingly brought on by the state that soldiers get into in a war. But if they believe that Gawaine did it, they might think it was something even uglier, as I did."

"Also," Guinevere continued, frowning, "it is not right to have secrets about such a thing. If a girl has been killed, everyone should know who did it."

Lancelot felt even more affection for her than ever. "You're right. I should have told you long ago," she said in a voice full of appreciation. She dared to smile.

"Yes, you should have." Guinevere's voice faltered in an unaccustomed way. "You trusted Gawaine more than you trusted me."

"Not any more," Lancelot assured her, although the words admitted it. She saw Guinevere flinch, and felt ashamed of her lack of trust. "He has seen me at my worst, but you generally see me at my best."

"You trust someone who has seen you kill more than someone who has known your love?" Guinevere shook her head and sighed.

Lancelot echoed her sigh. How could one who had never killed ever comprehend what it was to be a killer? "Please understand. Don't you know how much I feared to lose you?"

"That will never happen." Guinevere's hand stroked the hair back from Lancelot's forehead.

Lancelot kissed her, then dressed, for she had to leave before dawn, as always. Her heart was full of gratitude for Guinevere's love. She was relieved to have shed the burden of one of her secrets, and wondered whether she should tell Guinevere the rest. But no, Guinevere would never believe that Gawaine would keep silent about Lancelot's sex, and it would be wrong to worry her.

Too weak to get out of bed, Guinevere remained there. Rosy dawn streaking through her window did not charm her. She did not want to see the too bright light of day. Her heart felt heavy, as if someone had died.

She had never struck, never even slapped, anyone in her whole life. How could she understand so much killing?

Lancelot was unknowable, unreachable. The expression on her face, the tone in her voice, had been like those of a person returned from the dead.

Guinevere had believed that Lancelot had mostly recovered from the war. Lancelot had jested more as the years passed, had rejoiced in their tender play. But now she could see that Lancelot had not healed, would never heal.

Those gentle hands had held swords that sliced through so much human flesh, not just the girl's. Guinevere was used to fighting contests, where serious wounds were not too many, and often were the result of accidents.

Lancelot hardly ever injured her opponents much. Guinevere had never allowed herself to see Lancelot as a killer, but she had deceived herself.

Not just Lancelot, of course – all of them. Her father, her husband, almost all the men she knew were killers. She had seen them as defenders against the Saxons, which was true, but she had not admitted just how brutal that defense was. She had told herself that Gawaine was a beast, as a way of not seeing that they all were. Yes, Gawaine had taken the blame for Lancelot's killing, but why? Likely he had bloody secrets of his own.

Probably all of them did, even Bors. If Lancelot could be brutal, any warrior could.

Guinevere shuddered. The dawn had been replaced with a bright light that shone into her eyes. She would not cover them. She sat down to dine every day with a pack of wolves. None of the women wanted to know what the men they embraced and comforted had done in the name of protecting Britain, she thought. They did not want to see beyond the smiling faces and the jests. If the men were brutes, the women chose not to comprehend.

Even Lancelot, even a woman, the kindest person Guinevere had ever known, had done unspeakable things, and been shattered by them.

Guinevere let the grief flood through her, for she wanted to be able to smile as usual when her wounded sweetheart returned at night.

That evening, Lancelot, Peredur, Bedwyr, and Bors were in Arthur's room reminiscing about the Saxon War.

During a pause in which they were thinking of fallen comrades, Lancelot spoke up in a sober voice. She trembled. Would these men who now smiled at her ever smile that way again?

"The death I think most of is not a warrior's." Lancelot looked at the dark window rather than her friends' faces, but her voice did not falter. "Do you remember that poor British girl who was struck while she hid in the undergrowth? I, not Gawaine, was the one who struck into the brush and killed her. Killing her is the most terrible thing I have ever done, but letting Gawaine take the blame is the most contemptible. I should not let myself be called the greatest warrior in the world. Instead, I should call myself The Warrior Who Has Done Wrong."

Everyone was silent for a moment, and Lancelot wondered whether they would drive her out of the king's room.

Then Peredur said, "It was a terrible thing, and as the father of a girl not much older, I was horrified, but you shouldn't worry that anyone thought less of Gawaine. After a little reflection, all of us knew that you must have done it, because you were half mad at the time. We were too worried about you to blame you. We understood that Gawaine was protecting you."

Knocking over her goblet of wine, Lancelot exclaimed, "Holy Mother, you knew all the time, and knew that I was too cowardly to own it!" It was incredible to her that the warriors would not have shunned one who had done something so terrible. They even had maintained Lancelot's reputation as the best of them!

Her wine, red as blood, ran across the table and onto the floor.

Setting the goblet right, Peredur said soothingly, "Now, now, we know it was an accident. Don't believe that we think less of you."

Bors put a hand on Lancelot's shoulder. "We all have done terrible things, especially in war. It's right to be ashamed of them. I don't know whether it's better to talk of them or not. I could say what the worst thing is that I have done, and so could every man here, but I won't because it could become almost a contest to see who has done the worst."

Lancelot's head spun and her heart raced. She could hardly believe that any of them had done anything as bad as she had. "We should tell the young men about these things, as a warning. Why should we pretend to be better than we are? How will that help others to avoid our mistakes?"

"No, we should not tell them," Bors shook his head vigorously. "Young men need to believe that it's possible to be good, and to be inspired to do better than the best that we have done, not crueler than the worst. You should not tell any other warriors about what you have done, because they should believe that it is possible to always be good, as they think you are. But of course we must warn the young warriors in a general way of the moral dangers involved in fighting."

"You are both right," Peredur said. "But I couldn't bear to let my son know the worst that I have done. I must hope that telling him the best will be enough."

Although the others looked calm, Arthur was staring at Lancelot. She averted her gaze from him. Evidently he had not known that she had killed the girl. What would he think of her now?

"None of us is pure," Bors said, then his voice became warmer. "But at least some women are, and they will pray for us. I would not want my wife or any others to be disillusioned."

Lancelot groaned. "Women are only human. Why expect them to be any better than men are?"

"Why of course they are! How could you, the courteous one, say otherwise?" Bors's eyes widened.

"So men can sin, as long as women are innocent, and save men with their virtue?" Lancelot asked. "Women are either bad, and men can do anything to them, or are good, and must redeem men, in large part for what they do to other women?"

"Of course a good woman would want to," Bors replied.

"So women's purpose is to redeem men?" Lancelot sighed. "I doubt that anyone can redeem me."

Bors gasped.

To save his feelings, Lancelot quickly added, "Other than the Christ, of course." But she wasn't sure she believed it.

Her soul seemed weighed down with sins, including those she would never give up.

Bedwyr, who had drummed on the table during this talk of virtue, spoke up. "Don't worry, Lancelot. Nothing happened to Gawaine.

"He's too important to punish, and so are you, no matter what you do."

"What?" Lancelot fell back in her chair.

She wanted the king to yell at Bedwyr and insist that he would punish anyone who committed a crime, but Arthur said nothing. Bors and Peredur merely frowned.

After a long pause, Lancelot bade them goodnight, and left. She almost wished her friends had condemned her. What, if anything, would they condemn? It occurred to her that the most dreadful thing she had done, killing a girl in war, was perhaps not so uncommon after all. What Bedwyr had suggested was so repulsive that she couldn't bear to think about it.

She did want to redeem men, at least her good friends, but she had not realized it was expected of women. She knew that being a warrior was based on terrible moral compromises, and now she had discovered that being a good woman was also. What was left? She had to continue being a warrior to stay with Guinevere.

Now she had required Guinevere to share the burden of knowing her guilt. Was that kind? Lancelot asked herself. Should one ask that of a lover?

When Lancelot entered Guinevere's room, the handsome warrior's face was more careworn than ever. Even in the candlelight, she looked pale. She moved slowly, as if reluctant to see Guinevere, and she seemed to have difficulty looking Guinevere in the eye.

Moved almost to tears, Guinevere took her hand and led her to a chair. "Tell me everything about the war. Tell me all of the things that haunt you."

Lancelot put her hand over her face.

608

"How can I burden you with such horrors? It's not right that you should have to think about them."

"It is right." Guinevere looked into those sad brown eyes, eyes so grieved that the word "sad" was inadequate.

"You are so good." Lancelot pressed Guinevere's hand to her cheek, which was soon damp with tears.

Guinevere steeled herself to bear whatever Lancelot would say. It would be terrible, but not so bad as Lancelot's having to depart the next day.

In the spring, when Gawaine had returned to Camelot, Guinevere reluctantly approached him in the courtyard and gestured for him to follow her into the walled garden.

He grinned as if he wanted to make a jest about their having an assignation. No doubt he would make apologizing difficult for her. Guinevere gritted her teeth. It galled her to have to make an apology to the man who had gone to a woman and pretended to be Lancelot.

As soon as they were within the walls and she could see that no one else was there, Guinevere spoke. She wanted to make the conversation as brief as possible, overheard only by the robins hopping about the garden.

She gave him the barest of nods. "Lord Gawaine, I regret my mistake about the girl's death."

Gawaine bowed his head to her. "Thank you, Lady Guinevere. I understand. Certainly a man who intentionally killed a girl should be shunned at first and hanged afterwards. I assure you that I never would have told Queen Morgause anything about the death of the girl or your words."

Guinevere nodded to him and moved away, indicating that it was time to end the conversation.

But Gawaine did not leave. He lowered his voice. "Lady Guinevere, I doubt that Lancelot told you that after he accidentally killed the girl, he turned his sword on himself, but I grabbed his arm and restrained him."

Guinevere gasped.

"Even later, he came near to killing himself in grief," Gawaine continued in a solemn voice. "The only reason he didn't throw himself in the river is that a camp follower also had gone there to kill herself, and he saved her life instead."

Guinevere sat down on a bench to keep from falling.

Gawaine remained standing. "Later, he often tried to get himself killed in battle, but of course he did not succeed, thank all the gods. Lancelot has suffered a great deal. It would go very hard with him if he had to endure any more great suffering. I thought you should understand that."

Guinevere said nothing. Her heart seemed to stop.

Gawaine bowed to her and left the garden.

The thought that Lancelot had tried to kill herself was almost beyond bearing, but remembering all that Lancelot had told her about the war, Guinevere could understand it. She of course would never give Lancelot any great hurt – did Gawaine imagine that she would? But she could not keep Lancelot from going out to battle again. She wanted to fold Lancelot in her arms, to cover her as a mother hen covers its chick, but that was impossible.

She stared almost unseeing at an apple tree that was beginning to bud. The robins' song seemed to be coming from far away.

Lancelot, Lancelot, Lancelot, she repeated silently, over and over.

As if in a dream, Guinevere rose and walked towards the stables to see her horse and perhaps ride. Not much to her pleasure, she saw Gawaine ahead of her.

"Gawaine!" she called.

He turned to her. "Yes, Lady Guinevere?" Gawaine waited while she walked up to him.

"You can call off your pursuer now. I'm right tired of being followed by your horseman," Guinevere said.

Gawaine stared at her as if she were mad. "What are you talking about, Lady Guinevere? I certainly would not have anyone follow you. Has some man been disturbing you?"

For once, Guinevere believed him. She groped for words.

"If not you, then who? Some warrior has been following me for years, whenever Lancelot is away and I ride alone. When I let my horse run, he appears and follows me. But when I go off into the woods, he disappears."

"Gods, why haven't you told anyone?" Gawaine cried. "How dare this man try to frighten you! He must be stopped." He touched the pommel of his sword.

"I thought he was sent by you."

"No! We must tell Arthur and Lancelot."

Guinevere drew back. "Arthur will never let me ride alone again."

"Forgive me, Lady Guinevere, but he might be right." Gawaine inclined his head in apology. "There could be men who would want to capture you because you are the queen."

She grimaced at that.

"Please, Lady Guinevere, let me follow you and find out who this is. We must know." Gawaine's tone was urgent. "He might be mad. Even though he hasn't tried to injure you yet, he still might. And one of the stablehands must be informing him when you go out to ride; we have to find out who the informer is, also. Tell Lancelot, and he and I can handle these wretches."

Guinevere's stomach sank at the thought of telling Lancelot that a man had followed her for years but she had never disclosed it. Yet she had to admit that Gawaine was right.

"I suppose I must tell him." Guinevere understood that Gawaine would tell Lancelot if she did not, though he didn't say so. She would not show fear in front of Gawaine, but the realization that the pursuer was unknown to anyone unnerved her. So did the idea that one of the stablehands betrayed her.

That evening, Guinevere told Lancelot as calmly as possible, or so she thought.

Lancelot stared at her as strangely as Gawaine had. "A man has pursued you for years and you never told anyone? Why not, in the name of heaven?"

Reluctant to say she thought Gawaine was behind it all because she didn't want to tell Lancelot how she had threatened Gawaine, Guinevere searched for a reason. "I didn't think he was dangerous."

"Not dangerous! What would you say if the same thing happened to another lady you know, and she had said nothing?"

"I would say she took a foolish risk," Guinevere admitted, annoyed that Lancelot's first show of anger was aimed at her. "Are you angry at me, or at the man who pursues me?"

"I'll kill him." Lancelot shook with rage, but her voice was steady, and deadly. Her hands were clenched fists.

Guinevere had never seen her beloved so furious. Or heard her speak in that tone. Taken aback, she could not reply.

"I'll pretend to go away, but I'll stay nearby. Then, when you go out, Gawaine and I can follow at a distance. I don't like using you as bait to catch this cur, but we have no other choice."

"I'll be fine," Guinevere insisted.

Lancelot took up a goblet of wine, then set it down. She choked. "Do you understand what all this means? I wasn't imagining things when I saw a man pursuing you the day we became lovers." Her face flushed. "I pray he didn't see our first embraces."

Guinevere touched her hand. "Surely not. Such a man would have tried extortion if he knew our secret." The mere thought of being spied on nauseated her.

"Very likely." Lancelot put her arms around Guinevere and held her tight. "Please don't take chances. I don't want anything to happen to you."

"A strange warning, coming from you. I wish you also would not run so many risks." Guinevere put her head on Lancelot's shoulder.

On a day not far distant, Lancelot said farewell to everyone and left Camelot. She had told Bors to let Guinevere ride alone three days later.

On the appointed day, Guinevere set out. She glanced at the stablehands: young and freckle-faced, older and brawny, old and gray. Surely it couldn't be Cuall the stablemaster who betrayed her, but who could it be?

As she rode, new leaves and birdsong were far from her mind. All she could think of was the plan, and whether it would succeed.

Was it possible that the man might hurt Lancelot?

Guinevere rode alone in her favorite meadow, where the grass had not yet grown tall. Her horse enjoyed the activity far more than she did.

A rider came in sight. Guinevere kept on as usual, but didn't turn off to the woods. The man seemed to be gaining on her. She tensed, anxious for Lancelot and Gawaine to appear.

Two riders charged out of the forest in front of her and headed towards the pursuer.

He turned and fled, but before he could leave the meadow, the blunt end of Lancelot's spear had knocked him from his horse.

Guinevere hastened in their direction.

Lancelot and Gawaine were on the ground beside the pursuer. Gawaine held the man's arms.

"Take off your helmet, or I'll cut off your head first and find out who you are later," Lancelot demanded, her sword at the man's neck.

Gawaine let him pull off his helmet, revealing a face that was older but unmistakable.

"Melwas!" Guinevere cried.

"Yes, it's Melwas," the man said, cowering. His hair was graying, but that gave him no more dignity than he had before. "Melwas whose daughter you stole and whose land the king took."

"How dare you harry the queen!" Lancelot's eyes were bloodshot with rage.

"I'd have done more than that, but I feared the king's wrath if I abducted her. You can't punish me for just riding and doing nothing," Melwas whined.

"I can and will kill you." Lancelot apparently pressed the sword in a little more, for Melwas squealed. "But first, tell me who informed you when the queen was going riding."

"It was Budec," Melwas said, naming a stablehand. "He was in my service. But after the war, when the king's men were fewer, I told Budec to get a place at Camelot. That was why I had to wait years before I had a chance to follow the queen. But the first time I tried, you appeared and rode after me, so I fled and vowed to follow her only when you were away. Budec sent me a dove with a message when the queen went riding alone."

"Budec will meet the same fate you do," Lancelot exclaimed.

Guinevere let out a sigh of relief that Melwas knew nothing of what she and Lancelot had done that first day, or he would have flung accusations in their faces. She was surprised that Budec, a man whose face was so blank that he seemed innocuous, was the one who had helped her pursuer.

Melwas whimpered. "Is this King Arthur's justice? Take me to the king."

Gawaine grabbed Lancelot's arm. "Let's take him to Arthur. It will gain him only one more day of life."

"One day too many." Apparently unmoved, Lancelot did not withdraw her sword.

"No, don't kill him. Take him back to Camelot for punishment," Guinevere's voice cracked. She realized how much she did not want to see Lancelot kill a man, especially one who was already defeated. This Lancelot was different from the one she knew.

"If you say so." Lancelot spoke reluctantly. "But that's one execution I want to see."

Guinevere gasped. "Have you changed so much?" The difference in Lancelot shook her more than anything Melwas had done.

Lancelot looked away from her. While she was tying Melwas's hands behind his back, Lancelot said, "I shall accompany you to your quarters during the execution as usual, my lady."

Guinevere sighed with relief.

Guinevere entered the great hall first, followed by Lancelot and Gawaine, who had to drag Melwas, and guards dragging Budec. Melwas had soiled his breeches, and the smell was most unpleasant. Budec was panting like a dog.

Arthur rose from his chair.

"My Lord Arthur," said Gawaine. Guinevere had seldom heard him use such a formal address to his cousin. "Lancelot and I caught this man following Queen Guinevere. He admits that he has followed her for years, whenever she rode out alone, so that he might frighten her. He even admitted that he thought of abducting her, but he was too cowardly to do so, for which I thank all the gods."

Arthur's face reddened to the point that Guinevere wondered whether his heart might be strained. He yelled at Melwas. "How dare you!"

"My Lord Arthur, I meant no harm," Melwas whimpered. "I never hurt the queen."

"No harm! You have plotted against the queen, and against my honor. That is treason. You will be executed at dawn." Arthur shook his fist. He looked as if he wished he could strike down Melwas with his own hands.

Melwas burst out sobbing.

Lancelot's face was as purple as Arthur's. She regarded Melwas as if he were an insect she wanted to crush.

"And Budec the stablehand sent Melwas signals to let him know when the queen was riding out alone." Lancelot's voice was so choked that the words were difficult to distinguish.

"Another traitor. He, too, will be executed tomorrow morning," Arthur proclaimed. "Take them away," he commanded with a sweeping gesture.

When Lancelot and Gawaine had dragged the men away, Arthur approached Guinevere. Only a little of the raging color had faded from his face. He took her arm, and guided her to her room. "Are you well, my dear?" he asked, but his voice was not warm.

"Yes, my lord." She knew she had incurred his wrath.

Arthur said no more until they were in her chamber, with only the cat to hear them. "You did not heed my request that you never ride alone." His tone was outraged, because no one ignored his requests. His hold on her arm was firm, though not tight enough to hurt her. "Now I command you never to ride alone again. If you disobey this order, you will never ride again with only one man to guard you. There will have to be several. And even now, if you have only one escort, you can ride no more than five miles from Camelot. Do you understand?"

"Yes, my lord." Guinevere did not let her face show her feelings. He threatened her with never being allowed to ride alone with Lancelot again. And he confined their rides to five miles from the caer. She swallowed her anger at being punished for Melwas's crime, as she had known she would be.

"You are the queen, and your honor is my honor. If anything happened to you, it would be a great blow against me."

Finally, her husband released her arm. But her life still seemed to be within his grasp. Once again, she was reminded that what she symbolized was more important to him than she was.

Lancelot asked Gawaine to speak with her out by the horse pasture. The horses looked to be calmly enjoying the spring day and the new grass, but she could not. Even the scent of the grass did not please her as much as usual.

"I told Arthur and our friends that I killed that girl in the war," she confessed, hardly daring to look at Gawaine's face.

"Arthur told me. Good of you, but you did not need to. It was years ago." His tone was subdued. "You have suffered for it more than I did."

"I cared too much about my reputation." Lancelot shook her head. "I liked being called the best of Arthur's warriors. That's all over now."

Gawaine smiled. "No, it's not. You've become a legend, and you'll stay one, lady warrior."

Her shame began to vanish. It was impossible to be solemn with Gawaine for long. "Cease mentioning that I am a woman."

"Of course, noble warrior. Watch out for the horseshit." He stepped around a clump of it, using a tone that hinted at the paternal, a tone he had never used when he thought she was a man.

Lancelot flared up.

"Don't give me any of yours. It was bad enough saying that I bedded Etaine though you're the one who did. Don't come up with any new tales about me."

"How little you appreciate me," Gawaine sighed as if in pain but grinned like a boy whose prank has just been discovered. "That was the best thing I've ever done for you."

"The best for whom? You?" Lancelot complained. "The stories say Etaine was a maiden. What maiden would have done such a thing?"

"A maiden who wanted to marry Lancelot. That part's not so hard to believe. Camelot is probably full of maidens who wish they'd tried it. And they all think, 'If I'd been the one, Lancelot would have married me.'" Gawaine whistled a few bars of a popular love tune.

"Maidens aren't like that," Lancelot protested. "Only a man would think so."

"A man who's had many maidens throw themselves at him. And don't tell me that maidens haven't thrown themselves at you, too, because I know they have." He picked a flower and began tearing off petals in imitation of a maiden seeking a lover.

"That whole episode makes me tired of pretending to be a man," Lancelot said, sighing.

"You could always tell everyone that you are a woman," Gawaine teased.

"And lead a life like most women's? Of course not." Lancelot raised her voice. "I don't want to be either like a woman or like a man."

"You are different, no doubt."

"Then I want to be just as I am." A yearling filly trotted up to them and Lancelot patted her. A blackbird warbled nearby. "Not many people know that I am a woman, so everything can be just as it was, and I can always live just as I want."

"Yes, just as you want. Always." Leaning against the pasture's fence, Gawaine smiled.

Lancelot was still in a serious mood. "Don't repeat stories that are untrue. What if they are all that people ever know about us?"

"What of it?" Gawaine offered a dried apple to the filly, which munched it eagerly. "If you don't like the stories about you, make up tales of your own."

"How can I?" Lancelot asked, knowing there was no good answer. "If I tell about my life, I must give it up. I cannot both have it and tell about it."

Gawaine shrugged his shoulders. "Well, then, in all the tales I'll have the last word."

Lancelot grimaced.

But Gawaine said, "Come along, let's go for a ride in the woods."

Lancelot smiled. "Of cour . . ." Then she saw the queen walking to the stables.

"Of course not." Gawaine rolled his eyes. "You'll go riding with her, Lance."

Nodding to Gawaine, Lancelot went off to greet her beloved. She was certain that, for her, the first and last words always would be "Guinevere."

The End

LANCELOT AND GUINEVERE

1 Camelot

The great hall at Camelot blazed with torches and fires in its huge firepits. Lancelot felt her face blaze even more as Gawaine said, "So, Lancelot, how is Etaine? Why don't you visit her before she gives birth? I look forward to drinking a toast to your son or daughter. What did she say she was going to name a boy? Galahad, was it?"

Lancelot cast an angry look at red-bearded Gawaine, who was clearly the tallest man in the hall even when they were all seated at the spokes of the round table. The gold torque around Gawaine's neck showed that he was high-born, son of the late King Lot of Lothian and Orkney and Queen Morgause, who had succeeded her husband. The torque was only a little less grand than the one King Arthur wore, but the difference was enough to be noticeable.

"I have no intention of seeing Etaine, now or ever." Lancelot thumped her goblet on the table. As Gawaine knew well, Etaine had pretended to be Guinevere so she could lie with Lancelot and claim that Lancelot was the father of the child she was carrying. Gawaine had lain with the lady instead, and guessed that she was already with child, but had persuaded Lancelot to refrain from denying paternity. That was his idea of protecting Lancelot, now that he had discovered she was a woman. She had been right not to tell Guinevere that Gawaine knew, for Guinevere would have cringed at his jests even more than Lancelot did.

"As you won't marry the lady and have no wife to fatten you up, I must do what I can to keep you from starving." Gawaine cut off a shank of mutton and threw it onto Lancelot's plate.

Lancelot was almost angry enough to fight Gawaine if he kept talking about her supposed fatherhood. Would Gawaine's love for teasing and jesting lead him to reveal her secret unwittingly?

Lancelot shuddered inwardly, remembering how recently the king's exiled sister, Morgan, had threatened to reveal her sex. The thought of losing her place at Camelot made Lancelot so upset that she did not want to eat the meat that Gawaine had tossed to her, but it smelled so appealing that she began to slice it.

Some warriors laughed with disbelief at Lancelot's denial of attachment to Etaine.

"No doubt Lancelot has good reasons for refusing to see the lady," King Arthur said. The slightly graying red-haired king, who knew that Lancelot had not lain with Etaine but not that Lancelot was a woman, cast a sympathetic look at his queen.

If only Guinevere were not Arthur's wife, Lancelot wished, as she had wished every day for many years, for Guinevere was her own true love. It pained them every day that they could not acknowledge the fact.

The king was not the only one looking at Guinevere. Half the hall was staring at Lancelot, while the other half watched the queen, to see her reaction to the talk of Lancelot being the father

2

of another woman's child. Although almost no one knew that Guinevere and Lancelot were lovers, people constantly watched them for signs of love for each other. How difficult it was to try to hide their affection.

At least Guinevere knew that Lancelot never looked at any other women. She didn't need to be reassured, especially not in public.

Then Bedwyr, a thin-lipped man with a left arm that had lacked its hand since the Saxon War, chimed in.

"Lancelot says that he has no call for congratulations, but Bors does. His wife just gave birth to their twelfth child, the eighth boy! Let's toast him."

The warriors bellowed their congratulations and swilled their mead in Bors's honor.

The gray-mustached warrior who was their object beamed, nodded his thanks, and said, "Another gift from God."

Gawaine added, "You helped, Bors," and the hall was filled with such loud laughter that the harper, who was playing a song about Arthur's defeat of the Saxons, paused.

With the warriors' attention focused on Bors, Guinevere and Lancelot looked at each other with relief. They knew that no taunts or jeers could ever come between them.

The sage Merlin, whose once-gray beard had turned white, did not join in the warriors' laughter. Instead, he sighed. "Such a show of merriment," he said to the king. "I hope it will last."

"Why, of course it will last. Let the hall be filled with joy," Arthur replied heartily, then took a swig of mead.

"Have some mead, Merlin. You've been looking a little pale."

The old man took only a sip.

One of the king's wolfhounds, padding about in the rushes on the floor, approached and thrust her head in Lancelot's lap.

Lancelot cut off a bit of the mutton and gave it to her.

Later in the night, Lancelot went as usual to the queen's bed chamber. In spite of Gawaine's silly teasing, Guinevere thrilled at the sight of her warrior. Being alone with Lancelot was always a celebration.

Guinevere enjoyed the warm fire in the brazier and the scent of her beeswax candles. But she scarcely noticed her cat, Grayse, sleeping on a chair heaped with cushions, or the tapestries on the wall that depicted women picking apples and gathering wheat.

Lancelot's beauty outshone everything else, for Guinevere. Lancelot's long, angular face framed by wavy black hair led many of the ladies to cast eyes her way, for Lancelot was just as appealing for those who believed she was a man. Her large brown eyes, touched as ever with a hint of sadness, looked at Guinevere as if she were the fairest woman in the world.

Lancelot's movements when she first entered Guinevere's room were always tense, as if she feared being sent away, though she never had been. After a while, she seemed to relax.

"I'm tired of this tale about your being the father of a child." Guinevere sighed. She also disliked the way Arthur had looked at her when everyone talked about Lancelot fathering a child.

Must she worry about keeping her husband at bay? She had stopped lying with Arthur before she began with Lancelot, and she liked her husband much better now than when she had been required to go to his bed. Arthur knew that she and Lancelot loved each other, and did not mind overmuch. He imagined that it had been his idea, so Guinevere would conceive a child, but Lancelot had been her lover well before Arthur had suggested the affair.

"Gawaine's just jesting, as he likes to do. What does it matter? I love none but you," Lancelot said soothingly. "Be not angry, my queen, for you are my forest as well as my love. Let me comb

4

your hair and visit my trees," she said, brushing a stray strand of Guinevere's black hair from her forehead.

"If I may visit your water-meadow later," Guinevere teased, removing from her neck the golden torque that showed she was queen.

"Water-meadow? Is that a swamp? Oh, lovely. How sweet are your compliments, my lady!"

Lancelot laughed, undoing Guinevere's black braids, which were dark as her own hair.

"Fair, indeed. A water-meadow in which an orchid grows. I prefer moors to mountains."

Lancelot kissed her neck. "What, do you think of mountains as men? No, they surely are breasts. And here is my forest."

She pressed her face into Guinevere's hair. "Here are the oaks, the alders, the hazel, and the rowan. I am jealous of anyone else who has ever combed your hair."

Guinevere laughed slightly. That, at least, Arthur had never done. "Including my old nurse Macha, who always complained about the tangles?"

"Including her, of course. I wish I had seen you as a child."

Guinevere swished her head back and forth so the hair flopped across her warrior's face. "You would have seen many tempers if you had."

"Stay still, or I cannot comb your hair," Lancelot complained, trying to pull a silver comb gently through the long strands.

"I can't enjoy it while your poor breasts are bound." Evading the comb, Guinevere turned to her. "Let me unbind them."

Surrendering the comb, Lancelot pulled off her crimson tunic, then stood while Guinevere unwound the thick cloth that held down her breasts. Guinevere pressed her lips to that beloved chest as Lancelot held her tightly.

"Bind me to your bosom," Guinevere teased, and Lancelot, who was much taller, kissed the top of her head.

"Would that I could. How soft your cheeks are. If only mine could be soft for you." As Guinevere knew, Lancelot rubbed them with pumice every morning so it would look as if she had shaved.

"If they were any softer, I would faint when I touch them, so it is well that they are not." Guinevere reached up and caressed Lancelot's cheek. It was far softer than Arthur's cheeks ever had been. Now he wore a beard, and the hair in it was stiff, like a boar's. She was glad that she could just brush her husband's cheek with her lips and be done with it.

She had wanted Lancelot ever since the day they met, but it had taken years to win the sweet warrior to her bed. Lancelot hadn't realized that Guinevere could see that she was a woman. Even when she learned that Guinevere knew the truth, Lancelot had feared the sin of adultery.

The sin didn't worry Guinevere greatly, though perhaps it should. She suspected that Lancelot, who had not received the sacraments since the day they first embraced, said prayers that were haunted with guilt. But how could such a deep love be wrong? Rather, it had been wrong to lie loveless with Arthur.

The night passed all too quickly, and at a dark, early hour, Lancelot had to bind her breasts and clothe herself again. Dawn was the one time that they could not see each other. Guinevere imagined how the rosy light would look illuminating Lancelot's face.

Guinevere called her lover back to the bed and pressed her lips one more time. She gently touched Lancelot's left hand, which had lost two fingers in the Saxon War. It was amazing that Lancelot could still use that hand for many things, fighting included. "'Til tonight," Guinevere murmured.

"A thousand things will happen before we can be together again in the dark," Lancelot said, sighing.

She walked to the largest tapestry, a scene of women gathering fruit, and pulled it back, revealing the hidden panel to the passageway she used when she visited her love.

Guinevere returned to sleep. When dawn had passed and sunlight streamed into the room, her white-haired serving woman, Fencha, who had the only key to the queen's room other than Guinevere's, entered and greeted her.

"Did you sleep well, Lady Guinevere?"

"Indeed. And you, Fencha?"

"Tolerably well, my lady." She smiled because Guinevere had asked her.

Guinevere slid out of bed and took the damp cloth Fencha handed her to wash her face.

A series of mews, increasingly desperate, startled Guinevere.

"Here, Grayse," she called, looking about the room. The cat was not under the table or the bed, nor was she hidden among Guinevere's gowns.

The mews became louder.

"She's in the secret passage," Fencha said, moving to free the cat.

Grayse bounded over to Guinevere, who reached down to pat her. "God's eyebrows, what if someone else had heard her and discovered the hidden door, and the fact that I was using it!" Guinevere exclaimed. Fencha had always known about the door, had in fact told Guinevere about it when she came to Camelot.

"Such a simple thing. How near we came to being discovered." Guinevere gritted her teeth and tried to dismiss the thought.

Arthur did not object to their love, but he would care very much if anyone else learned that his wife was unfaithful to him.

7

Indeed, he would have to punish them. Guinevere did not want to contemplate just what that punishment might be.

Mordred crept through the darkened brothel. He knew what door Dunaut, the owner, slept behind. With a whore, of course. Sometimes when Mordred was younger, he had been the one who was forced to lie with Dunaut. Raped. Now was the time for his revenge.

He wished he could torture the panderer, but that would rouse the others. Mordred clutched the sharpest kitchen knife, the only weapon he was allowed to touch. He was sorry that Dunaut would die in his sleep and would never know that Mordred had killed him, but there was no time for the luxury of confronting him. It was necessary to act as quickly as possible. Mordred understood necessity.

Mordred knew every inch of the brothel, for he had been raised there. He was ignorant of the rest of the world, but he would remedy that.

He wedged his knife through the crack in the door, springing the latch noiselessly. He stole his way to the bed.

Dunaut was far enough away from the girl so that Mordred could probably kill him without killing her, too – not that he cared. Not when every scar on his back had come from Dunaut's beating. For an instant, he regarded the sleeping panderer. Then he slashed Dunaut's throat neatly.

The girl opened her eyes.

"Make a sound and I'll kill you, too," Mordred whispered. She cowered, and shrank to the corner of the small bed.

There were two other panderers to kill, though Dunaut had been the chief one. All of them had mocked Mordred for being a king's son, born to a whore. If his so-called mother, who was only

8

a whore, hadn't died when he was a small child, he would have killed her too, Mordred thought.

Drunk with elation, he moved to the second panderer's room. His bloody knife was ready for more work. Now for Tudy, who had liked to kick Mordred, when he was a boy, and watch him fall. And then kick him again. Tudy was heavier, and might require a deeper thrust of Mordred's blade.

This latch also opened easily – Mordred had of course tried them earlier. He entered. Tudy stirred in his sleep, so Mordred bounded across the floor and stabbed him. The girl beside him screamed before Mordred could warn her not to and leapt from the bed.

"Shut up, fool! I'll be the owner now, and you dare not disobey me," Mordred said, checking to make sure that his knife had gone home and Tudy was dead.

"What's up?" came a shout from outside the door. Coan, the third and youngest panderer, not so many years older than Mordred, was on his way. Coan had liked to shame Mordred by throwing the food Mordred served back in his face.

Mordred waited. The girl shivered in a corner.

Bearing a rushlight, the panderer peered cautiously through the open door. His other hand held a club.

Mordred grabbed a chair and threw it at him.

Dropping both torch and club, Coan fell. Mordred was on him in an instant, holding down the thrashing man until he could slash his throat. Coan screamed and tried to get away, but Mordred kept slashing until he fell silent.

Kicking the corpse, Mordred grabbed the chamber pot and doused the fallen torch. The brothel was his now, and he didn't want it damaged.

Emerging from the doorway, he yelled, "Here, every one of you! Come here. I'm the master now."

9

He had waited for a night when there were no customers. Only the whores and assorted rough men who worked at the brothel were there.

"Light the rushlights," Mordred commanded.

Men and women scurried to obey him.

Mordred held his bloodied knife before the assembled throng. "I've killed all three of the masters. Now I'm the master here. Obey me, and you'll live as you did before. Disobey, and you'll follow them. Which will it be?"

Several cracking voices called out, "We'll obey."

"You'd better. Now clean up these rooms. Throw the bodies to the pigs. And bring me some mead."

Mordred took a seat at one of the tables in the front room and waited to be served, for a change, instead of serving. He did not wipe off the blood that had splattered on him. It pleased him.

This was only the first step. He would have money now, plenty of money. And he would find a man to teach him sword-fighting and the ways of the High King's court. He would go to his father, the king, someday, but only when he was prepared.

He was young, strong, and clever. His whole life was ahead of him. King Mordred had a good sound to it. Mordred Rex.

ABOUT THE AUTHOR

Carol Anne Douglas is a lifelong student of Arthurian and Shakespearian lore. Please review *Lancelot: Her Story* on Amazon and Goodreads, and subscribe to the RSS feed on her blog at **CarolAnneDouglas.com** to receive updates about Volume II, *Lancelot and Guinevere* (978-0-9967722-2-8) as well as other books to come.

Made in the USA
San Bernardino, CA
19 June 2016